— TRAPPED! —

▼

The Gryphon barely had time to recognize the wolfhelmed figures surrounding them, arms raised, before he and his allies were surrounded by an even greater number of the threatening figures. He discovered that he could not speak, could not move.

From somewhere beyond the Gryphon's vision, someone chuckled in great satisfaction. The sound of a heavy pair of boots echoed in the dark chamber and a large hand with a powerful grip took hold of the lionbird and spun him around. The face he saw was not a pleasant one.

"Welcome to Canisargos, Gryphon. I am your host. My name is D'Rak, and I am so VERY pleased to finally meet you."

D'Rak smiled. It was the smile of a predator who is about to eat his prey.

▲

THE DRAGONREALM
WOLFHELM

ALSO BY RICHARD A. KNAAK

Firedrake
Ice Dragon

Published by
POPULAR LIBRARY

THE DRAGONREALM
WOLFHELM

RICHARD A. KNAAK

POPULAR LIBRARY

An Imprint of Warner Books, Inc.

A Time Warner Company

Special thanks to
Gail H. for reading chores
above and beyond
the call of duty—
she claims to like the stories, too!

POPULAR LIBRARY EDITION

Copyright © 1990 by Richard A. Knaak
All rights reserved.

Popular Library®, the fanciful P design, and Questar® are registered trademarks of Warner Books, Inc.

Cover illustration by Larry Elmore

Popular Library books are published by

Warner Books, Inc.
1271 Avenue of the Americas
New York, N.Y. 10020

A Time Warner Company

Printed in the United States of America

First Printing: June, 1990

10 9 8 7 6 5 4 3

I

R'Dane caught his foot on the uncovered root of the huge oak, tripped, and fell flat on his face. It was not that he was a clumsy man; it was simply impossible to keep one's mind on the path when there were Runners on one's heels.

He could hear them now. Not the sounds of their great clawed paws striking the ground with each lope or the snap of their toothy jaws, but rather their growls of anticipation, their hunger. The Runners were always hungry, if only for blood and violence. Were they not, after all, the *true* children of the Ravager?

Rising to his feet, R'Dane once more pleaded silently to his master, the true one. It was not his fault that the latest excursion toward the Dream Lands had ended in complete and utter failure—well, not entirely his fault. He *had* led the expeditionary force, but the plan had been approved by his superiors.

"Come on, you fool!" he muttered to himself. There was no time to dwell on past mistakes. This was a time to run and keep running in the hopes that maybe—just maybe—his former enemies would be his salvation.

Why he hoped for any assistance from the lords of Sirvak Dragoth was beyond him, but the desperateness of his plight made their aid the only possible solution. No one outside of the Dream Lands was about to come to his rescue. Nothing existed on this continent now save the Dream Lands and the empire he had once served, the empire that now demanded he pay the price, stripped of his rank, reduced to the R' of the common soldiers, and let loose as prey for the Runners in a race that no one to his knowledge had ever won.

He had begun running again while thinking of this. What was most frustrating was that he did not even know if he was near the Gate. He was just running in the general direction of where he believed the Dream Lands to be, hoping that someone would see him, realize his plight.

The Runners were closer. He imagined he felt their hot, fetid breath on his neck.

The Pack Master and a handful of his aides sat watching the lone figure stumble through the wooded region that separated the eastern edge of the Aramite empire from the outskirts of the Dream Lands. Occasionally, something would interest the Pack Master and he would lean his huge, armored form forward as if in anticipation. All but one of his aides would follow suit, hoping they, too, would see whatever it was that interested their emperor so. Only one aide—the only one standing—seemed to have little interest in the doings shown by the keeper's crystal.

The room was dark, the better to view the scene in the crystal, and the darkness gave those within the chamber the look of fearsome specters, for all wore armor of the purest ebony and blended in with the shadows. Physically, the Pack Master looked no different from the rest, save for his incredible size and a long, flowing wolfskin cloak. He wore no other symbol of his station than that. The armor was plain, flexible—very well made—and covered every square inch of his body. No one had seen him without it for years, and, if any of them had been asked, it was doubtful they could recall his face.

He leaned forward again, and none of those present could say exactly what the Pack Master might be thinking, for he, like the rest, wore the face-concealing wolfhelms that were a symbol of the Aramites' devotion to their god, the Ravager. The leering wolf-head design on the helm was only a depiction of what their god supposedly looked like; only the Pack Master and one other possibly knew the true face of the deity. Most of the others had no desire to know. They were quite satisfied to serve and leave it at that. Small wonder. There were few, if any, with the courage, let alone the power, to challenge the somber dictator. On a physical scale alone, the arms of their leader, twice as thick as anyone else's, revealed the strength that could snap a man in two—whether he wore armor or not.

One helmed figure sat away from the rest, his hands above the crystal, guiding the scene along. There were no markings to differentiate him from the others, but no one in the room would have mistaken him. Keepers were just that way. They could be nothing else.

"How far is he from the estimated borders of the Dream Lands, Keeper D'Rak?" one of the Pack Leaders grumbled.

Keeper D'Rak was the only one in the room, other than the Pack Master, who could, if need be, flout tradition during council. Whereas the others were required to wear the ceremonial helms during such meetings, he was allowed to wear the more open helm, with the wolf's head a crest rather than part of the face mask. A length of fur ran down the back. This helm was preferred when not in council, for it was much cooler. In this instance, D'Rak, a slightly overweight Aramite with a mustache and one long brow across his forehead, had chosen the open helm in order to concentrate better on the manipulating of the crystal.

"He might already be within the borders; it is impossible to say with the Dream Lands." D'Rak could not keep the irritation out of his voice. The Pack Master would have not asked such a stupid question; nor would have the aide standing near him. Of all those in the room, only they understood the difficulty in pinning down the borders of a place that existed as much in the mind as it did geographically. That had been R'Dane's problem; he had acted as if his foes were as precisely located as, say, the Menliates had been. The Menliates had had an obsession with precision that only conquering them had finally been able to cure. The lords of Sirvak Dragoth, on the other hand, controlled a region that appeared as flexible in form as mist.

"Let us see the Runners." A hand fully capable of containing *both* of D'Rak's own clenched tight, the only other indication of the Pack Master's growing interest in the chase. The *voice*, on the other hand . . .

More than one member of the council stirred uneasily at the sound of that voice. Even the keeper shuddered. There was something about the Pack Master that disturbed even the most formidable of the Leaders and Commanders. It had an echoing quality, as if the man actually sat elsewhere. Again, the only exception to this uneasiness was the aide who stood near the Master, but then, there were enough stories about that one as well.

Nodding, D'Rak whispered something and waved his hand over the crystal. Keepers were attuned to their respective talismans and, as one of the seniormost keepers, D'Rak had control of the Eye of the Wolf, one of the most powerful of the artifacts of the raiders. The Eye of the Wolf had many abilities; its present use involved one of the most minor of those abilities.

The picture shifted. At first, the scene appeared to be little more than a dark blur. It was a moment before even the keeper realized that the blur was actually the Runners. Focusing the power of the crystal did little to increase the detail of the creatures. It was that way with the Runners.

A thing fairly lupine in shape hesitated a moment by a tree's roots, apparently on the scent of its prey. It was darker than the armor of its masters, darker than the night. An impossibly long, narrow maw opened wide, revealing daggerlike teeth that glistened in harsh contrast to the monster's form. A tongue, more like that of a serpent, lolled. It raised a splayed paw and scratched at the tree with arched claws as long as a man's fingers. The claws ripped easily through the roots. The Runner should not have been swift, built as it was, yet there were few creatures it could not catch.

Another joined it, and then three more sought to share the discovery. There was no way to see where one creature ended and another began; they seemed to blend into one another. All that was evident was that the Runners had very good noses and very large jaws. At points, there seemed to be nothing but teeth and claws.

The discoverer of the new trace left by their prey bounded off in the same direction R'Dane had gone only a minute or two before. It was joined by the second one and then the others. A number of the creatures howled or barked, alerting their fellows nearby.

"Return the view to the hunted."

"Yes, Pack Master." D'Rak manipulated the power within the Eye and turned the scene once more to the fleeing man. R'Dane's face—which D'Rak thought sourly was too ruggedly handsome for his own good—was a study in fear. He knew that the Runners were only a short distance from him and that sanctuary was nowhere to be found.

"How long has he been out there?" the Pack Master asked almost casually.

"More than a day, milord," said one of the commanders.

The huge figure shifted in his seat, apparently contemplating. However, only a few seconds had passed when he leaned back to the aide behind him and said, "End this game now."

"Milord." The aide brought his wolf's-head mask forward as he stared at the crystal. D'Rak suppressed his irritation. He, like all keepers, disliked when outsiders, especially this particular outsider, fooled with the talismans the keepers were bound to. A keeper's talisman was his existence. The Pack Master had chosen to honor this one with the kill, though, and there was nothing the senior keeper could do.

A frenzy of howling built up among the Runners as something stirred them. The Pack Master's aide continued to stare, and, as seconds passed, the howling rose to such a level that some of the raider leaders were forced to put their hands over their ears.

"Enough."

The armored figure stepped back, bowing to the Pack Master as he did.

Turning to look behind himself despite knowing he should not, R'Dane stumbled over uneven ground and tumbled down a small slope. He rolled to a stop only when his body collided with a tree. The shock of the collision knocked the air out of him, and he was unable to rise.

They have me! Curse the Ravager! What kind of god—

Softly but surprisingly, strong hands took hold of him. At first, he thought that the Runners had reached him at last, but those creatures would have torn him to pieces by now. His eyes refused to focus, and his lids were, in fact, becoming too heavy for him to keep open. The last thing he saw before the world faded to black were two indistinct figures who seemed to be without faces. Then, nothing.

Oddly, the assembled wolf raiders did not see this. What they saw was a hapless former comrade who had failed his lord. They saw the Runners come upon that failure and, with great glee, circle the fool. Then, one by one, they jumped at R'Dane, snapping at him, biting him, cutting him with their foreclaws, but always retreating, though their circle grew tighter each time.

At last, the lead Runner broke from the circle, snarling and glaring at the man with what could only be described as both anticipation and disdain. It circled him once and then stepped back a few paces before coming to a halt.

The cowering figure in the middle might have bought himself a few moments more if he had stayed motionless, but such was not the case. R'Dane took a step away from the lead Runner, a sign of weakness to the creatures.

The lead Runner took three steps and leaped at the former wolf raider. The other creatures, howling wildly, followed suit.

When there was nothing left, not even a piece of bloodied cloth, the Pack Master rose, indifferent to the horrible execution he himself had ordered and then watched. ''D'Rak, recall the Runners. The rest of you—remember this.''

The Pack Master departed without fanfare, followed immediately by the one aide. D'Rak watched the others file out. He could have controlled the Runners himself all that time. His lord had only had the other raider do it to show that the latter was once more in his good graces.

No surprise. D'Shay had always been his favorite.

The keeper made contact with the Runners, who were reluctant to return. Probably in a blood frenzy. One rabbit was not enough for so large a pack. Perhaps it could be worked out so that they had two or even three. Now, that would be entertaining.

The Runners milled around aimlessly, their prey suddenly lost to them. When the keeper's summons reached them, they hesitated, baring their teeth and disliking both the fact that they had been cheated and the thought that something out of the ordinary had happened.

Fear and loyalty won in the end. The lead Runner howled and began the run back to the kennels. The rest of the pack followed close behind.

They did not see the two figures standing beside them, carrying the unconscious Aramite between them. Even when one Runner brushed against the pale gray cloaks they wore, it did nothing more than unconsciously move aside to a clearer path.

When the last of the Runners had vanished in the distance, the two figures turned to the east. The air before them shimmered, and a gaping hole opened up in the fabric of reality itself. Had D'Rak still been watching, he would have glimpsed a great tower in the distance and a massive gate around which unidentifiable things swarmed, protecting the Gate to the Dream Lands from outsiders.

The two carrying R'Dane stepped through, and the hole vanished.

D'Rak had been essentially correct in his assumption. The Dream Lands were indeed as much a state of mind as anything else. And R'Dane, in those last seconds, had finally become attuned to them.

II

"Are you certain that this 'safe harbor' of yours is truly that?"

Beseen, the captain of the Irillian privateer *Korbus*, smiled, revealing his sharp, draconian teeth. Most Irillian ship captains were either members of the ruling drake clans or humans who had served faithfully under other drake captains. Unlike many of his kind, Beseen was a short, almost stout drake. While his appearance was that of a bluish, humanoid, armor-clad warrior whose face was nearly completely obscured by a helm, he was far more comfortable commanding a vessel than fighting wars —odd, considering that the *Korbus* was one of the most successful privateers.

"Truly that, Lord Gryphon, truly that. My crew and I have used it more than a dozen times. The Aramite wolf raiders, who pride themselves on their own enterprises at sea, decided that this place was useless, being too far south of the bulk of their empire and lacking any unconquered villages to plunder. Then again, their needs differ from ours."

The Gryphon did not ask him to elaborate. Too often, drake needs consisted of things he would rather not hear about or even try to imagine. It was difficult enough to comprehend why drakes would want to become sailors. Overall, the race seemed to have an unconscious obsession to become more and more like the humans they sometimes so despised. Why risk their lives as privateers when they could shift into their original forms and swarm over their prey as dragons?

Beseen, more open than most of his kind, had given him several reasons over the course of the voyage. Odds were, he had said, that a dragon attacking a foreign ship would have to be so careful that his powers would almost be useless. There was nothing to be gained from a drifting pile of smashed timber. It was also extremely tiring for most dragons of his clans to be airborne for very long—and where would a full-grown creature land in the middle of the ocean? The drake would drown while trying to shift back into humanoid form. Dragons did not float very well for some odd reason. While the Blue Dragon's clans were seagoing, they were still land-based creatures like their cousins.

There were other reasons as well, and the captain had gone into them in some detail, but the Gryphon found the explanation as a whole somewhat suspect. He had studied the drakes aboard the *Korbus* throughout the entire journey, and Beseen's tone more than his words had finally convinced the lionbird that the true reason was that the drakes had actually come to *prefer* their humanoid forms. From their manner and some careful questions, the Gryphon knew that some of the crew could not even recall the last time they had shifted to their original shapes. More important, drake hatchlings, especially after contact with humans, were learning to transform themselves at a younger age and with more success. He could foresee a time, not too distant, when all drakes would be able to pass for humans—even better than some humans themselves.

He thought of suggesting this to Beseen, but quickly decided against it. The crew already watched him warily. Telling a drake that he wanted to be more human was an invitation to disaster, and the Gryphon knew how low his odds of surviving were with so many of the race aboard.

The past weeks on the ship had been grueling ones. Putting aside his theories for a more leisurely time, the Gryphon squeezed the rail with both clawed hands as a light spray dotted his face. Both his fur and feathers were damp, and he could not blame the crew when they sometimes chose to stand to one side of him when the wind blew. It was enough to rankle even the lionbird's senses, and he had lived with the problem all his life.

All his life. That was another problem, possibly the greatest. Over a hundred years before, the Gryphon had washed up on the shore of the Dragonrealm region belonging to Penacles, the City of Knowledge. A creature human in form, but with the face of a bird of prey, a mane like a lion, and clawed hands that sometimes were covered with fur, other times with feathers. He was truly a human version of the beast, with vestigial wings and lacking only a tail.

He had power, though, as well as fighting skills from some forgotten past. With his magic and his ability to command, he raised a mercenary army. Despite his appearance and his decision to avoid working as much as possible for the reptilian Dragon Kings, he and his men had prospered. Throughout all that time and the turbulent period following those mercenary days, he had always avoided the sea whenever possible. It brought on a chill within him that few things could match. He knew his past lay across the Eastern Seas, but only until recently had he discovered both bits of his past and the courage to cross the vast body of water separating the Dragonrealm from the lands of his birth.

That courage had not made the crossing any easier. Memories of being tossed about the seas before finally washing up on land, three-quarters dead, remained with him even now.

The privateer turned so as to make its way into the hidden harbor, forcing the Gryphon to move to another part of the ship. To all appearances, he walked as any human, elf, or drake did. His boots seemed a bit wider, but, other than that, he moved like a well-trained hunter. The loose clothing he wore served another function than the obvious, for it hid the tiny knobs that were his wings and covered the fact that, like a cat or bird, his legs bent the opposite way at the knee. His wide boots hid the fact that his feet more resembled a cross between the paws of a lion and the claws of an eagle than they did those of a man. After all these years as ruler of Penacles, it mattered only to him, but it mattered. His subjects had accepted him as one of their own, and he tried to return the favor by dressing the part. A silly notion, to be sure, but no worse than many he had seen.

Recalling Penacles, he closed his eyes. What must they think of him? he wondered. Abandoning them when the whole continent was caught in the midst of change. The Dragon Emperor was dead, killed by one of his own kind—who was also dead. The northern lands had been ravaged by that same Dragon King before his death and were still recovering. A total of six of the ruling drake lords were dead, and only one had had a ready successor. Despite their sudden surge in influence, the human kingdoms within those regions were little better off. Mito Pica still lay in ruins, its citizens slaughtered or scattered by the would-be drake usurper Duke Toma, who was still at large. Talak's king, young Melicard, was a crippled fanatic who had lost part of a face and one arm during an attempt to kidnap the hatchlings, the children, of the late Dragon Emperor. The hatchlings had been under the care and guidance of Cabe and Gwen Bedlam, two of the most powerful mages living and close friends of the Gryphon. They were also under the protection of the Green Dragon, only Dragon King allied with the humans on a friendly basis.

Beseen was shouting orders to the mixed crew of humans, drakes, and assorted others. The *Korbus* entered the tiny harbor slowly, almost tentatively. The captain liked this harbor because one had to follow a straight path or else take the risk of running across one of the many underwater ridges. Beseen claimed his divers had uncovered countless traces of hapless ships that had tried that trick.

"Duke Morgis on deck!" someone shouted.

The Gryphon turned. After the wolf raiders, specifically the aristocratic D'Shay, had attempted to assassinate both the Blue Dragon, master of Irillian, and the Gryphon, the Dragon King had extended his temporary truce with the lord—now former lord—of Penacles. The Blue Dragon had ships that now and then harassed the Aramites, and he had the *Korbus* make room for the Gryphon, who was determined to discover the truth about himself after the final confrontation with D'Shay had revealed things the Gryphon had been unable to remember before.

D'Shay had died in that encounter, willing himself to death apparently. The lionbird still had trouble believing that, but he had witnessed it with his own eyes. Yet, each night, he thought he saw the wolf raider's face as D'Shay laughed at him. The Aramite was an important link to his past—even dead.

Duke Morgis stepped into sight. The Blue Dragon trusted his ally only so far, and had sent one of his newly appointed dukes along as companion and adviser to the lionbird. Like his predecessors, Morgis was one of Blue's own hatchlings, though lacking the markings that would have allowed him to succeed his sire if something occurred. Dragon Kings were sticklers about the royal markings. It had been that which had nearly killed the Dragon King and had resulted in the death of two of his other sons—one by the hand of the other, who had then died from a single blow by the Blue Dragon. A blow that had torn out his throat.

Morgis was a true drake lord, despite the lack of markings. He stood almost a foot taller than the Gryphon, who was above average height himself. He was green with a tint of the sea blue common among his clans. Many of the drakes not marked tended to be green in scale color unless their clans chose to do something about it when the hatchling was young. Some bred for the colors or symbols their clans represented. The clans of the Red Dragon—the new Red Dragon, since the old one had perished long ago at the hand of Cabe's mad father, Azran—were all bloodred in color.

The helm and armor effect were just that—an effect. The armor was actually the scaly skin of the drake, fashioned through natural draconian magic into the form of an armored knight, the closest most male drakes could come to human shape, although it improved with each successive generation. Morgis, like many of the younger drakes, preferred the handier humanoid shape so much over the one he had been born in that he, too, refused to shift unless it was a life-and-death situation. And even then he would have hesitated.

"My Lord Gryphon," the drake rasped. The Gryphon admitted that some of his dislike for the duke was due to the fact that, other than color, Morgis resembled Toma too much. Like Toma, the lionbird's companion was a throwback, having the long, forked tongue and sharp, tearing teeth that in no way could be described as human. The dragon-head crest was also elaborate, though that was more a symbol of the drake's power than anything else. The Gryphon had seen drakes shapeshift before; had Morgis done so, the dragon's face would have melded into his own, eventually becoming his true visage. Morgis, he suspected, would be one large dragon.

"Duke Morgis."

"Have you made a decision as to where you wish to head once we land?"

That had been troubling the former lord of Penacles all trip. Should he attempt to sneak into Canisargos, the sprawling capital city of the Aramites' empire, or should he seek out the Dream Lands and Sirvak Dragoth, two places that D'Shay had mentioned and that now nagged at memories still locked away?

"East, then northeast."

"You want to find these mythical Dream Lands, then." It was a statement, not a question, and an indication that the drake had known the Gryphon's decision before even he did.

"I do—and I don't think they're mythical."

Morgis turned to Beseen, who, satisfied his men had the situation under control, was coming to see to his two passengers. "What do you say, Captain? Do *you* know where the Dream Lands are?"

Beseen hissed in thought. "They mussst exissst." He concentrated harder. Drakes, being perfectionists at times, were determined to speak the common languages without flaw. That was sometimes difficult for a reptilian race, especially when emotions soared. Lapses were common. "They must, or else the wolf raiders would not spend so much time and manpower trying to conquer them."

"Spoken like a realist. I concede the point." Duke Morgis smiled. It was not a pleasant sight.

The Gryphon cocked his head to one side, the better to view the shore. He could, if he greatly desired, shift temporarily into a human form with human eyes, but his own vision, similar but far more advanced than that of a true bird, was more than satisfactory. Better to leave form-shifting for when he needed it. It was a tiring spell if kept up for long periods of time, and he suspected such a situation would materialize before his quest was completed—*if* it was completed.

There was a good possibility, a definite possibility, that he would die before he even found a trace of the mysterious Dream Lands and Sirvak Dragoth—and a gate, it suddenly dawned on him. A gate of some importance. Another door in his memory, long barred from him, had opened. While he welcomed the return of such memories, they also annoyed him, because, more often than not, he could not connect them with anything else.

One day I will remember everything, he swore.

Beseen was speaking. ". . . shore, the boat will return. We cannot afford to stay here too long. There is always the chance some adventurous raider will head this way, perhaps thinking his predecessors have missed something. We also have a quota to make. You'll find a friendly village some ten miles due east. They'll sell the two of you horses."

That stirred the Gryphon to full attention. He turned on the drake lord, focusing on the glittering eyes within the false helm. "The two of us?"

Morgis was smiling slightly. He refused to return the Gryphon's glare. "My sire's orders were to accompany you. He felt it would be inopportune to mention it to you then."

''Because I would have refused in very graphic terms.''

The drake's tone was one of amusement. ''That was mentioned, yes.''

''I still refuse!'' The fur on the Gryphon's back rose.

Morgis shrugged indifferently. ''Then Captain Beseen will turn the *Korbus* around, and we will head back as soon as we pick up supplies.''

From what the Gryphon could see of the captain's face, the stout drake had not been consulted about this second choice. It was not his place to protest, however.

There was no turning back. The hint of memories still locked away haunted the lionbird day and night. To return to the Dragonrealm now would drive him to madness. Even now, the land before him called to him with a siren song so compelling that he was half tempted to swim the rest of the way, regardless of his intense dislike for the seas.

''All right, but just you.'' He pictured himself riding with a fully armed party of drake warriors and trying to look inconspicuous. Even disguised, such a party would have drawn attention.

''Of course. I'm no hatchling, Lord Gryphon.''

We'll see about that, the ex-ruler thought wryly. He, at least, could cover himself with a cloak or shift to human form when necessary. How was he to hide a tall, massive drake lord resembling a fully armored knight?

The duke was ahead of him. ''My sire gave me two of these. To ease our trek, he said.''

One of the crew, a human, brought forth two cloaks. The Gryphon had to admire the choreography. Morgis, or perhaps the Blue Dragon himself, had set everything up so that his ''ally'' would have no time to think out any solid argument—if there was one.

''Illusion cloaks. They took quite some time making, I understand, but they should give us the safety we need.'' The cloaks would provide them with the appearances of whatever they mentally imprinted on them. Simple in looks, the cloaks were difficult magic.

For a brief moment, the Gryphon contemplated the new possibilities opened by the use of the garments. With one of these, he could probably enter Canisargos without too much difficulty, and from there . . .

From there, what? Surrounded by enemies, some of whom

probably had greater power than he did, what would he do? No, better to continue with his original plans and seek out the inhabitants of Sirvak Dragoth. The wolf raiders could wait—but not forever. They owed him, if only for the memories they had stolen from him.

Beseen took the cloaks and handed one to each of his two passengers. "The styles of clothing vary as much here as they do on our own continent. If you choose clothing from, say, Penacles or Irillian and avoid distinctive markings, you should be fine. The physical forms I'll leave for you two to decide."

The Gryphon studied the cloak. It was loose-fitting but cut so that it would not interfere if they had to fight. There would be no trouble wearing weapons. It was possible to imagine weapons, but, should trouble rear its ugly head, illusionary swords tended to prove pretty useless.

Morgis and the Gryphon donned their garments. For several seconds, the lionbird found it hard to focus on his companion. The duke was an indistinct blur that eventually reshaped itself into a tall, dark-haired man with arresting blue eyes. There was, however, a self-confident smirk on Morgis's face, and the Gryphon could not help thinking how, even disguised by illusion, the true personality of the wearer so often revealed itself. That made him wonder what it was that the duke saw when looking at him.

Captain Beseen, ever helpful, called for a looking glass. Someone located one among the "treasures" the privateer had yet to sell and brought it on deck. Morgis inspected himself first, seemed satisfied, and handed the mirror to the Gryphon.

It was a slight variation on the face he normally used when shifting his form. His memory apparently had proven faulty, but he could not complain about the look. He had what could appropriately be called a hawkish look. His nose was aristocratic, but fortunately falling in the region of size where it enhanced his appearance rather than detracted. His hair was blond, almost white, and his eyes were narrow and dark. Unlike the drake, who had chosen to go clean-shaven, his illusionary self sported a thin, well-groomed beard.

That brought up a notion. "We'd best not be with anyone untrustworthy for too long, else they'll wonder why we never have to shave or why our hair is never out of place."

"Agreed. We shall also keep the mirror—just in case." While the garments should keep their present forms locked into whatever spell had been cast, a strong will, either conscious or sleeping, could alter one perceptively. That was the danger of such a cloak. It was far from perfect.

The Gryphon adjusted his garment. The illusionary powers of the cloak extended to itself. Instead of the oddly cut cloth it was, it now appeared to be a normal riding cloak with attached hood. The Gryphon could only marvel at all the work the Dragon King or his mages had put into it.

A crewman walked up to Beseen, stood at attention, and saluted. "The boat is ready, Captain."

"Excellent. My lords?" The drake bowed and indicated which direction they were to go.

The boat was large enough for a good dozen men, though only the Gryphon, Duke Morgis, and four rowers were going to make use of it. Their supplies were already in the boat, and the vessel itself had been lowered to the water. The four crewmen waited patiently while their charges climbed down.

Above them, Beseen shouted, "May the Dragon of the Depths watch over you!"

The duke returned the farewell, and then the tiny boat was moving toward shore. As it rocked, the master of Penacles shivered inwardly. Water! The last time he had been in a situation such as this, it had been on his way to confront the Blue Dragon. He cared for this no better. The *Korbus* at least gave him some sense of security. This boat—this boat was so light that he expected each and every wave to be the one that would capsize it. It did not capsize, however, and soon the crew was preparing to pull it ashore.

They waited until one of the crew signaled that it was all right to climb out. The Gryphon silently cursed the feel of seawater around his boots and the spray in his face. Morgis, human or not, looked no more pleased—an odd thing considering his was a maritime domain. Unlike the ruling Dragon King, Morgis was evidently land-oriented.

The crew members transferred the supplies to shore, saluted the duke, and then pushed the boat back out to sea. The Gryphon and his companion watched them row out to the ship, then picked up their gear and turned to scan the land around them.

They were at the bottom of a gently sloping ridge dotted with grass and a few trees along the side. Had it not been on such a precarious angle, it would have made good grazing land. Beseen had said that a friendly village lay ten miles east. A fair walk, but nothing terrible. Had this been some region in the volcanic Hell Plains, ten miles might have proven an impossible task.

Glancing briefly back at the *Korbus*, which was just now beginning to get under way, the Gryphon sighed and, making certain his gear was secure, he sunk his clawed hands into the earth. The ground was firm and gave him a good handhold. Morgis followed suit, and it then became a sudden contest to see who would reach the top first.

The drake won, but only because of his relative height and the sudden realization to the Gryphon that the first one to the top might find himself staring at the boots of some wanderer who might not prove to be friendly.

Standing at the top of the ridge, they discovered that the grasslands gave way to a lightly wooded region that seemed to thicken the farther one went east or north. The grasslands themselves extended only about a mile or two in any direction. The Gryphon thought it beautiful; the drake thought it dull and turned back to glance at the *Korbus*, which should have been out in the open sea by then.

"Gryphon!"

The lionbird whirled at the surprise in his draconian companion's voice.

The *Korbus* was just out of the natural harbor and heading west. Unfortunately, there were three other vessels on the horizon and, though it was impossible to say from so far away, both of them doubted that these were drake privateers.

"They must see him," Morgis cursed. "Look! They're trying to cut him off!"

It was true. Vast expanses of sea separated the three newcomers from the privateer, and the captains of the trio were moving to block all paths of escape for the *Korbus*. If Beseen attempted to return to the Dragonrealm, he would have a ship coming from all sides. He could hope to outrun them or turn to the south and keep going until they gave up. If there were other choices, the Gryphon could not think of them. He was, admittedly, in the dark where naval warfare was concerned. It couldn't be *that* different, could it?

"Why don't some of them shift to dragon form? They're close enough to the land that they could return here when the battle's done."

Morgis shook his head. "A dragon would make a very nice target for the Aramites. They *do* have surprises of their own, I understand. Beseen is a good captain. If he thought he could win the other way, he would have already begun.''

"Oh.'' The Gryphon grew uneasy, wondering what sort of countermeasures the wolf raiders had that would make a dragon reluctant to attack.

The drake froze, then hissed angrily.

"What is it, Morgis?''

"We'd best not wait around to see if Beseen can pull his ship out of this mess. Better to give ourselves as much distance from here as possible. They know the *Korbus* came from here. I don't doubt that they'll want to see what its business was.''

The Gryphon nodded. It was wise for them to not underestimate the Aramites. Doing so had cost more than one life. Only General Toos, the lionbird's former second-in-command and now his successor, had saved both the Gryphon and the Blue Dragon from a slow death at D'Shay's hands.

Tearing their eyes away from the scene, the two started east. From the captain's explanation earlier, they assumed the village would be easy to find, which, of course, meant that any wolf raiders following them would find it, too. That meant that they had to reach it, buy some decent animals, and move on. Only when they were deep into the dark woods that Beseen claimed were much, much farther east could they truly rest.

The trek was a quiet if unnerving one. The Gryphon could not say just what it was about the ever-thickening woods around him that so disturbed him. Whatever it was, it had put Duke Morgis on edge as well. The closest the lionbird could come to describing it was the feeling that there were a million eyes—no exaggeration—watching them from all around. Eyes that were not necessarily friendly, either.

The two weary travelers were more than a little thankful when they finally came across the village.

Resal was the name of the village, a pitiful-looking place even from where they first spotted it. This was the village that Beseen had said would sell them horses—if they had any. There were no more than a dozen or so structures that could loosely be called buildings, and several others that should not have been but evidently were. Most were made from stone, mud, and thatch, and the closer the duo got, the more haphazard the buildings looked. It was as if someone had thrown Resal together without care. There was nothing in the way of a road; the Gryphon and Morgis chose to walk in the wild grass rather than trudge through the muddy stretch running through the village. A few worn-out animals wandered aimlessly about, but none of them were horses. No horses were visible anywhere. The people were clad in simple cloth outfits and, while everyone seemed to be actively involved in some task or another, many appeared to just be going through the motions, as if they cared very little about their lives. That changed when someone finally noticed the two newcomers.

Friendly was not the way the Gryphon would have described the unfortunate inhabitants of Resal. Morgis saw nothing wrong with their attitudes, but that was most likely due to the fact that they practically fell over their feet to help the two. As a member of the ruling drake family, this was what he was sometimes accustomed to. The Gryphon wondered how helpful the people would have been if Morgis had revealed to them his draconian form. From brief conversations with Beseen, he gathered that the drake captain sent only a few trusted humans in to deal with the inhabitants.

These were a conquered people, he realized for the first time. They had little spirit when encountering anyone with any true self-confidence. Children who had been playing when they entered had stopped to stare with sullen eyes. Adults ceased all activity and women went inside while men stood silently, expecting the worst. When it was learned that the two would not be staying the night and all they wanted were a couple horses, supplies, and food, the people were all too happy to give them what aid they needed—quickly, so as to get the strangers out of their lives as soon as possible.

The privateers obviously did not care about these people, but the Gryphon did. When one elderly man, apparently parting with a prize animal, almost tried to give it away, the lionbird was forced to almost threaten him in order to make him take more.

This was what the Aramites had wrought. Perpetually frightened children and cowering adults willing to give up everything. His mane bristled as his anger grew. One more mark against the wolf raiders—as if he needed any more reasons to despise them.

"We should be moving on. We can't have more than two, maybe three hours until sunset." Morgis was already mounted. He, too, had seen more than enough of the village. It was too dirty. Better to chance the unknown woods than stay in such a filthy place—even if the people did know how to show respect.

The Gryphon read some of what the drake was thinking in his face, again amazed at how the illusionary visage revealed as much as the real thing—which suddenly made him realize that his own disgust at the duke's attitude was probably just as visible. He forced himself to relax.

They told no one where they were going, though they did hint they were moving north. There was no way of knowing for certain whether there were spies or loyalists in the village, but it might at least throw anyone pursuing them off the track for a short while.

As they rode out of the village, the inhabitants greatly over-doing their farewells, Morgis spotted an odd pole sunken into the ground. It was as thick as a human's trunk and at least a foot taller than the drake. On the top was a crudely carved representation of a wolf or some similar creature.

"An interesting piece of work, wouldn't you say?"

Its eyes seemed to draw the Gryphon's attention. He stared at it even after they passed it, turning away only when it became impossible to see it without riding the horse backwards.

Another door opened, releasing yet more memories.

Morgis, who had been moving ahead, looked back and slowed his mount, no easy task since, unlike the humans, it could tell the difference between what the drake looked like and what he actually was and continually fought him. "Gry—what's wrong?"

"Ravager."

"I beg your pardon?"

"The Ravager. The Aramites' chief god. They call him the living god." The Gryphon felt cold. He urged his steed to a faster pace. Morgis's horse matched it.

"It's just a totem. Besides, why worry? It's been my experience that most gods tend to let things run themselves. What's the point of being a god if you have to work so much?" Morgis smiled, looking no less pleasant than he had before the illusion.

The lionbird shook his head, trying to lose the feeling he'd had when caught by the thing's gaze—no, that was ridiculous! It was, as his companion had said, only a totem. Yet, something in his new memories bit at him—and he knew what it was though he had no memories to back it up.

"The Ravager," he finally said, "is different, then."

"Different?"

Something . . . a story someone had told him long ago. A story he could not remember. "The Ravager takes a personal interest in his people. Controls them quite well. All in all, the ultimate source of the wolf raiders' actions is said to originate from the Ravager himself."

Morgis frowned. "You're not suggesting . . ."

The Gryphon nodded, his eyes on the vast expanse of land before them, a land all under the eye of one being, so it was said. "I am. We may soon find ourselves stepping on the feet —or paws—of one very real, very dark god."

III

Had it not been for the fact that they were on a foreign continent where anyone or anything had to be counted as a potential threat, both riders might have been bored. There was a certain uniformity about the countryside that sometimes made it seem as if they were traveling in a circle. Everything tended to look the same. The Gryphon almost looked forward to the coming sunset, if only for the fact that it would give the land around them a different look.

Morgis leaned back in the saddle. "Shall we make camp here, or would you prefer to go on for a little while? I have no desire to stop, and the horses certainly seem eager to keep moving on."

That was certainly true. Both riders were experiencing some difficulty in maintaining control of their mounts. The horses wanted to run. Neither the Gryphon nor his companion had any intention of allowing them that. Riding wildly through a darkening wood was not the wisest of moves.

The Gryphon considered the duke's question. "Let's ride on for a little longer." He pointed up at the sky. "Only Hestia is going to be out in any strength tonight, and she won't even be half there. I've no desire to travel through these woods too long if I can't see."

"We've seen nothing. These woods are empty."

"Then ask yourself *why* they're so empty."

Morgis quieted at that, and the Gryphon was once more able to concentrate on the situation at hand. What he had asked the drake was what was troubling him a bit. The woods *were* fairly empty. Even the normal sound of nature—the birds and the night animals—were muted. Was it just such a sparsely populated area that this was normal? Perhaps the Aramites' initial conquering of this region had so decimated the wildlife that they had not yet returned in great numbers. That seemed odd, for he would have expected the landscape to have suffered as well. With so many warriors in his hypothetical army, there should have been wide-scale destruction. Trees cut or burned down, items such as that.

These trees were far too old. In the length of time it had taken them to grow to such heights, the animal life should have long replenished its numbers.

He stiffened then, for the forest had become completely quiet. Dead quiet.

In the gloom, he could make out Morgis, who had reined his steed to a halt, signaling to him. Something to the north. The Gryphon came to a stop, concentrated, and, thanks to the quiet, he heard it. A very faint sound, but unmistakable. The clink of metal against metal.

Running would be foolish. The lionbird peered around, his eyes coming to rest on some heavy foliage to the right of him. Indicating what he wanted to the drake, he dismounted and slowly led his animal toward the spot. Morgis followed with his own mount. They led the creatures around and then forced them down.

Visibility was nearly nonexistent, but that worked to their advantage as well. In their present position, it was more likely that they would spot the newcomers than the other way around.

They did not have to wait long. Now the clink of metal against metal was more obvious, as were the sounds of both men and horses. Morgis put a hand on the Gryphon's shoulder to alert him. The first of the riders, resembling only an indistinct blur, passed by.

He could not see their helms, but he knew they were wolf raiders. There was just a way about them, a way so much a part of them that, even now, he could picture what they must be thinking. There were at least ten, probably twice that many. It was difficult to say, but he doubted his estimate was off by very much.

At one point, he felt a probing in his mind. Subtle, almost unnoticeable. The Gryphon formed a barrier, diverting the probe so that it seemed he did not exist. He turned anxiously to the drake, but Morgis was already nodding; he, too, had felt the probe. A sorcerer of some sort was riding with the patrol. Like the one with D'Shay that last time. The one who had seemed to wither up and die when one of the Gryphon's unliving bodyguards had accidentally crushed the talisman the man had been utilizing. Keeper? That was the term. The Aramites had a keeper with them.

He also knew where they were going now. They were on a direct course for the village where the two had purchased the horses, which meant that they were, at the very least, trying to determine whether the *Korbus* had left anyone behind.

The last of the wolf raiders went by. The duo waited, the Gryphon mentally counting the seconds. Morgis finally tired of waiting and was about to stand when the Gryphon pulled him back down. It was a fortunate turn, for no sooner was the drake back behind the foliage than several more wolf raiders appeared, their route identical to their predecessors'. It was as the Gryphon had suspected. The second group served as backup. It was a way to draw a foe from cover and then hit him from two sides. Let him think the patrol had passed and then catch him by surprise when he rose from cover.

It was clear they had even less of a start than they had assumed. Somehow, word had traveled from the raider ships to one of the outposts in less than a day. The lionbird had no doubt word would travel equally fast around the area the moment the patrol discovered the existence of two unknown travelers who had been forced to purchase horses only ten or so miles from the harbor. They could not even assume that they had the time needed for this patrol to reach the village, question the inhabitants, and turn around to pursue them. If communications were this efficient, another patrol might already be waiting to cut them off at some point ahead.

This time, they waited much longer before even thinking of standing. Finally, the Gryphon rose silently, scanning the surrounding woods. A strange feeling coursed through him—as if they were not alone despite the certainty in his mind that all the Aramites had passed by. It was similar to when he had felt as if they were being watched by countless eyes, only this time it felt as if they were surrounded completely.

Morgis rose, stretching sore muscles. The drake was not one

built for skulking. "I suggest we go on for as long as the horses are comfortably able. We *have* to give ourselves as much breathing room as possible."

"We could use the illusion cloaks. Make ourselves resemble the foliage—No, we'd have to give up the horses, then." The Gryphon nodded. "No choice. We keep riding—but we stop the minute one of us begins nodding off. No carelessness for fear of losing face. If one of us grows too tired, he tells the other."

The duke nodded. "Agreed."

They mounted and, after only a short debate, continued directly east. Morgis suggested the southeast, but the Gryphon was certain that what he sought lay more to the north, if anywhere. Moving northeast, however, was chancy, as it would take them too close to the more populated regions of the wolf raiders' empire.

Hestia continued her way across the skies, shedding only a little light. The duo was thankful for the cover it gave them, but, at the same time, they would have liked to have been able to see more than a few yards ahead at a time.

All the while, the feeling of being watched continued to nag at the lionbird.

Time dragged. The Gryphon glanced up at the single moon now and then, trying to estimate both their speed and how long it was until sunrise. On the third glance, his eyes narrowed. Hadn't the moon been on his left all evening? What was it doing behind them? A moon was nothing if not constant. It followed a path and stayed on that path. It did not go traveling this way and that like some errant youngster.

So, if the moon was not at fault, that meant that they were now heading . . . south?

"We have a problem." The words were the Gryphon's, but they were uttered by Morgis. The lionbird pulled his gaze away from the misplaced moon and stared ahead where the drake was pointing.

"There's no way we can get through that tangle."

"Tangle" was a kind word for what blocked their way. There was no path. Instead, they found themselves facing a vast, twisted growth of tree and vine so thick that it would have taken days to clear it.

"Don't use magic," the Gryphon warned.

"I know better than that," Morgis hissed. "Any spell sufficient to break us a path through this mess would be like blowing a horn so that our friends in black can find us. Likewise, fire is out. Do you recommend we chop our way through it?''

"I recommend we go around it."

"Where?" The duke spread his arms. "It goes on and on. Why didn't we see this before?"

The feeling of being watched was growing even more intense. "I . . . don't know."

A sigh. "We'll have to . . ."

The Gryphon did not bother to ask. Morgis was staring behind them. The lionbird turned in his saddle—to find himself face-to-face with a wall of vegetation as thick as the one in front.

"Dragon of the Depths!" The drake cursed quietly. "A trap!"

They turned their horses to the right—west. Another wall greeted their narrowed eyes. Reversing direction, they found that their last route of escape had vanished as well.

That was when the whispering began.

At first, they ignored it, more concerned with finding a way out that did not require the use of magic powerful enough to alert the Aramites. Then they thought it was the wind creating sounds through the tangled limbs and vines. Only after a few minutes of frustration did they come to notice that there was no wind to speak of.

"We *have* fallen into a trap," Morgis muttered.

"Not the wolf raiders', though."

"Then who?"

The Gryphon did not answer, more concerned with trying to make out what the voices were whispering about. It was impossible, however, for the voices spoke so quickly that he could make out only one or two words, and even those he was not certain about.

. . . have . . . Tzee . . . certain it is . . .
. . . why . . . dead . . . Tzee . . . back . . .
. . . chance . . . redeem . . . revenge . . .
. . . revenge . . . Tzee . . .
. . . power . . . offer . . . Tzee . . . gain . . .

There was no order to the whispers, and most of the time they spoke simultaneously. It was as if one person had been divided into several parts and was trying to hold a conversation with himself.

He heard the rustling of cloth and turned to see the drake removing his cloak. The illusion of a human vanished as the duke pulled the cloak over his head. The whispering came to an abrupt halt, as if their captors had not been expecting this.

"Take this." Morgis threw the cloak at him.

The whispering picked up again, although now there was a different tone to it—as if the speakers were being forced to come to a rapid decision.

. . . dragon . . . one of his . . . Tzee . . .

. . . both then . . .

. . . I/we will . . . grow . . .

. . . power . . . Tzee . . .

. . . power . . .

. . . power . . . Tzee . . .

The whisperers grew ominously silent once more.

Morgis dismounted quickly and handed the reins of his horse to his companion. "Pull back. I'm going to shift my form."

The Gryphon would have protested, but the drake was already transforming. The armor softened and twisted. Arms and legs bent at impossible angles and grew. Hands became claws. Tiny wings burst from the duke's back, unfolded, and continued growing. Morgis fell forward so that he was now on all fours. Already he was taking up most of the space they had available.

The intricate dragon face on the duke's helm slowly slid downward, gradually revealing itself as the drake's true visage. Morgis, almost completely now a dragon, continued to expand.

Looking heavenward, the Gryphon frowned as he watched a canopy of twisted vegetable matter form across their prison. The invisible whisperers continued their odd conversation, a new intensity, a new confidence, in their voices. The lionbird suddenly had a terrible feeling about all of this. Fighting the two frantically struggling horses with one hand, he pointed the other at the nearly completed canopy and manipulated the fields of power.

Nothing happened.

There was a scream, and then the voices of the whisperers took on a tone of triumph, of mastery.

. . . ours . . . Tzee . . . at last . . .

The Gryphon's horse bucked suddenly, throwing him violently into the air. He had not survived years of mercenary service, however, without learning to adapt whenever possible. Striking the ground, he rolled to soften the impact. His momentum threw him against the side of their living prison, and he collapsed there. The Gryphon opened his eyes and rolled to the side just in time to avoid being accidentally trampled by the drake's steed.

As for Morgis himself, the Gryphon found him where he had originally stood, hands clutching the earth, moaning. He had reverted completely back to his humanoid form, and the shock of the sudden reversal had nearly thrown him into a catatonic state.

The whisperers were practically gleeful, and their constant, now completely undecipherable patter began to weigh unnaturally heavy on the ex-monarch's mind. He began to withdraw within himself, to seek some escape from them. His hands, fumbling aimlessly, came across a ring with two tiny whistles that had fallen from a pocket. A memory of another time, when the Black Dragon's clans and his fanatical human followers had laid siege to Penacles. Dragons had covered the sky one night, and all of them belonged to that Dragon King. Penacles would have surely fallen that night if he had not used the third whistle that had originally hung with these two. That had summoned birds from all around. So many that the dragons could not hide. Dragons had destroyed birds, but they had destroyed each other as well. Vast swarms of birds enveloped whole dragons, a thousand tiny knives cutting away at the hapless monsters.

The attack had failed miserably. With it had gone the Black Dragon's possibility for a swift victory.

He did not care which of the two whistles he had in his hand. The Gryphon brought the whistle to his beak, knowing all too well how much easier it would have been with a true human face rather than an illusionary one. Like the writhing Morgis, however, he could not bring about a change, especially now, when it was hard even to stay conscious. All he had to do, he remembered, was force air through the whistle. Just force air.

It proved to be much more difficult than he could have imagined, and he knew that their unseen captors had something to do with that. Every time he nearly made it, his head would begin to pound uncontrollably from the mad mutterings of the hidden creatures. Once, he almost dropped the whistles.

With what little conscious thought remained, he forced himself to build a mental barrier across his mind. It was much more difficult than it had been earlier, when he had blocked the random probe by the wolf raider. Nevertheless, it slowly took shape, gradually strengthening faster and faster until control was his once more. He tightened his grip on the whistle and even succeeded in shifting to a semihuman form.

The whistle planted firmly in his newly created lips, he blew. Blew until he nearly passed out from lack of air.

Its work done, the whistle crumbled in his hand, leaving nothing behind but a light ash.

The whispering pounded with renewed force at his barrier, but there was now an uncertainty in the maddening whisper pervading everything. The Gryphon wondered whether any wolf raiders had heard either his whistle or Morgis's shriek of agony. He was still certain, somehow, that this was not one of their traps. No, the Gryphon and his companion had stumbled into some dark corner of the very Dream Lands he sought.

A memory blossomed. More of a sentence, actually. *Sirvak Dragoth guards the Dream Lands, but it rules only those who wish to be ruled.* A way of saying that the lords of Dragoth welcomed all and hindered no one who did not care for their ways.

Caretakers, that's what they are, the Gryphon decided.

The constant mumble of the whisperers suddenly became a disjointed babble of anger and anxiety. The pressure on the lionbird's mind ceased abruptly. A stirring nearby told the Gryphon that Morgis was also no longer under attack. The horses, though, stood frozen where they were, their sides heaving in and out in fear. Herd instinct had taken over and they were now side-by-side, waiting for something to come at them, something they could lash out at to relieve their terror. The Gryphon made a note to watch them if the living prison weakened. In their present states, the animals might bolt off at the first chance, forcing their riders to travel on foot in a most definitely unfriendly forest.

Something snarled outside, something feline, thankfully. That meant that the whistle had done its work, for whatever was outside there was a symbol of a part of him. As the Gryphon rose cautiously to a sitting position, he fingered the remaining whistle. What was the third one for? The first had been related to his avian aspect. What did that leave?

The walls of the prison heaved inward. As the Gryphon once more flattened himself on the earth, his hands covering his head, he realized that he still might find out before this was over—providing he lived.

When the massive wall of vegetation did not crush him after several seconds, he dared to open his eyes and look around.

There was no evidence that the prison had ever existed. The feeling of being watched by all those eyes had vanished. The whispering had ceased.

Sharp ears picked up the faint noise of something moving through the brush, something moving in all haste to the east. The Gryphon leaped to his feet and immediately regretted it.

The struggle for his mind had given him a powerful headache. He swayed but did not fall.

"Gryphon?" Morgis had avoided calling him by that name for fear it would reveal their true identities. They had never agreed on another name, something the lionbird planned to take care of the moment the world stopped having it out with him. He clutched his head and turned to his companion.

The drake was on his knees, his first act being to scoop up the cloak that the Gryphon had dropped at some point. Other than being a little dirty, it was fine. The moment Morgis donned it, he once more became the tall, burly human. "What happened? What did you do?"

Carefully pocketing the remaining whistle so as not to reveal it to his "ally," the former monarch replied, "I . . . called on a onetime spell for aid, a spell from my oh-so-murky past. With it, I was able to summon something from my feline cousins."

It was not quite a lie, yet it was not the truth either. Regardless, Morgis seemed to take it at face value. Not knowing of the final whistle, he had no solid evidence that his companion might have omitted anything.

"What happened to our unseen friends or our green prison?"

"I really don't know."

"Have we found the Dream Lands, then?"

Seeing that the drake was all right after all, the Gryphon turned his attention to their mounts, which surprisingly enough had not run off when the trap vanished. The Gryphon stared off in the direction that he had heard their savior depart. "Not a part we wanted to find. I'm having some new thoughts on the subject."

"New thoughts or old memories?" Morgis asked wryly. He was on his feet now, seemingly no worse for his ordeal. The lionbird knew better, though. Whatever pain the drake felt was going to be kept a secret from the Gryphon. Too much pride.

"What were those things?" the duke asked as he took the reins of his steed.

"I don't know. I feel I should, but I don't know. Not all my memories are so willing to come back."

Morgis hissed his understanding. "You were saying something about new thoughts. . . ."

"I was thinking that we should follow this path." The Gryphon pointed east along their mysterious benefactor's path.

"Any special reason?"

"Our savior went that way. I've gotten the idea that he, she, or it is definitely linked to the Dream Lands—the part we want to find.''

The drake mounted with more than a little grunting. He was hurt far worse inside than his companion had first supposed. ''Then let's be gone from here, friend. I've no desire for a return match with our soft-spoken acquaintances—at least not during the night. Let them come in the daytime. . . .''

He indicated what he would do by slowly squeezing a fist tight.

The Gryphon refrained from commenting on the drake's chances, considering what they had already faced. Instead, he mounted and said, ''Forget about that for now. I want to put some distance between us and this place—maybe an hour. Then I recommend we set up camp, taking turns. We're both going to need some rest soon.''

Even though it was barely visible, Morgis's face seemed to radiate relief. He was definitely worse off than he was willing to reveal. The Gryphon had already decided that the drake could have second watch—which would not start until the lionbird was absolutely certain his own exhaustion was starting to get the better of him.

With a backward glance that was supposed to assure himself that they were free of the presence of the whisperers, the Gryphon urged his horse toward the east. Morgis followed suit immediately, hands tightly gripping the reins. They had little trouble encouraging the horses; the animals had no desire to remain in this area either.

It was fortunate, then, that they were far from the spot when the two figures stepped out of what could only be described as a tear in reality. Tall, slim figures, who moved with arrogance where the unseen, whispering creatures had lurked. Had the Gryphon been there, he might have recognized the two for what they were, recognized them even though they had no faces. Only a white, blank area where eyes, nose, and mouth should have been. The two did not seem to be gazing at their surroundings so much as waiting for a third being.

They were joined but moments later by that third, a sinuous, feline shape that blurred as it neared the two, at last becoming something human—or at least humanoid. She—there was no mistaking that even in the dim light of Hestia—pointed to the east where the two riders had gone in the supposition that they were following a trail. A trail that she had purposefully laid.

No word passed between her and the two faceless ones, but they nodded. The female blurred again and became once more a menacing cat of some sort. She loped off into the woods, trailing behind the Gryphon and Morgis.

The other two watched until she was gone, then reentered the rip, which healed itself the moment they were through.

A moment later, the whispering began again. There was a new tone to it, and one word—a name—was repeated over and over, a sign of their anger and eagerness to someday soon wipe the smug arrogance from those who had just departed.

Tzee. It was their own name for their kind, the only one they knew. It was a power of sorts itself, and they drew strength from it.

Tzee. The Gryphon would have remembered that name had he heard it. Remembered what they could do when their full strength was marshaled, which was being done even now. The Tzee remembered the Gryphon as well. They had made the mistake of believing surprise could overwhelm him. Past experience should have reminded them of that fallacy. The misfit had always proven tricky. He had apparently even risen from the dead.

Soon, the Tzee promised themselves, it would be different. *He* had said so—and *he* had the power to *make* it so.

IV

They were not disturbed the rest of that night or the following day. The trail of their mysterious benefactor had, admittedly, vanished long before, but they continued in the same direction regardless. The woods eventually gave way to hilly fields, which proved to be the grazing areas for a farming settlement. The sun burned bright in the sky, and the land was alive with the wonders of nature—small animals, birds, flowers. Only the people seemed incongruous to the beauty of the region. Morgis actually sniffed in disdain upon sighting them, an act that the Gryphon was certain he must have practiced often to achieve such perfection. It would have been almost comical under other circumstances.

Here the people moved listlessly, completing their chores but seeming to take no interest in the work they did. No one really spoke, and it was amazing that there were even any small children, all things considered. The townspeople paid no attention to their appearance, some wearing clothing that obviously served little practical purpose, while others had definitely not washed in weeks.

"Living dead," the Gryphon muttered.

"Scum," retorted Morgis. "These people are scum. Do we have any real reason to stop here?"

"No."

"Then let's move on. I'd rather not spend too much time in their company. They probably carry something."

The lionbird shook his head at his companion's uncaring attitude but acquiesced. There was nothing they could do to help these people. Like the others, their spirit had been broken by the wolf raiders, so much so that they did whatever their masters wanted them to do. The Gryphon understood what was going on. These villagers and others like them were probably the supply source for the Aramite forces in the southern regions. The fields were too vast to be merely for the use of the settlement. Odds were that patrols made regular stops at each such settlement, which was another good reason to depart. The patrol that had passed them during the night might head this way as part of its normal routine.

They urged their horses to a faster pace and soon left the dismal place behind them. Ahead, they saw, lay more woods and, if it was not a trick of the eye, there was the faint outline of a major town or small city to the northeast. The Gryphon slowed his mount and turned to his companion.

"We've . . ."

What he was about to say vanished from his mind as he stared at the thing behind Morgis. A gate—no, the Gate—loomed beyond. The Gryphon had seen it before, though the memory was still a shadow. He had passed through it, too, though when also escaped his grasping mind. Long ago. That was all he could say with certainty. That and the belief that this portal was the path to and from the Dream Lands. The path the Gryphon had been looking for.

He felt a tie with it, a thin, tenuous tie, but one that stretched farther back than his fragmented mind could accept. What link could he possibly have with . . . with such as this? The Gate stood perhaps twenty yards back and was taller, far taller than both riders combined. It was an ancient thing, but the only visible sign of its age were the slight traces of rust at the hinges of the two massive wooden doors. Its appearance suggested marble, but that might not be the case, he felt. What caught his interest the most, though, were the fanciful and frightening sculptured figures—

" 'We've' what?" Morgis broke the seductive spell of the artifact. The Gryphon blinked and saw the Gate fade away much like the morning mist. By the time the drake was able to turn, it was gone.

Morgis turned back to the lionbird. "What was it? Did you see something? Are those damn things back again?"

Despite arguments to the contrary, the duke was still not fully recovered from the wrenching agony of being forced to shift his form.

"It—the Gate! The way into the Dream Lands! It was over there!" The Gryphon looked to his ally for some sign of understanding. Morgis studied him curiously and then squinted at where the Gate had supposedly been. His eyes widened, and at first the Gryphon thought the doorway to the Dream Lands had returned. When he turned to see for himself, however, his mane—fortunately disguised—bristled.

"I see no gate, but I do see something I'd rather not."

A wolf raider patrol was riding toward them at a more than moderate pace. There were at least twoscore men, a very massive patrol indeed. They could only have been looking for one thing—spies dropped off by the drake ship. The Gryphon felt the gentle probing that he now knew was always the work of a keeper. He allowed the false surface thoughts that he and Morgis had discussed to be tapped. The keeper would find two men of slightly dubious background traveling about in search of new opportunities—opportunities of any sort. Beseen had told the Gryphon earlier that the Aramites encouraged free enterprise of the illicit sort if it profited them. They were also acknowledged as being of the lowest of the free castes, not even worthy of the low-ranking R' designation that all Aramite warriors began with. Insignificant beings to the patrol—unless, of course, they were on a recruiting raid. If that were so, the two were about to become involuntary volunteers, an irony that the Gryphon could have done without.

Neither fighting nor a foolish attempt at flight would have profited the two. Therefore, they remained as still and as calm as they could. The touch of the keeper had withdrawn, but both the Gryphon and Morgis knew better than to assume that it might not happen again.

The apparent leader of the patrol, a wide, muscular figure, raised his left hand in the air, a signal for the group to come to a halt. The entire patrol was clad as the Gryphon had last remembered seeing D'Shay, including the visor so akin to that of the drakes but that, in the case of the Aramites, served only the normal functional purpose it looked to be designed for. The wolf raiders were human—as far as the broadest definition of the word was concerned.

Several, including the leader and one who must have been the keeper, removed their helmets during the halt. The leader was an ugly, scarred veteran with a beard as ragged as his face was ravaged. A complete contrast to the impeccably groomed D'Shay.

The keeper—it *was* the keeper, for he held something tightly in one hand that emanated power of great potential—was something of a surprise. He was barely into his adulthood, but his eyes radiated a confidence and knowledge that told the lionbird that here was the final authority on matters involving the patrol. The Gryphon wished briefly that his golems had not turned the other keeper's artifact to so much dust during the struggle in the former monarch's former quarters.

"I am Captain D'Haaren, Fifth Level, working out of Luperion, the gateway to the southern regions." He indicated the city off in the distance. "Your names?"

"I am Morgis, of Tylir," the drake replied first. No one here would recognize the duke's name, and Beseen had often commented that Tylir was a good place to claim to have originated from because it was so far north that few people had ever visited it. It would be just their luck if the captain or the keeper hailed from that region.

"I am Gregoth, also of Tylir." For safety's sake, the Gryphon had chosen a name beginning as his did, but common enough, again according to Captain Beseen, on this continent to prevent someone who had knowledge of him from making the connection.

"You are of the pack," the keeper suddenly uttered in what they supposed was his way of awing two civilians. They pretended to be properly awed, nodding their heads slowly but saying nothing. The keeper seemed satisfied.

Captain D'Haaren was not. "Where have you two come from? Recently."

The Gryphon shrugged. "Here and there, Captain. We've traveled the country a lot lately."

In his mind, the lionbird created a layer, a shield, of false memories of a deal gone bad and the need for a quick retreat to the south. Far south. He had discussed the possibilities with Beseen, who had suggested the sort of things that would lose a keeper's interest. The memories were colored in favor of the Gryphon's character, who, naturally, would be somewhat biased. If the keeper believed those thoughts, he might not delve deeper. This young one, though, fresh to his duties, might push just to prove himself.

A tingle went through his mind. The keeper, though he looked almost bored, was actually probing them once more. A moment later, he could tell by the slight curling of the young raider's lip that the keeper had taken the bait and was now sympathetic.

"Forget them, Captain. They're all right. I, for one, would like to return to Luperion and get some rest. We've been out here for almost a day."

The patrol captain grunted, but said nothing that might have endangered his position. He did not care for the keeper, that much was obvious, but he knew better than to push one. Physical appearance was nothing compared with the strength of a keeper's mind in proper conjunction with his chosen tool.

The Gryphon blinked. He was remembering far more about such things than his experience with D'Shay's comrade, the keeper D'Laque, warranted.

"Very well, then," D'Haaren said politely. "Since both parties are headed for the same destination, I invite you to ride along with us. I *insist*, in fact."

Morgis might have been able to settle this entire matter by shifting to his dragon form and overwhelming the entire patrol, keeper and all, but such an action would not only have aggravated his injuries, it would also have alerted anyone with power that they were here.

It was also not a certainty that they *could* defeat the patrol. The keeper might not be the only one with powers. D'Haaren lacked the silver streak in his hair that marked sorcerers in the Dragonrealm, but such a trait might not exist on this continent.

"We shall be happy to join you," the lionbird replied politely in turn. He hoped that the captain would not insist on accompanying them once they were within the city itself.

The Aramite donned his helm, his men following suit immediately. The keeper took more time, brushing his own helm off and even taking a moment to admire the wolf's-head crest before finally putting it back on. The captain was visibly annoyed, but pretended not to have noticed the act of independence.

D'Haaren raised his arm and signaled his men to move. The Gryphon and Morgis were given a place of honor, so to speak, next to the captain. The keeper, much to the annoyance of the three, urged his mount forward so that he could join them.

"Have you ever been to Luperion?" D'Haaren asked much too casually.

"No," the Gryphon replied. "Nor have we been to Canisargos. I understand the capital is quite impressive."

"It has its points," the captain returned somewhat sourly. "You'll find that Luperion is quite a place itself. The only decent bastion of civilization in these parts. Like stepping into another world, you might say."

The Gryphon hoped that no one was paying too much attention to him, or else they might have noticed how he twitched at the last statement. D'Haaren evidently meant nothing by it, but the lionbird's mind had immediately turned to the Dream Lands. It was ridiculous to think that the wolf raider was *that* suspicious of them—wasn't it?

The captain continued asking seemingly casual questions that both newcomers knew were an attempt to cross them up and reveal them as something else. It took a while to realize that Captain D'Haaren's major reason for this was his desire to be transferred north, preferably to Canisargos. He was no doubt hoping that he could find something important enough to gain him notice from his superiors—the same superiors who obviously knew enough about him to have a longtime veteran shipped to some place where he would be out of their sight.

A bitter man was a dangerous man.

Luperion slowly became a distinctive form. It was a fair-sized city, about two-thirds the size of Penacles, and surrounded by a protective wall. They could tell little more about it at this point. A few tall, rectangular structures rose above that wall, one bearing a banner unreadable from this distance.

"Have you two run across any strangers in your travels during the past few days?" D'Haaren asked abruptly.

The Gryphon felt a sudden probe, barely discernible, at the edge of his conscious mind. Fortunately, it was a ploy that both he and Morgis were familiar with, and they replied easily and calmly.

"We met a few of the villagers. Unpromising bunch."

The keeper's probe withdrew, having obtained only false thoughts of superiority concerning cowering farmers—typical Aramite attitudes.

The patrol captain chuckled. "You wouldn't have said that if you'd fought them way back. The T'R'Layscions gave us a worse fight than anyone in the south. We had to set the keepers on their magic men. Almost failed, too."

"Not our fault," the keeper added smugly. "*Someone* decided not to wait until we were done. A third more casualties than we were supposed to have. The Ravager hates stupidity.''

"Then he should do something about some of his keepers. Laziness is also a failing in his eyes.''

Everyone had quieted completely. From the looks of the other Aramites, this was not the first time these two had argued so.

"There was no one out there. I checked.''

"They have to be.'' D'Haaren glanced back at the two new-comers and then returned his gaze to the path before them. No one spoke for some time afterward. Suddenly, Luperion seemed quite an attractive place to the Gryphon and his companion. Anything to be away from such a volatile situation. Nothing good could come from being caught up in the personal confrontation between a bitter veteran soldier and a smug, young keeper.

It was the keeper who broke the silence, and his choice of subject worried the two almost as much as the argument had.

"Do they talk of the Dream Lands where you come from, friend Gregoth? Tylir, you said?''

"A little. I've never really paid attention. Who cares about some blasted place that isn't always there?''

It was apparently the right thing to say, because more than one Aramite, including both the captain and the keeper, nodded their heads in agreement.

"There you have the gist of the matter,'' the keeper continued. "They want us to fight shadows. Nothing. Why bother? The Dream Lands, wherever they are, have no armies as we know them. They rarely take the offensive. We'd be better off sending an armada across the seas and striking at those new lands they keep talking about. Of what use do we have for a place like the Dream Lands?''

Morgis innocently asked, "These new lands, do you know anything about them? We've heard rumors about monsters, but you're the first one to mention the lands themselves.''

The young Aramite shrugged. "A bunch of petty, barbaric kingdoms, I hear. Monsters—nothing the children of the Ravager cannot handle.''

It took both Morgis and the Gryphon a moment to realize that the "children" the keeper spoke of were the wolf raiders. Fortunately, no one realized the reason for their confusion, putting it down instead to talk of the new lands.

The two nodded agreement. The Gryphon would have asked another question, but his eyes were suddenly drawn to a figure far off to the right of the patrol. A figure clad in gray robes with a hood that covered the face. It seemed to stare at the party for several seconds, then calmly turned away.

He pretended to be looking over the landscape. The figure might have been someone or something from the Dream Lands, or it might have been something else. What memories he had regained drew a blank on this incident, and no new memories had arisen because of it. Best not to speak of it to anyone until he and Morgis were alone.

"Can you tell us of Luperion, Captain?" Morgis asked. "What sort of entertainment we might find—or better yet, good food and drink?"

D'Haaren went into amazing detail about the sights of the city, an indication of how long he had been stationed here. The Gryphon listened with only one ear. His concerns were with getting out of the city as soon as possible.

As the gates of Luperion came into sight, a chill coursed through him and his concern grew even greater. It was not the city itself that disturbed him so much as the single sculpture adorning the top of each gate. A savage wolf's head. Not just a normal wolf, either, but something almost manlike. That was the horrible thing about them. Each head revealed a combination of savageness and cunning that promised terror and destruction. There was no question as to what the heads represented. The feeling that washed over the Gryphon was the same as the one in the village.

The twin faces leered down at him, inviting him to join in the delights of the city.

The Ravager's city.

"She claims she was summoned," the two identical voices harmonized, "by one with guardian whistles."

"Impossible. All major guardians are accounted for. None of them made use of their talismans." The new voice belonged to a tall, narrow figure who seemed to glide across the room, though the effect was actually the result of the long, flowing robe of white and red he wore. His face was veiled, for it could prove hazardous to those around him if they happened to glance his way. Such was the price of power.

"Could it be, Haggerth," the two voices continued, "that someone found those of a past guardian? There have been those who died, or at least vanished."

"If a guardian dies, his personal talismans—all of them—die with him. The whistles would have been nothing more than ash. They could have found a way to copy the sounds, I suppose. . . ."

"Come now." The twin speakers scoffed at such a thought. "You know that true communication with the Dream Lands is beyond the Ravager. It is against the laws set down in the beginning."

"There is Shaidarol. That one knew the secrets. That one was one of us once."

"Shaidarol forfeited the knowledge when he allowed himself to be seduced by the Ravager's promises. The Brotherhood of the Tzee are also unable to make use of those powers, having put themselves beyond the normal boundaries of nature in their own mad quest for dominance. I understand that they were, in fact, the ones seeking to capture or kill those two."

The veiled figure called Haggerth reached up a gloved hand in an unconscious manner and tugged the masking cloth in thought. "Does Troia have any suggestions?"

The twin figures nodded simultaneously. "She thinks we dare not hesitate. The problem must be *dealt* with in a very final manner. Better to be safe than lose all."

"A bit drastic, wouldn't you say?"

"No."

"That would make us little better than the wolf raiders. Doesn't that bother you?"

"We often become our enemies in time of war. When the Aramites and their mad dog of a god are washed away into the seas, we will forget this terrible time and remember again the pleasures of life—all of us except the annoying Tzee, that is."

Haggerth sighed. "I think that your dreams of a return to the ways of the past are too much for even the Dream Lands. I have a suggestion. The not-people have entered Luperion. I think they will help us in this matter. It will mean summoning the aid of the Gate. Then, when the ones we seek are alone . . ."

The twin figures leaned forward as Haggerth explained his plan. In moments, they were both smiling identical smiles.

For just the briefest span of time, it woke. The bonds still held it prisoner, as they had done for ages. Why, then, it wondered, had it awakened? It reviewed the past, which was always open to it, and discovered the presence of a mind of a type it was familiar with. Far away, but nevertheless the closest any had ever come. Perhaps, it thought briefly, the time of release would soon come. Perhaps.

One portion of its mind became active. It was a trick the prisoner had long been skilled at. That part of the mind would monitor and inform while the prisoner as a whole would continue his age-old slumber. If the faint trace went away, that portion would also return to sleep. If it moved nearer . . .

. . . the game would begin anew.

The great leviathan closed its eyes.

V

The city within the walls was indeed impressive, but more so for the throngs of people and animals than anything else. There were groups of all sizes, and they were packed together so tightly that the riders looked as if they were leading their mounts across a river.

"Is it market day?" Morgis finally asked.

"Market day?" The keeper smiled smugly. "Hardly. This is what it looks like every day in Luperion!"

"Oh."

Though darkness was descending, Luperion had no intention of settling down. Torches, lanterns, and such lit most of the areas already. People continued to haggle or wander about, and the Gryphon suspected that the crowds would still be here hours from now.

Luperion was a contrasting mixture of function and fancy. In the market areas, tents and structures of all shapes and sizes abounded. Beyond, where the military might of the wolf raiders watched, the buildings became boxlike and dark. Banners with wolf-head emblems fluttered fiercely in the wind. Ebony-armored figures stood watch or marched back and forth. Everything seemed to be either black, gray, or white, a distinct difference from the open market region where countless colors vied with one another, including even the skins of the inhabitants themselves. Most were familiar to the Gryphon, but the blue men gave him pause. Beseen had mentioned them briefly, but the lionbird had assumed the blue was merely some sort of dye. It was not, he discovered. What proved more important was that they were from a place near Tylir. Beseen had chosen that area because visitors from there were supposed to be rare here in the south. Apparently, the drake's information had been sketchy. The Gryphon wondered what else Beseen had missed.

He expected hard going through the living sea of people, but the crowds flowed away from the patrol whenever it neared and flowed back after it passed. They moved with such precision that it almost seemed they had practiced for this—which, in a sense, they had. That said something about the Aramite empire, that the patrol should be so accepted an obstacle.

It was D'Haaren who suggested an inn, the Jackal's Way, where the two might find a room and food. The Gryphon thanked him for the information, careful not to reveal his suspicions about the captain's more tolerant attitude. The inn, no doubt, housed a spy or two, but it was not a great danger as far as he was concerned. There were ways to evade spies.

As they broke off from the Aramites, only one member of the patrol—the keeper—bid them farewell. He simply nodded and said, "May your endeavors reach an appropriate end."

Neither the Gryphon nor Morgis cared to dwell on the implications of the statement.

"Do you have something in mind?" Morgis hissed once they were out far away.

The lionbird nodded, pretending to comment on some sight. He whispered, "Yes. We'll go to the Jackal's Way and pay for a night's stay, but we won't be coming back. I want to leave here before dawn. Just in case we need to separate for a time, I want to find another inn—or some other crowded place—for us to meet at."

"Sounds reasonable, providing your plans also include an honest meal in the near future. I have a yawning chasm for a stomach."

The Gryphon knew how he felt. "It does . . . believe me, it does."

After eating and drinking their fair shares at the Jackal's Way—the ale was good, but, in this case, the spice was uncalled for—they wandered deep into the city with the pretense of looking over the local entertainment. Under this guise, they studied the city around them and, during their sojourn, located the second inn. The going was rough; without the patrol or even their horses to break open a path for them, they were forced to go around and about the waves of pedestrians.

There was one close encounter. Morgis, trying to wheedle information from a merchant, mentioned Tylir in passing. Only after that did they realize that one of the blue men was nearby, looking over some animal skins. Fortunately, he appeared not to hear them. After that, they tried to mention the region as little as possible and always kept an eye out for the distinctive color of the northerners.

They were on their way back to the second inn when the Gryphon again spotted a long, robed figure like the one standing in the field outside of the city. The hood obscured all traces of the person's head, and the lionbird was briefly reminded of Shade, the warlock who had been cursed to live an eternity of alternating lives, good and evil. But Shade was gone now, exiled to the endless Void by the only creature capable of defeating his darkest persona yet.

Morgis, too, had seen the figure. As they watched, they noticed one thing in particular: no one blocked the path of the hooded one for more than a second. Even Aramite soldiers on horses steered clear. It was quite obvious as well that the mysterious figure was not popular with the citizenry, though he or she was definitely respected.

"Someone we should know about, perhaps?" the drake whispered.

"Several we should know about. Look." The Gryphon pointed down the street.

Two more hooded figures strode through the crowds with the clear intention of joining the third, who stood waiting for them. In size, they were identical. Shape was debatable; it was impossible to say just what might be under those robes. Whatever it was, people avoided it like the plague.

The Gryphon studied the crowd. "It might not be a good idea to talk to anyone about this right now. From what I've seen, they're all too worked up about them. Besides, we're supposed to know who they are, apparently."

"I know one thing about them," Morgis commented, eyes on the now-distant trio.

"What's that?"

"They're heading toward the other inn, the one we're staying at."

They were, indeed. Worse yet, one had detached himself—again, the Gryphon could only assume they were men—and was now standing outside, gazing at the crowds from the murky depths of his hood.

"I think we have a problem," the duke hissed.

"I *know* we have a problem. To your right."

Much to their dismay, Captain D'Haaren and a handful of his men were making their way toward the duo. The look in the veteran raider's eyes was not one that appealed to them.

Slowly, casually they turned away, pretending not to have noticed the Aramite soldiers.

"What now?" Morgis hissed. Had it been up to him alone, he would have been sorely tempted to pull out his sword and fight. True, there were more than half a dozen of the soldiers, but the crowd would slow them long enough for him to take care of one or two.

The Gryphon frowned. "Down that side street."

The side street in question was no less crowded than any other avenue of the city. The former ruler of Penacles hoped that they could turn off into yet another side street before the Aramites got too close. It was his hope, a slight one, true, that they might lose the patrol long enough to recover their belongings, including the horses. The next problem would be to see if they could escape the city itself.

"What gave us away?" the drake whispered. It did not seem to matter how loud they spoke; everyone else was too caught up in their own activities.

"I really don't know. Maybe they ran into some of our neighbors and questioned them," he replied, thinking of the bluish men. Maybe there was something about Tylir Beseen had forgotten to tell them or had not known at the time. The Gryphon's eyes settled on another side street, almost an alley by the looks of it. "Down that way. Hurry, but don't run."

They turned the corner—and found themselves facing an oncoming party of four wolf raiders.

The knife was into and out of Morgis's hand before the Gryphon could stop him. The Aramites coming toward them were obviously on routine patrol and not part of any concerted effort to capture the two. They probably could have walked right past the soldiers.

It was too late for that now. The lead soldier went down

without a sound, the hilt of the knife sticking out of his neck. The other three hesitated only a moment from surprise and then drew their swords, long, wicked blades that curved slightly.

Cursing, the Gryphon pulled his own weapon. Morgis already had his out and was moving swiftly toward the trio. One of them shouted something, but whatever it was became lost in the noise. The drake matched blades against two of the Aramites while the Gryphon arrived barely in time to save his companion from the third. The street was very narrow, and the lionbird was able to catch the man at an awkward angle. The point of his blade cut a deep gash along his opponent's shoulder where the armor of necessity had a break. The wolf raider gritted his teeth and switched hands, proving himself to be just as excellent a swordsman with his left as with his right.

Morgis thrust his blade through one of his two opponents, but got his sword stuck in the collapsing form. As he struggled, the remaining Aramite pressed his advantage, cutting the drake on the left side near the collarbone. The duke hissed more out of anger than pain, but his response so startled the soldier that Morgis had enough time to free his blade before the wolf raider pressed again.

With each breath, the Gryphon expected Captain D'Haaren and his men to cut them down from behind. Even if the captain had lost them, the noise of the battle would surely have been enough to alert him or some other patrol. If not the noise, then the crowd of people rushing from this particular street would have been a good sign that something was amiss.

The Gryphon parried a wild attack by his adversary, who apparently felt his left-handed assault would throw the other off, and followed through with a death-dealing thrust of his own. As the soldier fell, the former monarch turned and caught the drake's opponent from the side. The Aramite parried, but in doing so left himself wide open to Morgis. The duke dispatched him with ease.

Still D'Haaren and his fellows did not appear.

They were, however, being watched from the direction that the wolf raiders had come. A lone woman, there was no denying *that* form was feminine, studied them from behind a veil. When she realized that they had seen her, she stepped back gracefully but did not flee. It was almost as if she wanted them to chase her.

Morgis took a step forward, sword raised. "We have to take her. She'll warn the patrol captain."

"Will she?" The Gryphon matched gazes with her. She did not seem like any Aramite. Even through the veil, he could see that she had large, dark eyes. Entrancing eyes, but not like those of most women. More like a cat. A predatory cat.

She stared back with equal curiosity, almost as if she knew what actually lurked behind the illusion. The Gryphon might have stood there for hours if Morgis had not broken the spell.

A heavy hand gripped his shoulder as the drake tried to shake him back to awareness. "If you can tear yourself away from that woman, I thought I'd warn you that we have more company."

"What?" The lionbird whirled, expecting to face Captain D'Haaren. Instead, two of the hooded figures stood at the intersection, calmly waiting. Their hands were buried within their cloaks, leaving no portion of their bodies uncovered. It would have been impossible to tell whether these two were part of the trio that had gone to the inn they were staying in or whether they were two new ones.

The Gryphon turned his attention back to the woman. His eyes widened. She was now accompanied by two more. The Gryphon found himself hoping that D'Haaren and his men might show up after all. The Aramites, at least, were a fairly familiar danger; these cloaked figures, figures whom even the wolf raiders gave wide berth to, were not. Given a choice, he preferred the known to the unknown.

The two figures with the woman stepped past her and walked side-by-side toward the duo. At the same time, their counterparts moved forward from the other side.

"Back-to-back," Morgis hissed. "And if you have a spell ready, please use it. Shifting my form in this narrow place could prove quite uncomfortable."

Nodding, the Gryphon raised his free hand—and found he could do nothing else. He was frozen in place. When he tried to say something, nothing happened, not even a moan.

"So interesting," a distinctly female voice near his ear said. "Not one of the Ravager's kind, but something different."

She moved to his front. The veil was gone and, while she was breathtakingly beautiful, she was certainly not human. Her eyes were indeed dark and like a cat's, even down to the pupil. It added rather than detracted from her looks. Her hair was short and pitch-black, and she had a tiny, well-formed nose that twitched on occasion for no apparent reason. Her lips were long and full—quite inviting until she smiled. It was not a smile of friendship, but rather the smile of a cat as it plays with its prey.

Of her form he could tell little, since she stood too close. The Gryphon did not doubt that she was lithe and strong, and under other circumstances he would have been very attracted. Even now, it was impossible to totally ignore the flirtatious looks she gave or the caress of her hand on the side of his head. He reminded himself again of the feline toying with its meal.

"I can feel the true shape of your face; your illusion does not completely fool my eyes. A strange creature you must be, but no less strange than your companion, I notice."

She ran her long fingers along his cloak. "It would be a waste to destroy this. I'll let you keep it for the moment."

The female stepped away, and the Gryphon saw that his assumption about her form was correct in essence but had not done her justice at all. Though she was looking at the two hooded figures before them, she seemed to be walking for his benefit—or perhaps it was just natural for her. If she was what he thought she was, then everything she did was a normal part of her nature.

"You won't tell me anything, will you?" she asked both of the figures. Neither responded with so much as a shake of the head, but the woman shrugged and turned to look once more at her two prisoners.

"They want you alive—not these, the Master Guardians. The not-people never say what they want. You just ask them something and hope they respond in the way you want. Sometimes I wonder who really runs the continent."

She frowned and then pointed at the Gryphon and Morgis. As if on cue, the others removed their hoods. It was fortunate that neither the Gryphon nor Morgis could move, for what met their eyes was one of the strangest sights either of them had beheld. The not-people, as the woman had called them, looked human in form—as much as was visible—but they lacked any feature on their head. No hair, no eyes, no mouth, no nose, no ears—nothing. A clean slate upon which anything might be added. It was impossible to imagine how they they breathed, let alone how they ate or drank. They had to have something related to sight or hearing, for they moved in smooth motions that even the Gryphon, excellent as he was in matters of stealth, would have found impossible to copy.

When they were no more than an arm's length, the two creatures raised their hands high. He could not see them, but the lionbird suspected the other two were repeating the process behind him.

The tremendous tug on the fields and lines of power astonished him. Surely, the use of such intense magic would alert every keeper in the vicinity—wouldn't it? That train of thought was cut off as a familiar sound briefly reappeared. A chill ran through him.

"Not last time and not this time, you cursed Tzee!" Raising her left hand as a cat might raise its paw to bat something, she muttered a phrase that the Gryphon felt he should recognize. The whispering, which had threatened to increase, vanished abruptly instead.

"Stupid shadow creatures."

Tzee. The name opened new memories for the Gryphon, and none of them were good ones. The woman was wrong if she considered them stupid creatures. He prayed he would not be around when the Tzee proved that to her.

Whatever it was that the faceless not-people were doing was completed swiftly. One of them glanced—at least the front of its head turned—at the Gryphon, and the lionbird suddenly found his body moving without his willing it. As he turned, he saw that Morgis was in like straits; only his eyes were able to show any of the frustration both of them felt.

That frustration melted away when he saw where they were headed. One of the walls was missing an entire section, and that section had been replaced by the Gate. It looked different than before, but the Gryphon remembered that part of its nature was change—for was it not the way into the Dream Lands, where change was the norm and stability more of a freak occurrence?

The doors of the Gate were wide open. Things climbed all over the frame of the artifact, tiny things, but no less deadly because of their size. These were the watchers, the guard dogs of the Gate. There once had been more of them. He was certain of that. Something had happened to them. They had been turned.

Those memories escaped him, not that they mattered at this moment. Only the Gate and where it led mattered. As his body obediently made its way to the artifact, he could not help thinking how desperately he had wanted to find the Gate and enter the Dream Lands. This had been his home once. No more, apparently. He was returning a prisoner; it was quite possible that all those who had known him were dead and that others now controlled Sirvak Dragoth. It was quite possible that he had traveled across the Eastern Seas and a fair portion of this continent only to die at the hands of those he had been seeking.

For some inexplicable reason, he could not help but picture D'Shay laughing, mocking his adversary for his foolhardiness.

The Gate swallowed him.

The novice keeper knelt before D'Rak. D'Rak frowned briefly, but decided that it must be important if the novice was willing to interrupt his senior. Novices who disturbed their superiors for minor matters never completed their training. They were usually shipped home in a small box.

This one knew better, for he was one of D'Rak's students. The senior keeper pushed aside the notes he was making and leaned back.

"Speak."

"Keeper D'Wendel reports the presence of a foreign ship several days ago near the southwestern coast—approximately due west of Luperion."

D'Rak grew annoyed. "So? This is the news you thought important enough to break my concentration? Probably Xeenian privateers. There are still a few independents left. Another year and we'll have them all. Why bother me with this? Is D'Wendel having some sort of difficulty? You said it was several days ago?"

There was a slight tremor in the novice's voice. "It was not a Xeenian ship, Master. The keeper did not report it earlier because he did not know himself. Pursuit ships were out of range for their associate keepers."

Associate keepers were those who had risen above novice stage. Most of them were assigned minor patrol duties. Despite their youth, they actually outranked anyone captain or lower. It was a symbol of the keepers' power in the Aramite empire.

D'Rak, however, was not concerned with the matter of communication. He had still not been given a reason why his own novice had interrupted him. "I gather there was something significant about the foreign vessel? Something worth saving your miserable hide if you delay any longer?"

The senior keeper's tone was even, but the younger keeper knew how serious he really was. Swallowing heavily, he replied, "After a long hunt in which one pursuit ship perished in flames and another was finally abandoned due to damage, the keepers aboard banded together and succeeded in destroying both ship and crew, save a few scattered survivors."

This did capture D'Rak's attention. "A formidable adversary, indeed. You are forgiven for now. Carry on."

Somewhat relieved, the novice continued. "The pursuit ship that perished in flames was the victim of a dragon, Master. The creature died at the hands of the keepers, who set up a field nullifying its power. The thing fell from the sky and sank like a stone. It was believed at first that the dragon was some sort of rare pet or slave, but some of the survivors fished out of the sea proved to be—to be humanoid, reptilian monsters. Dragon men, Keeper D'Wendel said."

"Dragon men." D'Rak rubbed his chin. "Dragon men."

"He swears it is the truth."

The master keeper smiled vaguely. "Oh, I believe him. I'm just trying to decide what the proper course of action would be."

"Master?"

D'Rak leaned forward. "You've not heard the tales of the new continent west of our domain, have you?"

"No, master. I've been studying here for the past two years. I intend to finish my novice training at least a year early."

The elder man nodded in satisfaction. This novice—D'Rak made it a point to never use or even think of their names in order to prove his impartiality—would be a fine keeper if he survived his years as an associate.

"Be sure to remind me to tell you of them sometime soon. We know of these drakes, but I doubt anyone actually thought they were this bold. I shall have to speak to the Pack Master. Was there anything else?"

"Yes, lord. As I understand it, Keeper D'Wendel believes that they might have set one or more persons on shore. He said traces were found by the keepers present that indicate something of that sort. That was all he knew when he sent the message. He said he would relay any new information the moment it arrived."

"Thank you, novice. You may go."

"Master." The young man stood and backed out, bowing all the way.

D'Rak turned to the Eye of the Wolf. The Pack Master would be interested in this. Why were the drakes seeking to infiltrate the Aramites' empire? Did they know what the wolf raiders planned? The inconsistent war with the Dream Lands was putting too much of a strain on things. The Pack Master was without rival, but it was his responsibility to create results. Until the Dream Lands, no one had been able to stand up to the raiders.

As long as that place existed, the empire could not expand. Armies sent east lost their way and began marching every direction but that. Scouts and spies sent out to investigate possibilities beyond those areas under the Dream Lands' protection never returned. Ships sailing around the northern and southern shores of the continent reported storms so fierce and ice so thick that it was impossible for them to proceed any farther, even with the aid of senior keepers and high-level sorcerers.

The Ravager could not possibly be pleased. The last time he had shown his anger, Qualard, the former capital, had vanished in the worst earthquake anyone had ever seen. Some claimed that to have been the work of the lords of the Dream Lands, but D'Rak knew better. The Dream Lands could not possibly have such power, else they would have used it again. But that was the past, more than two centuries ago. No one cared about that now save a few of the near-immortals.

D'Rak ran his hands almost reverently over the Eye. The pride within him swelled, for only a handful had ever truly mastered an artifact as powerful as this. It was one reason why he had grown to be the unofficial third power of the empire—fourth if one counted the Ravager himself.

The question of who was first and second was debatable, as far as he was concerned. The Pack Master was *supposed* to be, but more and more . . .

What is it?

The voice was within his own mind, as he had expected, but it was not the voice of the Pack Master.

"D'Shay!" the keeper snarled. "This is for the Pack Master's attention, not yours!"

He could almost see the confident, aristocratic face. *All things are my concern, Keeper D'Rak. Do you think that the master will not consult me on whatever it is you wish to discuss with him? Has he not said in the past that my ear is his ear?*

The question of who was truly in charge briefly reared its ugly head. D'Rak squashed the thought, for fear that D'Shay might catch it. Though the keeper spoke, it was more his thoughts that were transmitted than his words.

He sighed. Regrettably, his rival was correct. After all, D'Shay was the one who had dealt with the drakes most. He relayed what his novice had told him, pretending that he did not know that D'Shay had scored a victory of sorts over him.

To his surprise, the other wolf raider genuinely thanked him. *At last! I told him that he would come eventually!*

D'Rak realized that he was picking up some of the other's thoughts. He said nothing, though. It was possible that *he* might learn something of importance from D'Shay.

No doubt he thinks I am long dead! Wonderful! The Ravager will have his head and the key to the Gate as well!

The keeper became uneasy. D'Shay always spoke of their god as if he were a personal friend.

Keeper D'Rak! I will inform the Pack Master, but I have a request of you!

"What is it?"

Order the keepers in the region of Luperion to do nothing but observe! They will indeed find at least one stranger, possibly more! If they find someone who seems too different, they should allow him to go unmolested!

"What are you saying? What do you plan?"

It is not for you to know right now.

The keeper stood without realizing it. "Only the Pack Master can decide that!"

He will.

Contact was broken. D'Rak seethed, but he knew there was nothing he could do—for now. D'Shay had the Pack Master's ear, but there were other ways to discover things; he was not a senior keeper for nothing. D'Shay was only a man like any other—wasn't he?

He was not, and D'Rak knew that. Still, the keeper had amassed too much power of his own to allow himself to be ordered around like this. He would do as his rival said—and then some. D'Shay obviously believed that the drakes had dropped off somebody important, perhaps even the one who seemed to prey on the Aramite's mind at all times. What was he called? The Gryphon, that was it. A refugee from the Dream Lands, apparently. It had to be him. No other news would have struck D'Shay so.

Dream Lands. D'Rak smiled. He knew just what was needed to hunt down someone from the Dream Lands. Someone who obviously must be returning there and who might be leaving a trail of sorts.

The Pack Master would not fault him, regardless of what D'Shay might say. The keeper moved his hands slowly across the Eye of the Wolf, observing all until his second sight came upon the kennels. Carefully, for they were an unruly, high-strung lot, he sought out the pack leader and disturbed its slumber.

The Runner woke.

VI

He had blacked out.

Eyes still closed, the Gryphon started to raise his head, only to discover that it now weighed at least as much as a full-grown dragon. He gingerly returned it to the soft cushion beneath him and decided to try his eyes.

The light was blinding at first, but his eyes soon became used to it. Unfortunately, his vision refused to clear up, giving everything the appearance of being viewed through muddy water. He blinked several times, and things finally came into focus.

He was in a room of extravagant tastes and proportions. Everything seemed to glitter with gold, silver, and crystal. Tapestries so lifelike that he was tempted to think they watched him hung on every wall. There were sculptures of many fantastic creatures, including his namesake. The room was lit by a single, glowing crystal in the center of the ceiling. He heard tales of such use, but could not recall ever seeing it, though he suspected he had long ago.

With some trepidation, he dared rise from the couch again. This time, he was rewarded with only an incessant pounding in his forehead, a vast improvement over his previous attempt. The Gryphon stumbled to his feet, one hand on the side of his head, and took a deep breath. The pounding lessened.

There were drapes to his left, which meant a window. His strength slowly returning, he made his way to the drapes, which were made of the finest silk, he saw, and pulled them wide open.

He found himself staring at a mirror.

"I am not amused," he muttered, although he knew that it was not necessarily the designer's intention to have played him for a fool.

The Gryphon stared at his reflection. His cloak had been taken from him, and so his true features were revealed. There was something odd about the other him, something not quite right. It was almost as if it were not so much his mirror image, but an independent entity. He could not prove it, but he was certain that its movements did not quite match his own.

One of the faceless creatures stepped into the background of the reflection. The Gryphon released the curtains and whirled. There was no one there.

He turned back to the mirror, only to find that the curtains had completely covered it once more. The lionbird was about to reach out when the door to his room opened. It was one of the faceless ones, clad exactly as the image in the mirror had been—which meant nothing. The Gryphon could not have told one from another even if his life had been at stake.

The garments it wore differed only in color, being a combination of blue and black, with the latter making up the shoulders and hood. The hood was down, fully revealing its frightening lack of any feature. It almost seemed to float as it stepped into the room. The Gryphon thought briefly about assaulting it, then changed his mind when he remembered with what ease the foursome in the alley had captured him.

That thought led to ones concerning the safety of Morgis and the question of just exactly where he was. Not in Luperion. The Dream Lands, he remembered now, but where did one truly exist in a place not quite real?

"Where's my companion?"

The creature gestured at the open doorway behind it. The Gryphon understood that, at least, but was it answering his question or did it have some other destination in mind?

A second of the faceless not-people, as the woman had termed them, entered the room. Evidently, the Gryphon was going to come with them one way or another. There seemed no point in being obstinate; he would have been left lying in the streets of Luperion if it was his death they wanted.

With one creature leading and the other behind the Gryphon,

they departed. The lionbird studied the halls, occasionally dredging up some fragment of memory as he spotted various objects. He had been in this place before, but the name escaped him for the moment. This was where he had sought to go.

"Lord Gryphon!"

He turned to see Duke Morgis, also monitored by a pair of the not-people, being led toward him. Apparently, the two of them were on their way to a confrontation with the masters of this place.

"Have you any idea where we are?" The drake was anxious. The Gryphon had not tried his own powers, but he suspected that Morgis had—and had found them wanting.

They were allowed to walk with one another so long as they kept the pace set by their escort. The ex-monarch nodded. The name had come back to him, and he now wondered how he could have ever forgotten. "We've reached Sirvak Dragoth, the citadel of the Dream Land's guardians."

Morgis turned to study the blank visages of their guards. "Aren't these people supposed to be your friends?"

"Times change. It *has* been well over a hundred years. Maybe much longer."

"Four against two is not bad odds for us," the drake suggested quietly. He was not terribly confident about their chances with whoever was in charge.

"Eight against two," the Gryphon replied. "And I think we've reached our destination."

Four more of the creatures stood watch over a massive, intricately patterned wooden door. Eyeing the new complement, the lionbird came to the sudden realization that these beings were not servants of a sort, but rather a group with a purpose of its own that presently coincided with that of the Master Guardians of the Dream Lands. The Gryphon corrected himself; it was not a realization, but another memory unleashed.

He was irritated. So many memories of things and people around him, but very few useful ones about himself.

The two nearest to the doors opened them wide. The Gryphon and Morgis were ushered through without ceremony into a room as opulent as the one the lionbird had woken in, but obviously designed for holding court . . . for four figures awaited them on a dais. Only one of those figures was recognizable. That was the dark-haired woman who had coordinated their capture. She seemed ready to devour them both.

An identical pair of near-human males in their late years

stood to one side in the brightest part of the room, which, the Gryphon thought idly as he glanced up at the skylight, meant that it was daytime. The two moved with such uniformity that one would have thought they were puppets controlled by the same master. When one blinked, the other blinked (even their breathing was in unison). That they were not human was evident by their eyes, which were wide and multifaceted, like those of an insect.

Seated on a chair in the center of the dais was a long, humanoid figure clad in red and white and wearing a veil that completely obscured his or her features. The Gryphon hazarded the guess that it was a man, or at least male. It was this figure that seemed in charge of the situation.

"I trust both of you have rested well," he said by way of an opening remark.

"We rested," Morgis replied angrily, "because we had no choice."

"Ah, that!" The figure shifted somewhat uncomfortably. The two identical men frowned simultaneously, and the woman bared sharp teeth. "Forgive me, but it wasn't supposed to be that way. The not-people had agreed to confront you in your rooms, but you chose to flee and fight the wolf raiders instead."

"Fools," the twins chorused.

"Mrin/Amrin, please." The veiled figure raised a hand in an attempt to regain control. "The Aramite captain had no idea who you were. He was actually heading to one of the buildings near where you happened to be standing. It seems one of the merchants wasn't paying his fair share, so to speak."

The Gryphon and Morgis glanced at one another. The lionbird turned back to the speaker. "Would—Pardon me, first. You seem to know us—at least you haven't asked us our names—but we don't know you."

"Forgive me. I am Haggerth." He rose, being careful to keep his veil in place. "To my right is Mrin/Amrin, and to my left is Troia, whom you have already met." There was a hint of mischief in his voice.

Taking a deep breath, the Gryphon said, "You are, if I recall, Master Guardians, are you not? All four of you?"

He was almost sure that the expression on Haggerth's hidden face included a frown. "You are partially correct. Mrin/Amrin and I are Master Guardians, but Troia is not."

"I am *merely* a Guardian," she purred, her tone implying she was anything but.

"There are only *three* of us, for that matter!" the twins shouted. "There is Haggerth, Troia, and myself!"

Morgis hissed. The Gryphon studied the two identical Master Guardians. They were so much alike that he could not deny that they might not be the same man. Was it possible that in the Dream Lands a man could be in two places at the same time?

"Easy, friend," Haggerth was saying to the entity Mrin/Amrin. "You know how the power of the Guardianship affects us in the eyes of others." He turned back to his "guests." "We are all changed by our nature. Mrin/Amrin took pride in his individuality; now people see him as more than one person—not a true individual. Myself, I was a presence that sometimes commanded by sheer appearance alone. My decisions were not always based on deep thought, merely the fact that I knew I could turn people to my point of view. Now, unless I wish to possibly destroy everything I've worked for, I have to rely on ability alone."

Haggerth flicked the bottom of the veil in emphasis.

"We have all given something to protect our land, even if not all things appreciate it," Troia added, smiling invitingly at the Gryphon.

"I see." Beside him, Morgis said nothing.

"Let us now return to the question of these two," Mrin/Amrin chorused. Both bodies had the right arm raised and were pointing at the Gryphon and Morgis. "Let us discover the truth about this hybrid—this misfit."

The Gryphon started at the vehemence behind the words, so much akin to that of D'Shay. "Am I being condemned for my existence? If so, I would like to know the reason why."

Haggerth and even Troia seemed unsettled by Mrin/Amrin's attitude. The veiled guardian shook his head carefully. "You must forgive us at times. We find ourselves in troubling situations of late, and things better left unsaid tend to rear their ugly heads. It was nothing to concern you. Isn't that so, Mrin/Amrin?"

The double man's multifaceted eyes dimmed a little. "My apologies. It was uncalled for."

"Now, then. The crux of this meeting is your existence and its origins." Haggerth reached into a pocket and removed from it a small whistle. The Gryphon's eyes widened, and he frantically searched his own pockets. It was his remaining whistle. His mane stood on end, and the sound that escaped him was more that of the king of beasts than the bird of prey he more resembled.

Troia reacted in kind, becoming more feline as she stepped forward. Oddly, while he became wary of her sharp claws, he also became more and more aware of how desirable she was.

"Cease! Both of you!" Haggerth rose from his chair and, with one smooth movement, tossed the whistle to the Gryphon, who caught it with one clawed hand while holding off the cat-woman with the other.

"I said CEASE!" Haggerth pulled the veil from his face. Mrin/Amrin, as if knowing what to expect, turned away quickly. The Gryphon, Morgis, and Troia, unprepared, all stared at what the Master Guardian hid beneath that veil.

Neither the lionbird nor the drake would ever be able to recall just what the face of Haggerth looked like. They would only remember that it was something that threatened to tear their sanity from their minds. They were fortunate in that the guardian had almost immediately replaced the thin, protective cloth.

The not-people, to no one's surprise, had not been affected.

Haggerth waited while the three stricken beings recovered. He hated the necessity of having had to do that, but he could see no way of avoiding it. It was no less horrible to him than it was to those he unleashed his curse on.

There were times when the guardianship hung heavy.

"Again, our apologies. Knowing what our guardians are like when their own prizes are taken, I should have realized—"

The Gryphon cut him off with a curt wave of his hand. "This is dragging on, and I can't take it anymore. I have a few questions of my own that I'd like to ask, the first of which is do *any* of you know me?"

All three—four, if one counted both bodies of Mrin/Amrin —shook their heads. Haggerth added, "It was our hope that you could clear up the mystery of your existence. You are a guardian of the Dream Lands; that much is obvious. But the question is, who and when?"

"Who and when?"

The Master Guardian sighed. "You know the name of this place—Sirvak Dragoth?"

The Gryphon nodded, his eyes gleaming. "I thought it must be, but to have it verified is like opening another door in my mind."

"You remember very little, I take it. Let me explain more. It is the erroneous belief of the Aramites, or wolf raiders, that we are the lords of the Dream Lands. By that they mean that we control the place."

"And don't you?"

The twin forms of Mrin/Amrin both laughed. "The Aramites and their god find it difficult to fight a land that exists as much in the mind as it does in reality. They should try maintaining some control over it. It is impossible. If anything, the Dream Lands control us."

"A slight exaggeration," Haggerth corrected. "Let us say that we coexist with this place, and in return for what it gives us we aid it against those who would see it destroyed."

"That's what guardians do?" the Gryphon inquired, staring at the trio. Even with their individual skills—and the skills of the double man were still a question mark—he could not see the guardians holding off the concerted efforts of the Ravager's children. He refrained from expressing the thought out loud. Quite obviously, they were doing just that. "I understand that I am—was—one of you. What happened? Why doesn't anyone remember me? Why don't I remember—Wait—I stand corrected. There *was* one who knew me. A wolf raider named D'Shay."

Had he told them that the entire Aramite military was coming through the Gate, along with the Ravager himself, he could not have asked for more startled looks from the trio. Even Haggerth, with his face covered, evinced utter shock and horror.

"I told you!" Mrin/Amrin was shouting madly. "He's one of those!" The double man stared at the Gryphon with wide eyes and clenched both of his right fists.

Something began to churn within the lionbird, and he felt as if he were about to explode. However, an angry shout from Haggerth made the other Master Guardian pause. The sensation, which Mrin/Amrin must have caused, ceased.

"Because he knows of Shaidarol does not make him like that one! Let not your memories cloud your judgment!"

Shaidarol.

Some of it was coming back to him. Not all of it, the Gryphon cursed silently, but some very important pieces fit together now. D'Shay—he could not bring himself to use the other name, for that had been a friend—had betrayed the guardians, had *been* one of the guardians.

It seemed impossible that D'Shay could have been that other. Yet . . . "He was changed the day he took up the mantle of guardianship. I remembered how different he seemed, how much . . . darker his moods became."

"And no one remembers you," muttered Haggerth. "Curious.

This must be due to whatever it was you were forced to give up by taking on the burden of the guardianship. The Dream Lands shape the all guardians, sometimes in ways we don't understand until much later.''

"You believe this one?" Troia glared at the Gryphon. "You believe what he says when you yourself do not even remember him? There is no record of his existence. You told me."

"No record save Shaidarol himself," added Mrin/Amrin.

"He is certainly not going to tell us anything useful!"

"The Tzee know of me." The Gryphon returned Troia's glare. "You know it. They knew who I was, and they tried to kill me."

She frowned. "That is true. Even I could feel the recognition in whatever passes for their minds—but that's certainly no recommendation!"

"I wish the other Master Guardians were here." Haggerth sighed. "Perhaps they might have a suggestion."

"Others?"

"There are six of us. It is terrible trying to maintain order where none was meant to be. We need all six, plus the other guardians."

The heads of Mrin/Amrin turned toward Morgis. "This one has said nothing for quite some time. Are we to believe that he, too, is a guardian come home?"

"I am not one of your guardians. I am Duke Morgis, son of the Blue Dragon, Lord of Irillian by the Sea, which lies far to the west."

"Across the seas?" asked Haggerth.

"That is correct. It is part of the Dragonrealm, though each Dragon King's region can also be called by that name as well."

"It's your vessels that harass the wolf raiders."

"It is."

The veiled Master Guardian straightened, looking more official than he had since the two had first been ushered into this room. "And why have you traveled with our lost guardian here? Are you a friend?"

Morgis glanced at the Gryphon, who shrugged lightly. If the drake wanted to tell the truth, then that was up to him. If he wanted to lie, the lionbird would not hinder him, but neither would he support the duke.

"At best, Lords of Sirvak Dragoth, I would say we are uneasy allies. Perhaps a little more than a year ago, our lands were threatened by one of my own kind. My sire and the Gryphon made a pact and, with the aid of others, destroyed the mad traitor.''

Not exactly the truth, the Gryphon thought, but not far enough from it to be of any concern—so far.

''During that crisis, my sire and the Lord Gryphon, who ruled Penacles at that time, were also confronted by the evil of the one called D'Shay—or Shaidarol, as you called him.''

''His evil grows!'' Troia hissed, stepping away from the column she had chosen to lean against. ''Master Haggerth, you should have let me go after him! I can still hunt him down! The Runners will not find me!''

''Be quiet, young one. You never met Shaidarol before or after he was tempted by the Ravager. You would have found either form more than you could possibly handle.''

''But . . .'' She trailed off. It was impossible to argue with Haggerth. Not that the young guardian had any desire to truly battle her superior.

The Gryphon frowned and ran the last few bits of conversation through his mind again. There was something wrong.

Morgis continued. ''There is no need to worry about D'Shay. He died during a mad attempt to assassinate the Gryphon and my father.''

''Died?'' Mrin/Amrin looked puzzled. ''When did this occur?''

''It happened a month or so prior to our voyage. We were actually planning on leaving immed—''

Haggerth shook his head. ''D'Shay is alive, all too well, and has been back here quite some time.''

That was what the Gryphon had noticed in the conversation. In a nearly toneless voice, he said, ''He's alive after all. I didn't think suicide was his way—but we burned his body.''

''There are a few ways to get around that, if need be, and all of them are unspeakable. D'Shay is more than capable of doing something like that. He no longer has any regard for life. His only duty is to the Ravager.''

''D'Shay. Alive,'' the Gryphon muttered as he turned away from the rest of them, ignoring his faceless escorts as well. He stared blindly at some of the tapestries and statues in the chamber. Mrin/Amrin started to speak, but Haggerth waved him quiet. Finally, the lionbird faced the Master Guardians and continued, ''Where is D'Shay?''

It was Troia who answered, despite a look from the veiled guardian. "In Canisargos. Everything the wolf raiders do is coordinated out of the capital."

"Canisargos? The capital?" Something about that did not seem accurate.

"It's the center of everything. That's where the Pack Master, their emperor, holds council. D'Shay stands at his right side."

That settled it, then. "How do I get to Canisargos? Do you have a map of the city?"

Mrin/Amrin shook his heads. "I think you presume too much. We have not even settled the problem of whether you are one of us or not."

"Come now." Haggerth turned to his fellow guardian. "I think it safe to assume he is. This is just another of the Dream Lands' tricks. We've seen worse, Mrin/Amrin. Far worse. The Lands do what they have to do to survive."

"Nevertheless, if he is interested in finding out why his 'enemies' remember him but his 'comrades' do not, there is another way."

The Gryphon chose one of the Master Guardian's twin faces and matched gazes with him. It was, nonetheless, slightly unsettling to have the other returning his gaze as well. "I'm going to Canisargos. Whether you believe me or not, there is still a matter to be settled between Shaidarol and myself. A matter put aside for far too long."

He did not notice that he had made mention of D'Shay's original name, but the others did. Mrin/Amrin's faces screwed up as the Master Guardian contemplated something he did not care to think about. Haggerth waited, silently watching the duo. Morgis, who had stood by quietly, was so tense that the Gryphon could literally feel it.

The double man's faces became bland. He scanned each individual in the chamber before returning his attention to the Gryphon. "When . . . D'Shay . . . turned from us, he did not leave us unscathed. We shall never fully know everything he did before he was at last cast out, but I, personally, shall remember one incident in particular."

"Mrin . . . ," Haggerth began.

Mrin/Amrin went on, ignoring his counterpart. "You shall have my full backing in your endeavor to seek out the traitor—and a guide who knows the city—if you agree to furnish the final proof I need in order to believe that you are not yet another ploy on his part."

The Gryphon straightened and studied the guardians. The veiled Haggerth said nothing; he had chosen to withdraw from this discussion until he knew more. Troia appeared oddly anxious for the lionbird, even to the point of giving him a nervous half-smile.

It was between the Gryphon and Mrin/Amrin. "What is it? What sort of proof do you want?"

"Go to the Gate. Stand there and tell it you have come for judgment—"

"No!" the cat-woman shouted.

"—and ask it to give you the proof you need to convince others of your loyalty." The Master Guardian looked at Haggerth for confirmation. The veiled figure nodded his head slowly.

"And that's all?"

A peculiar look passed over Mrin/Amrin's face. He almost smiled sadly. "Oh, no, Gryphon. That's not all. I truly hope you succeed, but to do so, you'll have to do more than just stand there. When I say you have to face judgment, I am talking about a judgment that, if you fail to measure up, means you won't be going to Canisargos."

The Gryphon eyed Haggerth for confirmation. The Master Guardian seemed very tired, but he acknowledged the truth of his fellow's statement and added emotionlessly, "Or anywhere else, for that matter. If the Dream Lands find you wanting, there may not even be anything left to burn."

VII

The smell of death and carnage overwhelmed all else. Here in the dark, one could imagine that all the scavengers of history had gathered, adding to the stench with their rotting meals. Boots kicked at oddly shaped rubble that might have been bones cracked open. There was no light. Those who had a reason for being here knew where they were to kneel. Those who had no right to be here added to the debris scattered on the floor.

It was here that D'Shay had formally sworn his existence to his one true master. It was here that all Pack Leaders, keepers, and even the Pack Master himself came to swear their allegiance.

My prize pup. My hunter. How are you today, Shaidarol?

D'Shay did not look up at the use of his old name. If his master chose to use it for some reason, that would be made clear before long. If not, it was not for D'Shay to know.

"I am well, my lord. The body is stronger than I expected. It will last quite some time."

Something huge stirred in the darkness. *What reason brings you to me?*

"Milord, the Gryphon is in your domain. I am certain of it." D'Shay's mouth was set in a predatory grin, giving him a feral look.

I know. I knew soon after he stepped on this continent.

The wolf raider did not question that, for he would have been surprised if his master had not known.

"D'Rak's people are seeking him now. I ordered him to tell his underlings to do nothing but observe if they find him. I do not want him suspicious."

D'Rak has let loose a Runner pack. They are already nearing the countryside near Luperion.

"What?" D'Shay was standing before it registered on his mind that this was something his master normally forbade. Quickly, he fell back into a kneeling position.

You are forgiven. D'Rak serves his function well. You will not speak to him about this. It is possible that, with the Gryphon searching for a home, he obviously remembers little about how he might accidentally open the Gate. If the Runners gain a pawhold, the Dream Lands are mine.

"And the Gryphon?"

If possible, he shall be saved for your pleasure. If he has forgotten so much, then it must be that he has also forgotten the purpose of his existence. If he did remember, he would be here now.

"Qualard," D'Shay could not help muttering. The old capital of the Aramites' empire had sprung unbidden to his mind.

A savage rage threw him backward. The thing in the darkness shifted angrily, stirring up the ghastly remains about it. Had his wolfhelm not been padded, D'Shay would have cracked his skull on the unseen debris around him. An annoyance for him, yes, but nothing more. What did disturb D'Shay was the anger his master had directed against him. An anger still fresh after more than two centuries.

Qualard is never to be mentioned, the voice howled in his head. *Even you are not indispensible, Shaidarol. The Tzee would gladly take your place.*

"Forgive me, my lord!" D'Shay trembled, and with good reason. Swords and bolts did not bother him much, but the one he truly served had the power to erase him from existence with no more than a breath. It was also true that the Tzee would be more than willing to step in and take his place.

Forgiven. Listen to me, my Shaidarol. The great lizard stirred recently. He has not done that since—since Qualard. It may be that some of his kind are here; it may be that he feels the presence of the Gryphon. Whichever the case, I have no intention of losing my advantage in the game. I am the hunter, not the hunted. I will be the final victor—no one else. If it means forgoing your own pleasure, you will kill the Gryphon the instant he comes too close to the truth.

"I will do so."

Your existence is tied to my existence, Shaidarol. I am the only thing keeping you together. Put your interests ahead of mine . . . The thought did not have to be completed.

"I exist to serve you."

Literally. You would do well to remember that. Go now. It is time for the Pack Master to meet with his council. We would not want them to worry about him.

D'Shay rose and bowed. It may have been that he saw two huge, bloodred eyes staring out at him from the darkness, but he could not be sure. He could never be sure. Even on that night, when he had cast off the laughable guardianship and chosen a new master, he had not been certain. It really did not matter. All that mattered was that his continued existence depended on his value to his master. His only master.

He continued his bow until he was out of the cavern. The cavern beneath Canisargos. A cavern that had once served as a home to gods—and still served as home to one. The only true god, as far as the Aramites were concerned.

The Ravager.

"Who is this guide that the Master Guardians have promised me?" the Gryphon asked as he stepped over the fallen tree.

Troia shrugged. He was disturbed by his response almost as much as he was disturbed by what might prove a very fatal ordeal. "I don't know. The not-people brought him in. He might have been a wolf raider—disgraced probably, if the Runners were after him."

Runners. Shadows of the Ravager's own being. As close as the dark god was said to have true children. No one knew where the Runners had come from, though it was suspected that at one time they had been, like the Tzee, creatures of the Dream Lands. They served their master well, from what Troia had said earlier of them.

She had volunteered to be his guide, and the two Master Guardians had not objected. Haggerth had been reluctant, perhaps fearing that the she-cat might suffer whatever fate befell the Gryphon—not that he claimed to believe that the lionbird was anything but the guardian he said he was. She had insisted. Her initial distrust of the Gryphon had given way to a new, mysterious hope—that, somehow, he would prove of great importance. It was only then that the Gryphon had realized how young she actually was. He was more than two centuries old—maybe more—while she was not even into her third decade, barely an adult.

Or too much of one, the ex-monarch thought wryly as he watched her climb up the side of the hill. She wore little clothing, her soft, tawny fur protecting her from the cold. The only clothing she wore was due to necessity and conventional morals. In Luperion, she had worn clothing that allowed her to look completely human from most distances, but that was not necessary here.

She said little about her kind as they made their way along the winding path that Haggerth had said would definitely lead them to the Gate. They had been dubbed sphinxes by some unknown being far, far back in history, though the term was not quite correct. In appearance, most looked nearly human—though their features were quite exotic and the fur would, of course, not go unnoticed. In slave markets, their beauty and their strength would have brought them the highest prices. Unfortunately, or perhaps fortunately, they refused to live long in captivity, for they either simply died or fought until they were killed. In battle, their sharp teeth and tearing claws became all too evident and their humanity seemed to vanish.

Perhaps it was due in part to that portion of him that was leonine in nature, that the Gryphon felt a kinship, an understanding with her. He tried to convince himself that it was this reason alone he was attracted to Troia.

Still, she made a much better companion than the drake Morgis had. Despite the growing closeness between the duke and himself, the Gryphon had been relieved when Mrin/Amrin had said in no uncertain terms that the drake was not allowed to go with them. Morgis's first duty was to his father, and so it was still debatable how far he could actually be trusted.

They came at last to a small thicket of woods. The Gryphon grew anxious when Troia rose and looked around, but she only laughed lightly when he warned her that wolf raiders might be on the prowl. She shook her head and smiled at his worries.

"You've forgotten so much, haven't you? We're in the Dream Lands now. This isn't the same land that the Aramites see. They could be standing right next to us and they would see only trees and birds. As long as we exist to give it strength, that is the way of the Dream Lands—or have you forgotten why the first ones dubbed it that?"

"Then what do we fear from the Aramites?"

The smile vanished. "We fear the 'truth' of their Ravager. We fear that his dreams will overwhelm ours. As he grows in strength, the Dream Lands dwindle. Faster and faster his reality overtakes ours." She stretched her arms wide. "Once, the Dream Lands *were* this entire continent. That was before the coming of the Ravager."

" 'And the Game began in earnest. . . .' " The Gryphon quoted without thinking.

"What was that?"

He shook his head, trying to gather the memories together. As usual, they sank back into the mire that was his mind. "I don't know. A quote from somewhere . . . but I can't say where." His hands were clenched in frustration. "It's like that all the time! I understand now how Cabe must have felt!"

Troia stepped closer, her worry obvious. "Cabe?"

"A friend. One of the few close ones I have—had. He had a memory problem of sorts as well; perhaps that's why I understood him so well."

"What happened to him?"

The Gryphon glanced around, but the woodlands around seemed to hide no menace greater than a few annoying insects. "Cabe's problem was that he had been born the sickly child to a madman. The Bedlams were the greatest of sorcerers, but Azran was crippled in his mind. He killed his brother, and tried to kill his father. He would have raised Cabe in his image or, more likely, destroyed the poor boy. Cabe's grandfather, Nathan, stole the child and placed it in the care of another. But Nathan saw that the boy would probably not survive and, knowing that he himself was likely to die, gave the lad a part of himself. A part of his soul or essence. In that way, Nathan himself also lived on."

The cat-woman could only shake her head in amazement. "I've never heard anything like that."

"At one point, it was as if two different personalities lived in his head. He grew up not knowing who he was—Azran still lived, you see—and often recalled memories of a life that was not his own. Like my past seems to me."

She gave him a comforting smile. "Perhaps the Gate will take care of that."

"Perhaps the Gate will take care of what?" a soft, but regal voice asked. There was no visible being to accompany the voice.

The Gryphon crouched, ready to use either claw or sorcery, but Troia put a hand on his shoulder and squeezed reassuringly.

The lionbird was not convinced; friendly strangers did not leave themselves unseen.

"Relax!" Troia hissed. "It's Lord Petrac, the Will of the Wood!"

While he puzzled over the odd title, a figure that had somehow not been noticeable earlier stepped closer. The Gryphon tilted his head, trying to understand how he could not have noticed a being that his mind now said had been there all the time but had just been ignored.

How one could ignore Lord Petrac—what Will of the Wood meant, the lionbird still could not comprehend—was beyond him as well. Petrac stood as tall as Morgis, with the head of a full-grown stag and a rack of antlers that would have brought any real animal to shame. Most of the remainder of his form was human, though his hands were shaped oddly—more like those of a raccoon—and his feet were cloven. He wore a loin-cloth, a cape of what appeared to be green leaves, and a belt from which hung several pouches. In his left hand he held a staff, which he utilized at present as a walking stick.

Troia knelt and, with great respect, said, "Hail, Will of the Woods."

Despite—or perhaps because of—having the head of a stag, Petrac's visage was one of power, of purpose. It was a different sort of strength than most leaders revealed, the lionbird thought. Petrac was at peace with his power, a rare, enviable thing in anyone who ruled.

"I do not insist on ceremony, kitten. That I leave to Haggerth and the others."

"If anyone should deserve it, Lord Petrac, it's you."

The mouth of the stag curled up slightly. "That is debatable. But come, your companion and I are strangers, and I would like to know why you and he seek the Gate."

The Gryphon belatedly bowed and introduced himself. Petrac nodded to him, then added, "Mrin/Amrin need not have concerned himself. I can see you are one of us. I daresay that he and Haggerth are becoming much too paranoid of late."

"Haggerth didn't—" Troia began.

The Will of the Woods waved off her objection. "You can be certain that this was as much the veiled one's idea as it was Mrin/Amrin's. He is a good man, but he gives his trust grudgingly. Such is the price of leadership to some."

"I'd still like to go on."

"What need? I will vouch for you."

Shaking his head, the Gryphon explained, "Not for the Master Guardians' sakes, although I would like to make them happy as well, but for my own peace of mind. I'm hoping that a confrontation with the Gate might bring to light some of the essential memories I still lack."

"Sometimes memories are best left forgotten. The Gate is an essential part of the Dream Lands. It is older than any record indicates. You could very well die. I assume they made *that* clear." Petrac shifted his staff, and the look in his eyes indicated that Haggerth and Mrin/Amrin had better have, that otherwise, there was going to be a discussion.

"They did. I still *want* to go there now."

"Then you need not go much farther. It's just over that rise in the woods."

Troia and the Gryphon glanced the way the Master Guardian indicated. The cat-woman frowned. "I was under the impression, Lord Petrac, that it was still much farther."

"I have some advantage being who I am," the Will of the Woods responded in light amusement. "Let us say I know a few shortcuts. Come. I will lead you there so that you make no wrong turns."

As they traveled through the lightly wooded region, the Gryphon began to understand Lord Petrac's unusual title. Animals and birds would come to greet the stag-man. Even creatures normally hostile to one another would forget their instincts in their desire to touch the hand of the Will of the Wood. Yet, they did not approach the Master Guardian as one approached a lord or even a deity. They came to him as they would a loved one. Petrac did not rule them; he was one of them. His interests were their interests—which, coincidentally, were the Dream Lands' interests as well, for what was this wooded area but a portion of the magical region itself.

It was a fascinating walk, made only nerve-racking when two of those who insisted on trundling up and greeting Lord Petrac were full-grown bears. Troia automatically unsheathed her claws, and the Gryphon prepared to cast a spell. The Will of the Woods shook his head at their actions and stepped up to touch the heads of the two beasts. They sniffed his hands and rubbed the sides of their bodies against his. It was a wonder they did not knock him over, but he stood there as if nothing touched him. The Gryphon could only watch in amazement, understanding now why Troia held this particular guardian in so much more awe than the others.

"Be careful where you step over here," the Master Guardian commented, his staff directed at the right side of the path. "The Ravager's reality is pressing forward. You might find yourself in the midst of an unknown woodland with his Runners on your trail."

"I was under the impression that the Aramites were losing ground," the lionbird commented, recalling a remark by the Black Dragon sometime far back. It had been implied that the Aramites' empire had met its match, since D'Shay was cutting off the Dragon King's source of living war material.

"So, too, were we until I noticed that our borders were becoming more indistinct than normal. The Dream Lands are contracting. Somehow, the wolf raiders are winning despite the stalemate."

"They also seek a permanent base of operations in the Dragonrealm," the Gryphon muttered, more to himself. There was a reason for that, too. The wolf raiders did nothing without reason. D'Shay did nothing without reason.

"Here we are. This should do." Petrac indicated an open field ahead of them. There was a strange, almost illusionary feel to it.

"Are you sure it's safe?" The Gryphon eyed the field uneasily. This was the Dream Lands as they once had been. This was a region nearly untouched by the presence of an intelligent race. A region where nature truly ruled.

Would it recognize him as a friend? Would he be, according to its ways, a true friend of the Dream Lands?

"I don't see the Gate."

"You haven't stepped into the field yet."

"Oh." The ex-monarch moved forward. Troia began to follow, but Lord Petrac held her back with his outstretched staff. He shook his head, indicating that this was to be the Gryphon's task alone. She growled quietly but acquiesced.

Each step stirred the field. That was the best way the Gryphon could describe the feeling. He could see the spectrum of lines running this way and that, but they were not as well-organized as in the Dragonrealm. By the rules he had learned, this should not have been possible; it would have made it too difficult to manipulate any of the powers, light or dark. The lionbird had never fully agreed with any of the accepted theories about magic, but this was almost too much even for his radical mind. Nathan Bedlam, Cabe's grandfather, would have had fits if he had been alive.

The waist-high grass whispered as he cautiously made his way through it. Not the mad whisper of the Tzee, but a harmonious whisper of curiosity, as if the Gryphon were as much of a wonder to the field as the field was to him. He noted absently that there was no wind and, therefore, no normal reason for the grass to be swaying to and fro.

When he was in what he reckoned to be approximately the center of the field, he came to a dead stop. If the Gate was going to materialize for him, it would be somewhere about here. At least, this was·as far as he planned on going. The rest was up to the Gate.

As if responding to his unspoken challenge, the scene before him ripped open. A gap in reality appeared. First, only an odd, floating line of energy, then a vast hole through which he could see, not the rest of the field, but another land *entirely*. Perhaps the woods that any wolf raider would have noticed if he had come riding over here. Once more, the Gryphon was struck by the truth of what others had said about the Dream Lands. They *were* as much a part of the mind as of the geography.

Standing in the midst of the tear in reality was the Gate itself.

It was changed once more, which only emphasized again its relation to the Dream Lands. It now resembled an arch under which were two huge, wooden doors trimmed to follow the shape of the doorway. The doors had a touch of rot in them, and the metal hinges were covered with rust. The lionbird suspected this was a bad omen. Nevertheless, he had every intention of continuing on.

With time on his side now, he began to notice more. The things he had glimpsed on the Gate were there in greater numbers than before. They crawled all over the stonework, never ceasing for even a second. They had long snouts and great, saucerlike eyes that saw everything. Whether they were reptiles or mammals or even demons was impossible to say. They resembled nothing he was familiar with. Skin color appeared to be black or dark blue; it was difficult to say. Not one of them was exactly like any other, though they all had enough traits in common to prove kinship. It was as if a thousand variations of one creature had been raised just for this purpose—and who was to say that might not have been the case?

He knew that the odd creatures were guardians, and he also knew that they watched him as well as everything else. There was no sense putting it off any longer. The Gryphon raised his hands into the air—the act was not one he had planned, but it seemed the appropriate thing to do—and called out to whatever entity controlled the Gate.

"I have come for judgment. I come as a guardian lost. I come as a friend to the Dream Lands and ask that my claim be proven!" He hesitated, then added, "I also come in the hopes of regaining my own past, good or ill! If I have betrayed a trust in the past, let me me work to regain that trust as well!"

The Gate was majestically silent. The minute guardians—actually, some of them were more than two feet in length—continued their hectic pace up, down, and around the artifact and ignored the lionbird save to glance his way as part of their duties.

The Gryphon stood where he was, arms raised, for a good five minutes. He lowered his arms, took a few steps back, and looked back at Troia and the Lord Petrac. The feline woman gave him a quick smile; evidently, she believed that no response was a good response. The Master Guardian's animal visage was almost as hard to read as the lack of reaction on the part of the oh-so-legendary Gate. He merely returned the lionbird's gaze.

The Gryphon turned back to the object of his trek, closed his eyes in exasperation, and then opened them when he realized the Gate was opening.

Troia hissed and Petrac shouted a warning, but the Gryphon was already far more aware of what was now coming through the open Gate than he wanted to be. Not simply one what, either. At least six, maybe seven vicious whats that all fell under one collective name that the Gryphon recalled even as the first of the creatures leaped at him.

Runners.

VIII

Morgis did not care for the fact that he had been forced to remain behind while the Gryphon pursued what the drake considered an imbecilic and highly dangerous quest merely to prove himself to the Master Guardians. It should have been the other way around. He knew from his father's talk and the reports of spies what the ex-ruler of Penacles was like. There was much to admire, and their travels together had only emphasized many of those traits that the duke had first noticed. Under other circumstances, Morgis might have called him friend, but drakes were not like that. The Gryphon was a momentary ally, he kept telling himself, and when they returned to the Dragonrealm, the truce between the lionbird and the Blue Dragon would at last come to an end.

He had not told his companion about the small device he carried in one of his pouches. The Gryphon would have surely grown suspicious if he had known that Morgis had been reporting everything back to his sire. It was the drake's duty, after all, but the Gryphon would perhaps see it as a sign of distrust or even a betrayal. All this had been explained by the Blue Dragon, although Morgis had trouble understanding it all. Despite his physical appearance, despite his knowledge and experience, Morgis was still young compared to both his parent and the

Gryphon. The violent death of both of his predecessors had shunted him into a position of power he could have done without.

Like most communication artifacts, it was crystal in nature. Morgis did not pretend to understand how it worked; the point was that it did. A thought struck him. Did the use of such items mean that the Crystal Dragon himself might be following everything they said? Was that the secret of the other Dragon King's tremendous power? He shuddered at the thought. With the Ice Dragon dead, his glittering brother in the far southwest was now the eldest and probably the most powerful of the reigning Kings.

He was letting his mind wander again. It was something he had begun doing more and more since first sailing with the Gryphon. The latter called it free thought, an ability that had allowed humanity to rise and spread the way it had. Morgis had reminded him that Toma was a free thinker. That had started a discussion that . . .

He was doing it *again*! With great deliberation, the duke forced his attention to the crystal. The sending would be weak, Morgis knew from past experience, but it had not originally been ensorceled for such a vast distance.

The drake concentrated, willing his mind to seek that of his sire. There was a time difference to consider, but he doubted it would play a major role at the moment. Still, the duke did not want to disturb the Dragon King from his slumber if it was at all possible.

The image refused to come. He had an impression of mist— no, a dense fog—that seemed to shroud the Dream Lands from the outside world. Morgis cursed. Was that why the keepers had left him the crystal? Did they know it would not work?

Abruptly, he made contact with something else. What it was he could not tell, but it was a kindred spirit of sorts. Draconian in nature and so overwhelming that the duke was almost forced to cut the connection himself.

It was a mind and more. The mind of a dragon, but what a dragon!

Then the connection gave way to another image. An image of a gate—the Gate—and the Gryphon standing before it, arms raised. After a brief time, the lionbird lowered his arms and looked behind him, most likely at the female who had accompanied him, Morgis thought sourly. He had a healthy distrust of females, being a drake. If a female drake did not have young to care for, she was often out trying to seduce a male or, worse yet, trying to seduce a human. He could not see what fascination the latter had for the females; it was not just because they could be tasty . . . not that the duke had ever tasted human flesh. The Blue Dragon kept such things to a minimum. It was why his own humans were so honestly loyal.

The Gryphon turned back, a look of consternation on his avian face. Something dark and shadowy was leaping at him—

A pale hand came down and smashed the crystal from his hand. It struck the floor sharply and cracked. A shoe crushed it to fine powder.

Morgis gazed up into the emptiness that was the face of the not-people.

He was not fooled by its soft appearance. The power of the creatures had already made its impression on him. He was not without power of his own, however. Spells had been prepared for just such an occasion, and the first of these the drake unleashed almost automatically. Eyes that saw into the other world where the spectrum of power lay watched as a portion was manipulated and bands of force sought out the ghoulish intruder.

It was impossible to say if the thing could see as humans and drakes did, but the not-person—a tiny part of the duke's mind cursed the Master Guardians for not giving these monstrosities a real name—looked down at its body and seemed to study what the drake was doing. As his control strengthened, Morgis allowed himself a slight smile.

The blank-faced creature stepped through his bands as if they were naught but illusion. The bands closed upon themselves and disintegrated.

Very bad, Morgis thought absently. *Very bad, indeed*.

He let loose with another, more violent spell. Subtlety was a thing of the past; preservation was important at all cost. What he unleashed would tear apart the front half of his room and scatter his adversary in a dozen different directions.

At least, that was what it was supposed to do.

The air around the intruder sparkled brilliantly, blinding the drake. He covered his eyes and stumbled back. The explosion that should have resulted from his spell did not follow.

Morgis was not a subtle being, but he began wracking his mind for some trick with which to take out the not-person. The magical assault had failed miserably. Perhaps, he thought quickly, the physical was called for. Shifting to his dragon form would leave him open far too long to attack. That left his sword—and the duke's prowess with a blade was well known in his region.

The sword was out in his next breath. He had gone beyond defending himself now. Morgis wanted the faceless creature's blood; it seemed likely that nothing short of that would save the drake. He was pleased to see that the robed figure had come to a halt when it became aware of his intentions; that meant that it recognized the blade as a true threat.

He smiled and lunged.

The not-person stretched out a soft, pale hand—and caught hold of the sharp edge of the blade. The specially honed edge, which, combined with the drake's strength, would have nearly cut through a three-foot-thick tree trunk, did not even so much as nick the intruder's palm.

The being pulled the blade toward it. The drake had the forethought to release his grip, at least; otherwise, he would have fallen into its arms. Even so, he was running out of both ideas and space. The faceless creature had slowly and methodically backed him into a corner. Morgis gave into the inevitable and swallowed his pride.

He shouted. At least, he tried. There was nothing wrong with his voice; he was certain of that. Yet, the shout came out as little more than a whisper. He did not have to guess who was responsible for that.

His backside struck against the wall. There was nowhere else to go. Morgis hissed. Very well. If the thing wanted him, it could have him—all of him. He lunged, clawed hands reaching for that blank visage, his form melting and reshaping, calling forth his birth shape. Morgis leered as his jaws widened and he lost all traces of humanity. Now it would be seen whether his assailant had taken on more than it had bargained for.

The hand that reached out and caught him by the face was the same one that had stopped his sharp, deadly blade with so little effort. It expended no more in bringing the drake to an abrupt halt, reversing the change in much the same way the mysterious Tzee had done. The duke's snarl became a cry of pain and he fell to his knees, once more in humanoid form. Fighting the agony, he reached up and tried to tear the other's hand away. He might have been trying to pry the entire Dragonrealm from the earth for all the success he had. Panic set in; Morgis had never come across so helpless a situation.

The not-person appeared to gaze down at its defeated opponent. There was no hint of satisfaction, no hint of anger. If anything, it seemed to be curious about him.

Morgis felt the world slip away.

The faceless being removed its hand and studied the blank-eyed drake. Morgis, oblivious of the world, remained on his knees, staring blindly ahead. The creatures reached out with its left hand and drew a pattern on the duke's chest. Then, satisfied, the not-person stepped away, gazed without known sight at the room in general, and then quietly and calmly departed through the doorway.

Less than a minute passed before the drake rose and opened his eyes. He blinked once, then reached into one of his belt pouches.

His crystal was missing. Morgis thought for a moment and then took a step toward the rest of his belongings, his boots at one point stepping on the very spot where the object of his search had been crushed. Now there was no trace. Ignorant of this fact, Morgis searched thoroughly among his few items. At last, he gave up and sat on the edge of one of the chairs in the room. Apparently, he thought, the Master Guardians had recognized the crystal for what it was and decided to confiscate it.

Since there was evidently nothing he could do, Morgis rose from the chair and shifted over to the bed. On his way, he noted the odd placement of his sword on one of the other chairs. For the life of him, he could not recall taking it out. Chiding himself for his carelessness, he retrieved it and placed it where he could reach it on a moment's notice.

The bed was soft. Where a human would have never been able to rest comfortably in full armor, the drake had the advantage in that, since he was only mimicking it, he could adjust it as he needed. Morgis settled back and relaxed.

His last thought before drifting off to sleep was that he hoped the Gryphon would come back soon before boredom drove him crazy.

Runners are very good at their tasks, and, when presented with a sudden, almost miraculous opportunity, they adapt easily. Thus it was that the first one to discover the open Gate was through it almost a breath later and his fellows were right behind him. It was also this adaptability that allowed the shadowy stalker to size up the situation and attack the nearest target all in the space of a few seconds. It was only the fact that the particular target was the Gryphon that spoiled an otherwise perfect execution of steps.

Where the dark shape assumed its victim would be was not where that would-be victim was in the next instant. The Gryphon had survived a period as a mercenary that had lasted longer than many humans lived. He had not survived through dumb luck. His already well-honed skills, in great part natural to him because of what he was, had reached a peak few could match. The lionbird had not allowed himself to grow soft, despite an equally lengthy period as monarch of a thriving region.

The Runner sailed over his head and landed gracefully some four yards behind him. Its eyes caught sight of the two figures watching from a short distance. A Master Guardian! The Runner, an indistinct, lupine shape, appeared to quiver with anticipation. How the Father would reward it. . . .

Under other circumstances, the Gryphon would have attempted to deal with the creature. His attention, however, was being demanded by several more of the eager, dark shapes, and his acute hearing had already informed him that the first Runner had chosen to attack Troia and Lord Petrac. He assumed that between the two of them they could handle one of the monstrosities. Considering he had at least half a dozen to himself, that was only fair.

The Runners were disconcerting horrors. He caught glimpses of teeth, of glowing, bloodred eyes, and forms akin to lean, swift predators. Yet, they were not ordinary animals. Runners mixed and passed through one another as if they had no substance or as if they were the same creature. If they attacked him, however, the Gryphon knew that they would feel all too real.

They were circling him, some clockwise, some counterclockwise. Four or five. He could really not say how many had come through the Gate before it had decided to close. At least one more must have gone past him to join the first in an attack on the lionbird's two companions. Another, the first to leap at him after the initial attack, was dead—or at least vanquished. The Gryphon had caught it with his claws as it had gone for his throat. Apparently, when solidifying to attack, the Runners were susceptible to retaliation.

He knew it was only a matter of moments before they would attack again. They were trying to cross him up, make him turn the wrong way at the wrong time so that one of them could catch him in a vulnerable spot. The others would close in on him while he fought off the first. It was a simple strategy, but an effective one. One that would have worked against most other adversaries, but not the Gryphon.

He was reaching into the realms of sorcery—a particular spell already in mind—when he noted something astonishing. The

Runners awaited him there as well. At least, a portion of each of their minds lay in contact with the very powers he sought. If not for his careful attention, he would have ensnared himself there. He withdrew before the creatures' minds could take notice of him.

An intricate dilemma. The Runners watched on both levels, physical and magical, and knew what to wait for. If he attempted to use sorcery, they would have him. If he used physical force . . .

What? The one that had perished so far had died from a physical assault. Could it be that while the Runners could maintain watch on the two separate planes, they could only attack on the physical? Did that mean that at all other times they were merely harmless phantoms?

The entire thought process had taken place over a span of only a few seconds without taking any of his attention from the danger at hand. It was something he had developed to perfection through countless campaigns; the mercenary who could not think while in a life-and-death situation was one who died early.

There were sounds behind him, sounds of battle, but he knew it was too dangerous to turn for even a moment. Still, if what he had worked out was true, it was quite possible that he could turn the shadowy creatures' wraithlike ability to his advantage. If physically unable to touch him . . .

He let them circle twice more and then left his right side vulnerable. The Runners were intelligent, but they were still animals, not sentient creatures. Instinct took over and the nearest of the lupine forms leaped at his unprotected side.

With a speed impossible for most creatures, the Gryphon took hold of the startled Runner and, before it could phase back into incorporeality, threw it into its fellows. They, of course, still retained their own wraithlike states—which was exactly what he wanted. Even before the airborne Runner regained enough wits to act, the Gryphon had moved with the creature so that when it landed, he was already out of the circle. The Runners bayed, and the one that had been tricked tried to snap at the lionbird, forgetting that it no longer had solid form.

Free of the circle and having roused the anger of the Runners sufficiently, the Gryphon whirled and, snaring what power he could as quickly as possible, unleashed a sloppy, raw burst of energy at the nearest of his pursuers. The lead creature melted in the bright eruption of power, fading to nothing in midlunge. The one closest behind it had only enough time to begin a hasty halt before it, too, vanished like a pebble of ice tossed into a blazing bonfire.

A third of the indistinct, lupine forms succeeded in turning and dodging most of the blast, but the amount that caught him was enough to shear off his back end and both hind legs. The Gryphon was startled to discover that, despite its noncorporeal nature, a Runner bled when wounded badly. At least, something dark and moist poured freely from the rapidly dying monstrosity.

There were still two remaining Runners. They had apparently had enough time to consider their chances, which meant that they had turned tail and would escape momentarily unless he did something. In control of the situation now, he summoned up a spell from his memories and focused on the field in front of the two escaping horrors.

The grass approximately ten yards in front of the Runners bent toward the two with evident purpose. As he had thought, the Runners ignored the physical threat and continued on without ever breaking stride. He watched as the waving field enveloped them. When nothing reappeared, he nodded his satisfaction. As he had not wanted to cause any more damage to the field, he had cast a small gate behind the illusion of a physical attack. The Runners had gone through the gate without a moment's comprehension, and the portal had been designed to close the moment they were through.

Unfortunately for the Runners, there was no exit. The Gryphon had cast them out into the endless, empty Void, a dimension of nothingness that could swallow the entire world and still be no less sated. There was little chance the two creatures would ever find a way out before something else floating in the Void got them, wraithlike or not.

The Gryphon had conceived the trick after he and the Blue Dragon had almost suffered a similar fate at the claws of one of the Dragon King's own sons. The lionbird and the Dragon King had been using a gate much like this one (termed a blink-hole for some ancient, obscure reason), and were just onto the path formed through the Void when the Blue Dragon's rebellious offspring had cut off the gate. Only experience and quick thinking had saved them. Morgis now held the title that had once belonged to that particular drake. The dead, after all, had little need for rank.

He recalled suddenly the two that had gone past him to attack Troia and Lord Petrac. The Gryphon paid no attention to the fact that his thoughts were first and foremost for her. If he had indeed noted them, he would have assumed it was because she was not a Master Guardian like the stag-headed Petrac.

To his relief, they seemed none the worse for wear, although the Will of the Wood looked oddly downcast. Troia was trying to soothe him about something. She looked up at the Gryphon's approach.

"He's never been like this before," the cat-woman whispered.

Petrac stirred. He raised his head to look at the lionbird. The deer visage only made his sadness that much more tragic. "Forgive me. As the Dream Lands wane, each violent action I take becomes more repulsive. They were horrors, true, but they lived, they savored life—such as it was. Can they help it if the Ravager made them what they are?"

The Gryphon had not considered it from that point of view, and he determined that he would not try to. War was terrible enough, but to consider the life of one's foe to the point where it threatened your own existence . . . it was a thought too disturbing. He knew that if it came down to his life and his beliefs against his enemy's, he would battle to protect them.

There were no black and white answers, he knew. The Gryphon mumbled something to that effect to Lord Petrac, but it sounded terribly incomplete even to him.

The Master Guardian had calmed. He nodded his thanks and managed to produce a weak smile. "I know we do what we must. The Ravager and his children, the Aramites, will not accept compromise. To give in meekly would be a fool's gamble. The wolf raiders would just trod on our corpses." He shook his head. "I cannot explain what came over me. When I raised my staff and cast them from existence, I was overwhelmed by the loss. I fear the long war is catching up with me."

Relief washed over the Gryphon. Things were bad enough without having to try to take care of a morality-stricken Master Guardian. Petrac's role was one he would never wish upon himself. He sighed and turned to face the Gate once more.

The Gate had not changed appearance during the battle. The dark creatures on the sides continued to swarm up, down, and around. The heavy, massive doors of the Gate were sealed shut. There was a faint glow surrounding the huge artifact.

Pleased with yourself? the Gryphon mentally raged at it. *Was that my judgment—letting in a pack of those terrors? What kind of games are you playing?*

He was not certain if the Gate was a direct part of the Dream Lands or if it was merely a device created by someone long ago.

Nevertheless, it was the most solid thing at which he could direct his anger.

Troia took a step toward him. "Gryphon . . . no."

He shrugged off her warning. "Let me be. Lord Petrac has his burdens to shoulder; I've got a few burdens to dispose of. Just what are we protecting here? Do the Dream Lands really care about us? I want some answers."

The Gryphon stalked toward the Gate. When he was within three yards of it, it winked out of existence, leaving him to stare at a few wild trees and more field.

Yet, before it vanished, he had a glimpse of something—as if whatever it was had chosen that moment to send some sort of message through. He might have been imagining it, he knew. It had only been for a second, and the Gryphon could not have described it save to say it gave the impression of being huge and powerful. Not the Ravager. He would have recognized the foulness of that creature. No, this was something more.

And it was imprisoned. Bonds of vast skill had been weaved about it; the Gryphon had felt that, too.

Old memories teased at him from the recesses of his mind. Like so many of those that hinted at dire need and events of great import, they turned and buried themselves once more within the mire of his unconsciousness. He was left standing there, quietly and bitterly cursing himself for returning to a land that threatened to make the Dragonrealm seem peaceful and understanding.

Now, more than ever, he was determined to go to Canisargos—even if it meant confronting the Ravager himself.

With his luck, he knew, it probably would.

IX

Dark as the room was, it could not mask the anger of the figure seated in the lone chair.

D'Rak glared down at the young keeper he had ordered to monitor the Runners' moves during his rest. The other Aramite was bowed in cowering obeisance. Senior keeper D'Rak was not known for his kind mercy.

"What do you mean, more than half the pack has vanished?"

The associate keeper, mindful of the fates of some of his predecessors, carefully kept his eyes focused on his own feet. "Master, it is as I said. One minute, they were all there; the next, there were only three."

"And you saw nothing?" D'Rak clenched his fists in impotent fury. Runners lost! The Pack Master would be displeased—*very* displeased. What was worse was that it would only strengthen D'Shay's position. The keeper had hoped that a successful hunt would shake his rival's death-grip hold on his favored position.

"Nothing," his subordinate replied meekly for the third time. He was not concerned with power plays. He was only concerned with getting out with his skin still attached to his living body.

Muttering a number of dark curses concerning his underling's family tree, D'Rak closed his eyes to meditate on the sour turn of events. Nearly a full pack seemingly wiped from existence, the three survivors ignorant of what had occurred—they were animals, after all, despite their intelligence and cunning. Could it have anything to do with the incident in Luperion that had left a small city patrol dead? There had also been reports of increased activity among the not-people, those faceless sorcerers that the Ravager tolerated for some unknown reason. Still, those creatures had always been effectively neutral. Why change now? He knew a little about the Gryphon and his importance, but he suspected that the not-people knew much, much more—as did D'Shay. If they were playing a game, it was one of their own, for even the slightest hint of the Gryphon's true value would have had every guardian of the Dream Lands out looking for him.

The Ravager's spell, then, still held.

There had to be some way of saving face. Offering up the body of the incompetent young keeper was a step in the right direction, but it was far from sufficient. He could have the three remaining Runners scour the area for their brethren; they were already eager to do just that. Trouble was, from past experience he knew that they would find no clues. Still, the very disappearance of the creatures indicated that something was up. The denizens of the Dream Lands never bothered with Runners unless they had to.

He opened his eyes and stared down at the associate keeper who had wisely remained in the same position. ''Summon the three surviving Runners back to the Kennels. Alert me when they have returned. I want the keeper in charge to probe their memories, conscious and unconscious. Dismissed.''

''Master.'' The younger Aramite backed out, outwardly unemotional but inwardly jubilant. He did not know that his sacrifice was already ordained. D'Rak planned on cutting his losses as much as possible.

It was nearing that time when he and D'Shay would be at one another's throats, and he knew that for him it was an uphill struggle. He was not concerned over his adversary's special place in the hierarchy of the empire; if D'Shay could not defend himself in the subtleties of Aramite political intrigue, all the favor in the world would gain him little aid from the Ravager. Survival of the fittest.

Still, it would be nice to have something to present to council— that would wipe the perpetual smirk off D'Shay's visage. The senior keeper sighed. It was time to display his own claws, to show the others in council what a force he truly was to be reckoned with. Most of them knew, but it was always good to give them a reminder.

With no more than a thought, he summoned the Eye of the Wolf from its hidden resting place. The planning for this moment stretched back more than two years—two years since that accidental contact with them. That contact led to the other outsider, the one with the amazing proposition. D'Rak had scoffed at it at the time, believing it a trick, but subsequent months had proven the truth of the offer. In the past few weeks, it had become his top priority, something he had been holding back for the best opportunity available.

D'Rak placed his hands over the top of the crystal and performed the necessary patterns. Another keeper would have noticed intricate differences in each major pattern, and the order of those major patterns would have differed from standard teaching. They had to be; there was no way he could contact his "allies" and still maintain a cloak of secrecy otherwise. There was also the little fact that the minds of the creatures were so different, so alien in their own patterns, that normal procedures would not even have drawn their attention.

He knew he had made contact when the whispering began. D'Rak allowed it to grow, hearing both their name and his own and knowing from past experience that this was necessary for the things. Secretly, the Tzee disgusted him, but they had their uses, the most important of which was their own connection to the one he sought. If the Tzee performed their function, they would be rewarded—and then crushed. An abomination was an abomination, especially when it was no longer of any use.

Tzee . . . Tzee. . . . The whispering built up to such a frenzy that it could hardly be called whispering anymore. D'Rak was thankful he had cast a spell to deaden such noise. He did not want to draw attention to himself. Even the slightest rumor would make its way to D'Shay, who had an amazing knack for drawing out the truth.

A tiny black dot materialized in the middle of the Eye. Slowly, it swelled, like some disease, becoming a black cloud from which countless tiny eyes seemed to stare out in every direction. This was not the true form of the Tzee; they had no true form that he knew of. This was merely how the Eye chose to perceive them—and how the crystal perceived them was based on the mind operating it. He smiled. They looked disgusting, all right. The senior keeper would be happy to be rid of them.

The keeper allowed the Tzee to build to a moderate strength

and then quickly imposed his will upon them. It would not be unlike the nebulous colony of creatures to try their hands—or whatever they used—at a little betrayal. He knew they coveted the Eye of the Wolf, among other things. It was what had brought about initial contact. What they wanted it for, he could not discover. That alone, however, was enough reason to maintain a wary vigilance. Any idea the Tzee protected with such secrecy was one that promised dire fates for anyone else. Besides, he thought wryly, it would have been truly ironic to have prepared for his confrontation with D'Shay for so long only to fall prey at the last moment to a living mass of insubstantial paranoia calling themselves the Tzee.

The Tzee were not pleased with his reaction, but they knew better than to struggle. D'Rak eased off his control just a bit. Enough to seem willing to give in a little, but not enough to endanger himself. He had not reached and maintained his position by behaving like a fool.

Over a period of less than a minute, the Tzee related their message to him. The senior keeper's demeanor altered from disgust and disdain to near glee. Where his own aides had failed him at every turn, the Tzee—the damned annoying, insufferable Tzee!—had given him far more information than he could have dreamed!

The Gryphon and one other were indeed here! Foolishly, the Tzee had jumped right in, never planning properly, thinking that their foolish displays would be sufficient, and, of course, failing miserably in the end. He did not relay these thoughts to the Tzee, of course. They had provided him with much of value.

He digested the information over and over in his mind. The Tzee queried whether he still sought contact with the traitor within the Dream Lands. It was odd that the Tzee never saw *themselves* as traitors. Then again, they were merely following their own coarse nature. D'Rak thought for a moment, then broke contact, watching uninterestedly as the image of the whispering mass dissipated. Courtesy was not something the Tzee understood. It was simple enough for them to know that he obviously did not want to include the third party at this time.

D'Rak rose, joyful. He waved one hand over the Eye, returning it to the place that only he knew of. At last, he had his rival. What had seemed a terrible loss of prestige had become his most powerful weapon.

Various creatures he had collected and caged stirred uneasily as he passed out of his private chambers and into his miniature court. The keepership was semireligious, being connected so deeply with the Ravager. As a symbol of the keepership's influence, especially since he had taken office—murdered his way, actually—he held court twice a week. Court consisted of petitions by novices on up for an increase in status. It also consisted of trial for those who had failed, those in the empire found wanting in loyalty, and special cases where only the skills of a keeper could unlock the truth.

Several wolf-visage masks glanced briefly his way and then turned quickly away as the guardsmen snapped to attention. They were handpicked. D'Rak knew that his rival had spies within the keepers' organization, but not among these men. They owed their very lives to him. If he died, they died. It was similar to a Ravager's Tooth, the artifact used by most keepers to monitor soldiers in a particular Pack, only the blood of the individual served a second purpose. Not only did it allow the senior keeper to maintain contact with his own underlings, but it had created a life-bond between them. If that life-bond was severed, they died. D'Rak was careful not to have it a two-way bond. He did not like the thought of suddenly keeling over because one of his guards had fallen victim to a knife in the throat during an off-duty street fight.

"D'Altain."

"Master?" A short, narrow figure materialized at his side. D'Altain had survived for years as one of the senior keeper's top aides solely because of his fanatical desire for efficiency. The underling rubbed a scraggly beard and bowed low. D'Rak was not fooled; he knew that beneath the cowardly exterior was a calculating mind. That suited him fine as long as D'Altain remembered his place.

The guards stirred uneasily at someone being so near their master. There was nothing to worry about, however. With his own prowess with the sword and the nearby protection of so many able men, any physical attack would fail. As an added measure, the senior keeper was covered from head to toe in a complex arrangement of wards that he himself had designed.

"D'Altain, I want you to cancel court tomorrow. I'm going to be much too busy. Do you think there'll be anything you would have trouble rescheduling?" Utilizing the tone of his voice, D'Rak hinted that there had better not be.

"No, master. I shall take care of it immediately." The aide did not depart, sensing, perhaps, that something was still on the senior keeper's mind.

D'Rak turned and made his way to a balcony overlooking the capital proper. The massive city of Canisargos seemed to go on forever—or at least to the horizon. It was a breathtaking sight, the more so because of his own power over so many people. A power that would soon grow.

"Master?" D'Altain had seen his master this happy only twice before, and neither of those two occasions had left pleasant memories. The aide personally thought D'Shay and D'Rak deserved one another. He squashed the thought instantly, knowing that the senior keeper often had others secretly probing the minds of those around him for loose, possibly traitorous thoughts. Not to mention thoughts that he found merely insulting.

D'Rak nodded, more to himself than to his second. "I want two teams of keepers, working in coordination, monitoring an area surrounding the royal district."

"We have such a team already."

"Then we will have two more. Besides, I have special instructions for them. One more thing . . ."

"Master?" D'Altain tried to keep the misery from his face. D'Rak was planning something of major proportions. That meant that someone would die at some point. It always did in Aramite politics.

"I want a special team—handpicked sensitives—to go to Qualard and await my instructions."

"Qualard? The ancient capital?"

The senior keeper gave him a rueful but threatening smile. "Careful, D'Altain. Qualard was still the capital when I was born."

Only a handful of the upper rank still lived who recalled the city of Qualard as a flourishing metropolis. Only D'Shay really knew everything that had happened the night it came tumbling down. D'Rak knew some, and what he knew he considered enough for his plans.

An idea struck him. "Have the sensitives marked."

"Marked?" This time, the other Aramite could not keep the surprise from his face. "But that means . . ."

"There will be no further use of their services when this is done."

"Yes, master."

"Dismissed, D'Altain. Do not tarry and, above all else, do not fail me in these tasks."

"I will not." The aide scurried away.

D'Rak watched him depart, the ghost of a smile briefly making an appearance on the senior keeper's face. Then he turned his attention back to the city and its milling crowds. Thousands of people, many of them among the controlling forces of the Ravager's empire. All going about their business as he watched them—and watched over them.

The smile returned, this time lingering for quite some time.

A brief passage of time, ending with the disruptive clang of metal upon metal as D'Shay closed the cell door behind him. He had gotten nearly all the information he could out of his prisoner. It had been an intricate wolf-and-fox game, with D'Shay's hands tied because he wanted his prisoner in one piece and his prisoner knew that. Now, though, he suspected the fountain of knowledge had at last run dry. A good thing, too, for D'Shay had begun to notice a graying of his own skin, the first sign that time was catching up to him.

Two armored figures stood by the cell. From far away, they would be taken as Aramite soldiers wearing wolfhelms. Close up? D'Shay smiled, looking much like the images of the wolf god he obeyed. Anyone foolish enough to come down here deserved what they got.

Another armored figure coldly stalked up to him and held out an oval crystal, a crystal that D'Shay's agents had pirated out of D'Rak's citadel, his self-styled empire within an empire. He took the artifact from the servant, who continued to stare in his direction. What the wolfhelm did not obscure revealed only darkness, as if the suit of armor was empty. D'Shay knew better, though.

He waved a hand in dismissal and waited until the servant had departed. Raising the crystal to his face, he stared into it, concentrating. Another visage appeared. D'Altain, his spy, his traitor in the ranks of the fool who would dare be his rival. D'Shay enjoyed turning his rivals' own people against them. It was a tribute, of sorts, to that day when he had turned on the Dream Lands and its inconsistency for the power of the Ravager.

"Speak."

D'Altain relayed everything he had either been told or overheard. D'Shay's mind raced, different ideas raised, pursued, and dropped as his spy continued. When it was over, he broke contact with the treacherous aide without a word, his thoughts deeply ensconced in what his rival was plotting.

He handed the crystal back to the dark, armored servant. It departed as silently as it had arrived.

Qualard. While it was not forbidden to go there, it certainly was not something the Ravager would have approved of had he been asked. Still, if the senior keeper could justify his actions, the savage, lupine god might not only agree, he might reward D'Rak for his vigilance.

It must be the Gryphon, D'Shay thought. No one else would create such an interest in the rubble that was all that remained of the former capital. Add to that the interesting fact that the keepers had lost nearly an entire Runner pack. As much as he distrusted D'Rak as a person, he could not fault the man's abilities. The senior keeper was up to something, perhaps even the major confrontation between the two of them that they both knew would someday come.

D'Shay had been walking while he pondered the new developments, and his travels soon took him to the nearest thing he could call a home. He did not sleep like normal beings. Therein lay his true advantage over his rival and all former rivals. No matter what his power, they still believed him one of them now. Long-lived, yes, but that could just as easily have been a reward for serving the Ravager well. He had sorcery—of a sort—but no one knew the true extent of his abilities or how much he had lost that day he had turned on his former comrades.

The room was decorated sparsely, its occupant having little interest in frivolities. Various trophies of past victories, artifacts gathered—a moderately sized but potentially powerful display.

Two creatures hissed fiercely from cages in the room. D'Shay had had to separate them when it became apparent they would kill one another. Savage creatures made the more savage by his careful mistreatment of them. One of the monsters spread its wings as best it could in the cramped quarters and let loose with a cry that was a mixture of a bird of prey's battle call and the roar of a deadly, huge cat.

They were his special treat for the Gryphon, these creatures. They were the beasts from which he had taken his title, the true gryphons. Trained for one purpose—to seek out one of their own and tear him to shreds. A poetic piece of work, in D'Shay's opinion. This particular pair represented the tenth generation he had bred, and it pleased him that such perfect killers would be granted the opportunity.

D'Shay leaned toward one of the cages. "What is it you wish to do?"

"Kill! Kill!" the gryphon parroted. The other joined in, recognizing a call that was natural to it, thanks to its owner.

"Kill! Kill!"

The wolf raider let the two monsters squawk several times before calling for quiet. It was an example of his power over them that they grew silent almost instantly. Despite their bravado, the two animals feared him as they feared no other creature—which proved how advanced their powers of reasoning actually were.

Like some birds, they could be trained to repeat dozens of phrases on command, and D'Shay had taught them a variety, all designed to strike at the mind of the Gryphon.

"He is the last of the old guardians, your cousin is," he whispered to the creatures, which stared at him with baleful eyes. "The last of the misfits, the true children of the Dream Lands. The rest . . ." D'Shay waved a hand as if dismissing them. The gryphons cowered, fearing he was about to strike them. He chuckled. ". . . a race of usurpers, also-rans. Not half the power he truly controls—if he could only remember." His eyes lit up with a fiery passion. "The last of the *lizard's* get, the last danger to my existence and that of the lord I serve. With him gone, the bonds are eternal."

The gryphons' feathers and fur were bristling at the tone in his voice. He switched to a tone of soothing that fooled no one and that he expected to fool no one with. It was a mockery, nothing more.

"Do good, children, and I'll reward you as no other has ever been rewarded. Perhaps I'll feed you a nice, plump senior keeper—if he hasn't rotted away by that time."

He did not lie to himself; the Ravager would turn on him if D'Rak proved more efficient, more . . . predatory. The senior keeper was the exact opposite personality of D'Laque, the keeper who had accompanied D'Shay across the seas to the Dragonrealm. Losing D'Laque had been costly in more than one way. The keeper had been powerful; he had also proven accessible and would have made a good ally if he had returned. A mistake that had cost D'Shay much favor with his lord.

No, he thought sourly, *I cannot underestimate you, D'Rak. Despite his words of praise to me, the Lord Ravager has great interest in you as well. Perhaps it is because you and I are so much alike . . . just as the Gryphon and I are so much alike . . . that we are destined to bare our fangs against one another. A pity. Together we might have even toppled a god.*

At the last thought, D'Shay scanned the room guiltily. Gods were notorious for their great ears even when the words were thought and not spoken. He glanced at his slightly grayed flesh once more. Now of all times he dared not annoy his lord. Not until he had passed from this suit of flesh to the next. Not yet, though. To transfer too soon would leave him too weak—and with both D'Rak and the Gryphon meddling in things, that could prove fatal to him.

One of his two prized pets squawked angrily, a garbled "Kill!" escaping from its beak. They were waiting for a chance to stretch their wings, and even their fear of their master could not hold back their eagerness.

As if on cue, two of the armored servants dragged a naked, stinking form in. A convict, most likely. D'Shay generally asked for convicts; they had a survival trait that made them perfect exercise for the gryphons.

D'Shay stalked over to the glaring figure, reached out a gauntleted hand, and harshly pulled the man's head back by the hair. For a second, he imagined the eagle visage of his oldest adversary and former companion.

"We're going to play a little game," he finally began. "A game that *could* offer you freedom . . ."

X

Lord Petrac insisted that they come with him to the grove where he made his home, if only to stay long enough to eat something. The Gryphon was chafing to return to Sirvak Dragoth and be on his way to Canisargos, but Troia quietly implied that what the Will of the Woods offered was an honor few received. Though Lord Petrac was a Master Guardian and friend to the forest around them, he was still a private soul. Even his fellow master Guardians had to contact him prior to any desired visitation.

It turned out, however, that Petrac was not the only inhabitant of that particular grove. Much to the surprise of both of his guests, there also existed what passed for a village in the Dream Lands, the first one that the Gryphon could recall seeing. It could only be called a village because of the fact that there were contrived habitats and a population of at least three dozen. The Gryphon was at a loss as to whether the people were elves or some mixture of elf and human. They did not resemble the elves or half-elves he knew, but it was known that the race came in more than one size and was as diverse in society as humans. At least these did not seem to resemble the more annoying, tinier wood elves that their taller brethren referred to as sprites.

They were fair in face and form, as an old saying the Gryphon knew went. Out here, among the wonders of nature, they went more or less unclothed. What little they did wear—and it was little enough to make Troia appear overdressed—was purely decorative and usually of a color that complemented the colors of the grove itself. The Gryphon and Troia received only cursory glances and friendly smiles, but the presence of Lord Petrac was enough to send a few to their knees in what the lionbird could not help thinking was rather imperialistic homage to the stag-headed guardian.

They had barely passed through the village when Petrac stretched out his arms and said, "Here we are. Do you like it?"

From past experience with other dwellers of the forest, the Gryphon had come to expect something combining nature with civilization. Cabe and Gwen Bedlam lived in the Manor, a vast, ancient home that was a complement of stone and the trunk of a massive tree. It was difficult to say where the stone ended and the tree began, so skillfully had the original craftsmen worked. He had expected the Will of the Woods to be housed in something at least as grand.

What the Master Guardian called his home was no more than a tiny, open field in which, from vegetable matter, had been formed an overhang. The wall of plant life was uncomfortably close in design to that constructed by the Tzee, the Gryphon noticed, but here it served a more benevolent purpose. Crude chairs of straw and wood created a primitive court of sorts with a large couch obviously serving Petrac's personal needs. There was a bowl of fresh fruit, twigs, leaves, and such on a waist-high, flat rock next to the couch. The Gryphon glanced from the bowl to his host, realizing then that the stag aspect of the guardian was more than just show. He wondered how the human part coped with such a diet.

"Please. Be seated. Have some fruit." Lord Petrac took Troia's arm and led her forward. Like the Gryphon, she was at a loss. From the expression on her face, it was evident that she had expected a more regal residence for one she respected so much. From her side, the lionbird watched as her mouth tightened. He knew that she was assuming there was an unfairness about the situation. Haggerth and Mrin/Amrin lived in the vast, elegant Sirvak Dragoth, while Petrac eked out an existence in a place that could not possibly give him shelter from a moderately strong rain. The Gryphon hardly expected that was the case, but he decided it was best left up to the Will of the Woods to explain such things.

Lord Petrac led the feline woman to one of the chairs and

aided her in sitting down, an act that revealed how much she respected him. The Gryphon doubted she would have acted so demurely with anyone else. Oddly, he felt a pang of jealousy, but it was forgotten when he noticed that Troia's chair was *moving*. No, it was *changing*. Unprepared for this, she was clinging on for dear life, as if expecting to be thrown off any minute.

The Will of the Woods laughed, a surprisingly deep laugh at that. "It is only adjusting itself to your contours. I suggest you relax; it will finish sooner if you stop fidgeting."

The Gryphon turned to study the chair beside him. Like the others, it appeared to be a crudely made piece of furniture. He wondered if it had been designed that way, or whether this was merely a sample of the guardian's sense of humor. With some reluctance, he seated himself. The sensation beneath him was astonishingly pleasant. It was warm and soft and, if he remained relaxed, shaped itself perfectly to fit his form. When he found it to his liking, he nodded his approval to his host. Troia, still fidgeting, fumed in his direction.

"Fruit? I apologize for not offering you any meat, but you will, I hope, understand."

Friend that he was to the wildlife of the forest, slaughtering an animal for food probably would have seemed like murder to the Master Guardian. He understood the needs of others, though, and knew that many of the animals he befriended hunted one another when his influence was far away.

Eyeing the piece of fruit, the Gryphon debated over proprieties and finally shifted to the more convenient human form. Lord Petrac watched almost uninterestedly, but Troia stared as if the lionbird had turned into the Tzee. She had never seen him eat and, therefore, did not know of either his ability to shift shape or preference for a human body for certain things.

"You are a versatile being, Gryphon," the Master Guardian commented as he chose a piece of fruit for himself.

"That's the same face you wore when I captured you—only, that was illusion."

"Based on fact. I find myself changing without thinking sometimes. This is the only other form I can transform into. Anything else requires great sorcery or intricate illusion. I'm sorry if I disturbed either of you."

"By no means," Petrac replied. He bit into a handful of grass and leaves, a disconcerting sight to both of his guests.

Troia's eyes appraised him. "It takes a little getting used to. Not bad, though."

The Gryphon allowed himself a smile. "Glad you approve."

To his surprise, she looked away, suddenly intent on the piece of fruit she held in her hands. He quickly changed the subject. "Lord Petrac, I do thank you for your hospitality, but I cannot stay. Regardless of the risk, I *must* go to Canisargos. D'Shay is the key to my background and, I believe, the key to much of the present crisis."

"The endless war of attrition, you mean."

"As you say. I grant you, he probably already knows I'm here, and he probably knows that the moment I discovered he was still alive I swore I would track him down."

"Then why bother going? He will have certainly set several novel traps. Shaidarol was always imaginative about such things."

The Gryphon hesitated, then replied, "Because the very fact that he knows I'm coming after him is my ticket for safe passage through the Aramite capital."

"What?" Troia looked up from the contemplation of her piece of fruit. "That's absurd!"

"Is it? D'Shay and I are very much alike in many ways. He wants me for himself, Troia. This is something personal. Forget the wolf raiders. D'Shay has made my life his, and I've begun to do the same with him."

"The deadliest wars are those fought between 'brothers,' " Lord Petrac commented. He shook his head. "The confrontation between you two could possibly prove more of a danger than the Ravager himself."

"Or it could be the end of the wolf raider threat. I want to know why they remember me and no one here does."

There was an uneasy silence after that which was not broken until a bird, a raven, landed suddenly on the left shoulder of the Master Guardian.

Lord Petrac stroked the bird. "I believe Haggerth must be concerned about the results of your 'judgment.' "

The Gryphon frowned. "It was pretty inconclusive, I would say."

"On the contrary, you faced off against a number of the Ravager's children and vanquished them all. You could have just as easily joined them and killed both of us—or tried to, anyway."

"He wouldn't have done that!" Troia spat, her claws out with astonishing speed. She looked down at them and grimaced. "I'm—I'm sorry."

"You believe in him, kitten, as do I." The Will of the Woods took the raven onto his right hand and whispered something to it. The bird squawked several times. Petrac nodded to himself and then whispered again. When he was finished, he held his hand high in the air and let the raven fly off.

"It *was* Haggerth. I think the message I give him will convince him. You have only one more problem, and that concerns your guide, one Jerilon Dane."

"Him!" This time, the feline did not apologize when she unsheathed her claws. "I lost clan to him! He had kittens butchered!"

"He did not. Yes, he is responsible for the deaths of many, but in battle. Jerilon Dane was one of the more civilized Aramite officers. That was his downfall. That was why he was made the fox in a Runner hunt. He failed to make any true headway—at least in the Pack's eyes—and he showed compassion, a trait the wolf raiders have been trying to breed out of their soldiers for centuries."

"I'll leave my judgment of him for when I've spoken to him," the Gryphon said. "Beings can change. Is that the problem? Don't they trust him?"

"Haggerth seems to. Mrin/Amrin . . . I suppose so. The other Master Guardians are not involved with this, and they would likely go along with what we decide. No, the problem is that Dane refuses to go back with you. He says that traveling with you is certain death for him. One miracle is enough. I cannot say I blame him, if you consider his point of view."

The Gryphon *was* considering the former wolf raider's point of view . . . and some of the intriguing possibilities his presence in the Dream Lands meant. "This man was an Aramite commander. High-ranking."

"He was."

He stood. "Then I have to beg your pardon and depart now, Lord Petrac. Whether or not I can convince this man Dane to come with me to Canisargos, I have to speak to him, if only for my own sanity!"

The Master Guardian frowned as best his features allowed. "I don't follow your logic. . . ."

The Gryphon looked at Troia, but she shook her head, indicating her own lack of understanding. The former monarch of Penacles indicated both of them with his hands and said, "You two—no one in the Dream Lands retains any knowledge of me. It's been said time and time again."

"And it's very, very true," the Will of the Woods interjected. "Despite the fact that few of us are old enough to remember so long ago—the war has done what nature could not—some of us should have remembered."

"And who does remember?"

"Shaidarol, of course, but that's because—"

The Master Guardian broke off as the Gryphon nodded. "—Because he was one of the Ravager's servants. As Jerilon Dane was once." The Gryphon folded his arms and smiled without pleasure. "Jerilon Dane may hold the knowledge of my past, and I'll get it from him even if I have to wring it from him with my claws!"

"I can't help you," the former wolf raider stated flatly. "There is nothing I can say to you."

There had been times during his long, colored past that the Gryphon had come close to losing all control. Times when the beast within him had threatened to take permanent control. He prided himself on having never given in completely, although there had been a few occasions where he had teetered on the brink.

He reached such a point now.

They had assembled in the chamber where Haggerth and Mrin/Amrin had questioned him the first time. Aside from the two Master Guardians, there were nearly a dozen others. Many were not-people—or "the Faceless Ones," as Morgis, who disliked the awkwardness of the other title, had started calling them—who waited with their seeming indifference for whatever outcome arose from this meeting. Morgis and Troia were there also. Two other figures of significance to the situation were there as well. One was yet another of the Master Guardians, a thin, balding man who sported a long flute. He sat to one side of his counterparts and said nothing. Neither Haggerth nor Mrin/Amrin made any attempt to introduce him to the others.

The remaining person in the room was, of course, the former wolf raider Jerilon Dane.

Dane was not a cowardly man. While he was younger than the lionbird had expected, he carried the look of a man who had spent years on or near the front, a look the Gryphon saw every time he looked in a mirror. If he was not a coward, then he was holding back because he had no desire to tell what he knew.

The Gryphon had reverted to his normal form, and he made use of his predatory appearance. Reaching out with one clawed hand, he pulled the veteran commander by the front of his shirt and dragged him until the Aramite's nose came within an inch of his very sharp beak. To his credit, Dane did nothing more but swallow very loudly.

"You"—the Gryphon emphasized each word precisely—"will tell me what it is about myself that so concerns your former masters and has been stolen from the memories of my own people, or I will show you exactly why the gryphon of the wild is a beast most others learn to shun—even the largest of the other predators."

Jerilon Dane gave him a dangerous sneer, dangerous to the Aramite for daring to do it at all. The former wolf raider reached up and purposefully removed the hand from his shirt. The Gryphon's mane had risen, and the urge to strike out was becoming difficult to ignore. Yet, Dane still pretended that there was little danger to him.

From behind them, Haggerth said, "There will be no bloodshed in this chamber, Gryphon. Even if it means we strike you down by some other means."

"There won't be any need for *that*," the Aramite snorted. "If the misfit will just *listen* instead of squawking, he would understand what I'm saying."

"I understand quite well, scavenger."

Now it was Dane who bristled, albeit in a different fashion, of course. "You are *not* listening! I can't tell you what you want to know, because I can't remember any of it now!"

The Gryphon stepped back in shock. No one else was making a sound. It was even impossible to detect any breathing.

"What?" was all that the lionbird finally succeeded in blurting out.

Jerilon Dane sneered again. "From the moment I first woke in one of the rooms in this citadel, I knew there were gaps in my memory. Things I had been willing to offer in exchange for asylum—including things dealing specifically with you, as a matter of fact. When I realized what had happened, I stalled, fearing that the lords of Sirvak Dragoth would return me to the Runners."

"We would never do that," Haggerth assured him.

"None of you has grown up under the rule of the Pack Master or, for that matter, the Lord Ravager. I couldn't be certain. I thought maybe that some of you had retained some piece of knowledge—that's a thought held by many on the council, if I recall *that* correctly."

"There have been many casualties among the elder guardians," Mrin/Amrin commented bitterly. There was a personal conflict inherent in the tones of both his voices, but he did not elaborate and no one wanted to bring it up.

Dane nodded. "Then you are even worse off than we imagined. What I can remember is that there was always the fear that you *people*"—the sarcasm in his voice was unconscious, a throwback to his life as a wolf raider—"would—would—would . . ." He took a deep breath. "I find it hard to formulate the thought even from what has been explained to me and what I can deduce—*that you would search for and find whatever it was that was so important to your cause.*"

The former officer cursed at the exhausting effort of merely making the statement. "I—I'm sorry. That's the best I can do."

"Very strong sorcery," Haggerth muttered.

"Impossibly strong," added Mrin/Amrin.

The other Master Guardian stroked his flute and nodded, nothing more.

Jerilon Dane smiled bitterly. "Can you expect any less from my Lord Ravager?"

"You would do best to remember that he is no longer your lord, Aramite," Troia hissed. It was quite obvious she cared nothing for the man.

"I shall endeavor to do so."

"We can do without futile bickering," the Gryphon interrupted. "What we need is a direction to turn. A course of action. Canisargos."

"I already stated that I will *not* go back there. Luperion is nothing compared to Canisargos. When it became the capital after Qualard's destruction, the keepers were ordered to enshroud the city in such a complex web of sorcery that not even the least of a hearth witch's market wares would escape notice. Can you imagine what your materialization in or near the city would do? More alarms would sound—silent to all save the keepers, of course—than if the Ravager himself had come calling."

"You remember that much, do you?"

"My *former* lord," Dane replied with a glance at Troia, "apparently sees nothing wrong with advertising such precautions."

"I sssshould sssay not," Morgis hissed, so disturbed by events of late that he was allowing his speech patterns to slip. He corrected himself immediately. "Such a defense would be very costly, but certainly effective."

"It *was* costly. I understand most of the keepers involved died under the pressure of binding it."

"More likely they met with 'accidents,' " the drake concluded. "Not an uncommon practice in some places."

The Gryphon eyed his companion closely. In retrospect, it should not have surprised him that such things were practiced by the drakes. The gods knew that more than a few humans had eliminated the possibility of secrets leaking out by eliminating the only other possessors of that knowledge.

Something clicked in his mind. "You mentioned Qualard. The old capital."

Dane shrugged. "What of it?"

More than one of the Faceless Ones—the lionbird found the drake's phrase more comfortable—seemed to stir at talk of the devastated city. They were only slight movements, a flicker of a finger or the twitch of the body, but the Gryphon, a veteran predator, could read the change in the normally ambivalent creatures. He decided to press on.

"What happened to Qualard?"

"Even I can answer that," Troia said, one clawed hand running leisurely along her thigh. The Gryphon forced himself to keep his eyes on her face. "The wolf raider leaders at that time had failed their doggy god miserably. He punished them—and everyone else in the city. Goes to show what a great mind the dog soldiers obey."

The ex-raider whitened, but then remembered where he was. He nodded. "More or less, that's the truth."

The Gryphon was not so sure. "Seems a little extreme, even for what little I recall of what the Ravager is supposed to be like."

"If there's anything else, I can't recall."

"Do you recall how long ago it happened?"

That brought a slight smile. "I'm not an elder like you, bird. Before my time. Still . . . at least a couple of centuries, I think."

"About right," the Gryphon muttered. He reached up a hand and rubbed his neck in thought.

"What is it?" Mrin/Amrin asked Haggerth. "What bird-brained pattern of thought is he following now?"

Haggerth shrugged, but it was possible a smile was hidden

beneath his veil. Certainly, he did not seem to share his fellow guardian's worries.

The third Master Guardian, not asked for an opinion, took out a cloth and began to polish the intricate designs on his flute.

"Dane, do you know anything about the layout of Qualard? I know it's unlikely, but—"

"I do, Gryphon."

"You do?"

"Part of military history. In the early days, it saw its share of war. Some of the greatest battles were fought near it. I admit I studied a little more deeply than necessary, but until its fall, Qualard was considered impregnable."

Mrin/Amrin muttered something unintelligible. He did not seem inclined to repeat himself, so no one bothered to ask him.

The Gryphon turned back to the Master Guardians. "With your permission, I've changed my mind. I'd like to go to Qualard."

"Of what use would it be to go to the ruins of a city dead these past two centuries?" Mrin/Amrin asked disdainfully. "It hardly seems that anything of value would remain after so long."

"That may be true. Do I have your permission?"

Haggerth looked at Mrin/Amrin, who shrugged both sets of shoulders in surrender. The veiled guardian turned to the Gryphon. "I don't see why not. I doubt forbidding you to go would keep you from finding a way. Still, Qualard may itself be dead, but you could encounter something that scavenges in the ruins. Even the Aramites tend to steer clear of the place."

There was a glint in the lionbird's eyes that old comrades, such as his former second-in-command Toos (now supposedly King Toos I of Penacles), would have recognized. It was a glint that hinted of what had made the Gryphon successful as a commander and had earned him the respect of any man who served him. "Which is one of the reasons I want to go. Something occurs to me—or maybe it's a memory nagging at me." He held up a hand to forestall what he knew the Master Guardian was going to say. "This would best be done with as few as possible. I've no desire to pull anyone away from their duties. We've not been attacked, besides Runners, since I've been here, but I suspect you've been defending against an assault of sorts all this time."

At that, the guardian with the flute looked up. He did nothing more, merely looked up at the Gryphon.

Haggerth nodded, his veil fluttering slightly. It was weighted in the bottom to prevent breezes from pushing it aside and revealing what no one wanted revealed. "Keepers hound us day and night, though that has lessened a little lately. They cannot touch the Dream Lands itself, but their power strikes at individuals, sapping our strength slowly but surely, as if their soldiers were marching on us. I fear that the stalemate is truly at an end. Senior Keeper D'Rak, who may be D'Shay's only true rival for power, wants this to be a victory for his kind. It is a precursor, I suspect, for a major assault on both the physical and magical planes."

The Gryphon nodded. "I thought as much. If there is no objection, I'd like to take Jerilon Dane and Duke Morgis and leave it at that."

Haggerth looked at the former wolf raider, who closed his eyes in thought and finally, reluctantly, nodded. Apparently, Qualard was a much safer prospect in his mind, and he no doubt knew that, one way or another, he was going to end up traveling with the Gryphon somewhere.

"Very well," the Master Guardian began. Troia cut him off.

"Master Haggerth, Master Mrin/Amrin." She did not mention or even glance at the third member of the august group, who was at that moment back to work on his flute. "If I may, we are sending out two who are unfamiliar—or can't remember—with the way of things in the empire of the Ravager. They are being led by one whose loyalties are recent—which is, of course, not to say I distrust him," she added quickly.

Morgis, who had moved nearer the Gryphon, whispered sarcastically, "Oh, no. By no means is she saying such a thing."

"Hush."

"We need to send one of our own, especially if there is need to return quickly. There is some question as to whether they can summon the Gate if needed. I volunteer to be that one."

"You?" Haggerth asked needlessly. He did not even turn to his counterparts. "Very well. Go. All of you. Go before anything *else* comes up."

"Geas," Mrin/Amrin called out, and the Gryphon realized it was not just a word, but the name of the third Master Guardian. The man looked up indifferently. "Can you bring the Gate here?"

Geas nodded and put the flute to his lips. He began to play a melody. As it developed, those hearing it for the first time felt a stirring, as if a wayward child were being called back by a loving parent—or perhaps a wayward parent being called by a loving child. As the guardian played, his face grew flushed, but it was not due to exertion but some deep emotion.

The not-people took hold of the Gryphon, Jerilon Dane, and Morgis and pulled them aside. The air began to ripple not far from where the three had stood. A tall, wide blotch began to form from the ripple.

"Couldn't we have made a gate of our own?" the Gryphon asked Troia, who had just joined them.

"None of us have been to the city. This is the only sure method. The Gate"—the capital letter was quite evident in her tone—"does not need to have been there."

"Why not use it against Canisargos?"

"There are limits to *our* power. To Geas's ability to persuade it to do this."

"Persuade it?"

"Another time," she said, for the Gate was now fully formed. It was cast completely from iron this time, and the rust was growing. The insane creatures still scurried about, but there was something more anxious in their movements.

The Gryphon shook his head and whispered to Troia, "I'm not so sure about this part. Remember last time we made use of the Gate. . . ."

"That was different."

"Was it?"

Geas suddenly played a questioning note, and the massive doors of the Gate began to slowly swing open. The assembled group seemed to hold its breath—even the Faceless Ones, if they truly breathed.

A scene of ancient but very complete destruction was all they could see no matter what angle they viewed it from. There was no question that this could be anything but poor Qualard. The wind could be seen to be blowing harshly, and the sun was hidden behind a gray haze of clouds.

"Qualard was never a very hospitable place, I understand," Haggerth commented. "You four had best go now. There's no telling how long the Gate will stay open. We rarely ask it to open to such places. It will not stay so for very long."

"What about food and water?" Dane asked, and then grimaced as four of the empty-visaged creatures stepped into the chamber, bearing with them four packs. The Aramite shuddered and whispered to the Gryphon, "Helpful they may be, but they give me shivers the way they seem to anticipate or know things."

The Gryphon nodded and then took the proffered pack from

the Faceless One. He slung it over one shoulder and, when he saw that his companions were ready, started toward the Gate.

"No horses?" questioned Morgis.

"Too rocky a region," Troia responded. "Besides, we won't be traveling too far—I think."

"What do you hope to find when we get there?" Dane asked the Gryphon.

"I'll be depending on your memory and mine to answer that. There's something there—I'm fairly certain of that."

"Oh, fine. Perhaps, I accepted too soon."

Morgis stumbled into them. He had been staring intently at the scene before them. His eyes darted to first the Gryphon and then Jerilon Dane. "He's right. There *is* something there."

"You, too?" the former wolf raider muttered.

"Good hunting!" Haggerth called.

They stepped into the Gate—

—and into the desolation of Qualard—

—and barely had time to recognize the wolfhelmed figures surrounding them, arms raised, before—

—they were sent *elsewhere*—

—where they were surrounded by an even greater number of the wolfhelmed figures and discovered that they could not speak, could not move.

From somewhere beyond the Gryphon's vision, someone chuckled in great satisfaction. The sound of a heavy pair of boots echoed in the dark chamber. A large hand with a powerful grip took hold of the lionbird by the shoulder and spun him around. The face he saw was not a pleasant one.

"Welcome to Canisargos, Gryphon. I am your host. My name is D'Rak, and I am so *very* pleased to finally meet you."

D'Rak smiled. It was a smile frighteningly akin to the one the Gryphon recalled D'Shay had worn during their last encounter. It was the last thing he saw before consciousness vanished abruptly.

It was the smile of a predator about to eat his prey.

XI

The Gryphon woke.

Anyone glancing his way would have seen no change in his appearance. His eyes were still closed, and he breathed with the regularity of sleep. He did not even stir. Nonetheless, he was awake . . .

. . . and chained. Beyond him, he could hear one other person nearby. Judging by the consistent hissing each time the other took a breath, he knew it had to be Duke Morgis. The drake was still out. The Gryphon tuned out the pattern of his companion's breathing and sought out other sounds. He heard the distant marching of feet and the mumbled words of male voices, probably guards. The normal sounds of an ancient structure revealing its age, the creaks and groans, were ignored. Occasionally, Morgis moved in his sleep, causing the chains on his wrists, ankles—and, yes, even around the neck—to rattle.

The Gryphon opened one eye and peered around.

Neither Troia nor the Aramite Jerilon Dane were to be seen in the tiny, cramped cell. The lionbird had already known that, but it was always good to have visual evidence as well, especially when dealing with sorcery of one sort or another. He opened his other eye and studied the place in detail.

His surroundings were not what he had grown accustomed to

as monarch of Penacles, but neither were they the worst he had ever found himself in. At least it was decently warm in here, if a bit moist. The smell of rot was prevalent, but, to a soldier who had spent most of his life on one battlefield or another, it was little more than an annoyance. Moss grew on most of the walls, and tiny creatures of every shape and form scurried about. The Gryphon shifted uneasily. At least a few of them had decided to check his potential as a host.

Unsheathing his claws, he bent his fingers forward and allowed the tips of the claws to brush against the manacles holding the wrists. Hard and sharp as they were, his claws were also sensitive to the nature of things, something that those who did not have them would never have understood. Claws were more than just weapons to animals; they were tools that aided the senses.

The manacles, as he feared, were enshrouded in a number of binding spells. They had also been cast in an alloy that defied understanding save that it was very strong. The chains were, of course, of the same design. Knowing what sort of work creating such bonds would have entailed, the Gryphon knew that he and his companions—at least Morgis, that is—were not being held in one of the common cells. No, this was a private prison, a dungeon.

He stiffened suddenly, for his mind had finally cleared enough to recall the single whistle he still had. Tiny as it was, it was difficult to tell whether the artifact was still on his person or not. He tried to reach his chest with one hand, but even with his claws he lacked the length needed. It had been bad enough to see it in the hands of Haggerth, but now it might be the prize of one of the highest-ranking wolf raiders—a man supposedly every bit as deadly as D'Shay himself.

D'Rak. The name had come up in conversation at various times. D'Shay's apparent rival. Senior Keeper D'Rak. A man very much like D'Shay.

What could have happened? he wondered. They had arrived in Qualard and there had been wolf raiders. Not ordinary soldiers, but men like D'Laque, bearing tiny artifacts similar to the Ravager's Tooth that keeper had carried before his death. There was a brief moment when it seemed the entire world turned to the side—and they had been teleported here, frozen like statues, unable to defend themselves in any way.

He heard footsteps nearing his cell and realized that they were stopping at the door. There was the rattle of a key in the lock of the heavy wooden door, and then it was shoved open. A hulking, monstrous figure clad in a black apron, trousers, and boots, his face covered by a hood—with no eyeholes!—turned his head in the direction of both prisoners, saw that the chains still held, and stepped back. The jailer moved aside, and a second figure stepped into the cell. The lionbird recognized him immediately, though his only other glimpse had lasted no more than a few seconds.

"Awake. Good. You know who I am? You remember?"

"You're D'Rak."

"I am. But before we begin negotiations, I would like to thank you for your timeliness. My men had barely gotten into position before you and your two companions stepped through the Gate. That was *the* Gate, wasn't it?"

The Gryphon, who had been mulling over the word "negotiations" and then the fact that the keeper's subordinates had captured only *three* people, nodded silently. Had Troia escaped somehow? Was this Mrin/Amrin's way of disposing of three unwanted guests? The Gryphon quietly cursed himself for not using his time with Lord Petrac to ask about the double-bodied Master Guardian. Petrac would have told him everything had he asked. Yet . . .

He *shrieked* in agony as it seemed a million of the tiny vermin crawling about the cell suddenly chose to eat him alive. That was the feeling. Thousands upon thousands of tiny mouths biting—*everywhere*. The very abruptness of it was the worst part. Even as he fought the incredible pain, the Gryphon felt the shame flowing through him. Shame at the weakness he had revealed to an enemy.

D'Rak stood over him, grinning with sadistic pleasure at his torment. No matter what their normal facial structure, the Gryphon could not help noticing that *all* of the Aramites he had studied closely had a definite feral look to them that revealed itself wholeheartedly in moments of anger or dark pleasure.

Children of the Ravager, indeed.

"When I speak to you," D'Rak said sweetly, "I expect the courtesy of a reply." The senior keeper's left hand was on a pendant that hung from his neck. It looked very much like the sharp, wicked tooth of a wolf carved in crystal.

A sharp hiss and a terrible rattling of chains informed both of them that Morgis was awake and furious. He was trying to transform, the Gryphon realized, but, as with the trap of the Tzee, he was being forced back into his humanoid form.

D'Rak turned and gazed at the drake with the look one reserved for a fool. "If you like, I'll give you the ability to shift to your dragon form, but I should warn you that neither the manacles nor the chains will break, and you will be dead from asphyxiation—or possibly decapitation—long before you can do any damage. I made certain to have the collars fairly tight."

Morgis hissed unhappily. "I am growing tired of finding myself in compromising positions. Give me my sword and let me fight to my death! If not a sssword, then at leassst unbind me ssso that I can go down asss a warrior!"

"A true warrior's spirit. Perhaps I'll oblige you later, although, if your companion comes to his senses, there may be no need for your death." The keeper turned his attention back to the Gryphon, who had by now recovered. "I mean what I say."

"You talked about negotiation. . . ."

"I did. We have a mutual enemy, bird. You know who I speak of. I am offering you an alliance of sorts."

The Gryphon tilted his head to one side and gave D'Rak a disparaging look. "An alliance? I agree that it would be nice to be rid of D'Shay once and for all, but an alliance with you? You tell me. What would make me believe that you would honor any bargain we made?"

"Wolf raiders have no honor," Morgis spat. "My sire said so, and I have seen nothing to change that fact."

D'Rak rubbed his chin with one gauntleted hand. "I suppose I could merely promise you a quick, painless death. You, Gryphon, felt a taste of what a slow, painful death could be like. I would like your cooperation, though, for a full effort by both of us is the best way we can rid ourselves of the one you once called Shaidarol."

The lionbird appeared to consider. "What happened at Qualard, D'Rak? You must know; otherwise, you wouldn't have sent men there."

The senior keeper shrugged. "I know enough. That's neither here nor there. We were talking about D'Shay. He fears you, you know."

"What?"

"He fears you. Behind all that anger, that raging confidence, he fears you. I think I may be the only one who knows—other than my lord Ravager, of course."

The Gryphon wanted to reject the idea out of hand, but he was curious as to the Aramite's reasoning. He also hoped that the keeper might say more than he meant. At this point, information was the only thing the Gryphon had any hope of obtaining—and even then it might be of no use should D'Rak decide he didn't need him after all.

"D'Shay has never shown anything remotely resembling fear—and why *should* he fear me?"

D'Rak smiled thinly. "D'Shay fears you because your continued existence lessens him in the eyes of the Ravager. While you were lost for so long, he was given the benefit of the doubt. Now he has a time limit of sorts. The Ravager is not a patient god. Even the most loyal of his followers can fall from favor overnight. D'Shay owes his continued existence—I don't know how—to the Lord Ravager. An existence the Master of the Hunt may cut off at any time."

It was not the answer that the Gryphon had hoped for, and he knew there was another reason, but it at least gave him some information about D'Shay. He *had* hoped for a hint concerning the truth about his own past and his connection with Qualard—which at least had been verified by the senior keeper's trap. D'Rak had *known* that the Gryphon would definitely go to the shattered city.

"You talk about negotiation, but I notice that one of us is missing." The Gryphon prayed that Morgis would not correct him.

"The female is in another cell. I said I wanted your cooperation, but I will take your unwilling aid, if necessary."

The Gryphon turned to Morgis, who returned his gaze but gave no indication of his opinion one way or another. He knew the decision belonged to the lionbird.

Putting on a reluctant appearance, the Gryphon looked up at D'Rak, sighed, and said, "If you can guarantee our lives once this is over, then I'll accept."

D'Rak held out the Ravager's Tooth. "By this token of my lord, I swear that I will bring no harm to you while I live. Any more, I cannot promise."

"I understand." Knowing what D'Shay was like, the Gryphon could not fully accept the ease with which the Aramite had sworn the oath. It *sounded* like an honest oath, but the promises of a hungry wolf . . .

The senior keeper was looking down at them. "Do you two agree to what I have offered? Will you assist me in the downfall of our mutual foe?"

The Gryphon nodded, and Morgis, after some hesitation, did the same. The Aramite held out the crystalline artifact. "I want each of you to touch it. Be careful; it's very sharp on the edge."

"Wait . . ." Morgis clenched his fists and began to protest.

"You want your oaths, and I want mine. You can rot in here—or perhaps I can give you to D'Shay as a peace offering."

Before the drake could reply, the Gryphon reached forward. As he touched the Ravager's Tooth, he felt a slight prick of pain, as if something had cut his—There *was* blood dripping from his finger! He jerked his hand back. The glistening, scarlet liquid dripped onto the crystal—and was absorbed.

D'Rak withdrew the artifact without even offering it to Morgis again. "That will suffice. Now I'm guaranteed of your cooperation, and you of mine."

"What've you done?"

"It was a trick! I knew it!" roared the duke.

The keeper hid the crystal beneath his shirt. "Your destiny is now linked with mine, Gryphon. My goals are now yours. Should anything happen to me, then, through this bond we share, you will die."

If he had expected a look of shock to spread itself over the Gryphon's visage, the wolf raider would have been disappointed. Rather than protest, the lionbird merely looked deep into the Aramite's eyes and said quietly, "Then *both* of us had better be careful, or *both* of us will regret it."

"Indeed." D'Rak seemed a bit taken aback by the lack of what he considered a proper response. "With that done . . ."

He snapped his fingers, and the huge jailer—whom somehow both the Gryphon and Morgis had forgotten about—lumbered over to the lionbird. It was impossible to tell exactly what the hooded figure did or how he did it, considering he should have been unable to see, but the manacles around both wrists suddenly fell away. There was no click of a lock mechanism, and the jailer had only the key that obviously fit into the cell door.

As the hulking form continued his work, the Gryphon asked something that had been puzzling him. "A question, D'Rak. Don't you see any of what you plan as an attack against your own god?"

"By no means. I serve the Pack Master and, through him, I serve my Lord Ravager. D'Shay serves no one save the Ravager, and he does that reluctantly. Too often, his mind turns to other things and he loses sight of the empire's goals. As for you, I think that the knowledge that you will no longer be a threat to us will be sufficient. The Pack Master will grant you the means to return home—across the seas. There are ways we can assure ourselves of your cooperation, if need be.''

The Gryphon stood and stretched, casually checking for the whistle as he pretended to straighten his clothing. It was still there. Something inherent in its nature hid it from the sight of others unless the lionbird chose to reveal it. He had been worried that the ease with which Haggerth had taken it meant that it had lost that masking power. Apparently, though, the Master Guardian had only been able to see it because of what he was. Anyone who was not one of the Dream Lands' guardians still fell prey to its subtle power. That was fortunate, especially now.

D'Rak waited patiently, his eyes seeming to stare *through* the Gryphon rather than at him. When they were ready, he indicated the jailer. ''R'Mok will see to your kitten. If you two will follow me . . .''

Outside, they discovered that the corridors of the dungeon were no less unimpressive than the cell. The Gryphon gazed around at the other cells. Some of them were occupied, and he started to look in one. A strong, heavy hand pulled him back. D'Rak's eyes bored into his own. ''She's elsewhere. You didn't think I'd put her this close to you? I take no chances.''

Behind them, Morgis made a sound. The Keeper ignored it and turned to his left. Without any hesitation, he started off down the corridor, fully confident that his two associates would follow suit. Morgis and the Gryphon looked at one another and then glanced at the monstrous jailer, who watched them silently from behind the eyeless hood.

They started after the Aramite. Morgis leaned toward the Gryphon. ''Do you really believe everything he said? His promises, his reasons?''

''Of course not—and he doesn't expect me to believe him.''

''He doesn't?''

The lionbird shook his head. He watched D'Rak with one eye as he replied, ''He has us for now. He knows it. From what little I understand and remember of the wolf raiders, nothing compares to their political intrigues. They lie to one another's face worse than any human or drake. It's what makes them so deadly—sometimes even they can't tell where the truth ends and the falsehoods begin. D'Rak, because of his pivotal position in the empire, probably thinks they're one and the same now.''

Morgis paused. ''You remember more.''

The Gryphon took hold of his arm and dragged him on. D'Rak

was slowing, and it was obvious to him that the senior keeper was about to turn around and check on his new "allies." Hastily, the Gryphon whispered, "Some of it I learned as a monarch. I do remember more, however, especially about the keepers. I remember enough to know we have to keep alert."

"D'Rak may stumble on some steps, slip, and break his neck. What then?"

"You find your way home on your own. Swim, maybe."

"Hmmph. One thing. What happened to our Aramite guide?"

The Gryphon shrugged. "I don't really know."

"Gentlemen?" the keeper called out. The irony was evident in his voice. "If you please."

They hastened their pace.

"Gaze, if you will, upon Canisargos, the greatest city ever raised from the earth!"

D'Rak had led them through the citadel of the keepers, past rooms where men stared at artifacts of all shapes and sizes, others filled with exotic creatures and works of art, all the way to the balcony from which, he said, he watched over his people.

"The Pack Master is a military leader. He does not understand people. Thus it falls to the keepers to oversee the daily functioning of the cities. A keeper travels with each patrol whenever possible, and they may overrule any decision made by that patrol leader if they can justify it."

Justifying actually meant that a keeper generally found some way to coerce the captain, thought the Gryphon as he recalled Captain D'Haaren's patrol. It was not an easy alliance.

Canisargos—politics, madmen, and wolf gods aside—was a spectacle that, for once, daunted the Gryphon completely. The city seemed to go on and on and on all the way to the horizon. Like Luperion, many of the buildings resembled tall, sleek rectangles. Unlike the other city, wicked, jagged spires topped every other tower. What could be seen of the surrounding walls indicated that any would-be conquerer would need to build ladders and siege machines at least three times as high as was the norm.

The Gryphon glanced briefly in the general direction of the sun. A little more than an hour until sunset—of the next day, he knew. What had happened in that time?

There were watch towers everywhere, all manned. He sensed power emanating all around and realized it was not just from the keepers' citadel; it was *everywhere*. There was more use of the fields and lines of power—or the light and dark side of the spectrum, if one chose to believe that theory instead—going on in Canisargos than in most of the Dragonrealm.

"Look there!" Morgis hissed, pointing at the sky.

Men rode on the back of long, muscular, winged creatures that dove hither and yonder. With a shock, the Gryphon understood that he was staring at the beasts from which he had taken his name. There were only a few in the Dragonrealm, and he had never really come across any of them. Here, however, there seemed to be hundreds. He could not see the gryphons' being used for aerial guard duty if they were very rare. No, they would be saved for special, high-priority missions.

He felt a twinge of loneliness. Even the beasts had others of their own kind. He was indeed a misfit.

"Don't we take a chance, being out here?" Morgis was asking the senior keeper.

"Hardly. We are protected from the sight of nonkeepers. They will see nothing but an empty, barred window."

The Gryphon gave Canisargos one last look. From here, the crowds melted into one vast sea of life. He could make out little detail of the lower city. "We still haven't seen our companion. You said your lackey was going to get her."

"And he will." D'Rak snapped his fingers. An unsavory figure seemed to materialize from nowhere. "D'Altain, we would like something to drink, I think. Could you please see to it?"

"Yes, Master." The Aramite vanished into the inner chamber, but not before the Gryphon detected a hint of hatred in the man's eyes.

"You surround yourself with interesting people, Lord D'Rak."

The senior keeper was amused. "D'Altain? He is an efficient aide, if a somewhat unappetizing person."

"Not a servant?"

"I make him double as that on occasion." D'Rak smiled knowingly. "It keeps him in line."

"It breeds rebellion," Duke Morgis snarled. "I would not stand being treated as a menial when my status is much higher."

The Aramite leader gazed back into the chamber. "D'Altain does what I want him to do. Trust me."

"The words of many an assassinated leader," countered the drake wryly.

"My lord!" D'Altain rushed onto the balcony, wringing his hands as he looked at his master.

The amusement vanished from D'Rak's face. "You've for-gotten the wine, D'Altain. What is it?"

"The feline. The one that bear R'Mok was supposed to bring!"

Stiffening, the Gryphon pushed heedlessly past the senior keeper and took the underling by the scruff of his collar. *"What about her?"*

"She's gone!"

The lionbird whirled on D'Rak. "Is this more treachery, wolf raider?"

"Gryphon . . . ," Morgis began.

D'Rak shook his head. "Leave it, drake lord. No, my feath-ered and furred friend, this is not treachery on my account. If you'll let my aide breathe a little, we might get somewhere."

Without realizing it, the Gryphon had pulled D'Altain from the floor. The smaller man bounced a bit as his feet struck the ground, and he wobbled uncertainly for a second. When he had regained his senses, he glared at the former monarch and turned to his master. "R'Mok is dead, master. One of the novices discovered him lying near the cell. His head . . . his head was nowhere to be seen!"

"Damn!" the senior keeper cursed. "All that work! R'Mok was the finest one yet!"

The lionbird got D'Altain's attention again. "The woman—Troia—what about her?"

"No sign. The cell door was locked, and R'Mok's key was still on his belt—unless someone had replaced it."

D'Rak tugged on his mustache as his mind raced. "She must be in the building still, unless . . . Could she have summoned the Gate? Tell me truthfully, my friends."

"As for the truth"—the Gryphon's mane bristled—"how do we know that all of this isn't more of your intrigues, keeper? Aramites are famous on this continent for their games!"

The senior keeper's eyes narrowed, and the lionbird realized that D'Rak now knew that his "ally" remembered much, much more than had been indicated earlier. The Gryphon found he did not care; all that mattered at the moment was finding Troia.

"Master?" A very young man in keeper's robes—obviously a novice—stumbled out onto the balcony, blanched at the sight of first the Gryphon and then Morgis, and then finally remem-bered why he was here. "Master! There's a messenger here! Asking entrance!"

"Who's here, fool? What messenger?" Having just been

handed one piece of disturbing news, D'Rak lashed out far more angrily than necessary at the unfortunate novice.

"Lord D'Shay's man. He seeks an audience." It was astounding that the young keeper could find his voice.

The silence was overwhelming.

"How . . . timely," D'Rak finally muttered. "So soon." He turned to the Gryphon, who had unsheathed his claws at the mere mention of his adversary's name. "I think we have the answer to our questions, Lord Gryphon."

"What do you mean?" *D'Shay. He had to be nearby.* The lionbird forced his breathing to stay regulated. If he allowed himself to lose control . . .

"Isn't it apparent?" The senior keeper seemed surprised that the Gryphon did not agree. "The timing is too perfect. I would say the chances are very good that your friend is now a guest of D'Shay—and that this messenger is his way of extending to us an invitation to meet him in *his* domain."

XII

She had woken up in a dank prison cell, and her first thoughts, oddly, were not about her own safety but about that of the older, mysterious guardian who called himself the Gryphon. Troia could not say why his safety concerned her so very much; her kind, living as wild as they did, were a people of the moment who did not dwell on long-term matters. Yet, her time as one of those working with the Master Guardians of Sirvak Dragoth had changed her, and she did recognize some of her reactions based on what she had seen in that place. Not completely comfortable with what she saw within herself, she turned other thoughts.

The Aramite called Dane had betrayed them; she was certain about *that*, at the very least. How else could they start out for the desolate region of Qualard only to be waylaid by stalking wolf raiders and transported to . . . to Canisargos? Most likely Canisargos, the feline woman decided, her mind already darting to another track of thought. The Gryphon was the object of a wolf raider hunt, and now he was in their claws. The Gate only knew what they were doing to him even now! She struggled violently against the manacles around her wrists, ankles, and neck, but they refused to give even a little. Troia spat out a childhood epithet that had earned her more than one swat on the behind from her elders. It did nothing to gain her freedom, but it allowed her to vent some hostility. There was too great a possibility that she might lose control, become the wild cat she so closely resembled. Troia refused to allow herself that mental escape; if nothing else, she knew the Gryphon would be counting on her to free herself. She would not let *him* down.

There were no guards outside. If there had been, they would have made an appearance before now, at least to look in and yell at her to settle down. Occasionally, her acute hearing picked up the sounds of people walking down distant corridors. Soldiers, judging from the heavy, trampling sounds of their footfalls. She unsheathed and sheathed her claws automatically at the image of so many wolf raiders close by. If only she could find a way to work herself free of these manacles! She knew how they worked, for more than one dead prisoner had been discovered still wearing them. The chains and manacles were attuned to the strength of the prisoner. They drew their power from the very life of the unfortunate soul. Neither struggling nor remaining still was effective. Death was one possible solution, but a pretty pointless one. The only true key was knowledge of the bonding spell of the manacle itself—and that required a sacrifice on the part of the jailer that Troia understood was even less desirable than death. Something to do with the head . . .

She lost track of the thought when she noticed that someone was walking down the corridor, getting nearer and nearer to her cell.

A hooded head appeared in the tiny window of the cell door. There were no eyeholes, but Troia knew with a chill that ran down her spine and caused her to arch her back a bit that the being beneath the hood could see her quite well—with or without eyes. She hesitated to even think of it as a man.

The jailer stepped back from the cell, and Troia knew he was reaching for the key to the door. Then there was an odd thumping sound from one side of the corridor and the hooded figure was turning to see what was going on. The feline woman watched in shock as the huge guard was pulled bodily from where he stood by something she could not see.

A rough, muffled grunt, that same thumping noise—and then silence again.

When she heard the thump a third time—in her cell yet—Troia renewed her struggles with the manacles. Then the wall beside her opened up and Jerilon Dane, with something large under his left arm, stepped out of a portal. She hissed and spat into his face. He wiped the moisture off his cheek and slapped her once in return before seeming to collect himself.

"I'm here to *free* you, you damn sphinx! Hold still while I deal with those manacles!"

"How—" she began, and then saw that the burden he carried under his arm was the hooded head of the jailer. The head or, if what she had been told was true, something not quite real. Whatever lurked beneath the blank hood, it allowed the Aramite to open her manacles with no difficulty.

Dane rose and started to toss the grisly prize away, but changed his mind before releasing it. He tucked it back under his arm as he waited for Troia to stand. The portal flickered ominously.

The former wolf raider glanced back at it and, with a frown, said, "They've latched on to it sooner than I thought! Go through, before they track it to here!"

She shook her head and backed away, having gained a healthy distrust of portals of late. "I thank you for your aid, but I think I'll make my own way from here! I have to find the Gryphon—"

"From inside a locked cell? Don't be a fool! I'm not risking myself any longer for you! Go through! Your only other choice is to remain here!"

"Just get me the key!"

He scowled. "That's it! I'm leaving! Come now, or wait and see what tender plans Senior Keeper D'Rak has in store for you! Perhaps he'll let you play with the Runners!"

Dane turned his back on her and stepped into the portal. As he vanished, Troia took one last look around and, reluctantly, leaped in after him. It was a good decision; the portal vanished almost immediately afterward.

A shout erupted from the main entrance to the keeper citadel. D'Rak, who was in the midst of herding the Gryphon and Morgis into one of the side chambers, was forced to abandon them to D'Altain. "Take them somewhere safe from probing! I must deal with this messenger!"

"Master." The aide turned to his two charges. "This way. No arguments, please."

Neither of them cared for the brief gleam in his eyes. Morgis's hand strayed to his empty scabbard, while the Gryphon found his mind wandering briefly to the question of where the drake's sword went when he transformed into his dragon shape. He and

Morgis were racing to keep pace with D'Rak's second, who moved swiftly for such a small, ungainly figure.

"A strange, very annoying land you've brought me to," whispered the duke as they followed D'Altain down a flight of stairs. "People here have an irritating habit of not being where you expect them to be or showing up when you least expect it—and that includes ourselves! If I could just have a blade, I'd fight this Ravager myself rather than end up in one more place I wasn't expecting to or having one more person show up when they really shouldn't!" The drake sounded somewhat confused by the end of his complaint.

"You may still get the opportunity!" D'Altain hissed. "Quiet now!"

The Gryphon's heart threatened to pound his chest apart. He realized now just what a deadly rivalry he had been thrown into. Until D'Shay's discovery of the lionbird's continued existence, D'Rak must have been his greatest stumbling block. It said something that the keeper could preserve any secrets and grow so powerful despite D'Shay's favored position with the Pack Master and the Ravager.

The senior keeper's aide was leading them deeper and deeper into the citadel, and the Gryphon began to wonder if he intended to march them all the way back to their cell. D'Rak was going to be unpleasantly surprised if he believed they would voluntarily return to that place, Ravager's Tooth oath or not.

"Where *are* we heading?" demanded Morgis, who, like the Gryphon, was beginning to believe that they were returning to the keeper's private dungeons.

"Master D'Rak has standing orders for situations such as this. Lord D'Shay's man would not be here unless his master did not have a good excuse and, most likely, permission from the Pack Master to probe our people. He no doubt suspects you are here and, if he truly has your companion, then he has the proof he needs to gain that permission. You can be certain that D'Shay's servants will be very, very thorough. That's why we have quite some distance to go. What he knows, we cannot help; what he does not know, we can try to keep from him."

A hiss of annoyance. "Why can't we use a portal to reach this place of safety?"

"With Lord D'Shay waiting for just such an occurrence? Do you really think he would not have others secretly probing? We do not expect that all keepers are loyal, either."

"You seem to have this all worked out fairly well," the Gryphon commented quietly. The three of them had come to a long-neglected landing that he estimated must be at least on the same level as the cells, if not lower. Cobwebs decorated the ceilings and walls, and the only true light came from a crystal that D'Altain wore around his neck. The dust was so thick that he wished it were possible to not have to breathe altogether. Morgis, directly behind them, began to cough. Though he preferred dry land to the sea his father reveled in, this was a little extreme for the duke's tastes.

The aide kicked aside a dark form that squealed as it raced down the corridor behind them. "I try my best. Besides, we knew this day might come some time. Lord D'Shay has probably become very nervous with you running free." He brushed aside a very large cobweb from in front of his face. "Pardon the condition of this area, my lords; its appearance is deceptive. The look of disuse tends to discourage searching parties."

"Won't we leave tracks in the dust?"

"Have we?" D'Altain asked in return.

The two looked down at their boots and, even in the dim light, could see the dust reshaping itself. Footprints vanished after mere seconds. The dust in the air (what they had not swallowed, that is) did not float for very long, but dropped almost like lead the moment the trio was past. A few feet back, it would have been impossible for even the Gryphon to believe that they had actually passed this way.

"You see," was all the Aramite said. He continued on, and, like his master, did not look back to see if his charges were following him.

A few corridors down, they came to a dead end. Judging by the debris lying on the side, the lionbird came to the conclusion that this area had once served as a storage facility of some kind. He was not suprised, however, to see the unsavory D'Altain touch a stone in the far wall and then push the entire wall forward like a massive door. A secret panel in a place like this came as no surprise.

"Through here."

Perhaps it was because the Aramite had been *too* helpful, *too* polite after what the Gryphon had read in his eyes earlier that made the former monarch pause a moment. He could understand D'Rak's almost paranoid caution about D'Shay's resources, but something inside said that this did not ring true.

His patience was rewarded by the impatience of D'Altain. The keeper reached upward to his own chest, no doubt for his talisman. He was unused to the Gryphon's natural speed, however, and before his hand could close on the artifact, the Gryphon had the hand in one of his own. He pulled the hand back, nearly snapping the bone at the wrist. D'Altain shouted something, and immediately the corridor was spilling over with dark armored figures bursting from the passage the Aramite had been trying to convince his two charges to enter.

In the dim light emitted by the crystalline talisman, the Gryphon could make out at least half a dozen figures, probably more, clad in wolf raider armor and wearing full masks such as those worn by the senior keeper's own guards. It occurred to the lionbird as the first one came at him that these might actually be members of that unit.

The Gryphon did the only thing he could do under the circumstances: he threw D'Altain at the foremost man and then shoved the two tangled bodies into the next. In the confusion that reigned, he succeeded in freeing a knife from the keeper and trying to use it against its former owner. D'Altain twisted, however, and the blade found only empty space where the traitorous keeper's side had been. One of the armored figures knocked the blade away with the flat of a sword and closed on the ex-mercenary. The Gryphon unsheathed his claws and met him head-on.

Behind him, he heard the triumphant shout of Duke Morgis as the drake was finally presented with a situation within his powers. The Gryphon hoped Morgis would not enjoy himself too much and become careless. They were still outnumbered in close quarters, with no weapons but their claws and their sorcery still suppressed by the power of the keepership in general. Not that the lionbird had any spells in mind that did not require time. He doubted very much that Morgis had any, either, and the drake would certainly not have tried shifting form in these tight spaces.

The mailed fist that drove into the wall next to him warned that it was he who was becoming careless. He drove his own fist into the midriff of his adversary, the armor giving a little under the force of his blow. The wolf raider was pushed back a step, and, taking advantage of the extra space, the Gryphon drove his claws into the narrow, unprotected area of the throat between helm and armor, killing the Aramite instantly. Unfortunately, the dead weight was such that he found himself unable to extricate himself from his fallen foe as two more wolf-visage masks closed with him.

The edge of a blade caught his left arm, drawing a long, searing line across it. He finally freed his claws, but by then the Aramites were too close for him to raise his arms properly. With sudden clarity, the Gryphon saw his death coming.

Complete darkness filled the corridor at that point, a sign that D'Altain had either fled or been killed. The sudden lack of light made the two wolf raiders hesitate, if only for a second. The Gryphon, pinned as he was against the wall, found little comfort in the fact that he could now see his oncoming death more clearly than the two about to deliver it.

There was a garbled shout, half astonishment and half sudden fear, and then the wolf raider on his left was flying backward like some mad marionette whose strings had been pulled. The other Aramite could not help but turn in dismay as his fellow seemingly vanished in the darkness—which proved to be his own undoing. Freed, the Gryphon roared and, using the wall as support, threw himself forward, striking his adversary with the full force of his body. Both of them were propelled into the opposing wall. The wolf raider let out a painful grunt as he struck the wall. The lionbird raised his claw for a final strike, but the soldier was already sliding to the floor.

The Gryphon whirled, awaiting a new opponent, but a quick scan with his night vision informed him that only one other form still stood. That form proved to be Morgis, who was relieving one of the corpses of its short sword. The drake's night vision was not as good as his companion's, but he could see well enough to know it was the Gryphon coming toward him. There were at least five bodies near the duke, and the ex-mercenary realized that the drake had taken on the majority of their attackers.

"You should feel fortunate," Morgis began. "I'd say they had orders to take you alive, if possible. Not so with me. When the first one failed to kill me, the rest came charging. Still, only two could fight me at any time. I suppose close quarters has its advantages and disadvantages."

The Gryphon chuckled. It was typical of some drakes—and humans—to start analyzing situations that had been, mere moments before, a matter of life or death. At least, he thought, Morgis would stop wishing for a sword.

Morgis inspected the short sword. "Not much more than a knife, but it will have to do until I can find a *real* weapon. Do you see anything?"

The Gryphon shook his head, afraid that any verbal response

would begin a new battle—between the two of them. Some beings were never satisfied.

One thing he had noticed was the absence of one body in particular. D'Altain had vanished, and the lionbird suspected he had fled through the very passage their attackers had entered from. What the keeper's plot had been was still debatable, but it was obvious that D'Rak, paranoid as he was, would have eventually discovered the truth from his subordinate—which meant that D'Altain had been planning on fleeing once the deed was done.

There were only two people in Canisargos with the power to save him, and only one that would even consider it. It was even possible that D'Altain had arranged for the messenger to come at that time. It would explain the assassins; somehow, it seemed unlikely that they had been waiting here on the slim chance that someone would come down here eventually.

"Morgis, we have a way out of here."

Eyeing the darkness of the passage, the drake asked, "What about you? You're still linked to that arrogant warm-blood up there."

"I'll take my chances. I have to find Troia. The longer she's in D'Shay's claws . . ." He trailed off.

Morgis nodded silently. He glanced at his short sword, tested it again in his right hand, and then took it in his left. After a brief mental debate, he returned it to his right. Like many veteran fighters, he was skilled with both hands. It was then a question concerning the balance of the weapon. The wolf raider who had used this sword had used it well, and it was worn in the handle. The difference would have been negligible to many swordsmen, but not one with the skill and experience of either the Gryphon or the drake.

They searched the bodies for any clue concerning Troia and the Aramite capital. The Gryphon found a short sword that suited him and also some of the local coinage. He disliked robbing the dead, but, under the circumstances, there was little choice. They might prove of use. The tiny talismans that were the mark of keeper guardsmen they did not touch; there was too much of a chance that D'Rak could work his sorcery directly through them. There was nothing else of value to the two. Morgis pulled two of the largest cloaks from the bodies and tossed one to his companion.

The passage proved to be fairly straightforward, and the Gryphon could not help but wonder how the senior keeper could not know about it. Evidently, he left more in the hands of his subordinates than he should have. It made the lionbird wonder if there were passages back in his former palace in Penacles that he had never known about. Still, he had placed more faith in his second-in-command, Toos, than D'Rak had in D'Altain—and there was the difference.

Groping, they eventually found the hidden door leading out of the citadel. Pulling the cloaks over their forms as best as they were able, they stood with swords ready while the Gryphon pushed with his free hand. The door gave much more easily than he expected—likely from the fact that D'Altain had preceded them not long before—and the Gryphon almost tumbled forward. Morgis caught him by the shoulder and pulled him back. For several seconds, they stared in the direction of the partially open door. Then, slowly, the lionbird pushed it open enough to allow them access.

The sun was nearing the point when it would soon be no more than a memory. Dark shadows already enveloped this side of the keepers' stronghold. There was no one in sight. The two fugitives stepped outside and scanned the area for danger. Nothing.

Morgis turned and pushed the secret door closed. The hiss that escaped his scaly lips made the Gryphon whirl.

The doorway was gone. There was absolutely no indication that it had ever even existed. Even a careful examination of where they knew the doorway had been revealed nothing but grime. The designer had been a master at his craft.

"What now?"

"We have to find a place to hide you, or at least find something to disguise you with. That cloak is only good for nighttime and long ranges."

"What about you?"

"I'll shift—" The Gryphon halted in midsentence. He had foolishly assumed he still had the ability to transform himself to human form, even though Morgis had been prevented by the power of the keepers. While the drake watched expectantly, he concentrated. There was a brief, tingling feeling that he knew preceded the change, but nothing more. It was as if a block had been put on that part of his mind.

That was not the worst of it; it dawned on the Gryphon that he had quite possibly alerted any number of keepers to the fact that he was there.

There were cries from above, as if his flying namesakes patrolling above the city had suddenly become alert to a danger nearby. He did not doubt that he was that danger and that the beasts would be here, each bearing an armed rider, before long.

Glancing around, the Gryphon knew which direction he needed to go. "Follow me! Quickly!"

"Where are we going?" It was a credit to the drake's trust that he followed instantly.

"Into the center of the city. To the Pack Master's palace."

That almost made the duke halt in midstride. "Madness! We should be going the *opposite* direction!"

"Which . . ." The lionbird took a breath and increased his pace, heading for the protection of an unlit street to the right. He swerved into it and was joined by Morgis a moment later. "Which," he continued, "is the same thing the guards up there will be thinking. *No one* would be crazy enough to go running for the home of the mortal commander of the wolf raiders!"

"I hope you'll remember that statement when they feed us to those Runner pets of theirs."

"I'll expect you to remind me."

They heard the cry of several guard beasts and quieted. Something large flew overhead, but it was heading in the opposite direction, as the Gryphon had hoped. When they were certain that it was gone, they resumed their journey into the heart of Canisargos—and what some called the jaws of the Ravager.

The messenger from D'Shay had been ejected almost as quickly as he had entered. D'Rak took some small satisfaction from that, although he wished that it could have been his rival in form as well as in spirit. In a sense, things had turned out better than he had expected. From the few words he had allowed the man, he knew that D'Shay did not have the female who seemed important to the Gryphon—and that left him with only one other possibility, one he would verify at his own liking.

What pleased him more was that everything had moved as if he had choreographed it himself. D'Altain was a fool to have thought that the senior keeper did not know where the aide's true loyalties lay. He had acted far more swiftly than even D'Rak had estimated, but the end result was the same. Granted, the Gryphon should have been on his way to D'Shay in the custody of several traitorous guards and not loose in the city. However, the Aramite had faith that the lionbird's skill, combined with D'Rak's manipulation, would soon steer the guardian and his reptilian companion to their proper destination. There would be a purging soon, now that the senior keeper was so close to success. No more spies. No more D'Shay. Perhaps, no more Pack Master.

He smiled. Soon, D'Shay and the Gryphon would be face-to-face—and then it would all be over. As for D'Altain . . . he would leave the fate of that one to the aide's new master.

"You, there," D'Rak called out to the young keeper monitoring the watch on the Gryphon. "What was your name?"

The subordinate looked up. He had still not become accustomed to working directly under the senior keeper himself, and so he swallowed several times before his voice returned. "R'Farany, master. Third level."

"Incorrect." D'Rak smiled at the keeper's frightened confusion. "As of now, you are D'Farany, sixth level."

"Milord!" The newly christened D'Farany had the sense not to abandon his post despite the overwhelming promotion in rank and caste he had just received.

"Do your work and I will formally make you tenth level before the year is out. I intend to make you my new second-in-command, providing you know your place." The awed look in D'Farany's face indicated to D'Rak that he had chosen well. He knew that the young man was not only skilled, but a truly dedicated follower of his. Such men were to be cultivated. The older keepers were too long into their power. He could not trust any of them to succeed him. He wanted a pliable successor.

He turned to go, and then recalled one more thing. "Bear in mind, D'Farany, that I am always the one in command. When I say that those under my rule do as I wish, I mean it. *All* keepers and keeper guardsmen perform my desires—whether they know it or not."

Including would-be traitors, he added silently.

XIII

Can you hear me?

The voice whispered mockingly throughout the conscious portion of his mind. He quickly buried all thought of his intentions, not out of fear, but so that he would not have to begin the tedious process of starting from scratch. Not when the present situation still held promise.

I know you hear me. Cease the pretense of sleep.

He sighed and acknowledged the other. *I hear you. For what reason do you disturb my thoughts? You've chosen not to speak to me since that last incident. Why now? Does something bother you?*

He felt rather than heard the snarl. For some reason, it amused him. *What do you call yourself now? Ravager, is it not? Such a savage name for such a tiny mind.*

A mind great enough to ensnare you while you blindly toyed with your experiments, the Ravager replied triumphantly.

I grant you that. I also granted you a trust you betrayed.

I will win this game, you know.

You still persist in that delusion, do you? The sleeper visualized a great head shaking in sadness, and revealed it to the one called the Ravager. *This is not a game. This is not a competition. The others knew that, and so do you.*

The others have withdrawn. I have only your last, feeble pawns to remove.

I feel sadness for you, Ravager. I was wrong. Your new name is so very appropriate for you. I hope you enjoy it still after you no longer have your delusions to entertain you.

Enough! The psychic shout was enough to give even the imprisoned one a brief headache—or at least the equivalent of one. *I don't know why I bothered to speak with you.*

Perhaps you are realizing your own mortality, the prisoner suggested, but he realized immediately that the Ravager had already withdrawn.

With a sigh, the sleeper returned to his rest, that one conscious portion of his mind already at work on the next step toward freedom.

Though night had come at last, it appeared that Canisargos was not a city that quieted with the darkness. The throngs shrank, but not significantly. Torches, oil lamps, and even crystals lit the city. Shouts and music filled the air. Merchants continued hawking their wares under the lamps. Armed patrols grew larger, a sign that some of the evening festivities occasionally got out of hand.

If this were indeed a sample of life in the capital city of the Aramites, small wonder they were continuously on the move to expand their empire. The little the Gryphon and Morgis had seen indicated that keeping Canisargos supplied with its desires was a full-time project.

"Thisss empire will not fall to enemiesss," Morgis hissed quietly. "Rather, it will burn itsssself out."

"A possibility, but I doubt it will happen soon enough for our sakes."

They were lost, and they both knew it. Much to their mutual dismay, the two fugitives had discovered something important about the streets of Canisargos—their designers would have been masters at creating unbeatable mazes. It was impossible to believe that the citizens of the capital could move around with such assurance. Not even the Gryphon, who prided himself on his skills, could keep track of where they had been and where they should go. Streets that led directly to their chosen goal suddenly veered off to the left or right or, in one case, nearly back the direction they had come. Traveling by rooftops would have been much more straightforward, but airborne patrols still flew overhead every few minutes. It was a miracle that they had not been captured by now. Twice, gryphon riders had flown within a few yards of them, frightening ground dwellers and alerting every foot patrol they came across of two outsiders. Already, wolf raiders were assaulting anyone who looked overly suspicious to them.

Yet another patrol, this one composed of at least twenty men, blocked their only path. The captain, who resembled D'Haaren much too much, was questioning one of the blue-tinted men from the north. Behind the patrol leader, a young keeper, boredom the dominant emotion on his visage, absently stroked the artifact on his chest. It was an image that the Gryphon had noticed more than once tonight. Most of the keepers seemed to be doing as little as possible to aid the search. With so many of them, it should have been near impossible for the two fugitives to evade custody this long. The lionbird suspected that they had been given orders from D'Rak. The senior keeper wanted his two former guests to remain loose in the city—but for what reason?

He wanted them to reach D'Shay; that much was reasonable. But there had to be more. D'Rak was not the type of man to sit back and hope that one of his rival's other enemies might dispose of D'Shay. No, the senior keeper was a man who liked to be certain. The fur and feathers on the Gryphon's back rose in agitation. If he succeeded in defeating D'Shay, would he merely be clearing the way for someone just as evil? While the two fought and the Pack Master apparently was willing to wait for the outcome, the war machine of the wolf raiders moved slowly. With a sense of direction, that would change. The stalemate was almost over; the Dream Lands were losing.

His knowledge of the outermost regions of this continent was sparse, but he hazarded a guess that there were no other enemies strong enough to withstand the Aramites—and then they would turn their claws once more toward the Dragonrealm.

At long last, the captain completed his questioning and, with the look of one who has already had a weary day, ordered the patrol on again. The young keeper's face held a brief smirk, which served only to verify the Gryphon's thoughts. D'Rak *was* up to something.

A horrid sound rose from behind him, and the lionbird whirled, ready to take on what could only be a Runner sent to track them down.

Morgis somehow managed to look sheepish. "There's nothing I can do. We haven't eaten in nearly two days, and a drake's stomach is a demanding thing when he has been active continuously.''

At the mention of food, the Gryphon's own stomach began to churn. It *had* been some time. He could recall eating only twice during his stay in the Dream Lands, and both times it had been a few pieces of fruit. While both he and the drake could probably go for days without food, it might be a good idea to grab something while they could. It was impossible to say what might happen if—when—they did reach the Pack Master's stronghold. They might die or they might succeed. Either way, it would not hurt for them to build up their energy reserves—providing they found a safe way to get some food. The Gryphon did not like the thought of being captured because he had been spotted stealing some half-rotted produce from the back of an unsavory inn.

He scanned the street again. The crowd was thinning out, and it appeared that some of the establishments were closing. It made sense; even innkeepers had to sleep occasionally, not to mention clean up from the day's activities.

One annoying problem was that the blue-tinted man was still hanging around. He seemed to have gained an obsessive interest in the area since his conversation with the patrol captain, and the lionbird wondered if he was an informer or some such.

The blue man became a secondary matter, for a familiar form strode into sight. The Gryphon flattened against the wall, with Morgis following suit.

"A Faceless One!" Morgis reached for his sword.

"No! We leave him alone unless he comes for us!"

"I don't trust them! I don't care if they *are* aiding the Dream Lands!"

"I don't trust them, either, but I'm not about to take on something that has free rein in both domains. Whoever or whatever the not-people are, I plan to avoid them—at least until I've taken care of what I originally came for."

They fully expected the blank visage to turn their way, but the Faceless One instead paused before the blue man and stared intently at the startled figure. Within seconds of being under the disturbing perusal of the hooded creature, the blue man ran off wildly. The Faceless One watched (supposedly) calmly until the other was no longer in sight, then continued on its way without so much as a glance in the direction of the two hidden watchers.

"I can't help feeling it knew we were here," Morgis grumbled uneasily.

"Let's hope it didn't." The Gryphon peeked around the corner. The area was deserted for the moment, likely due in part to the brief presence of the blank-faced specter. Across and to their right was a likely spot called the Ravager's Table. The lionbird could not picture a god as savage as the Ravager using a table—or a knife and fork, for that matter—but he guessed that any establishment bearing that particular name had better sell good meals.

Which meant a higher quality of refuse.

It was now or never. "Come on!"

They darted across the street, hoods pulled tight over their heads. Any onlooker less than half drunk would recognize them as outsiders. But they were fortunate; the street remained empty. Only when they were safely across did they dare to breathe again. The Gryphon made his way to the back of the inn. The garbage pile was a disappointment. Scavengers were already at work on the few good pieces, and the rest stunk of rot. After one whiff of the odor floating about the refuse, the Gryphon came to the conclusion that they had been fortunate.

"Well?" The drake came up behind him, sniffed, and shook his head in disgust. "Never mind. I can tell."

Something stirred within the pile of refuse. Something the size of a small dog, but shaped like no dog that the Gryphon had ever seen. It resembled a large rat in some ways, but the face was all pushed in, and no rat had teeth like this creature did.

"If we cleaned it off, it might make good eating," Morgis suggested quietly.

The thing let out a harsh bark. Another rose near it. A name came to the Gryphon. "Verlok."

"Verlok?"

"Some fool's attempt to free the cities of rats. They succeeded, but now they have verloks instead."

A third verlok rose from the back of the rubbish pile. It was bigger than the first two.

"These verloks." Morgis put a hand on the hilt of his sword. "How large a colony do they usually live in?"

The same harsh bark rose from garbage mounds all along the back alley.

"Large enough." The Gryphon pulled out his short sword very carefully. The drake did the same. "Back out of here. We can't fight verloks, not in great numbers."

Morgis gave him no argument, but asked, "Why do the wolf

raiders let these vermin thrive? Why not hunt them down? They have the power."

"Why should they? The creatures take care of the garbage situation—probably even a few of the unfortunate souls that the Pack Master would rather ignore."

The creatures nearest to them had grown silent, but they could hear others, much farther away, calling out.

The Gryphon stiffened. "They're alerting others! They're passing along word about us!"

"Gryphon . . ."

At the drake's warning, the lionbird slowly turned. Verloks were slowly converging from the alleys behind them. He could make out at least two or three dozen indistinct shapes, and he knew there had to be more.

Morgis had his sword drawn and used it to ward off a particularly arrogant verlok. The creature let loose with a staccato of harsh barks that they were certain would bring every soldier in Canisargos to them.

The Gryphon glanced around. Not one torch or candle had been lit. The inhabitants of the nearby buildings might have been dead for all the interest they seemed to have in what was going on behind their establishments and homes. Canisargos was evidently a place where people minded their own business. What they did not see they could not be held accountable for—so they thought. For once, he was happy that such an ignorant attitude existed.

That, of course, did not solve their vermin problem.

Slowly, they were edging their way back to the side street from which they had originally entered. The Gryphon's memories would tell him nothing further about the verloks; it seemed that most of his sudden recollections occurred only at the last moment, when they were absolutely needed. He wondered when some memory would return just a bit too late. It probably would not matter; he would not be around to worry about it by then.

The verloks did not follow them down the side street, for which both of them were thankful. It rankled them, especially Morgis, to retreat from such creatures, but both of them were experienced enough to know when they were at too great a disadvantage. There was nothing to be gained from standing and fighting. Better they continue through the maze called Canisargos in the hopes of reaching their destination. . . .

And then . . .

The Gryphon wished he knew what D'Rak planned. Or D'Shay. Both of them wanted a confrontation, but on their own terms. D'Rak wanted to use the lionbird as bait; that much was obvious. Still . . .

A new wave of harsh barking filled the silence of the empty streets, this time with a malevolent touch to it. From behind him, the Gryphon heard Morgis hiss in consternation. He did not have to ask why; one glance told him. For reasons of their own, the verloks had decided to follow them. More than two dozen of the beasts were already in sight, and more were materializing around the corner.

"Do we fight them? I could still use a fresh meal." Despite his words, it was evident that the drake did not really desire to take on the ever-increasing pack.

"No. We move."

"A good plan."

They stepped out into the main street, which was still devoid of any other souls, and scanned the area. Morgis pointed at a path to the right. "That way?"

"We don't have much choice." He pointed to the left. Verloks were coming out of every other possible route in numbers that would have had the local inhabitants fleeing for their lives in complete panic. The lionbird would not have blamed them.

Lest they lose the only path still available to them, they dropped caution and ran for the street that Morgis had chosen. The verloks farthest behind gave silent chase; oddly, those nearest seemed to hesitate.

Morgis led the way down the other street. The creatures followed close enough behind to be a threat but not close enough to actually strike. Something bothersome nudged at the Gryphon's mind.

"There's another intersection ahead! Which way?"

"Try right again."

Morgis whirled around the corner—and then backtracked into the Gryphon as at least a dozen verloks came racing down the direction the two had chosen.

There were more coming from the path that had been on their left. With no other choice remaining, they continued on their original route. The verlok stampede grew as the newcomers joined the main pack. The only benefit to the entire situation was that so many beasts together in a narrow area slowed down the group as a whole.

It was the drake that said it first. He was breathing rapidly, more from frustration than exhaustion, and the words came out in bursts. "We—are—being—herded."

That was what had been bothering the Gryphon. For scavengers, the verloks were acting with great precision. The two were being given one route and one route only. It was also too much of a coincidence that no one—and in a city such as Canisargos, it was an impossibility—absolutely no one else had strayed into their path. The city might as well have been deserted. In the distance, they could hear the sounds of the city's night people. Even assuming that everything in this section was closed for the night, it was impossible to believe that not one Aramite patrol had even come within sight—with two fugitives on the loose yet.

"What can—we do?" Morgis breathed.

"Stand and fight—or see where they want us to go."

"Your choice?"

"We can't fight them all. Let's hope they have other plans than just tiring us down before dinner."

"If we were only not under the spell of the senior keeper . . ."

"We would've probably brought the full force of the Aramite empire down on us. This—this is their capital city, remember."

The verloks continued to hound them silently. In their own way, they were worse than the Runners. At least the shadowy, lupine forms presented a defeatable opponent. Here, one could cut apart the scavengers all day and not put much of a dent in their population. It was the futility of the situation that wore at the two the most.

"Gryphon, we're getting—closer to—the palace."

They were, indeed. Ominously close. He had wanted to enter this place, but under far different circumstances. He had wanted a fighting chance. Run into the ground like a hapless rabbit was not the way for him. The Gryphon was tempted to turn and make a stand here and now. Better to die fighting, even if it was against the stinking, garbage-scavenging verloks. He doubted a death in the claws of the Ravager's underlings would be an honorable one.

Verloks suddenly came rushing from the path before them. The Gryphon and Morgis were forced to turn to the left—*away* from the sanctum of the Pack Master.

"Where—" was all Morgis could say before a portal that had not been there a moment ago materialized directly in their path, swallowing them before they could even react to its presence.

* * *

"Welcome back. I'm sorry about that. I had to hurry."

The Gryphon rose angrily from the cold stone floor that the miniature gate had deposited them on from a level two feet above ground. The unexpected absence of a place to stand had sent both him and the drake tumbling across the room. Their new host apologized again.

"It was a rather desperate maneuver. You wouldn't have liked where the verloks were steering you. Trust me. I know what it is like."

They recognized the voice before the figure itself became distinct in the dim light.

"Jerilon Dane!" Morgis hissed madly and reached down for his borrowed sword, from which he had been separated in the fall. "Warm-blood!"

"Stay your hand!" The Aramite raised both hands high to show that they were empty. "I've no weapons, and the power I used to open the portals is depleted. Are drakes so lacking in honor that they would strike down an unarmed opponent?"

The Gryphon, who remembered well many of the atrocities certain drakes such as Duke Toma could perform, made no move to interfere—yet. He had no love for the former wolf raider, but neither did he kill out of hand. Morgis would have to decide for himself what value he placed on his honor and that of his sire. If the drake made the wrong choice, the lionbird would react then.

Morgis hesitated, the sword point wavering from one side of Dane's chest to the other, and then muttered some incomprehensible drake curse. With great visible effort, he sheathed the blade.

"Better. I mean you no harm."

"You abandoned us to the wolf raiders' senior keeper!" the duke protested bitterly.

"I did nothing of the kind—my departure was hardly by choice. I was rescued myself. By pure chance. It could've been any of us. He only had time enough to focus on one."

The Gryphon glanced around. They were in a dusty, abandoned chamber. The place resembled an old assembly room more than anything else. Much of the back end of the room was hidden under a curtain of darkness. The one visible exit revealed a stone corridor. It was almost as if they were back in the private dungeons of D'Rak. "Where are we?"

"The underworld of Canisargos—what some call one of the

three ancient homes of the gods.'' From the tone in his voice, it was evident that Jerilon Dane believed what he said. That was not comforting, considering what god was supposed to reside in this city now.

"And what about this 'benefactor' of ours? Who is he and what does he want from us?''

"You could ask him all that yourself,'' a familiar feminine voice added.

"Troia?'' Startled by the relief in his own voice, the Gryphon quieted, feeling fortunate at that moment that his avian features prevented others from plumbing the depths of his embarrassment.

Her face *did* seem to light up at his reaction. She stepped into the chamber, a torch in one tawny hand, her every movement seemingly measured for best effect. A true predator, she would have been able to turn the simple act of walking into an offensive or defensive maneuver.

"It's about time you two got here.'' Closer, she looked a bit strained, as if she had worried far more than her casual airs indicated. "He'll be so pleased!''

"Were you out there all the time?'' Jerilon Dane snapped.

"I'm sorry—I wanted—to be nearby in case something other than these two stepped through. You might've needed help.''

"Your concern is overwhelming,'' he snarled. "Unlike your trust!''

"My children, why must you bicker so? We are all allies in this.''

The Gryphon stared at the tall, regal figure making his way into the chamber. "Lord Petrac!''

"Gryphon.'' The Will of the Woods leaned heavily against his staff. He seemed a little haggard, as if the Master Guardian had been through great strain of late. If he had been the mastermind behind the successful escape of all four of them in the midst of the wolf raiders' capital city, then it was more of a surprise than he could stand—even with something to give him support. "Forgive me. I've been overtaxing myself of late, it seems.''

Troia went to aid him, but he waved her away.

Morgis, who had never met the Master Guardian before, eyed him critically. "You are the one responsible?''

"I am, Duke Morgis.''

"Is it not a little dangerous for you to be here in the stronghold of your enemies?''

The stag's eyes fixed on the drake, and it was Morgis who

finally looked away. Lord Petrac was exhausted, yes, but he was by no means weak. "There is a danger, true, but the risk is necessary if I am to salvage any hope for the Dream Lands. Besides, I could not leave you at the mercies of the Aramites."

He included all of them in the statement, but the Gryphon noticed that his gaze had turned to Troia. It was as if the Will of the Woods was speaking for her benefit alone. The lionbird instinctively bristled, then, ashamed at the thoughts running through his mind, he forced the dark emotions down.

"I think," the Master Guardian continued, "that it would be best if you departed Canisargos at once. D'Shay and D'Rak must both be after you by now. My ploy will not fool them long." He did not elaborate on what that particular ploy consisted of.

It was Morgis who surprised everyone then. He stiffened, pointed at Lord Petrac, and, in a voice loud and precise, said, "There is more to this than you have said. *Tell them about your dealings with the Ravager's spawn. Tell them about the betrayal you have concocted with the senior keeper, D'Rak.*"

The Gryphon looked from the drake to the Master Guardian. Instead of the incredulous shock that covered the faces of Jerilon Dane and Troia—not to mention himself—there was only a sadness in the proud visage of the Will of the Woods. He tapped the staff on the dust-covered floor.

"I don't know by what means you discovered this, reptile," he whispered, "but I *am* afraid it is going to cost all of you."

Morgis was looking at everyone in befuddlement. He did not even seem to remember what he had just said. While the drake looked from one person to another for some explanation, Petrac tapped the floor with his staff again.

To the Gryphon's growing horror, a familiar, incessant whisper began to rise throughout the chamber.

"I am *truly* sorry," the Master Guardian repeated softly.

XIV

"What am I to do with you, D'Altain?"

D'Shay reached out, took the traitorous keeper by the scruff of his neck, and threw him against the far wall. D'Altain struck with a heavy thud, only his armor and his talisman protecting him from severe damage. In the background, the two gryphons threw themselves at the bars of their cages and cried out again and again. D'Altain wished they would quit screaming about killing. He was not, he knew, in a very comfortable situation. D'Shay might save him from the revenge of D'Rak, but perhaps only so that D'Shay might punish him *himself*.

The master wolf raider reached down and pulled the hapless figure to his feet. "Again. What *am* I to do with you? You failed miserably, you've destroyed what value you had by playing your hand too soon, you've cost me others that I had planted in D'Rak's own guard unit. Can you tell me what I am to do with you?"

"Master." D'Altain was past the point of image. He was pleading now. "Master, I have served you well before this. Always I informed you of where, what, and when. Always you have maintained your favor with the Pack Master. Please, my lord, I know I have failed in this task, but I can still be of service to you! I cannot go back!"

"No, you can't." D'Shay smiled and released the traitor. As he did so, he noticed that his graying skin was now peeling as well. He had held on longer than necessary, hoping to arrange things so that he would not leave himself defenseless during the change. That could no longer be counted on. For a brief moment, he considered using D'Altain, but the Aramite had little enough of a form to work with. He would burn out too soon.

There was still his prisoner. It all depended on the Gryphon —who was nowhere to be found!

"I agree," he continued, noting the slight look of relief on his former spy's features. "You can't go back. You have to remain here."

"Thank you, Master!"

D'Shay looked behind the smaller man to where two of his unliving guards waited. On an unspoken signal, they stepped forward and took hold of the arms of the uncomprehending keeper.

"Lord D'Shay! What are they doing?"

His eyes suddenly turned to the cages holding the master wolf raider's two pet gryphons. Guards similar to the ones holding him prisoner were releasing the savage beasts. They were shrieking in joyous anticipation. The Aramite struggled desperately, but futilely.

"You've served me sufficiently well in the past, D'Altain, but your present failure is unacceptable, so I'm going to serve *you*—as one last treat before my pets receive the main course. The Gryphon." D'Shay reached forward and pulled both talisman and chain from the other wolf raider's neck. "You won't be needing this."

He watched with satisfaction and clinical interest as the unfortunate keeper was tossed into the midst of the two savage beasts. D'Altain proved, he noticed, to be less of a challenge than the last prisoner had. As the two gryphons continued their grisly game, he felt a chill in his hand. He looked down and noticed that the crystal no longer glowed with the power of the keepership. It was no more than a dull stone now. D'Shay dropped it by his feet and crushed it with one heavy heel.

It would have been so much more satisfying if the crystal could have been the senior keeper himself. D'Rak was no longer a constant nuisance; he had become a threat that nearly vied with the Gryphon for priority. Outright assassination was impossible. The Ravager expected more from those who served him. Even a successful assassination would probably lower him in the estimation of his master. No, first the rival had to be humiliated before his counterparts, stripped of his prestige and, consequently, his rank. That would satisfy the true lord of the Aramites.

It would also prevent possible repercussions. He knew that a number of D'Rak's people lived as if their lives depended upon the senior keeper's health; he knew that it was literally true in some cases. While it would rid D'Shay of some annoyances, it would also rid him of some allies that he might find handy in the near future.

Something major was afoot, and he disliked the fact that he knew so little this time. Things seemed to be slipping away from him. Not like the past. Now, he actually worried about his existence and its possible abrupt end. He also worried about the obvious fact that his lord the Ravager was distancing himself of late from his most favored servant. *That* was a warning sign if nothing else was.

Could that mean that the Ravager was looking at D'Rak as his new favorite? D'Shay shuddered at the thought of his master abandoning him. He did not want to end up as the Pack Master had. It was difficult to say whether nonexistence was worse or not.

"I've been a fool!" he muttered to himself. The unliving guards waited patiently for his commands. The gryphons were cleaning up after their meal. They were quick, voracious eaters. Only bits of armor, torn off like the skin of a fruit, left any indication of the late D'Altain's presence.

"A fool," he repeated more softly. He had allowed others to do his work for him, something he had generally shunned in the past. It may have been because of his own failures in the Dragonrealm. Perhaps that was why, he thought, he had started depending too much on others. There was only one being he could trust: himself. He could make others obey, but, in the end, it would have to be his hand that held the blade. That was what had raised him to his present position; that was what was required of him to remain the power he was. He had been a bigger fool than D'Altain not to see that.

As he watched the gryphons being herded back into their cages, their hunger temporarily sated, he wondered where the Gryphon was now. There were other players in this game, the grand game of the Ravager. Not just D'Rak and the Master Guardians of Sirvak Dragoth. He knew, for example, that more than one party was making use of the troublesome Tzee. If he—

D'Shay broke off. The Tzee. Now, *there* was a possibility he had not thought through. . . .

Tzee . . .

They were stronger than the Gryphon could have believed possible.

Tzee . . .

He was on his knees. To the side, Morgis was struggling to maintain a standing position, but his legs were quivering, and only a few seconds more passed before he joined the lionbird on the floor. Jerilon Dane, who the Gryphon was certain had been a part of this, was nonetheless writhing in agony under the savage assault by the nebulous multiple entity. Only Lord Petrac, of course, and Troia were left untouched. The Will of the Woods was speaking softly to her, as if to explain his reasons for what he was doing. Through bleary eyes, the Gryphon watched as she argued with him. The words were smothered under the constant, mind-numbing whisper, and he could only hazard a guess as to what they were actually saying. He could see that Troia was in terrible straits. On the one claw, she worshiped the Master Guardian as someone special, someone above the petty emotions that most beings allowed to control their lives. On the other, she knew that what Lord Petrac was doing went against everything she had been taught at Sirvak Dragoth.

The Gryphon fell beakfirst into the floor. Jerilon Dane had ceased moving. Morgis was still struggling feebly, and he would probably last a little longer than the lionbird himself. He took one last look at Troia. The argument was evidently over. With a wave of his staff, the Master Guardian sent her—elsewhere. The Gryphon could take a little comfort in knowing that Lord Petrac cared for her and would not harm her.

The world faded into black.

Oddly, he was not quite unconscious. Either that, or he was dreaming. If it was a dream, it was a lackluster one, for he floated in a place of nothing, much like the void, but pitch black. His body would not function, and he worried until he realized that, since this was a dream, it really did not matter.

He suddenly knew he was no longer alone.

Gryphon.

He tried to speak, but no words would come. Nonetheless, he somehow knew that the other understood him.

In a brilliant burst of fire, *he* was there.

More massive than any man the Gryphon had come across.

Both wider and taller, with a build that spoke of years of heavy conflict. This was a warrior, not just a man clad in armor—ebony armor trimmed with fur. His face was covered in a full-visage wolfhelm that left only the eyes, searing eyes, open to study. Nothing resembling humanity could be found in those eyes.

Gryphon.

"I—hear you." The sound of his own voice startled the lion-bird.

I am the Pack Master.

The Pack Master. As enigmatic a ruler as the Crystal Dragon, the Dragon King who had, in the end, been a telling blow against his own mad brother, the Ice Dragon. Other than that similarity, he could not class the two together. The Crystal Dragon he felt he could trust, but trust was not a word one could associate with the figure floating before him. Not the Pack Master. Not the hand that guided the wolf raiders.

Amusing.

The Pack Master knew what he was thinking. The Gryphon let him see much, much more.

I am tempted to withdraw my offer. Hear me out, misfit.

His dream self bristled at the insult, but could not move otherwise save to ask, "What offer?"

I will give you the prize that has eluded you so long.

"What prize?" Possibilities ran through his mind.

I can give you . . . D'Shay.

D'Shay! "I'm hardly in the position to take him."

Agree and I will free you. Take D'Shay, do with him as you will, and return across the seas.

"Forever, I suppose."

Yes.

"I won't bother telling you my decision. You know what it is."

He had come here in search of his past and to observe the potential threat of the wolf raiders to the Dragonrealm—especially that one region that had come to mean so much to him. The Gryphon had then discovered that his enemy was not dead, as he had supposed, and that gave him a third purpose. It was not his ultimate purpose, however, and he could no more depart this continent with those tasks undone than he could abandon the inhabitants of the Dream Lands to the dark hordes of the Ravager. D'Shay's death was not the point of it all, though the

Gryphon was the first to admit he could become obsessed at times with the thought.

Misfit! Mortal fool! I—I—

The image of the Pack Master seemed to melt. The wolf visage grew, became alive, and burst forth from the rapidly decomposing matter that had been the supreme commander of the Aramites. An enraged lupine face thrust itself high, growing and growing until the jaws were great enough to take the Gryphon whole. A vast, scarlet tongue lolled from the open maw, and saliva dripped in huge buckets.

You had your chance! It cannot be said I did not offer you that! I will win this game, though, and because you could not see sense, you will be crushed like all the rest! You will be mine dead or alive! Then he will never escape his bonds! The game will be mine!

Still howling, the maddening image vanished. The Gryphon, exhausted mentally, gave in to unconsciousness, but not before his mind noted one item of interest. Not the fact that, if what he saw was true, the Pack Master was no more than a vessel for the Ravager, but the simple fact that, from both his words and his tone, the living god of the wolf raiders was frightened.

Frightened of him.

He woke in a soft field of wild grass. He looked around drowsily for Troia and felt a pang of fear when he did not see her. Then he remembered the pond. It was her favorite place, of course. Unlike the cats she so resembled, Troia loved the water. She was no doubt swimming even now.

Rising from the grass, the Gryphon gazed up at the beautiful morning sky. A few fluffy white clouds dotted the heavens, but other than that it was like staring at a rich pageantry of blue silk. He could not recall ever seeing such a wonderful sight—

—and he could not recall how he had come to be here with Troia—

—which was all that mattered. She would be waiting for him. He yawned. It was a much easier process now that he had shifted to human form. There was something wrong with that, but what it was bothered him only briefly. Once again, it was Troia that made him forget all else. Why not? What else did he need besides her? They had the field, the trees, the pond, and the food that was provided them—what else, indeed?

A brisk swim, the ex-monarch decided, would do him good.

Clear the cobwebs from his overrested mind. He removed his tunic and tossed it carelessly aside. No one would take it. There *was* no one else.

Morgis?

He shook his head. No one else. Only Troia.

The pond came into view, a glistening, almost perfectly round pool of clear water. A few trees dotted one side. Someone had built a tiny platform that could be used for diving—who? It did not matter, for at that moment, *she* broke through to the surface of the water. Droplets flew all around as she shook herself. Her lungs filled with fresh air. She had removed the garments the proprieties of Sirvak Dragoth had forced on her, and the perfection of her face and form was enough to make the Gryphon question the unbelievable chance that had brought them together—whatever it had been.

He ran the rest of the way, discarding things along the path, landed on the platform, and, just when it seemed he was about to run straight off into the water, leaped into the air. The dive was not perfect, but it accomplished its secondary goal. Waves of water flew everywhere, but mostly on Troia, drenching her again. She sputtered and slapped at the water playfully.

The Gryphon rose to the surface, his smile matching hers. Then something large bumped against his leg. It was long and sinewy, not at all like the tiny fish that inhabited the pond. He felt it again, and the pleasure of the day gave away again to the uncomfortable feeling that something was amiss.

Coils of scaled flesh wrapped around his legs, tightened, and threw him off balance. As Troia watched, uncomprehending, he fell backward into the pond. His only comfort was that he had had enough warning to take a deep breath.

Claws ready, he tried to make out what the creature was— and especially where its head was located. It was a serpent of some sort. He could not recall ever seeing one here. The Gryphon slashed at it, but the water slowed him enough for it to shift, and the tips of his claws barely grazed it.

"Gryphon!"

A long, reptilian head materialized from behind him, the serpent's body wrapping itself around his forearm as the head twisted forward to better see him.

"Gryphon! Ssstop thissss nonsssensse!"

He had his free hand raised, and this time there would be no mistake. One swipe would shear the serpent's head from its body. One swipe.

"Gryphon, you fool! Look at me! Wake up! I am Morgissss!"

Morgis? The Gryphon shook his head. He knew no Morgis —yes—no! Trapped between conflicting memories, he did not pay heed to the fact that, by rights, he should have drowned by now. The serpent, however, was quick to use his confusion to point that out.

"Thissss isss an illusssion! One of Lord Petrac'sss! You've been under water far too long! Don't you sssee that thisss isss a falssse reality?"

"False?" He heard himself utter the words and then remembered it should have been impossible to do so. He blinked and watched the world flicker. From pond to dank, dusty, long-abandoned chamber to pond again. Then the chamber. Pond. Chamber. With a shriek, he forced the illusion of the pond out of his mind—and with it, the illusion of Troia.

He found he was on the flat of his back staring up at the ugly, half-hidden features of Morgis. The drake was looking at him with more concern than the lionbird would have thought possible for one of his kind to feel for an outsider.

"He's out of it. You've freed him."

The Gryphon twisted his neck until he could see the second figure. Jerilon Dane, looking more than a little disheveled. There was a hollow look in his eyes, and his skin was pale where it was not covered by a thin coat of black hair.

"What . . . happened? How long was I out?"

"That's two very good questions," the former wolf raider commander commented. "Blame the Tzee for the first. They—it—whatever the Tzee is, our 'good friend' Lord Petrac has given them more power—but he made them use it to ensnare us, not kill us. As for the second question, neither of us have an answer to that just yet."

"More than a day, if the fur growing on this Aramite's face is any indication," Morgis added.

The Gryphon closed his eyes for a moment, seeking the darkness in order to reorganize his thoughts. His conversation with the Ravager returned to him. *That* was no dream. He found himself pushing that incident aside, though, as false memories of the pond and his time with Troia intruded.

"Don't sssink back into it!" A scaled hand slapped the side of his face. He instinctively brought his claws into play. Strong hands gripped his wrists. The Gryphon forced open his eyes and saw Morgis, long, sharp, predatory teeth clenched, struggling with him.

"The Master Guardian must have given him something truly special," Dane remarked almost clinically.

"The pond . . ." The lionbird shook his head. *It did not exist!* he told himself. *It was a false dream!*

He rejected the memories—this time permanently.

"I'm better. Let me up."

Morgis shifted and, still holding on to the Gryphon's wrists, helped him to his feet. The former monarch gazed at his surroundings. It was the same chamber that they had been brought to by Jerilon Dane. He turned to the Aramite. "How did you escape?"

"I can't take credit for that. It was your scaly companion here who first broke free of the imaginary world the Will of the Woods created for him."

"*Lord Petrac*"—utilized by the drake, the Master Guardian's name became a slur word—"does not understand my people. Once he realized that I had no answers to any of his questions, he tried to set me down in some idyllic world." The duke laughed harshly. "He does not understand what an idyllic world is to a drake. I had to get out before I went crazy. I knew that I would never have consciously chosen a place such as he had created."

"His shouts brought me out of it. I've had keeper training. I understand these sort of traps a little. Once I recognized it, escaping proved simple. I woke just as he was rising to go to your aid."

"You were trapped more deeply in your dream," Morgis continued. "Lord Petrac must have wanted to be very sure of you."

The Gryphon nodded agreement, not wanting to elaborate on just what the Master Guardian had created. He forced his growing anger in check; despite everything else, he was certain that Petrac had been acting in kindness, that he had recognized a growing bond and had brought it to its ultimate conclusion in order to keep the lionbird securely under control.

It did not make the Gryphon any less unforgiving, though. Lord Petrac had much to answer for, especially the pact. . . .

"Morgis." The drake looked expectantly at him. "You don't remember *anything* you said before he turned on us?"

"Nothing."

"I've already asked him that," Dane interjected. "He remembers nothing."

"Interesting." He told them about his encounter with the

Ravager. Dane grew even more pale, and began to glance about as if he expected his former master to materialize in his full glory at any moment. Morgis, on the other hand, listened with growing interest.

"What you sssay . . ." He paused, correcting his speech. "What you say makes some sense, though I cannot think of any reason a god should fear a mortal."

"He feared me enough to offer me D'Shay on a platter."

"You should have taken it. I would have liked to see nothing better."

"In return, we would have departed for the Dragonrealm. I can't leave this continent to that bloodthirsty wolf lord and his horde of trained pets."

"The Dream Lands would fall," Jerilon Dane confirmed. "Two years ago, we would not have sworn to that, save to appease the general population and protect our positions. Now, even though my campaign was a farce," the former wolf raider looked bitter, but for which reasons he did not say, "the Dream Lands are slowly losing their reality. In three, maybe four years' time, the only Dream Lands will be those in the memories of the victorious war council."

"You're forgetting one thing," the Gryphon added angrily. "Lord Petrac's alliance."

"With the Tzee?"

"With D'Rak. What do you think he could possibly have offered the senior keeper to seal such a bargain?"

Morgis understood immediately. "The one thing that will secure the Aramite's place among his fellows! Sirvak Dragoth!"

"Sirvak Dragoth and his fellow guardians. I suspect that Petrac's reward for this will be control over whatever remains of the Dream Lands. A tiny preserve of his own where he can sit back and believe that some portion of the domain he was supposed to protect has been saved due to his valiant efforts—forgetting, of course, all those unfortunate enough not to be one of his chosen few survivors."

The Gryphon studied his two companions. They seemed ready for whatever he decided to do. Without their powers, he wondered if the three of them could do anything. The ex-mercenary sighed. What other choice did they have?

He turned to Jerilon Dane, who knew Canisargos better than either of the other two. "We need to find a way out of this city, and fast. Do you have any ideas?"

The look that spread over the former wolf raider's already darkened features told the Gryphon more than he wanted to know.

He closed his eyes in mental exhaustion. "Then I have a suggestion. . . ."

XV

Troia savored the last bit of ripe fruit and smiled, revealing sharp, white teeth more suited for tearing the flesh from prey than for biting into an apple or a berry. Nevertheless, she had enjoyed the fruit brought to her by one of Lord Petrac's helpers as she had never enjoyed a meal before. There was something about the things grown within the vicinity of the Master Guardian that made items grown elsewhere taste flat and bland. The cat-woman chalked it down to the inherent goodness in her host, her mentor. No other Master Guardian affected her the way the Will of the Woods did. With Lord Petrac, she felt confident, at peace with the wild beast within, and, best of all, protected from those threats that were beyond her capabilities.

"How are you feeling now, Kitten?" The Master Guardian, looking unusually worn, materialized from the woods surrounding her. He was leaning hard against his staff, and there was a distant look in his eyes. She could feel his concern for her. He cared for her much the way a parent cares for a beloved child.

"I'm well. Why do you ask?"

He frowned momentarily, then said, "I am always concerned with the health of my friends, Troia. Would you want me otherwise?"

"You could never be otherwise." She rose, thinking to depart, but finding instead that her host had, for some reason, moved to block her way.

"You've only just come. I insist you give me more of your time; I so rarely see you."

There was something wrong, something . . . that she had forgotten. Troia tried to make an excuse; she did not feel right being here. "Haggerth will be looking for me."

"Haggerth?" The stag head registered surprise—and possibly consternation. He recovered swiftly. "I doubt that he will be looking for you. When I last spoke to him, not more than an hour before, he indicated that he had no need for you and that you could stay for as long as you wish—or is that it? Have you tired of my company already?"

"Oh, no, my lord!" She felt helpless as he guided her back to where she had been sitting. Her movements were slow, hesitant, not like her at all. Something was not right.

Tzee . . .

She heard it only once, and might have dismissed it if not for the tightening of the Master Guardian's hands upon her. He summoned one of the villagers who aided him and requested drink for her. She did not protest, knowing somehow that he would convince her otherwise. He then rose and gave his apologies, saying he would return in a moment. Not once did he mention exactly what he had to do.

Troia had a great urge to sleep, but she fought against it. Try as she might, she could not accept what was happening to her. That brief whisper stirred something within her, memories that contradicted with the present. Memories that concerned Lord Petrac as well. Unsettling memories of . . . the Gryphon?

"Gryphon." She whispered the name as if by doing so it lent her strength. Memories of capture and escape and . . . treachery began to return to her.

"Lord Petrac." The name that had always meant honor and peace now disgusted her. Troia remembered everything, including the Tzee and Morgis's sudden, shocking declaration concerning a pact between the Will of the Woods and one of the Aramite lords. Her claws extended and retracted in growing anger. An unspoken trust had been betrayed. She wanted blood.

Rising slowly, silently, she moved down the path the Master Guardian had departed by a moment before. One of the villagers, carrying drink, stepped in front of her, openmouthed. She bared her claws, then realized that these people were probably more innocent than she was. The villager, a young male not quite yet into adulthood, dropped what he was carrying and turned. She caught him by the arm, pulled him back to her, and, with an apology that only seemed to confuse the situation further, struck him hard. In appearance, Troia seemed more supple and sleek than strong; in actuality, her strength was such that in hand-to-hand, she more often than not defeated opponents twice her size, veteran fighters all.

She lowered the unconscious boy to the ground, swearing she would make it up to him if she survived this mess. Troia found herself wishing that the Gryphon were here; he always seemed to maintain a presence of mind despite the hopelessness of a situation. She also wished he were here for other reasons, but they had nothing to do with the problem at hand.

Seconds later, she was cursing herself for being such a fool. At the very least, she could have questioned the boy to see if he knew where his master was and what he was doing. Tracking would not be too difficult, but, if there was an easier way, she would have been happy to take it. Only fools overflowing with pride sought the more difficult path.

Minutes passed, and she seriously thought about returning to her place of—captivity, she decided—and seeing if the boy was still there. The one thing she had forgotten was that in this region, Lord Petrac's scent was everywhere. Recent scents mixed with new scents, and it was almost impossible to tell one from the other after a while. She could not give up, though. Not with so much at stake. Not even if the traitor was Lord Petrac, who would very likely push aside her attack like one might push aside a leaf that had landed on the shoulder.

She heard a movement behind her.

"Well, what a delectable little cat we have here."

Without pause, she whirled and leaped at the source of the voice. Two figures clad in armor stepped into her path and, to her dismay and agony, she bounced off of them like a pebble, landing in a painful heap three feet back from them. The speaker laughed.

"Such a foolish little cat. Always look before you leap if you want to avoid broken bones and such."

Through tearing eyes, she glanced up in horror at the familar black, fur-trimmed armor. Wolf raiders in the Dream Lands! It was impossible—unless she had accidentally left the reality of her world and reentered theirs. No . . . she would have noticed that, wouldn't she?

The two figures she had struck gripped her by the arms. She

looked into their faces, hidden by wolfhelms, and discovered that nothing peered out from behind the masks. Her struggles increased, though still to no avail. They had a strength more than human.

The third figure stepped closer. It wasn't D'Rak, she knew that already from the sound of the voice. If not the senior keeper, then there was only one other wolf raider who moved with such presence, such confidence and energy.

He cupped her chin in one hand and, in a coldly polite manner said, "I am D'Shay. We haven't met face-to-face before, but you must be Troia, the Gryphon's female."

Troia found his smile far worse than that of any predator she had ever faced. There was no humanity in it and none of the innocence of a true animal. D'Shay was the worst of both worlds, a true apostle of the Ravager.

"Cat got your tongue?" The smile faded. "You shouldn't have come this way. I have this . . . obsession with things and people related somehow to the Gryphon. I like to take them and mold them to my will or maybe just see that he finds them unrecognizable—if he finds them at all."

She could no longer completely hide the growing fear within her, but she forced herself to reply, "You're pathetic, Shaidarol! Small wonder you and the *scavenger* get along so well!"

He released her chin and slapped her across the face with amazing speed. Blood dripped from her mouth, but she felt some satisfaction.

"There is no more Shaidarol! I am D'Shay, most loyal servant of the Lord Ravager!"

"Unhand her." This voice she recognized, but whether she should be relieved or angered the feline woman no longer knew.

Lord Petrac, a bear on his left side and a very large mountain cat on his right, came striding defiantly down the path. For just the briefest moment, it looked as if the two groups might come to blows, but then D'Shay stepped back and, with that earlier, disconcerting smile back on his face, he ordered the two armored . . . suits to help her to her feet. Once it was obvious that Troia could stand on her own, they released her.

The Will of the Woods held out one hand. "Come to me, child."

"Come to *you*?" she spat in his direction.

D'Shay laughed loud and long. "You seem to be losing the respect and confidence of your people, Master Guardian!"

Petrac looked more annoyed than worried. "Unless you would

rather go with Lord D'Shay here, I suggest you come to me, Troia.''

Given *that* sort of choice, she reluctantly joined the Master Guardian. Lord Petrac glared at D'Shay with disdain and disgust. ''Never touch her. Not even your master will be able to save you from my wrath if you do.''

The look on the master wolf raider's visage indicated he was anything but worried about such a threat, but he nodded agreement.

Troia looked up at the being she had once nearly worshiped and, forcing back her anger, whispered, ''What is he doing here?''

Shaking his head, the Will of the Woods sadly replied, ''He is apparently my new ally, young one.''

''Ally?'' Worse and worse.

Lord Petrac looked pained at the accusations in her eyes. ''I will do what I must to preserve *some* portion of the Dream Lands. If I do not do something, there will be *nothing*. Nothing.''

''But the wolf raiders! How can you deal with the spawn of that mad god?''

''I have dealt with them before.''

''You will deal with me from now on, Lord Petrac.'' D'Shay took great pleasure in that statement. The Master Guardian's eyes narrowed, then he agreed.

Troia buried her face in Petrac's chest. ''First D'Rak, and now this traitor—and is the Gryphon part of your contract as well? Have you given him to this—this—''

''Hush, child.'' The Master Guardian glanced warily in D'Shay's direction. ''You have my word, Shaidarol, provided you act swiftly and adhere to the same pact I made with D'Rak, though how you know so much . . .''

D'Shay stroked his goatee. ''You may thank the Tzee for that. They are the perfect allies; you know they will do what they can to achieve greater power. It's refreshing to have an ally that is so predictable. I contacted them originally in the hopes of using them to locate the Gryphon and to act as my eyes in regards to D'Rak. Imagine my surprise to quickly discover that, in exchange for a measure of power, they were all too willing to tell me about your own deal with my counterpart in the keepership. A good thing, too. The conquering of Sirvak Dragoth would have guaranteed his place as foremost among the Ravager's— that is, the Pack Master's—favorites.''

''Something you cannot afford.''

Troia listened with growing foreboding. There was no way D'Shay would actually adhere to his agreement with Lord Petrac. As long as one fragment of the Dream Lands remained, the wolf raiders would wonder, wonder if it might ever prove a threat again. The only certain way was to eliminate the problem once and for all. Eliminate the Dream Lands.

She knew Lord Petrac did not see it that way. Though he had already broken his promise to one wolf raider, he still obeyed some sort of code of honor, and he fully expected D'Shay, who was the last one the feline woman would have trusted, to maintain his part of the bargain.

"Something has to be done with her, you know."

At first, it did not dawn on her that D'Shay was speaking about *her*. Only when she felt Petrac start did she realize the danger.

"I have already told you. She will not come to harm!"

D'Shay sneered. "How do you propose to keep her out of the way? She's already proven her willpower. If she was able to escape one of your dream sequences, then she will be able to escape another. Best to give her to the Tzee. They would keep her occupied."

"I will do no such thing—and do not think to threaten me, Shaidarol! You need either myself or Geas to open the Gate long enough for your forces to come through, and I very much doubt you can convince *him* to do it! You also need the Gate to remain open so that the power of the Ravager can maintain your rather fragile personal existence!" The Will of the Woods smiled triumphantly as he watched the master wolf raider step back in momentary panic. "Yes, I know your plight just as I know what your servants are. Anywhere but the Dream Lands, the thread of your existence is safe. You are always in contact with your master. Here his power does not reach, and you must rely on either the Gate being open, allowing him continued access, or the good graces of the Tzee. How would they feel, I wonder, if they knew that you had perverted a portion of their being to create your *loyal* guards? Shall I tell them? It might save me trouble. Then I can go back to dealing with D'Rak."

D'Shay suddenly smiled, and both the Master Guardian and Troia, who had turned to watch the wolf raider's reaction, shivered at the sound.

"Very good, Lord Petrac! Not quite as clear-cut as you think, but close enough! I *will* point out that it would take me a very long time to die, and the first one to suffer will be the little kitten wrapped in your arm. But why should allies argue? This is the time for action, not bickering! D'Rak may, at any time, discover your duplicity. The Gryphon is still loose—''

"He is not. I have him.''

"You *have* him?'' D'Shay's face lit up with genuine joy. "But this is fantastic!''

"I . . . will turn him over to you, providing you swear to your end of the bargain by the word of your master—the Ravager, not the Pack Master.''

"My lord, no!'' Troia tried to pull free, but Petrac's arm was as unpliable as the manacles in D'Rak's private cells. The Will of the Woods put a hand over her mouth, holding it closed.

D'Shay ignored her outburst. Incongruously, he looked as if he wanted to hug his ally. "My master and I both thank you for the gift! In his name, I gladly swear to the bargain! Deliver the Gryphon to me and your private domain will forever remain untouched!''

Lord Petrac seemed satisfied with that. "The Gryphon is in a safe place and will keep. He and two companions are . . . resting.''

"Then let us begin.''

"Agreed.'' The Master Guardian gazed down at Troia. She tried to bite his hand, but he continued to hold her mouth closed. "I am sorry, young one, but it is time for Sirvak Dragoth to fall so that the Dream Lands may be at peace at last. You will have to sleep this one out. Forgive me.''

She hissed a protest. Lord Petrac released her mouth and reached for her forehead. Troia had only time to begin the most vile curse she had heard before the traitorous guardian touched the center of her forehead and consciousness fled. She slumped in his arms, forcing him to allow his staff to fall to the ground. He lowered her down onto the path and retrieved the wooden artifact. Straightening, he stared into the eyes of D'Shay.

"I give you two hours from the moment you depart. In two hours, you must have your forces ready. I will have enough to do to keep the Gate under control, since I expect the other Master Guardians to attempt to close it.''

"Two hours will more than suffice. Make it one.''

"One?'' Petrac blinked. "One hour to gather an army?''

One of D'Shay's unliving guards—it was debatable whether the Tzee or anything derived from them could truly be called life—stepped through a portal. The wolf raider acknowledged the guardian's question. "One hour. *We* have always been ready for this moment; where do you think Senior Keeper D'Rak was going to get his army?''

"I will never understand how such a society could exist."

D'Shay gave him one last smile before he and his remaining guard vanished through the Tzee portal. "I could say the same about yours, Master Guardian."

Lord Petrac watched as the Tzee withdrew. When the portal had dwindled to nothing, he took one last glance at the sleeping form on the path. The Will of the Woods frowned, but he knew that now was not the time to have second thoughts. He would be hated, reviled, but only until the survivors came to understand him. The constant pain of the half-real world called the Dream Lands touched him without respite. He could not let it suffer, and there was only one way to treat old, festering wounds. It was like trimming the trees in his woods so that they might grow better. There would be a new land, forever safe from the outside reality of such as the wolf raiders or the drakes who ruled the continent to the west. The Dream Lands would one day become more magnificent than ever.

Here the day was bright and sunny. He had no idea what it was like in this location in the other reality. Probably dank and miserable, he supposed. It really did not matter. All that mattered was preparing for the beginning of change. Just a little less than an hour before the new glory of the Dream Lands began its birth rites. Born in the ashes of blood and flame to become a stronger, free land.

His mind set at ease, the Master Guardian made his way toward his private place of contemplation. When the time arrived—and he would know exactly when that was—he would be prepared.

Someone was *not* doing as D'Rak desired.

He knew that, because the Gryphon and his companion were nowhere to be found. There were rumors that they had been seen near the Pack Master's stronghold, rumors that an army of the hideous verloks was on their tails, a rumor that they had even been eaten—which *was* possible, knowing the verloks.

There were also confirmed reports of the hooded, faceless creatures wandering the streets with a sense of purpose no one could recall them ever having. *That* worried the senior keeper. *They* were supposed to be neutral. *They* had never acted for or against the Aramites—at least, to no one's knowledge. Yet . . .

He had dismissed D'Farany so that he could think on these matters in the peace of a barely lit room. In fact, the only true illumination was that which emanated from the Eye of the Wolf. The glow was steady, something he was thankful for. Of late, it had been unreliable, as if . . . as if the power of the Ravager was coming into question. He had not told anyone of this, since it would only weaken his standing. With the capture of the Gryphon, the senior keeper had noticed a return to stability. It had flickered only once the other day, but enough to frighten him.

Still, despite the fact that the Eye appeared to work well, he could find out nothing concerning the Gryphon, his draconian companion, or the female from the Dream Lands. He knew that D'Shay could not possibly have them; his archrival would have made public news of this if he had. The Gryphon's capture would have spelled success for D'Shay and certain doom for the senior keeper.

D'Rak let the power focused by the Eye take him out of the chamber and over the city. He thrilled in becoming such an integral part of the very structure of the world. The hidden design of the world was open to him, and it was a great temptation to become a part of the design forever. He had long ago learned to control such a temptation, but that did not prevent him from basking in the feeling.

A thorough scan of the city proved once more that they were nowhere to be found. That should have been impossible for the Gryphon, at the very least. D'Rak had made certain of that with the smaller talisman around his neck. Like the guards, the Gryphon was marked. Where he went and what he did should have been open to the senior keeper's observations, but they were not. D'Rak doubted very much now that his own death would trigger the death of the lionbird—not that he was going to test that theory. It was just that someone or something seemed to be watching over the misfit, protecting him from powers awarded to the Aramite lord by the Ravager himself. Something on a level with the god—but that was absurd! There had never been and there never would be a force capable of reckoning with the true master of the empire!

D'Rak returned his thoughts to the original capture of the Gryphon. There had been that female who had vanished and the fact that the source of the escape portal could not directly be traced. Continual observation had indicated that it might have happened at least twice, once from within the city walls, but, again, the portals had all but defied study.

"Master!"

The senior keeper looked up in righteous anger, contact with the Eye broken by the interruption. No one, not even his new second-in-command, was permitted to disturb him during his contemplations. He summoned a guard and ordered him to drag the offending keeper to him.

D'Farany allowed himself to be escorted without hesitation. Anxiety was splashed all over his features, but not anxiety for his own precarious situation. D'Rak found that strange. The younger keeper certainly had to know that he had transgressed. Perhaps his news was worth hearing before he sent the boy down to the cells for a few days of . . . tutoring in the rules of the keepership.

"Speak—and you had better make it good!"

"Master!" D'Farany was still trying to catch his breath. He had run for some time, trying to bring the news to his lord in a way that would assure understanding. He no longer trusted his fellows. "Master, those units designated this month for standby duty are being summoned! Everyone! Gryphon riders, keepers, line soldiers, Runner controllers—everyone!"

D'Rak rose, shaking in anger and understanding. Nevertheless, he had to be certain before he did anything. "Are they being activated for maneuvers? What are their orders? Who gave them?"

The young Aramite kneeled, knowing all too well that his own lifespan might be cut short at any moment. "Master, the orders come from D'Shay with the permission of the Pack Master. He . . . he claims he will give them the Dream Lands! Master, is it possible? Could he—"

"Leave me! Return to your post! Your excellent work will be noted!"

Beaming at yet another sudden change in his fortunes, D'Farany saluted and rushed off. The two guards that had brought him in awaited orders of their own. D'Rak gave them one look. They turned and, to their credit, departed in a hasty but military manner.

Frantic, the senior keeper reached out and renewed contact with the Eye. Because of his growing fury, the connection was unstable, but he was able to observe that everything his aide had said was true. The Aramites kept a large force ready at all times purely for the possible invasion of the Dream Lands. The Ravager had so demanded it. Each month, soldiers from different units were assigned standby duty. They would rise, dress for war, and inspect all gear. Items were cycled in, maintained, and then cycled out if they began to grow worn. Rations were checked for spoilage and replaced before they became inedible. This was the preliminary assault unit. Even now, other units were organizing as men returned from wherever they had been. The senior keeper knew that, even now, his own men were preparing for their part. Some would continue to monitor the city's safety, while others would assault the Dream Lands on another scale. As for the senior keeper himself, his duty . . .

His duty was his own survival, and he knew it! Somehow, D'Shay would make certain that he would lose face, that another keeper, more pliant, would take his place.

I have been betrayed!

His supposed ally, the Master Guardian called Lord Petrac, was responsible. Yet, there still might be a chance. Whatever D'Shay offered him, D'Rak would match it and then some. Then the guardian would close the Gate, trapping those who had already gone through. D'Shay would be shamed for falling into a trap, and then the senior keeper would step in and save the day. D'Rak would prove the great hero—and it would cost only a few hundred line soldiers. There were always more of those.

With the aid of the Eye, he sought out the Tzee. He still needed the vermin to maintain contact with anything in the Dream Lands. That would change soon.

Tzee . . .

He was surprised at how readily they revealed themselves. The Tzee had always been a little hesitant, knowing who was the stronger. Even with the power he had granted them, they still knew their place.

Tzee . . .

The Eye shook, and D'Rak could not help but blink. That should have broken contact, but it did not. The Tzee were not only maintaining contact, they were beginning to *manifest*.

Tzee . . .

In his chamber! Why weren't the guards responding? Any unauthorized intrusion into the senior keeper's chambers was an automatic death sentence unless he chose otherwise.

Tzee . . .

A huge, black, nebulous cloud of matter and energy formed above him, pulsating like a living heart. D'Rak could feel a thousand million eyes upon him. Malevolent eyes. The Tzee had been waiting for this moment.

He summoned the power of the Eye of the Wolf and stared in consternation as the glow faded from the great, crystalline artifact. *Not possible!* He reached for the Ravager's Tooth around his neck, but it, too, was dead. Dead.

And still the guards made no move to aid him. They stood as if they heard nothing, as if they saw nothing.

Tzee . . .

There was only one thing left for D'Rak to do. . . .

— XVI —

"We leave these chambers, we leave Lord Petrac's protection. He dared only mask these three chambers from the sight of the wolf raiders. I don't doubt now that he didn't want his *ally*"— Jerilon Dane spat to the side as he said the word—"to know of his own duplicity."

The Gryphon's plan was to find one of the not-people, or Faceless Ones, and convince it to help them. He knew that location was no impediment to the blank-visaged creatures. The Faceless Ones could do what they wanted where they wanted. They were supposedly neutral, but that did not necessarily mean they couldn't interfere. Of all the puzzles crossing his path, the not-people were among the those that disturbed him most.

"We can't wait for one of them to come to us," the lionbird replied calmly, ignoring the latter portion of the Aramite's remarks. He had thought it over time and time again. It was their best hope.

"Why not? They seem to have an affinity for showing up when one needs a hand. I should know; the Runners would've had me if they had not."

"I'll not trust my luck to Faceless Ones," Morgis hissed. "I cannot explain it, but I don't trust them."

The Gryphon studied him. Morgis had the same look in his eyes that the lionbird suspected he himself wore when trying desperately to recall a memory. It would not be too surprising to discover that the not-people had plots of their own hatching. Nevertheless . . . "Have you thought of something else?"

"No." The drake's voice was flat, defeated. "Nothing feasible. I've had little experience in trying to escape from the capital city of an enemy empire. Perhaps next time."

From anyone else, it would have been an attempt at humor. From the drake . . . the Gryphon was not quite sure.

"We've no real reason for hesitating, then, do we?" The Aramite had the least reason to be happy with this situation. He had wanted to avoid his former home at all cost. Another chase with the Runners was all that awaited him here if he was captured.

Dane located the dead torch that Troia had been carrying before the discovery of Lord Petrac's betrayal and had apparently left behind when suddenly whisked away by the Master Guardian. While it was not entirely dark—a dim glow emanated from tiny crystals embedded, at regular intervals, in the walls—a torch gave them some security. The Aramite, who had no night vision whatsoever, was especially happy to be able to traverse the halls without falling into something he just could not see. With the torch lit—after some doing—they began their trek through corridors supposedly untouched for generations. *Supposedly* was the key word; the Gryphon recalled the passageway in the citadel of the senior keeper. "Are you certain these halls are unused?"

Dane nodded. "It's not something important enough to need to forget. The corridors date back to the early days of Canisargos, when it was little more than an outpost. As you can see, our ancestors built *very* well, though I don't doubt that this place has been improved on a number of times since then. These passages were more well hidden then. Later, they were used for storage. Many of them are still in use, but many are not." An odd smile flashed across his face. "I find it interesting that such a powerful city could be so indifferent or unknowing about an entire world beneath their feet. We've—*they* have grown too complacent. They think that there is nothing to fear, that they are invincible."

The trio were silent for some time afterward. They checked a few side corridors, but these always ended in some chamber. It was decided that the best thing to do was stay in the main passage and hope it ended at an exit.

They came across yet another side passage, and Morgis decided to give this one a quick look. He leaned in and let his eyes adjust.

"A stairway!" His shout brought the others running—mostly to quiet him in case they were not alone down here. "Leading upward!"

He could not be blamed for his excitement. It was indeed a stairway—what was left of it. Disuse had taken a greater toll on it than the rest of the corridor. It seemed to be an addition, and a late one at that. Dane stepped forward with the torch and, with his eyes, followed the ascent of the stairway up to . . .

The former wolf raider stepped away from the stairs, swearing by the god he claimed he no longer had faith in.

"What isss it?" Morgis asked angrily. He strode over to the steps and peered upward. "It's sealed off! They've covered it over with a wall. There's no door anymore."

Cautiously, the drake climbed the crumbling stairs and vanished into the dark. A minute passed, and then he came back down. "No hidden door—unless it's much more well hidden than any I've encountered, including the one in the keeper's lair. I'd say the work was completed years, perhaps decades, ago."

"There might not be another exit from this part of the corridor," the Aramite added in annoyance. "We might have to backtrack and go down the opposite direction."

The Gryphon considered it. "Would that take us deeper into Canisargos?"

"I couldn't say. I never saw the surface. I'm only assuming we're headed toward the outer walls because our 'savior,' Lord Petrac, gave me some indication that this was the proper way. Things he said, nothing specific and, at the time, I really couldn't be bothered with . . . with—What a forgetful fool I've been! We have to go back to the chambers we started from! He may not have taken it with him!"

"Taken what?" Morgis demanded, but the Aramite was already backtracking. The other two were plunged into near-darkness as their companion vanished in the distance.

"Follow him!" The Gryphon hoped that whatever Dane wanted was worth a return to their starting point. Every moment they remained trapped in the city, the danger to the Dream Lands increased. With his secret revealed once, Lord Petrac would not be able to help but think that someone *else* might know. Based on his own experience, the lionbird knew that whatever the Master Guardian had planned for his home and his people, it would occur soon. Only then could Lord Petrac rest easy.

* * *

They found the former wolf raider searching, not the chamber that the three of them had been trapped in, but a smaller one across from it. He was having difficulty pulling something from a shadowy corner because of the torch he held in one hand. That he had not bothered to do something about the situation pointed out how anxious he was about the object he had uncovered.

In the flickering light, the Gryphon could make out only a cloth-covered object approximately the size of a head—it was a poor choice for comparison, considering their situation—and apparently fragile, for the Aramite treated it like newborn child.

He held out the torch to the Gryphon. "Hold this while I get a better grip."

"What is that thing?"

"This, Lord Gryphon, is the head of your former jailer, a beast called R'Mok."

"Disgusting!" Morgis hissed. "We would not waste our times with such trophies! We leave our enemy's dead to the carrion creatures or our mounts, should they be hungry."

Jerilon Dane grimaced. "Much more civilized, of course. I have not kept this toy because of some hobby—though I won't deny that some of my former associates might have such keepsakes. Rather, I held on to it because I thought that the head of the keepership's jailer might prove of value to us. Besides, I doubt you really know what's underneath this hood."

The ex-soldier pulled the cloth, so akin to a tiny shroud in appearance, and smiled coldly. "Senior Keeper D'Rak was a master at crystalline structuring."

The head of the late jailer was a parody of a true human head. The entire thing appeared to have been carved from one great gem. A grinning mouth had been carved, but whatever humor it was trying to convey was lost upon the onlookers. There was a ridge that was located approximately where the nose should have been, but, of the eyes, there was not sign. Nor were there any ears or even holes in the sides of the head. In certain ways, the grotesque object was reminiscent of the not-people.

"The man is the foulest of necromancers. He is not even satisfied with merely raising the dead," the drake muttered in great disgust. "He has to mutilate them as well."

The Gryphon noted some markings carved into the side of the false head. "What are these?"

"Part of whatever spells the senior keeper utilized to create this abomination. This is not his first, gentlemen. Only the latest and the best. The others lived only a few months at a time.''

''What does he propose to do with these creatures?''

Dane shrugged. ''I don't remember. What I've told you is what Lord Petrac told me. He knew I'd need the head to free you. Since he hadn't said to leave it, I took it with me. I still find it hard to reconcile that someone like your Master Guardian could deal with the likes of Lord D'Rak.''

The Gryphon was studying the head. There was no discernible place where the neck would connect to D'Rak's terrible toy, but the lionbird knew only a little about magic involving crystal. Most of what he had learned had been derived from what little was known about the most solitary of the Dragon Kings, the self-styled Crystal Dragon. The power of the Crystal Dragon could not be denied. Only with his aid had the lionbird, Cabe and Gwen Bedlam, and the Blue Dragon been able to defeat the genocidal plan of the enigmatic King's closest brother in power, the mad, suicidal Ice Dragon. The Gryphon wondered briefly what the mighty drake lord would make of this.

He finally pulled his eyes away from the monstrosity. ''Cover that up until we absolutely need it. As for Lord Petrac, I suspect he would deal with the Ravager himself if he could be satisfied that his own little kingdom would remain. In some perverted way, he sees himself as the only hope for any part of the Dream Lands. All he'll end up doing is killing it.''

Morgis nodded. ''He's mad if he thinks he can keep the survivors under control. Eventually, they'll discover the truth, and that will be the end of it.''

The Gryphon blinked. ''Listen to us. We're talking as if the Dream Lands are lost already. We may still have time. Lord Petrac may not have even started.''

''We can't use this in here.'' Jerilon Dane made a sloppy attempt at covering up the ''face'' of D'Rak's creation. ''The vestiges of the Master Guardian's masking spell make this thing useless. We have to go out into the corridor.''

''Then let's do that. I'm getting tired of catacombs and such. I want to see the sky.''

Morgis went first, sword ready just in case something did show up. Dane came next. When he stepped out of the chamber, he yelped in surprise. The Gryphon, behind him, almost stumbled into him. When he finally had a clear view, he could not blame the Aramite for his lack of poise.

The crystalline head was glowing so brightly, it was a wonder that Dane's hands were not burning. The former wolf raider quickly pulled the hood over the gleaming object, but that did little to hide the intense light.

"It's never done this before!"

"What *is* it doing?" Morgis was unconsciously trying to protect himself from the glowing head by waving the tip of his sword in its direction. He realized what he was doing and, chagrined, quickly lowered the blade.

Shaking his head, the Aramite shoved past the Gryphon and dove back into the room. The blinding brilliance dimmed to a more tolerable level but did not die completely.

"I—don't—understand," he puffed.

"I think we've lost much of Lord Petrac's protection," said the Gryphon from the entryway. He pointed at the cloth-covered artifact. "And I think that thing did it. I think it's working against the spell."

"It shouldn't be able to!"

"Tell *it* that! Something's changed that thing! It happened the moment you took it into an unprotected area! If you know how to use that thing—if you still think we can *trust* that thing—then be prepared to do it fast! If the keepers locate us, you can be certain that they'll have soldiers here at any moment!"

That stirred the Aramite. He rose and stared at the glowing, cloth-covered object in his arms. "I think I can still manipulate it. My failure to become a keeper didn't stem from a lack of ability; it stemmed from being unable to bind myself with a talisman of my own. All keepers must bind themselves to talismans blessed by the senior keeper."

Morgis snorted. "Which is also a good way to keep an eye on any troublemakers, I imagine."

"Most likely. Give me a moment." Dane pulled off the hood and stared into the crude face of the artifact. He shivered. "I feel like I'm staring into the face of Lord D'Rak himself. This may prove more difficult than I imagined."

The Gryphon's fur and feathers suddenly stood on end. "You'd best do it quickly. I think our time has just run out."

The corridor abruptly filled with the sounds of many armored men running.

Someone with the voice of youth, who was not quite experienced in giving commands, shouted, "I want them alive, if possible, but *dead*, if necessary!"

Morgis looked from the frantic Jerilon Dane to the corridor

and then to the Gryphon. The duke broke into a horrific smile, showing great quantities of sharp teeth. "I'll hold them off! Call me if you get that thing working or can think of a miracle!"

He raced out of the chamber, shouting foul descriptions of wolf raiders that questioned the validity of their bloodlines. Dane could not help looking up at the Gryphon, who shrugged and then unsheathed his own sword. "Do you really think you can get that thing to work?"

"I have to, don't I?"

The lionbird nodded and went to join the drake.

There were Aramite soldiers everywhere. Most looked like members of the keepership guard, but there were two keepers as well, one of whom, much younger than the Gryphon would have expected, was evidently in charge. He, of course, was far from the battle. Still, both he and his companion were clutching their talismans tight while they tried to get a good view of Morgis.

The Gryphon knew then who his targets had to be.

Duke Morgis stood before the three foremost guards, his shortsword carving a wicked path before him. Two wolf raiders were already down, and a third looked to be injured. The corridors were wide enough for three men to move without bumping into one another and that would have meant the end of any foe but a massive, experienced drake warrior. Even with shields, the wolf raiders had actually begun to back away.

Glancing at his shortsword, the Gryphon cursed. There was no way he could get to the keepers, and it would not be long before one or both of them ensnared Morgis. At the very least, they might disrupt him enough for the soldiers to get under his guard. Without his powers, the duke would die as any warrior died. Heroic, yes, but still dead.

One of the dead wolf raiders lay on his back, and the Gryphon spotted one of the dark, curling daggers that seemed to be a favorite with the black-clad figures. He hurried over to the body and relieved the corpse of the weapon. A quick check of the other dead Aramite revealed no such dagger. He would have to make do with the one.

The battle had moved back much farther than the ex-mercenary would have believed. Morgis was a savage, skilled fighter, true, but he was battling members of a people born to war. It was almost as if they were purposefully giving way.

It was almost too late before he realized what they were doing. Only when he sought out the keepers and discovered only the commander still in sight did he recognize the trap.

They had passed one or two corridors and even a side chamber. Morgis, caught up in the battle, did not see the one keeper step into the next such chamber to the drake's right. By the time the Gryphon understood what was happening, the duke was already moving past the entryway to that room.

The lionbird flipped the knife, catching it by the flat of the blade. The twisted blade was weighed oddly, but not so much that he was worried.

As the drake, confident of his abilities, moved completely beyond the entranceway, the keeper stepped out from behind, fully intent on bringing Morgis down through the power of his talisman. Like the other keeper, he was young, which explained why he had not bothered to check for a second foe. There was a good reason why most veteran fighters were not fools. Most fools died young.

The Gryphon threw, forgoing some accuracy for the sake of speed.

The keeper must have heard him in that last moment, for he started to turn. Quite possibly, it prevented him from dying immediately when the knife struck, for, had his back been turned as it was, the blade would have sunk itself into his neck. Instead, it caught him along the throat and bounced off his chest plate. The keeper gagged, lost his grip on the crystalline artifact he wore, and reached upward in a desperate attempt to stem the flow of blood. The Gryphon realized that, despite not striking the neck directly, he had succeeded in cutting the jugular.

Success turned to disaster, for the dying keeper fell to his knees before the lionbird could reach him, stumbling into Morgis's legs and throwing the drake off balance. Wolf raiders swarmed over the duke, and several more came for the Gryphon.

"Gryphon!"

Jerilon Dane's scream was no indication of success. Even as the former monarch was thrown against the wall by sheer numbers, he felt the entire underworld shudder. A brilliant light burst forth from where the hapless Aramite had been working desperately.

The Gryphon felt power wash over him, and immediately understood at least what *that* meant. The only trouble was, there was little he could do pinned against the wall.

A fierce roar added to the pandemonium, and the chamber was almost instantly filled with a rapidly growing dragon.

For much too long, Morgis had been thrust from one situation to another without his powers and, especially, his inherent magical ability to shapeshift from his humanoid form to his birth form and back again. While he preferred the dexterity of the humanoid shape, to steal his right to transform from one to the other was like clipping a bird's wings so that it could no longer fly.

Much like a bird who has realized that his feathers have grown back, Morgis instantly knew his powers had returned.

The Aramites quickly forgot the Gryphon as they tried to cope with more dragon than they had ever seen in their lifetimes. Whatever Dane had unleashed, it was tearing at the entire system of spells that the keepers had woven about Canisargos. Morgis thrust his head toward the ceiling, and it was the latter that gave. Heavy stone, including full sections of ceiling and wall, caved in, crushing more than one wolf raider. Those trapped on the same side as the Gryphon foolishly tried to get past the expanding drake. They were either crushed flat against the walls or thrown by massive paws, eventually landing in broken heaps. One mad fool actually struck at the dragon with his sword, perhaps out of sheer frustration. The keeper that Morgis had originally fallen on was only a spotty memory on the floor.

The one great danger at the moment was that, in his fury, the dragon might inadvertently cause the Gryphon's death. Up until now, the lionbird had succeeded in avoiding the collasping underworld, but now portions of the building above were falling as well. In desperation, he stumbled back toward the blazing light.

It took a moment for his eyes to adjust even partially, but it was sufficient for him to see what was unfolding within the chamber. Jerilon Dane was standing in the center, clutching the false head in such a manner that it appeared he was trying to absorb all the energy flowing out of it. He seemed not to notice the instability of the walls and ceiling, but a single step by the Gryphon in his general direction made the Aramite look up.

Their eyes met. The eyes that stared into the lionbird's were *not* the eyes of Jerilon Dane.

A huge portion of the chamber's ceiling came crashing down within inches of the former wolf raider. He started to say something but decided against it. Then, what remained of the ceiling began to fall and the Gryphon was forced back out into the corridor. He was not able to see if Dane survived. A moment later, there was no more entranceway to the room.

"GRYPHON!"

The voice boomed from overhead. Walls and a portion of a

ceiling were all that remained of whatever structure had been on the surface. Morgis had done his best to ensure that his companion was not crushed by the collapsing building. The same could not be said of the Aramites who had attacked them. Perhaps a few had escaped if the other keeper had been able to open a portal in time.

Now was not the time to be concerned with that, however. By now, the entire city was aware of the fact that a full-grown dragon was in their midst, and the Gryphon doubted that the wolf raiders lacked the means of tackling such a problem. The keepers, especially, were a threat.

A massive reptilian head came swooping down toward him. Morgis shouted, "Dane! Is he dead?"

"I can only assume so! The chamber—"

The dragon cut him off. "We have not got the time to look! Climb atop my head!"

This was the first time he had seen his companion in this form, and it was truthful to say that Morgis was as grand, as overwhelming a dragon as any the Gryphon had seen, barring the Dragon Kings themselves. If they survived all of this, Morgis might one day be one of them. He certainly had the size. It would have been so simple for the dragon to swallow him whole. If ever there was an ally to have in a situation like this . . .

"Once we are out of this building, slide down to my neck. You will be more secure there."

Morgis began climbing out of the hole that was all that remained of the corridor and several chambers. People were screaming and cursing, and the Gryphon felt guilt at the damage and loss of life that must have been sustained. He knew that, like any other people, not all Aramites were evil. He wondered whether Morgis felt any guilt. Drakes had a more pragmatic view of such matters; in his eyes, he probably viewed the destruction as necessary to the preservation of his own existence. Unlike Duke Toma, however, Morgis did not seem to revel in carnage.

The Gryphon tightened his grip. It would be some time before he completely forgot what had happened here, if he ever did and if he managed to survive this day.

"Where are they? Where are their legions?" At last back in his natural form, the dragon was eager to prove his power. The Gryphon, on the other hand, had no other desire save to leave as soon as possible.

"Their legions will be here soon enough," he shouted at the dragon, although, in his mind, he, too, wondered at the absence of a ready force. There were a few single soldiers trying to make order out of the chaos, and one patrol with a lone keeper who looked as though he would have rather been elsewhere, but nothing vast and organized. That would not be the case for very long, of that the lionbird was certain. Canisargos would never be left completely unprotected, even during a major campaign, and since there was no major campaign on at the present . . .

But there *was*. It was the only explanation. They were already too late.

He leaned close in order to assure that Morgis heard him. The dragon was nearly out onto the surface, his vast body overwhelming and crushing buildings all around them. Most of the people had fled by now, and even the soldiers were starting to retreat. The Gryphon caught sight of the keeper again. The Aramite was staring at his talisman, which evidently was not working as it ought to have. They still had breathing room, then.

"Morgis! Forget the city!"

"No! I want D'Rak! I want this D'Shay! I want this city to know the power of a dragon!"

This was proving more difficult than he had expected. Morgis was building himself up into a frenzied rage. All the frustrations since his arrival on the shores of this continent were coming to a head.

"Morgis! They're attacking the Dream Lands! That's why we haven't been overwhelmed yet!" He did not mention his suspicions concerning D'Rak's toy. Whatever it was and whatever it had done, it was, hopefully, buried forever beneath the rubble, preferably in several thousand little pieces. Sooner or later, the keepers remaining behind during the invasion would regain control, and then that would be all for the two of them.

"Not here?"

"No! Hurry! If we leave now, it might be that we can find a way into the reality of the Dream Lands and stop Lord Petrac!"

"Lord Petrac!"

The Gryphon could see the sudden change in goals. Morgis wanted the Master Guardian as much as he wanted D'Rak, probably more.

"Slide down, Gryphon! We are going to fly!"

Just in time, too. The lionbird suddenly felt a presence, one that he knew could only be the keepers working to regain mastery of the situation. Regaining mastery meant disposing of the main problem, the dragon in their midst.

He slid down to the base of the dragon's neck even as huge,

membraned wings spread wide, damaging even more of this section of the wolf raiders' capital. The Gryphon wished the damage could have at least included the citadel of the keepers or the stronghold of the Pack Master.

"Hold tight!" Morgis shouted almost gleefully. He had not flown in too long a time.

The huge, blue-tinted behemoth rose into the air at an astonishing pace. Clinging for dear life, the Gryphon remembered that a dragon's ability to fly depended partly on sorcery, which was why they seemed to pick up altitude and speed at such an alarming rate.

When they were high enough, Morgis leveled out. The Gryphon dared to look down and was astonished to see that, despite the distance they had risen, the city still seemed to go on forever in every direction. They had not been near the outer wall! If anything, he suspected that they had been moving away from it.

"Gryphon! I sense some massive disturbance to the east!"

"It can only be what we're looking for! They have to be moving troops through still! We have a chance!" It seemed impossible that the dragon could hear him, what with the wind, but Morgis nodded.

"How will we enter the Dream Lands?"

"I don't know!"

The great beast *hmmphed*. "Well, at the very least, if we cannot get in, neither will many of the cursed Ravager's dogs!" Morgis twisted his neck and revealed a vast, toothy grin. "We shall see to that, eh?"

As the dragon turned his attention back to the task of flying, the Gryphon, still holding on as tightly as possible, wished he could share his companion's confidence. Somehow, he doubted things would be so easy.

After all, they never had been before.

XVII

D'Farany had failed and, worse still, had acted without the authority of Senior Keeper D'Rak. Now, with one entire section of the city in ruins and both the dragon and the one called the Gryphon free and out of the range of the Keepers' powers, he had to face his master and explain. D'Rak had not summoned him, but he knew better than to wait for such a summons. His only recourse was to go and explain his story as quickly as possible, before the senior keeper heard other tales. Perhaps he could get off relatively lightly if he could convince his master that he had attempted the capture in an attempt to prove himself worthy.

If he didn't, there was a good chance that he would be joining his predecessor, whom the crystals indicated had gone to his traitor's reward at the hands of D'Shay. *Why did the invasion have to take place at the same time*? he wondered. Because of that, D'Rak would be in the foulest of moods.

The senior keeper was sitting in near darkness, the Eye of the Wolf hovering silently near the right of his chair. The great crystal was ominously dim. D'Farany had heard stories about it. It had always been described as glowing, at the very least. The few times he himself had observed it, it had almost lit the room as well as a dozen of the seeing crystals and several torches combined might have. Was there something *else* amiss?

"Master?"

The figure sat motionless. The head was slumped forward, one hand attempting to keep it at least partially propped up. The younger keeper forgot his own predicament, suddenly fearing that D'Rak might be ill or, worse yet, dying.

"Master?"

The figure stirred. D'Farany breathed a heavy sigh of relief. Lord D'Rak had only been resting.

"What—is—it?" The voice sounded slurred, as if the senior keeper was drunk—an impossibility.

"Master, it's D'Farany. I'm afraid I have disturbing news concerning the one called the Gryphon."

"Gryphon?" The senior keeper looked up. Most of his face was obscured by shadow. D'Farany gazed into the darkness where D'Rak's eyes must have been, but only briefly, finding something unnerving about that area of the other's face. He felt as if the eyes must be watching everything, including what eyes could not normally see.

The senior keeper appeared to be growing impatient, so D'Farany started his tale. D'Rak was motionless during the whole story, as if absorbing the information was all that mattered to him. As he did not give any sign of anger, D'Farany began to relax and his narrative became more clinical. When he had finished, he stood there silently, awaiting the senior keeper's instructions—and possibly his final judgment.

"The Gryphon. He goes to the Dream Lands." D'Rak's voice was raspy. The younger keeper nodded in acknowledgment of the assumption. It made sense. Where else would the outsider go? It was said that he had once been one of the creatures guarding that elusive domain.

"Not this time."

"Master?"

"Nothing." The senior keeper might have been a statue, for all he moved. "D'Shay enters the Dream Lands."

"As you say, my lord." D'Farany was extremely uncomfortable. Perhaps Lord D'Rak was ill after all.

One hand rose, and a finger was pointed at the aide. "You obey me. Understand?"

"Your . . . your will is mine."

"It is. We—I want D'Shay gone. Gryphon gone. Master Guardians gone. The Gate must be closed."

Shock rippled through the other Aramite. "But . . . without the Gate, we cannot invade the Dream Lands!"

"Untrue." For the first time, the shadow-enshrouded figure showed some true confidence. He leaned back. "The power to control the Gate is now in here." D'Rak tapped the side of his head. "We have no need of the others."

"I . . . am overwhelmed, my lord! How did you secure it?"

"A change in thought was all that was needed." The senior keeper's voice was more its old self. D'Farany's fears began to subside.

"There are keepers in the invasion force. Loyal ones."

"Yes."

"Good. I—yes, I—want them to locate D'Shay's ally. A Master Guardian called Lord Petrac. He has the head of a stag."

"Ravager's Teeth! A stag's head?"

"They will kill him or, failing that, turn him against D'Shay. He has a weakness. Love for lessers."

D'Farany understood. A few hostages, utilized in the proper way, would either make the Master Guardian careless or make him furious, which would probably result in his cutting off those soldiers in the Dream Lands from any outside aid. "Those trapped in the Dream Lands will die."

"Possibly, but I will move to save them if timing permits. Go. Now. The instructions are simple enough. I will join you shortly."

"Master." The younger keeper bowed and, his spirits quite the opposite of what they had been when he had entered, departed to organize the betrayal. It did not occur to him that there were many loose ends in the plan outlined to him. As a keeper, he was used to his superiors' taking care of such things. If D'Rak said nothing more, then there was nothing more to be considered.

The shadowy form of the senior keeper rose from his chair. He studied his hands, as if seeing them for the first time. With his right, he guided the Eye to a spot before him. With his left, he summoned forth the power locked within. A few gestures brought him an image of the massive forces of the Ravager moving slowly through the Gate. Thanks to Lord Petrac, the Gate was at least ten times the size it had normally appeared as, but that still did not allow enough men to go through at one time. At least as far as D'Shay was concerned, no doubt. As for the traitorous former guardian himself, he would have been one of the first through. This was to be D'Shay's triumph, and the only way he could assure that was to lead it himself. So much the better. When the Gate closed, it would be the beginning of the end for him. If not through the keepers, then through the simple fact that he was unable to escape from the only place his master's power could not sustain him for very long.

Sirvak Dragoth would fall with the keepership's aid, leaving the Gryphon. But this time, they were prepared—more than they had expected to be. And with the Gryphon dead, the Ravager would reward them with even *greater* power, which was all they lived for.

"No, there is only 'I.' " A smile appeared on the visage of the senior keeper, an involuntary reaction, and one he was not familiar with. It was ignored. "Later, it will be 'we' again. When they are all dead, and only we remain."

Tzee . . .

A dragon flies more swiftly than any other creature, portals and demons not included. Thus it was that, when it seemed at first that Canisargos went on forever and ever, the eastern wall came into sight not more than half an hour later. That still said something about the size of the Aramites' mightiest city, the fact that it had taken Morgis even that long. Despite commenting once or twice about possibly leaving a major path of destruction in his wake, Morgis had flown without pause toward the great emanation of power that they could both feel long before they knew for certain what it was.

"The Gate of the Dream Lands! It's grown!"

The Gryphon followed the dragon's gaze. The Gate had indeed grown. It stood nearly as tall as Morgis did now, and the archway where the great doors presently hung open was probably just wide enough for him to squeeze through. Huge, dark shapes flowed over the sides of the Gate, and the lionbird recognized them as the tiny guardians of the artifact, albeit now nearly as large as a pony. He wondered why they did not attack the invaders.

A harsh squawking filled the air. The Gryphon scanned the heavens and spotted several airborne forms moving toward the two of them. "Gryphon riders!"

He counted more than a dozen, and hazarded a guess that there was at least twice that many. As the riders neared the dragon, Morgis let loose with a stream of smoking flame.

The gryphon riders separated in precise fashion, the column of fire continuing on harmlessly between what was now two columns. That separated farther into four units and then into eight tiny squads.

"Gnats! They try to beset me with gnats!" Morgis laughed. The Gryphon found the situation much more serious.

"Morgis! They're more dangerous than you think! Don't let them—"

"Worry not! I'll have them swatted aside in no time!"

Three came within range of his paws. He swung at them, claws extended, fully expecting to get at least two. The riders, however, controlled their beasts well and, by the time the dragon's paws reached where the targets had been, the riders were above and below.

Morgis suddenly screamed, and the Gryphon was barely able to hold on as the dragon writhed in pain. "I've been slashed!"

The Gryphon turned. Several riders had taken advantage of the deception in order to strike the unprotected flank of the leviathan. Morgis had twisted away immediately, but there were now several long, bloody gashes in his tail, his lower backside, and, most likely, his stomach region as well. Real gryphons had claws sharper than most any other creature and beaks strong enough to bite apart all but the strongest of metal bars.

As Morgis turned, one massive, leathery wing accidentally struck one of the beasts fully. Both rider and steed plummeted limply toward the ground. The rest of the riders pulled their animals back. Several began flying around the dragon in a circle going from left to right. Others began flying right to left. They were trying to cross Morgis up.

"If they'd stand still . . . What sort of warriors do they call themselves? They should fight in a more seemly manner!"

"They'll *win* if this keeps up, Morgis! You're already bleeding profusely!"

"One lucky strike! I was not prepared!" Nevertheless, the dragon sounded just a bit uncertain.

A rider darted in from the backside. The Gryphon heard the swoop of wings and twisted away just before the claws of the beast could tear him from his place on the dragon. He formed a fist with his left hand and, drawing from the less trustworthy lines of power that crisscrossed the skies, he created a spear of pure power that was his to control. The act of creation took but two seconds, a fortunate thing, because now several riders were daring the powers of the dragon in a deliberate attempt to get the Gryphon. He did not have to ask why. They obviously knew who he was, and both D'Shay and the senior keeper had undoubtedly given orders to capture him if possible—kill him, likely, if it proved necessary.

Those who knew the Gryphon well understood that his eyesight was much like that of an actual bird. The proof of his extraordinary eyesight was the skill with which he found his target. As he did now.

Three riders presented themselves as possibilities, but only one gave him full use of the strength in his arm. He did not hesitate. Sighting on the beast rather than the rider, he threw.

A direct hit. The spear passed through the animal so perfectly that it took several seconds for the creature to understand that it was dead. When it did understand, the eyes glazed over, the paws dropped, and the wings ceased to flap. The Gryphon watched with grim satisfaction as the beast fell like a stone, its rider screaming both in anger and fear. A fear was lifted from his heart; he had wondered if killing one of the creatures would feel like killing a part of himself. It did not. Regardless of resemblance, he felt no kinship with these monsters.

Morgis continued to shout his frustration. Time and time again, the gryphon riders moved in, barely staying out of the reach of his huge claws. Twice he had tried to burn them from the sky, but the beasts were too swift, too tiny. Yet, like a man bitten time after time by countless insects, the dragon was suffering, and it was evident which side would fail in the end. They had to get out of here.

"The Gate! You have to try for the Gate! It's the only way!"

At first, it seemed more likely that Morgis would refuse, that his rage had pushed him past reason, but, at last, he dipped his head in agreement. What happened next almost caught the Gryphon completely off guard. He thanked whoever was controlling his luck that he had gone back to a two-handed grip on the neck of his companion, for Morgis simply stopped flying.

A dragon is a large, massive creature. A large, massive creature that ceases flying can do only one thing.

Drop like a rock.

The gryphon riders watched, stunned. More than a few thought that their adversary had reached his limit and was falling to his death, which was exactly what Morgis wanted them to think. He allowed himself to fall a short distance, just enough to put the attackers out of immediate range, and then spread his wings and flapped with all his might. The inherent magic involved in the process of flying aided in what would have otherwise been suicide, and the dragon was almost immediately in control again.

The lionbird forced himself to look down. "We're going to have to get much, much lower if we want to go through the Gate!"

"Not until the last moment!" Morgis shouted. "I do not want to chance being struck down by the power of the keepers! I have had enough of their sorcery! Are you certain there is no other way of entering the Dream Lands?"

"Only the Gate and, apparently, the Faceless Ones, have complete control! The Tzee have always had partial control, but I think we can rule them out!"

"I, for one, would like to rule out those blank-faced demons as well!"

"Which leaves us with only one choice! The Gate!"

Morgis nodded determinedly. "The Gate it is, then!"

They heard shrieks of anger from behind them. The gryphon riders had not yet given up. In a long-distance race, the dragon would have left them behind easily. Now, though, Morgis was tired from the endless struggles and had to slow so as not to overshoot the Gate. The longer it took him to enter the Gate, the less chance he had of succeeding, especially when it meant entering in the midst of an invasion. Worse yet, there would literally be troops entering the vast portal at the same moment.

Below, the advance force was already turning to deal with the oncoming leviathan. The Gryphon cursed silently. There would be any number of keepers mixed in that army, and he doubted that even at full strength Morgis would be able to withstand their combined might. The lionbird knew that he himself had no chance whatsoever.

You can manipulate the gate yourself, a calm, commanding voice suggested.

"What was that you said?" Morgis shouted.

You, Gryphon, have the power to manipulate the gate. You can take it from the grasp of the one called Lord Petrac.

It was frighteningly akin to his confrontation with the Ravager, but there was a calmness here that the mad god had lacked.

No god. Neither am I. You should know that.

It was true; he did know that—now.

Time is short. The mad dog will discover me. You can manipulate the gate, old one. You merely have forgotten that, as you have forgotten so much. Would that I could bring all those memories back—but that must be your doing.

How? How do I manipulate the Gate? the Gryphon asked silently. This reminded him too much of the brief contact he had had with the Dragons Storm and Crystal. Both had sought to use him secretly against the dreaded Ice Dragon. Storm had failed. Crystal had not.

You can—

The voice was gone, contact abruptly cut off—and not by that other. Whoever, whatever it was, the Ravager had evidently discovered it sooner than it had hoped.

There is a thing I must ask of you, old one. This time, the words were not formed by an outsider. Rather, the Gryphon recalled another memory, one far older than any he had remembered before. Old one?

Manipulate the Gate. He had done so without thinking more than once. That had to be why he had seen it as he and Morgis had made their way to Luperion. An unconscious summoning. No. Not a summoning. That was Lord Petrac's way. More like the silent Master Guardian, the one called Geas. He had not really summoned the Gate so much as requested its aid in a matter of import. A matter of import.

"Gryphon!" Morgis's hissing cry freed him from his dreaming. "The Gate! It isss wavering out of control! The scavengers are fleeing from it!"

"I know!" A request for aid. A chance to end this madness, the madness of the Ravager. The madness of D'Shay. The madness of Lord Petrac the Betrayer.

And suddenly, dragon and rider were flying through an immense Gate standing freely in the middle of the air. Huge, black serpents with all-seeing eyes scurried about a massive stone arch with vast wooden doors that were swung back even as it appeared Morgis would crash into them. Though the dark guardians of the Gate hissed at them, it was somehow recognizable as an acknowledgment of an ally, not an enemy.

The Gryphon looked down before they entered, hoping to make out what was going on below. He was not permitted the time. There was only a brief glimpse of the eastern edge of Canisargos and countless ebony figures milling about in confusion—and then he was staring at a sloping hillside upon which other ebony figures were suddenly halting in panic as they realized there would be no reinforcements. Briefly, the shrieking of the pursuing gryphons rose, then the doors of the Gate closed. Not one of the beasts had made it through.

The appearance of a full-grown dragon brought welcome relief, no doubt, to the defenders of Sirvak Dragoth. From above, the Gryphon studied the assault. He was shocked to see, not only so many wolf raiders, but a great number of others that could only be the inhabitants of the Dream Lands. It was amazing to see so many. Not being able to recall memories of his time here, he had judged from what he had seen. In his last visit to the Dream Lands, he had come to think of it as an otherworldly wilderness with a handful of tiny communities and only the stronghold of the Master Guardians as any true defense. He saw then that he had assumed too much. The Gryphon wondered if D'Shay had assumed the same.

He was nearly thrown from Morgis's neck as the dragon ceased flying and, as he had done during the battle with the gryphon riders, began to plummet like so many tons of dead mass.

"Gryphon! I cannot d—"

Some might say that it was fortunate that the dragon had dropped lower to the earth before losing control. Some might have said that it lessened the impact and probably saved both their lives. *They*, as far as the Gryphon would have been concerned, knew nothing about what they were talking about.

The impact set every bone and muscle of the lionbird aquiver. At one point, he truly believed his skull and all of his organs had burst free from his battered body. The soft, numbing touch of unconsciousness offered him respite from the pain. He forced himself to refuse, knowing who and what lurked all about the two of them.

The Gryphon discovered he was lying several yards from the vast, motionless form of his companion. He forced his arms to work, then barely succeeded in smothering a cry when he realized that his right hand was broken. Not just the fingers, though three of those did hang limply. His wrist was, at the very least, fractured. The ex-mercenary leaned on his left side. While painful, at least he knew it would support him. It was still too difficult to raise himself into a sitting position. Standing was impossible for now.

Morgis presented a much, much bigger problem.

At present, the wolf raiders seemed more concerned with Sirvak Dragoth than the two newcomers. The dragon was down and still; that was good enough for them. Undoubtedly, they assumed it was the work of the keepers, although the Gryphon had his doubts. No, the keepers had their hands full just supporting their comrades at the moment, and, unless it had been either a senior keeper of comparable power to D'Rak himself or several keepers of lesser ability pooling their resources, then it had to be someone else. D'Shay or . . .

"It grieved me to do that to you, but you left me no choice."

Lord Petrac, the Will of the Woods (it might have been debatable at this point whether there was any truth to the title), stood over him, seemingly having materialized out of midair. He held his staff with both hands, the lower tip a foot above the injured Gryphon.

"It grieved me, but such is the price that must be paid for the welfare of at least a few of my children."

The hard tip of the staff came crashing down on the lionbird's injured hand.

If his wrist had not been truly broken before, there was no doubt of it now. He forced back the scream of agony, refusing to give the renegade Master Guardian any such satisfaction.

A leather boot was planted into his chest, forcing the Gryphon onto his back. He looked up into the dignified, oh-so-misleading features, into the "innocent" eyes of the stag, and discovered that his attacker actually did hate what he was doing. The self-disgust in Lord Petrac's eyes surprised him, but no more than the second blow from the staff. This time, the Master Guardian chose his left shoulder. There was intense pain, and then complete numbness.

"The Gate is mine again. You caught me by surprise; I admit that. But now, I understand about you. It makes sense. All of it. Qualard, Shaidarol, the not-people—all of it makes sense. If only it was not too late."

"Too late—for what?" the Gryphon croaked. Given a few minutes, he might have been able to stand and at least put up a brief struggle. At the moment, he could do neither that, nor concentrate. Spells were beyond him since the moment Lord Petrac had trapped them in the sky.

"It does not matter." The Master Guardian's eyes narrowed as he stared at the lower tip of his staff. The blunt end began to twist and grow. It tapered, thinned, until the Gryphon found himself staring red-eyed at a very sharp point. He did not bother to ask what the Will of the Woods planned to do with it.

Lord Petrac raised his staff high. The Gryphon tried to roll away, but he discovered he was now fastened to the ground. Even with the Gate under his control, Lord Petrac had power to spare.

"Understand, Gryphon, I *am* doing this for my children, so at least some of them will live."

The former monarch could not hold back. He glared in complete disgust at his murderer. "Will they want to after learning the truth?"

Lord Petrac gasped. The staff fell from his hands, clattering against the Gryphon as the Master Guardian reached up to clutch desperately at the river of blood flowing from the back of his neck—or what remained of it. His mouth opened and closed wordlessly, and his dark, round eyes stared without seeing.

The Will of the Woods fell forward, and it was only because his spell no longer held after death that the Gryphon was able to roll away before the lifeless body fell flat across the ground.

The Gryphon, blinded by both pain and splattered blood, wiped his eyes. He heard sobbing from near where the late Master Guardian had stood and knew who it was even before his sight returned.

Troia was on her knees, her right hand covered in the life fluids of one who had been her mentor, almost a father to her. The one she had finally forced herself to kill in order to save, not just the Dream Lands, but perhaps one even more dear to her.

In the middle of a battle, the sounds of her grief were lost to all but the Gryphon.

XVIII

D'Shay stood atop a hill and watched as countless ebony-armored soldiers assaulted the Master Guardians' stronghold. The line soldiers were almost a ruse; the real, more successful assault originated from behind him where more than fourscore keepers had combined their might in a battle of wills against the inhabitants of Sirvak Dragoth. They were the best his position in the hierarchy of command could buy. Keepers who believed he would reward them for their loyalty to him rather than to D'Rak.

On this day, he thought to himself, *I rid myself of all my enemies and . . . all my fears.*

And then the Gate had vanished and a dragon had appeared in the south, over the main bulk of the invasion force. D'Shay cried out, but then he realized that it was not the dragon he believed it to be, but only the drake companion of the most hated Gryphon. D'Shay smiled and then watched as the dragon suddenly dropped helplessly from the sky. The Master Guardian had apparently recovered quickly. He could not see where the great beast struck the ground, but he knew that it had done so with enough force to eliminate the dragon as a potential annoyance, possibly permanently.

Only then did he recognize how precarious his position was. D'Shay turned around and stalked quickly to a tent his creatures had constructed for him. Two of the armored beings stood guard at the opening. They saluted him mechanically. D'Shay ignored them and looked inside. The sight of his prisoner still chained relieved him. It meant that his emergency plan was still safe. The danger posed by being cut off from the will of the Ravager was still present, but not so immediate anymore. Still . . .

"My Lord D'Shay!"

He stepped away from the tent and glanced in unmasked disdain at the figure puffing up the slope to join him. Some nameless aide of the military officials coordinating the attack from the field. They did not understand that they could all die for all he cared. The work of his pet keepers was all that mattered. The army merely kept the defenders from concentrating too much on the actual threat.

"What is it?"

"Pack Commander D'Hayn and Pack Leader D'Issial are both requesting knowledge of the temporary disa—"

D'Shay held up a hand to quiet him. He glanced briefly in the direction of the Gate, which was back in place and looking as solid as ever. "Tell your officers that their minds should be on the assault of the enemy stronghold and not on—the—Gate. . . ."

He trailed off, staring in dismay. The aide turned, and his eyes widened, giving his otherwise unremarkable appearance the look of a frog.

The Gate was gone again. Somehow, D'Shay knew it was for good this time. *What had that guardian fool done?* Had he betrayed them? D'Shay closed his eyes. No, Lord Petrac had not betrayed the wolf raiders. Lord Petrac no longer lived. That much he could now discern, but . . .

His eyes opened, and he cursed at the aide for no other reason than that the hapless soldier was standing in front of him. *The Gryphon again!*

The ground rumbled, part of some desperate assault by the defenders, and D'Shay was forced to steady himself. Only years of paranoia made him turn in time to catch two keepers focusing the power of their talismans on *him*. Disbelief almost did him in; these were *his* keepers, their loyalty bought with promises of freedom from the power of D'Rak—and riches as well. Promises, apparently, were not always enough. He was only barely able to deflect their spell.

"Kill them!" he shouted at nobody in particular. The aide drew his sword, then screamed and shriveled to a dry husk. The assassins had turned the spell on him, but that proved their undoing. D'Shay's unliving servants came at them; this sort of spell was useless against something that did not really have a body. One of the keepers died instantly, a blow from a guard smashing his helm and head into one indescribable mess. The other assassin was not so foolish; he turned and ran. The guards began to pursue. During the whole incident, the other keepers, enraptured by their own part in the main battle, had not even noticed.

There was no feeling in D'Shay's right hand, and he quickly held it up. It was gray and shriveled, almost useless. At first he thought that the spell of the two assassins had somehow touched him, but then he realized that the problem was far worse than that. Even a short stay in this realm was too much for him; he was dying and would die within a couple hours unless he made use of his prisoner, his last resort. It would be more difficult here in the damned Dream Lands, but he knew he had the will-power because if he did not then he was dead, something D'Shay could not permit—not without the Gryphon to accompany him.

He turned back to the tent. Time was of the essence. It would mean burning out much sooner than he wanted, but, by then, another suitable "volunteer" would be found. All that mattered now was continued existence.

The prisoner, D'Shay's life, was gone. He had been spirited away, manacles and all, while the two assassins had kept the master wolf raider occupied.

D'Shay felt panic setting in.

I am beyond the terminal stage, he raged. *My mind is in a continuous fog! This should have never happened!*

He had to depart the Dream Lands immediately. Sirvak Dragoth no longer mattered. The Ravager no longer mattered. Even the Gryphon no longer mattered—for the moment.

Tzee . . .

D'Shay stepped away from the tent. The Tzee? Of course!

"I have need of you! Manifest yourself!"

Tzee . . . dying time . . . dying time . . .

The Tzee had yet to manifest themselves, but their harshly whispered words kept echoing in his mind. Dying time? They knew?

Tzee . . . dying time . . . enjoy . . .

"*What?*" D'Shay raised his fists into the air and shook them uselessly against the invisible presence of the Tzee. "Manifest yourself, or I'll see that you—"

Tzee . . . time to die . . . The last was followed by the quiet, mad laughter of countless entities.

D'Shay realized that the Tzee were departing. He grew desperate. "Come back! I can offer you more power!"

A last, faint reply reached his ears before they departed.

Tzee . . . not enough . . .

He understood then. The Tzee had stolen his prisoner. The Tzee, who had been given power by Lord Petrac, D'Rak, and himself. The Tzee, who everyone had not even bothered to think about, a wild card that had finally been played.

D'Shay stared briefly at his crippled hand. The Tzee were foolish if they believed he was finished. Not yet. Not while the Gryphon still lived.

"Milord!"

He turned, and his first thought was to slay the figure before him, for it was a keeper. This one, however, knelt in obedience and said, "Their defenses are weakening. A few more minutes and Sirvak Dragoth will be open to the advance forces."

D'Shay hid his hand from the sight of the keeper. "I want the Master Guardians at my feet within the next half hour. Alive. If any of them die, I will kill every man in the squad responsible—even keepers."

"Understood, milord."

As the man departed, D'Shay's servants returned. Blood dripped from their gloves. They came up to him and stopped, awaiting new orders. The master wolf raider felt strength return to him. As long as he remained near them, the process of decay was slowed. A few more hours, precious ones now. A few more hours was all he needed, though. Death had stared him in the face before, and he had laughed at it, mocked it.

As he would again.

"I'm sorry," Troia said as she gave him water. "It's the best I can do."

"It will help." The Gryphon held the cup with his one good hand, forcing himself to ignore the needles of pain stabbing his shoulder. His other arm was in fair shape, though, with a broken hand, it was of little practical use. Troia had wrapped up the hand with cloth from his shirt. There was nothing else she could do. Until the Gryphon's strength returned, he was unable to heal himself at all. Fortunately, he could at least walk, though running was definitely out. With the feline woman's aid, he had moved to a more secure place: The lionbird hated to leave Morgis behind, but there was no way he could drag so many tons of unconscious muscle and bone. At least, the Aramites had not come near, for they had assumed the dragon was dead, and that was becoming a distinct likelihood. Morgis was undoubtedly injured badly; the Gryphon had been fortunate in that the huge form had softened his own landing.

"I still don't understand why he had to kill me personally. It was a foolhardy thing to do."

Troia tried to cover the grief she still felt. She did not totally succeed, but the lionbird pretended not to notice. "I knew— thought I knew him, that is. I think your death was something horrible to him, something he decided was necessary, but yet could not leave to another. It had to be him. Alone. I think he wanted the guilt to fall on his shoulders alone."

"If you hadn't come when you had . . ."

He used his good hand to softly touch one of hers. She withdrew it, guilt on her face. "When you called the Gate to you, it disturbed his concentration so much that the spell keeping me asleep faded. Not completely, but enough for me to fight it. I —I followed him; I was there while he broke your hand. Even then, I couldn't believe he'd go any farther. I thought he'd take you prisoner and I could then release you. It wasn't until he raised the staff and I saw what he'd done to the tip that I realized what he had become." She covered her face. "I'm sorry! He could have killed you!"

The Gryphon pulled her hands away, one at a time. "You saved my life in the end. That's what matters. I can understand the way you feel."

"I'll never forget that" Still, she succeeded in smiling, albeit fleetingly.

He decided it was time to change the subject. "We have to get to Sirvak Dragoth," he told her. "It's vital."

"The citadel is under attack. I'm not injured. I can fight. You should stay here." Her eyes, red from crying, were filled with concern. Troia wanted badly to make up for what she had almost allowed to happen. "I'll bring help."

"You go alone and the wolf raiders will kill you."

"I have some magic—mostly enhancing my fighting. You know as a guardian I have certain inherent abilities. A few soldiers will only wet my appetite." Troia smiled, showing her fangs.

The Gryphon was not so willing to pretend. "Many, many

soldiers and more than a few keepers as well. Do you think you could take on a keeper?''

''I wouldn't back down.''

''That's not the same thing.'' He shook his head and tried to rise. ''I have to do something about Morgis. I cannot leave him out there. Even now, something could be happening. I've never abandoned a comrade before, and I have no intention of doing so now.'' The Gryphon tried not to think about Jerilon Dane. Dane had not exactly been a comrade, and it was almost a certainty that he had died, but there was still a little doubt.

She looked at him with an expression normally reserved for madmen. ''You can barely walk. What do you think you can do? It has to be me alone. I'll sneak past them, get into the citadel. Haggerth—''

''Has his hands full!'' The Gryphon leaned too much on one arm, and pain shot through his entire body. ''If only I could concentrate! Maybe bring the Gate to us! Where is it now?''

Troia shrugged. In the distance, the sounds of battle had taken on a new tone. She moved away from the Gryphon, intent on seeing what was happening. She had this dreadful fear that when she looked over the incline, she would see Sirvak Dragoth in ruins and wolf raiders clambering all over its remains like scavengers on a dead deer.

Sirvak Dragoth had not yet fallen, the feline woman saw, but it was obvious that it would hold out for little longer. Even cut off from their home, stranded in another reality, the Aramites fought with the same obsessive determination that they always had. The Dream Lands would soon fall, having no other organized resistance.

And she could watch it all unfold from an unobstructed view. Unobstructed?

''What is it? What's happened?'' From the tone of his voice, she knew that the Gryphon expected the worst. But would he expect what she herself could not believe, even after seeing— or not seeing—it?

Troia ducked back down, confused and afraid. ''Gryphon, your friend is gone.''

''Friend? Morgis? Gone?'' After several seconds, he understood what she was meant. ''*Gone?* An entire dragon? Unconscious and injured, yet! But why would they . . .'' He paused, and then a gleam that she had not seen for some time reappeared in his eyes.

"Why would they what? Why did the Ravager's hounds move him? It would take several keepers or hundreds of soldiers!"

"I doubt they took him. I think someone else took him. Correct that—I *know* someone else took him." His eyes narrowed, and he stared at something beyond her.

Troia turned cautiously around—and then nearly broke down in relief when she found herself matching the sightless gaze of one of three identical, familiar figures.

"The not-people!" she cried happily.

The Gryphon nodded. "Morgis and I have come to call them the Faceless Ones, but, whatever they are, they're very, very welcome at this moment."

He hoped he would not regret saying that at some future date—if there was any future.

The three featureless beings approached them, cowled robes swaying slightly as they seemed to float across the distance. When they were within arm's length, they came to a halt and the one in the center raised its right hand to a point level with its head, palm flat outward. The Gryphon looked at Troia, but the cat-woman had no idea how to reply. The lionbird hesitantly brought his one good hand up in a similar manner. The not-people nodded as one, but, for some reason, they seemed disappointed, as if they had been hoping for something more.

Whatever that might have been, it was evidently not important enough to keep them from their task. As the others—it might have been one or more of this group, but who could tell?—in the alley had done, the Faceless Ones raised their hands.

The Gate materialized, doors wide open.

Two of the odd beings helped the Gryphon to his feet. He already felt much better than he had, and he suspected that the Faceless Ones were doing more than simply assisting him to walk. It was with growing hope that he allowed himself to be escorted through the imposing edifice, Troia and the remaining Faceless One trailing behind.

It was with swiftly fading hope that he entered the central chamber of Sirvak Dragoth.

The room itself was a shambles. Anything loose had fallen to the ground. Marble from the ceiling and walls had broken loose and fallen to the floor. There were faults in the floor itself, and one was a foot wide already. Dust floated everywhere. There were perhaps a dozen figures in the room, not counting the Gryphon and his group. Mrin/Amrin and two women, one incredibly tall, beautiful, and wrapped in something like a long red shroud, and the other average in height with a face like an innocent child's. She was clad in a garment woven from some material that refused to come into focus.

The one called Geas sat in a corner, playing a somber melody on his flute. Haggerth sat in his usual place of authority, speaking to a male and female who resembled the folk from the village in Petrac's former domain. The veiled guardian looked up.

"Gryphon! How glad I am to see you, even if your timing could not be much worse!"

"Then you are losing." The Gryphon almost forgot his wounds as he stumbled away from his companions and toward the Master Guardian.

Haggerth dismissed the two, stood up, and hurried to meet the lionbird halfway. "How badly are you hurt?"

"I can live. You have Morgis?"

"He is resting. Someone saw to him the moment the not-people brought his body here."

"An entire dragon?"

"Dragon? No, they brought him in looking the same way he has always looked, albeit a bit worn. Speaking of damage, if you'll allow me . . ."

The Master Guardian examined the Gryphon's injuries, especially the hand. While his fingers probed, he said quietly, "We know what happened with you and Petrac. Difficult to believe—and yet, not so difficult to believe."

"Troia had to kill him to save my life."

The veil hid whatever emotion was coursing through the mind of Haggerth. "I'll be sure to speak to her later, if we're still around."

"What's happening?"

The guardian sighed. "While their soldiers batter away at our people, the keepers batter away at our walls and our minds. Combined, they are an imposing force. We almost lost control not more than a minute ago. Truthfully, I doubt if we'll last out the hour."

All the while, the Master Guardian had been inspecting the damage done by his former comrade. The pain in the Gryphon's broken hand vanished. He tentatively flexed the fingers. Haggerth had healed the broken hand completely. There was not even any stiffness during movement.

"Thank you, Haggerth. Do you really mean what you say?"

"Yes, but don't tell Troia or the others. Not yet. I've been doing some thinking based on Lord Petrac's betrayal of us."

"And?" The lionbird did not care for the sound of that. What was there to be learned about Petrac's betrayal except that many people were either dead or going to die because of him? That was the real lesson.

"I'll speak to you about it later. If you want to see Morgis, he's in a room down the hall. We have several here that have been brought in by either companions or the not-people."

The Gryphon glanced at one of the featureless beings. "They're on our side completely, I take it."

Haggerth laughed bitterly. "Take nothing at face value. I know. I've heard reports of them aiding enemy wounded as well. I don't think I'll ever figure them out."

The Gryphon thanked Haggerth, promising to return at the first sign of trouble. The veiled figure seemed to only half hear him. The lionbird watched him with growing worry. Haggerth had always seemed the most sensible and understanding of the Master Guardians that he had dealt with. If *he* had lost hope . . . the thought was not one that the Gryphon chose to complete.

Troia came to him. He stared past her at the Faceless Ones, who seemed to be watching him with great interest—though it might have been amusement or disgust and he was merely trying to read his own thoughts into their blank visages.

"Master Haggerth seemed worried," she commented. "I could tell from the way he was standing. I don't think he's rested for quite some time."

"Why bother. He might not wake up if he does." The Gryphon forced a change of subject. "Morgis is nearby. I have to see him before I do anything else."

"I'll help you." She put an arm around him and let him put one over her shoulders. He refrained from mentioning that, thanks to the powers of Haggerth, he could have made it on his own. The sensation of her body next to his was just too pleasant, too distracting, but there were so few things lately that had given him any pleasure at all.

Sirvak Dragoth shook. The Gryphon turned and looked for Haggerth, but the Master Guardian was nowhere to be seen. Troia pulled him to the side as the couple that Haggerth had been speaking to earlier moved past them with towels and water and hurried to where the other Master Guardians, save Geas, were working desperately to save the citadel.

The Gryphon was filled with a sudden sense of urgency. "Take me to Morgis. There's no telling how long this place has left."

They made their way over a rubble-strewn hallway. Part of one wall had fallen and, as they climbed over it, they discovered that someone had been caught under it. It only took one glance, however, to know that the victim was beyond help. Troia swore, and her claws extended, digging into the Gryphon's side. He said nothing.

The room that held the wounded was almost as vast as the central chamber itself. Furniture, unless useful, had been piled in one corner. While the injured filled most of the room, the Gryphon was surprised that there were not many, many more. He remarked so to Troia.

She corrected his misconception immediately. "Most of those with minor wounds are still out there fighting. There are also a few woodland healers. Those that can't be helped were left where they were."

It sounded like a cold thing to do, even to an ex-mercenary, but he knew that these were a people who lived closer to nature than even he had. He did not doubt that, like some elves and dwarves, they would prefer to die surrounded by nature than linger their last few moments in a crowded room with the smell of death instead of flowers.

"There's Morgis." Troia pointed to their right. The drake lay on a single blanket with a makeshift pillow keeping his head off the floor. It seemed incongruous to see a heavily armored figure lying there, apparently unscathed, surrounded by a variety of beings all looking badly injured. Yet, he knew that Morgis would not be here if the drake could help it. His imposing appearance, the only humanoid form he could create, hid the fact that he had suffered from internal injuries.

Volunteers moved to and fro, giving aid of all sort. There were maybe two healers in the entire room, trying desperately to keep up with the flow of injured. It was all to frighteningly reminiscent of his own past. His eyes scanned over the various patients as he and Troia made their way to Morgis. Broken limbs, sword and arrow wounds, concussions, shock—

The Gryphon froze.

He believed, though he tended to share it with no one, that, whatever powers did watch over the Dragonrealm and all other regions of the world, someone was going out of their way in the name of coincidence. People appeared suddenly, events changed without warning—all as if some great hand were manipulating everyone and everything. Each time he thought he knew who the manipulators were, he discovered that they, too, were being maneuvered. He could almost believe as had been said that the Ravager believed—that this was all some kind of game.

"What's the matter?"

If it *was* a game, a new piece had been added. He pulled away from her and squatted down by the figure that rocked itself continuously back and forth. A man, a fighter, who, even despite the shaggy growth of beard and the extremely pale skin, was familiar to him. Familiar, yes, but supposedly dead, slain by D'Shay prior to their last meeting in Penacles so long ago. The Captain of the Guard in the Gryphon's palace.

"Freynard? Allyn? Captain Freynard?"

The weathered, cadaverous face became visible as the man stopped rocking and looked up at him. The eyes, which had been staring nowhere, focused on the former monarch. Parched, cracked lips opened, and the ragged figure whispered, "At—at your service, your majesty. Ever—ever at your service."

For a brief moment, the Gryphon would have sworn that he heard D'Shay laughing.

XIX

Physical form was still something new to Tzee and, at the time, it proved annoying. It was necessary, however, for the mortal creatures who called themselves the wolf raiders would never take orders from such as them—at least, not knowingly. The Tzee could change that later, when they were more secure in their reign and the Ravager had given them the power they needed to truly be free of the constraints of the Dream Lands. It was the goal of the Tzee for countless centuries to escape from the bonds that kept them a part of the reality of that misty region and prevent them from extending their presence throughout the rest of the world, the Dragonrealm, for instance.

"Tzee . . ." They made the body whisper without thinking. The Ravager would change that, they were certain. When the true lord of the Aramites understood what they had done, he could not help but grant their request.

The body stumbled momentarily through the dark while they searched beyond human perceptions for the proper path. It was dark down here, even for the Tzee, yet, there was still a light of sorts. The Tzee could not comprehend this and were briefly awed. Yes, the Ravager would have the power.

They would offer him the Dream Lands and the Gryphon.

They had wanted the Gryphon, but not more than they wanted their freedom. The Gryphon had broken their power once, long ago, just prior to the near-calamity he had caused the Ravager in the human city of Qual—

The name is never to be thought of or spoken! The angry declaration was followed by a savage snarl, as if some great beast were lurking just beyond the darkness.

D'Rak's body stumbled over what the Tzee knew to be human remains. They made the head turn toward the presence they now felt. There was the impression of something large moving closer, and the eyes of D'Rak briefly caught sight of another pair of eyes, savage eyes. The Tzee themselves could see nothing, but could definitely not deny the other.

Tzee, little Tzee, you come to beg favors of a god?

In deference to the great power before them, the Tzee utilized the human's mouth and voice. It was their way of showing what an effort they were making.

"Great one." The voice was slurred. For a time, they had found their control of the body to be almost perfect. Now, though, it did not always function with its normal efficiency.

Your new form needs rest, little Tzee. Humans need sleep, and yours is a human body.

So that was it. "Great one," the Tzee continued, "we have striven—Tzee—to prove ourselves to you. We have shown our cunning. We have shown our power. We have shown that you need—Tzee—only us to achieve your goals. We can offer you—"

The Dream Lands and the Gryphon. I know, little Tzee. Am I not the Ravager? Am I not a god? I will win this game, little Tzee.

"We know of no game, great one, but—Tzee—if our skills —Tzee . . ." The Tzee found themselves growing uncomfortably nervous. ". . . can be of service to you, then that is what we—Tzee—wish. We seek only one thing in return—"

Power. I know you well. You desire power, little Tzee.

They became excited at such understanding. D'Rak's body quivered as the Tzee lost control of some of the motor functions for a brief spell. Then, realizing how they must look, the Tzee forced themselves calm. "Yes—Tzee—power."

I shall reveal power to you.

Something stumbled through the darkness and, at first, the Tzee had the terrible notion that the Ravager himself was coming toward them. They were partially correct. Though it was a human form that finally revealed itself in the odd light, there was no mind, not even any life. The Tzee knew of this. The Ravager had a fascination with dead forms, using them as its hands at times. The Tzee disliked the dead; they did not have such wondrous abilities as the wolf lord had. They could only overwhelm the living and force their minds down into some remote void the Tzee themselves did not understand. They just did it.

This one was only recently dead. The face it knew from somewhere, but that did not matter. What mattered was the object the corpse held before it the way flesh-and-blood creatures often held their young. A large, possibly oval object covered by cloth. It radiated power, enough so that the Tzee actually hungered for it. The unliving slave seemed to offer them the object. The Tzee looked away to that spot where, maybe, the Ravager waited.

It is yours to unveil. It is almost as if it was designed for you all along, little Tzee.

They could not hold off any longer. Anticipation got the best of them, and the Tzee raised the right arm and tore the cloth from their prize.

Power! Too much—Tzee!—power! In their panic, they no longer thought to speak through the mouth of their purloined body.

It is only power returning to its rightful place, little Tzee! A place you usurped! Do you think I would deal with anything spawned in the Dream Lands? Anything I planned to eliminate once its usefulness was at an end?

Power continued to overwhelm the Tzee. They could no longer maintain control of the body and the level of power, especially when the power itself seemed to be fighting them.

The Tzee reached their limit. Their essence, their . . . presence, for lack of a better word, began to break apart. The colony mind splintered, becoming vast numbers of weaker, less coherent thoughts. In a last effort, the largest remaining colony of the nebulous multiple entity withdrew completely from the body and abandoned the smaller, fractionating bits to their fates.

Tricked . . . Tzee . . . tricked . . . tricked . . . it whispered madly as it departed from the lair of the Ravager.

The body of the senior keeper swayed back and forth, and a hand went upward to tentatively touch the face. The voice was no more than a whisper. "They're gone! The cursed things are gone!"

You have rightful control of yourself once more. Remember who saved you.

D'Rak fell to his knees, his face pale, his tone one of incredible relief. "Master, I thank you!"

Thank me by serving me well.

The senior keeper glanced over toward the object that had been a part of his salvation. The crystalline head he had created—and held by one he knew, the failure R'Dane—but, R'Dane—

R'Dane was saved by those in the Dream Lands, but foolishly returned with the Gryphon! He perished during the escape of the misfit, trying to work your precious toy!

"Then that was what—" D'Rak stopped short, understanding now that he might have just betrayed himself.

Yes . . . say it. Say what you wanted to do with this toy!

"I wanted to . . . live forever. Just as D'Shay does. I wanted to be immortal!" He said the last defiantly. At this point, there was nothing left to lose. "The crystal was to hold my essence —but on death!"

You wanted to be immortal . . . like D'Shay.

"Yes." Was the Lord Ravager playing with him? Had he rid D'Rak of the Tzee just to pass judgment over the keeper? Despite the fact that he had been born while Qualard was still the capital, D'Rak knew that time was catching up to him. His position as senior keeper had given him access to the power he needed to extend his life, but not make him immortal, as D'Shay was. He would do whatever it took. He did not want to die, especially now that he had had a taste of something akin to it!

A mocking laugh echoed through the chamber. The wolf raider cringed.

You know your place now! You know you will obey! The Ravager seemed amused by his reactions. *You will do!*

"Do, Master? Do for what?"

Do you question me? There was a brief, angry snarl and, once more, the impression of two great eyes in the dark.

"No, my lord!"

Better! You would be immortal like D'Shay, my favorite hound.

"I—"

A silly notion, keeper. Silly because it is not true. D'Shay is not immortal; he is no longer even my favorite!

This time, D'Rak said nothing, but his heart beat faster. Did he understand correctly what his master had just told him?

You understand. The time has come, my faithful Runner. The

Dream Lands, though they have cut me off from my children, will still fall! Sirvak Dragoth is the only obstacle and, before the Gate vanished, it was understood that its defenses were crumbling!

D'Rak took this on faith. Much of that time he had been . . . elsewhere. "What of D'Shay, milord?"

If he is not dead, cut off from my will—which is what truly keeps him alive—then he will perish soon. His fate does not matter. He has served the purpose I originally planned for him. I have you now.

The senior keeper's chest swelled with pride. "What is it you wish of me?"

The Dream Lands will fall before the might of my children, but there is one danger that remains. . . .

"The Gryphon."

He will be forced to go to Qualard, believing it is the only way he may be able to save his friends, save the foul Dream Lands. He will go very soon, I think.

"I'll assemble an armed force. Hitai is the closest outpost to Qual—to that place. I'll—"

D'Rak rose and stumbled backward as a blood-chilling growl rose from the darkness. He could feel hot, fetid breath on his face, though nothing was there.

Fool! Pup! This is not why I saved you! An armed force? He will know of their existence long before you know of his! This is a creature with far more knowledge of war than you! Do you think he will come with an army of his own?

"A—a small group, then. Two keepers to form a triangle and half a dozen handpicked guards. No more."

Better, pup. This game will not be won with numbers but with craft. The Gryphon will be there, and he will, of course, bring his constant companion, that—that reptilian mongrel. Possibly his female as well.

"And a guardian, or perhaps . . . even one of the blank-faced creatures." Yes, D'Rak saw that. If there was indeed a guardian—a Master Guardian—then he might be "persuaded" to reopen the Gate for the wolf raiders.

Better, my loyal hound! Better!

He bowed, confidence restored. "I must depart now, if what you say is true, milord."

Go! This audience is at an end.

The senior keeper turned and started to make his way back to the stairway, when a voice called out to him. He froze, for the last thing he had expected to hear was the voice of R'Dane, the dead traitor.

"One last thing, my hound." Though the voice was R'Dane's, the eyes, when D'Rak turned to face him, were the fierce, red orbs of the Aramite's lord and master. "Fail me not, or else you will come to envy this ungainly puppet of mine!" The battered face of R'Dane smiled, revealing in the light that was not light its broken mouth and dried blood caked everywhere.

The body collapsed, falling upon the crystal it still clutched in its arms and shattering it against the mound of bones. *Fail . . . and I shall give you immortality of a sort. You have my promise.*

D'Rak stared at the latest addition to the Ravager's collection and swallowed hard. He turned and stumbled to the steps, which were to prove to be the longest flight of stairs he had ever climbed.

When he at last reached the top, the senior keeper ran as if his life depended upon it—which it did.

"Freynard! Gods above, Freynard! How did you come to be here?"

Captain Allyn Freynard had been a tough, young soldier. He would have taken the place of General Toos as commander of the armies of Penacles had he lived—or rather, had he not been spirited away, apparently by D'Shay.

Freynard's eyes darted back and forth, as if he expected to be reclaimed by his captors even now. The time he had spent as a prisoner of D'Shay could hardly have been a pleasant one. Beneath the beard, still partly visible, were old bruises and scars. Something that resembled a jagged pentagram had been carved into the upper portion of his right cheek. Other, less elaborate marks had been cut into his hands and neck. When he spoke, it was not to answer his lord's question, but to recall a terrible memory. "I held out for as long as I could, Majesty. After seeing what he'd done to the other man, I knew that the moment I was of no more value to him as a source of information, the ghoul would take me when next he needed a victim! I didn't mean to betray you, milord! It—it was just that it had been so long! Months, I think!"

It had been, in fact, longer, and the Gryphon felt a terrible shame grow within him. He had not bothered, not even considered that the captain might be alive. D'Shay had spoken of disposing of Freynard and one other guard, but the lionbird and General Toos had simply assumed that it meant they had been murdered, two more victims of the foul wolf raiders. There had been proper mourning, and then plans had been made by the Gryphon to journey across the Eastern Seas. Freynard had become a memory.

"This is really one of your men?" Troia whispered. She, knowing the Aramites better, thought it might be a trick.

The Gryphon nodded, self-disgust swelling within him as he spoke. "This is Captain Allyn Freynard. Like a fool, I took what D'Shay said at face value, forgetting at that moment that D'Shay had more than one face. Because of that, two men suffered and one of them died. I cannot say which was the luckier."

"He took him that night," Freynard was saying. The captain was making a visible effort to increase his newly discovered hold on sanity. "Transported us through one of those big portals you spoke of, Majesty. You called them . . . called them—"

"Blink holes. Not important, Freynard. Forget them."

"Yes, sir. Blink hole. I can't remember the other man's name, Majesty. I don't even remember if I ever knew it. I only knew that, when the horror came to him, I swore I would remember him!" The captain grabbed the Gryphon by the shoulders. "I swore it, and I can't remember! To watch a man lose his self and have no one able to remember even his name! It was . . . it was . . ."

A short female figure akin to Troia in appearance but with gray, mottled fur, came over and said anxiously, "If you excite him too much, I will have to ask you to go away. There are many here who need rest and, the Lands know, there's more than enough noise outside."

Outside. The battle. *How much time has passed since I came in here*? the Gryphon wondered frantically. He took hold of Freynard and made the captain look him in the eyes. "Allyn, I've got to go. There's danger, a battle. I still have one chance to possibly save the situation."

"A battle?" This seemed to excite the ragged man. "A weapon, milord! Give me a weapon and I'll fight at your side!"

"Don't be ridiculous, Freynard. You're not well, and I can't ask you to go out there, not after what you've been through!"

"Your Majesty,"—the captain's eyes burned—"it is because of what happened to me that I ask to go with you. You might have need of my arm. I've fought in worse physical condition than this, and I can assure, milord, that fighting at your side would only strengthen, not lessen, my mind—especially if my sword gets a taste of wolf raider blood.''

He had never abandoned a comrade . . . did this count? The Gryphon closed his eyes and reluctantly nodded. When he opened them, the young man was smiling. ''Understand, Freynard, that if you are not ready when we depart in a few minutes, I will leave you here.''

''I will be waiting—thank you, Your Majesty!''

The Gryphon could not help a short chuckle. ''That's another thing, Allyn. I'm no longer 'Your Majesty'. I gave that up when I sailed across the Eastern Seas. Call me as everyone who knows me does—Gryphon.''

Freynard shook his head. ''I shall call you 'milord' and 'Your Majesty,' sir. I'm sure that General Toos considers himself to be merely holding Penacles for you while you are away.''

It was too soon to talk about going back—especially when the lionbird was uncertain as to whether he wanted or would be able to return. Beside him, he had felt Troia stiffen at such talk. There was something he wanted to talk of, as well, when they were alone. For now . . .

He rose and patted the captain on the shoulder. ''You should be able to borrow a sword from someone; there are always more weapons late in a battle than there are children to use them. Also, see if you can locate some supplies. Enough for a day or two, no more. Wait in the corridor when you are done. Ten minutes, no more.''

''Yes, Your Majesty!'' Freynard rose with a speed and dexterity that was surprising in a man who looked as worn as he did. Serving his old master had rekindled a spark within him. The Gryphon knew that much of it was momentary; Freynard would weaken—hopefully to the point where the former monarch could keep him from going with. He did not want to cause a useless death. It was at times like this that he regretted the loyalty those men who had served under him always seemed to have. He did not like people dying for his sake.

While Freynard sought out a sword or some other weapon, the Gryphon and Troia finally made their way over to Morgis. The drake had not moved. He still looked like a warrior whose body had been readied for some death ritual. Only a faint hiss and the slow rise and fall of his chest proved that he was still alive.

Troia, who had never really paid attention to the appearance of the duke, tightened her grip on the Gryphon's arm. Even asleep and seemingly helpless, Morgis was an imposing figure that could easily unnerve more than one brave soul. The caretakers and healers had had to make extra room for him, what with an overall height of at least seven feet, but it was not his size that so fascinated her. Rather, it was the crude, partly human face that the drake kept half hidden within the dragonhelm that, so the Gryphon had explained, was as much a part of the duke as his hand or foot was. A blue-tinted, scaled skin covered the face, just as it did the entire body, but it was the incompleteness of the drake's visage that disturbed the onlooker. There was practically no nose, merely two slits that acted as nostrils, and the mouth was a long gash that, when opened, would reveal teeth far more predatory than hers. The eyes were narrow, and she knew that when they opened, they would be all one color. Troia wondered briefly if Morgis had ears—he heard somehow.

The Gryphon had made some mention about the Dragonrealm while she had bound his wounds. According to him, the drakes were slowly moving to a permanent, almost human form.

He had told her other things about the Dragonrealm, and she had secretly wondered what it would be like to go there. Now was not the time for such a subject, however.

Even as the Gryphon's hand reached out to wake Morgis, the drake's eyes opened, burning with life. Troia gasped. She was able to tolerate him, but now, seeing him up close, she could not fathom an entire race like the duke. There was nothing like the drakes in the Dream Lands.

She would have been surprised if she knew that Morgis had the same opinion of the Dream Lands. He had seen creatures and things here that he would not have ever believed existed.

"You are well. Good." The drake spoke matter-of-factly, but there was still a hint of strain in the tone of his voice.

"How are you?" The Gryphon gave Morgis a visual inspection, knowing, however, that most of the injuries were inside.

"I am well. The healers did what they could. Once they steered my body toward recovery, I took over. Sirvak Dragoth still stands, I take it?"

The lionbird nodded, more pleased than he had expected that his companion was better. He had come to think of Morgis as a friend. It was a shock, but true. "They're living on borrowed time. Each minute it looks like the wolf raiders will break through—there are a great number of keepers out there, not on a level with D'Rak, but they are working in concert, much like they did when we tried to go to Qualard. Where we need to go now, I think.''

"What *is* in Qualard? It is an ancient, ruined city. The place of the Ravager's wrath at his own people.''

"It holds the key, though. They tried to stop us once and almost succeeded. We have no real choice. I think Qualard is the place we have to go if we want to save the Sirvak Dragoth and the Dream Lands—not to mention ourselves.''

Morgis raised himself up to a sitting position, which made more than one head turn to look at him. He smiled, revealing those teeth that made even Troia shiver. "Then go we must. Things have been a little boring of late. This little quest sounds of interest—and perhaps I will yet get to run my blade through the senior keeper!''

"We can only hope—'' The citadel shook, as it had often before, but this time, there was a difference. It failed to stop shaking and, in fact, the quake—it could no longer simply be called shaking—was threatening to tear Sirvak Dragoth apart. A small crack in the floor suddenly yawned open, forcing those administering to the wounded to bunch them together even tighter for fear of some of the unconscious ones tumbling into the new crevice.

Haggerth came stumbling into the room. "Get everyone into the underground chambers and out of Sirvak Dragoth!''

Someone nearby asked a question. The Master Guardian's veiled face turned in the general direction of the speaker. "What do you think?'' he snapped irritably. Despite his generally calm demeanor, there was a point where even Haggerth could stand no more. "The citadel is falling! The Master Guardians will remain here in order to delay the wolf raiders as long as possible, but the first of them will be over the outer walls in little more than a quarter hour! That's all! Hurry, but, by the Lands' sake, do not rush out in a panic or no one will survive!''

It was to Haggerth's credit that the inhabitants acted more or less in some uniform fashion. Those who had the strength to walk helped carry those who either could not or were completely unconscious. The Master Guardian, meanwhile, moved through the crowds—which was difficult with the building still continuing to shake and a fissure large enough for a man to fall into now cutting through the center of the room—until he had reached the trio.

"You still plan to go to Qualard, don't you." It was not a question, but a statement. Haggerth had something in mind.

Morgis, who had just risen, nodded. The Gryphon did also, and then added, "Right now, I think it's the only way to save the Dream Lands—even if Sirvak Dragoth is lost."

Tiny bits of the ceiling began raining upon them. Haggerth looked up. "It has stood so long. I was beginning to think it would be here until the end of time—or at least longer than my lifetime."

"What was it you wanted, Master Guardian?"

The veiled man pulled himself together. "You will need help in Qualard."

"You want to go with me."

"I do not, Gryphon. The choice was made by my fellows. My . . . abilities"—Haggerth touched the veil—"are more useful up close. The others felt that one of us should accompany you; after all, you will need a Gate. Evidently, they felt I was the most useless here." The Master Guardian's voice had a touch of bitterness in it.

Troia shook her head at that. "Not useless, Master Haggerth. Not you."

A great block of marble fell from the ceiling. They could not see where it landed, but the screams that followed spoke of the terrible damage it had done. The rest of the ceiling was covered with ominous cracks.

"I would say," Morgis shouted over the din, "that there is no time to discuss this! Master Haggerth will come, yes? I think it's time someone called the Gate!"

"I'll do it," the Gryphon replied.

Both Troia and Haggerth looked at him, and the feline woman, growing awe on her face, asked, "You can summon the Gate? Only Master Guardians, not-people, and a few creatures like the Tzee, who are actually extensions of the Dream Lands themselves, can summon the Gate! When I saved you from the Tzee, I was only able to do it because one of the not-people agreed to help me!"

"I do not summon it; I ask it to help." He raised his arms and closed his eyes, not so much as part of the act of contacting the Gate, but more to silence the two guardians' questions.

Would it come this time? He had the brief inward fear that it would not respond to him, would not respond to anyone now that the guardians, himself included, had seemingly failed in their duties. The fear proved to be without substance, for he felt then the presence of the portal, a living presence, he knew now. The Gate *was* the Dream Lands, and it was an entity as well. Why it should have answered the summons of Lord Petrac that final time, the Gryphon could not say. He could only guess, from what he sensed, that the mind—or whatever it was—of the Gate was so different, so incomprehensible, that it must have ideas of its own concerning what was right and what was wrong. Perhaps, somehow, it had answered the Master Guardian's summons because doing so fit into some plan of its own.

The lionbird opened his eyes as the Gate materialized before them. It was taller than the chamber, yet it did not break through the ceiling. The same black creatures swarmed about it, but they seemed slower, possibly ill. The portal itself was open, but one of the massive doors hung slightly loose, as if the hinges were starting to come off.

Beyond lay a scene of desolation that the Gryphon had already seen before. It had, of course, not changed. Nothing had changed in Qualard for two centuries.

Troia put a hand on his shoulder. "Remember last time."

"I've scanned the area as far as I was able. I found no one."

They were alone in the room. The quake had subsided without the Gryphon's realizing it, but now it began anew. Haggerth uttered a curse.

"That can only mean the others are failing to hold the keepers. We haven't much time at all."

"Then what are we tarrying for?" Morgis asked, and then, without bothering to wait for a reply, leaped into the portal.

Troia looked at the Gryphon. He took a deep breath and, with a last glance toward her, followed after the drake.

The ceiling began to collapse.

XX

During the first tremors of what would soon become a quake to those inside, D'Shay waited silently, his mind brooding as he watched the results of the keepers' work. A watch tower had already fallen. Soldiers trying to overrun the walls of the citadel cheered at this, but the master wolf raider found little to be pleased about. Already, the predicted "victory in minutes" was dragging out longer than it should have. The gray had already spread up most of his arm, and now one of his legs was showing the first signs. Signs of decay. Signs that this body would not last too much longer.

He needed one of the Master Guardians. They knew how to control the Gate. They or the not-people. Forcing the latter to do something they did not desire to do was next to impossible. For some reason, they were willing to assist the Gryphon far beyond their normally neutral ways. In fact, since the Gryphon's arrival on this continent, the faceless beings had almost become allies to the Dream Lands in their efforts to aid D'Shay's enemy.

They must know more than I, he thought. *They know more than just the surface facts about Qualard. They know something about the Gryphon's origins and what makes him such a threat to the Lord Ravager.*

But what?

For now, the two servants he had brought with him supported him. Best to conserve strength. He had contemplated releasing these portions of the Tzee, turning them back into the colony creatures once more, but it was more likely that they would turn on him and, in his present condition, that might prove fatal. Yet, if they remained his slaves, it meant losing their ability to traverse from the Dream Lands to the outside world.

Cracks and fissures danced about the structure of Sirvak Dragoth. Some of the ground below the citadel had given way. At this rate, D'Shay supposed sourly, the great keep would tumble on top of his men before they were able to breach the defenses and overwhelm the inhabitants. If Sirvak Dragoth fell, odds were that the Master Guardians would die—which meant that *he* would die.

Not yet!

If nothing else, he would have the Gryphon. If it meant crawling into the struggle, then so be it.

The former prisoner, Freynard, had to be in the citadel. Either that, or he had been transported to the outside world by the Tzee. Whichever the case, D'Shay could not locate him. Matters were not helped by the fact that, without a direct link to the Ravager, his own abilities were greatly lessened.

He thought he heard someone speak, but, when he turned, there was no one near enough. Irritated at his own jumpiness, he ordered the two servants to assist him back to his tent. There was nothing he could do now, nothing at all until Sirvak Dragoth fell "in another few minutes."

Tzee . . .

"Hold," he ordered. The three of them came to a dead stop.

Tzee . . .

It *was* them! Faint, yes, but the Tzee had returned. Why? "What do you want from me now?"

Tzee . . . aid . . . will aid . . .

D'Shay hid his growing excitement. If the Tzee were willing to aid him, it was because they needed something in return. There was something wrong with them. They were very faint, almost impossible to hear at times.

Tzee . . . help . . . power . . .

It was hard to understand at first, but D'Shay finally comprehended. They needed power again. Something had broken the Tzee, literally fragmented it so that this was likely the largest coherent colony remaining. In return, they would aid him.

"If you wish to trade with me, I want you where I can see

you. Manifest yourself!'' He ordered the two servants away. For now, he would have to draw from his own strength. He could not show any more weakness than necessary.

Tzee . . . strain . . .

"Do it, or you will be left to dissipate here!'' It was a gamble, to be sure. If the Tzee did not obey, then D'Shay would eventually "dissipate'' himself. He had to know the extent of his power over the Tzee.

Slowly, a churning mass, dark as night, grew before his eyes. From a tiny point before him, it expanded and expanded until, at long last, it was a living cloud of energy and matter—but not as great in size as the wolf raider remembered it.

"So, the mighty Tzee have been humbled by someone. Was it D'Rak?''

Tzee . . . was all the cloud would say, but somehow D'Shay felt that his rival was involved.

"Where is he now?'' The senior keeper could not be in the Dream Lands. Lord Petrac was dead, the Tzee were not aiding him, and the not-people—well, that went without saying.

Tzee . . . Qualard . . . Even fragmented, the Tzee were one. What the tinier colonies, abandoned, heard and saw, the larger entity that had fled knew as well.

"Qualard?'' The surprise and realization in D'Shay's voice was enough to send the cloud scurrying back a few feet.

Qualard! It was all coming together now! A desperate attempt to save the Dream Lands by fulfilling his mission after all this time—but, then, what did time have to do with this? What the Gryphon sought was still there, still waiting.

"Come back here!'' he snapped at the Tzee. The cloud moved slowly forward, all those eyes seemingly downcast like those of children about to be punished. It paused at eye level no more than an arm's width from him. "Where is the prisoner you stole from me? Where is Freynard?''

Tzee . . . not Dragoth . . . not . . . here. . . .

"You turned him over to the Gryphon's allies?''

Tzee . . .

"But he's not there anymore?''

Tzee . . . not . . .

"Then he's with the Gryphon. In Qualard.''

Tzee . . . do not—

"I wasn't asking you.'' While the chastised Tzee floated impatiently, D'Shay's mind raced. He did not have time to go back to Canisargos, and he doubted that would be a good idea at the moment. With him supposedly trapped in the Dream Lands, it was not unlikely that the senior keeper's position had grown. D'Shay knew that he might return to discover that his private chambers had been ransacked by keepership guards.

His eyes narrowed on the Tzee. As if feeling this, the nebulous form tried to shrink inward. "You must transport me to Qualard. I will picture the exact location."

Tzee . . . need . . . power. . . .

D'Shay shook his head. He did not really have the power to give, but that was not for the Tzee to know. "*After* you deliver me to my destination."

Tzee . . .

"You have no one else who will deal with you—and in your present state, you're hardly a threat to anyone. Well?"

Tzee . . . yesss. . . .

As the wolf raider watched, the Tzee seemed to compact themselves into a tighter, thicker mass, as if preparing to sacrifice a portion of the colony itself. They were not summoning the Gate but creating a portal of their own, something the Dream Lands allowed only them to do. That was the only true power the Tzee really had. Yet, being a part of the Dream Lands, they no doubt drew their ability from whatever had created the Gate in the first place. D'Shay dismissed the theory from his mind. Now was not the time to be concerned with something that did not concern his own survival. He felt the Tzee touch his thoughts briefly, but only to draw forth the needed destination. He had only to wait a few seconds now.

D'Shay glanced around. The keepers were still at work, breaking down the last desperate defenses of the Master Guardians. Given time, they might be able to bring one to him—and the key word was *might*. Given the choice between a possible solution and a probable one, D'Shay would always choose the latter.

Tzee . . . Gate . . . hurry . . .

A portal that shimmered ominously materialized next to one of the unliving guards. D'Shay glanced up at the Tzee. It was struggling to maintain both the portal and its own existence, and he doubted it could do both for very long. He ordered the two servants through. While they passed through the portal, he took a quick look around. Victory was assured here, and no one would notice for now that the commanding officer was missing, not when that officer was D'Shay, known for his eccentric ways. All that mattered right now to the Aramites was victory over this, their only major stumbling block. They did not even realize what they were really fighting for.

He laughed, albeit a little bitterly, turned, and stepped through the portal.

The last person through the portal was a bit of a surprise. He came flying through, rolled forward once, and came up standing, somewhat wobbly, a short sword in his hands.

Morgis had his own blade ready and would have made short work of the newcomer if the Gryphon had not caught his wrist. "No! Captain Freynard is one of my men!"

The drake looked at him doubtfully. "One of your men? Here across the Eastern Seas?"

"I haven't got time to explain it. Suffice it to say that he's been a prisoner of D'Shay."

"Was he?" Morgis was still not convinced. "Then how did you escape? This D'Shay does not mark me as a careless sort."

Freynard opened his mouth to speak and then hesitated. After a few seconds, his shoulders slumped. He shook his head and said slowly, "I don't know how I escaped, Your Majesty. I only recall a sudden dark fog—and then I was wandering in the wilderness, my bonds hanging loose, near the place you call Sirvak Dragoth. Two of those—those faceless things took hold of me. . . ."

"And you ended up inside the citadel," the Gryphon finished. "It sounds to me as if someone wanted you away from D'Shay, but not dead. The dark fog sounds like the Tzee, but I do not recall them being quite so strong."

"Nor I," added Haggerth.

"I still don't trust this one."

The Gryphon finally snapped at him. "Then you question my judgment and you question the loyalty of a man who has always been willing to lay down his life for me—not that I have ever wanted such a thing to happen."

"I would do it anyway," Freynard added quietly.

"Let us hope you never have to. Well, Duke Morgis? I would like to continue with this mission."

The drake hissed, but he nodded. "So, where do we start?"

They took their first long look at what awaited them.

Qualard had been a vast metropolis with high towers and massive walls. What remained now spoke more about how much had been lost rather than how great the city had been. Even after two centuries of being worn down by the forces of nature—and that did not even include the initial quake that had destroyed the city (and may or may not have been the work of the Ravager; the Gryphon was skeptical)—the ruins of Qualard were still impressive. Many structures were now no more than great piles of unidentifiable debris. Most of the wood had long rotted, but marble floors and columns—what had not been crushed to pieces—were everywhere. Some walls, amazingly enough, still stood. A few streets were passable to at least some extent, though one or two dropped off into chasms. One portion of the city had been raised up at least twenty feet; a few buildings, minus roots, stood. To their right, a deep ravine was all that remained of one building, save a cornerstone.

No one said anything at first. Troia was the one to break the silence, finally whispering, "What it must have been like that day!"

"It was terrible," the Gryphon muttered quietly—and then jolted to awareness when he realized what he had just said.

"You *were* here when it happened."

He looked at her. Nothing, besides that admission, would come to him. No memory of that day, merely that it was terrible.

The place they stood must have been a square, for it was clear some distance around. The Gryphon turned in a full circle, trying to get his bearings with the phantoms of lost memories. "If I guess correctly, we're somewhere near the center of the city."

With a return to the task at hand came notice of the bitter wind that blew hither through the ruins of the former Aramite capital. Haggerth took hold of the bottom of his veil and held it in place with one hand while he used the other to secure one of the corners, which had a tiny loop, to a hook in his robe. When both corners were thus secured, he shook his head and made a comment about some of the more unsavory regions of the afterlife as he believed it.

Troia's fur was on end. Her reply to the Master Guardian's remark was unrepeatable, but she got her point across.

The cold would take its toll on all of them the longer they stood around. The Gryphon satisfied himself that they were near where he had wanted to be. He had no real memories of Qualard, but he had had a suspicion it would resemble the design of Canisargos—and it had. That alone confirmed what he had assumed prior to his first attempt to come here—that he would find what he was looking for in approximately the same region as the Pack Master's stronghold was in the present capital.

"Considering the time we have," he began, "we're going to have to split up."

"That's a bit unwise, wouldn't you think?" Morgis hissed.

"Any other time, yes. This time, we have no choice. We have to hurry. There are three probable areas. Troia, Master Haggerth, if you have no objections, I would like you to search over there." The Gryphon pointed to a fairly stable expanse far to his left.

Troia protested. "I . . . don't want to leave you—not here."

"There's nothing here but ruins. No life, no danger except from crumbling masonry." He shook his head briefly, as if unconcerned himself, though he felt the opposite. "Morgis, I'd like you and Captain Freynard to search toward the north where it starts to sink down. There might be passages underneath. If anyone finds anything, return here. At worst, we meet . . ." He looked up. Sunlight was not something common to this region. Clouds obscured the entire sky. "Try to estimate a half hour."

Freynard cleared his throat. "With all due respect, Majesty, I would be remiss in my duty if I did not stay with you."

"I'm no longer your liegelord. You have no duty toward me."

"Then"—Freynard managed a grin through the birds' nest beard—"you can't order me *not* to accompany you."

Morgis put a heavy hand on the man's shoulder. "And if *you* think I'm going to leave you alone with him, you are a fool."

Before anything could happen, the Gryphon separated them. "If both of you cannot follow directions—and I'm only asking this because of time, which is drastically running short even as we continue to speak—then stay here. I need people willing to work, not argue."

After a pause, both warriors gave in. He breathed a sigh of relief.

"Where will you go, Gryphon?" Haggerth asked.

"South. Now. No more talk."

They separated reluctantly, Haggerth having to encourage Troia to leave, and Morgis and Freynard watching one another as they walked. The lionbird refused to look at any of them, instead turning his back and moving resolutely southward. He made his way over jutting bits of street and long narrow chasms and did not stop until he was more than a hundred long paces from where he had started. He jumped down to a spot where the ground had sunk partially and turned back to check on the others.

Morgis and Freynard were out of sight. Once they became accustomed to the situation, they would start concentrating on the search. Both men were veteran warriors and pragmatic when all was said and done.

He could just barely see Troia and Haggerth. Not certain as to how old or how agile the Master Guardian was, he had chosen the easiest path for them. Even as the Gryphon watched, first Troia and then the veiled guardian disappeared over a rise that might have once been the first floor of a building.

The lionbird waited for several seconds until he was certain that no one was going to backtrack in an attempt to return to him. Then he climbed up from his hiding place, caught his breath, and began working his way—*east.*

He knew where he had to go, just as he knew that someone might already be waiting for him there. To kill him or be killed. The Gryphon knew these things, had known these things, the moment he had started to separate the group. He also knew a little more about what secret was hidden here.

It was not a thing he sought, but rather a prisoner. Some . . . entity . . . that had been ensnared by the Ravager long before the existence of the wolf raiders. An entity that had waited patiently, biding its time, knowing freedom could be its if it was careful . . . And now the time had come, but the Ravager's agents were here as well. That is, at least one was.

A short climb over some unidentifiable piece of architecture brought him to a relatively clear area. This had been the floor of the palace of the Pack Master, mortal ruler—in name—of the wolf raiders. The Gryphon wondered if the Pack Master of that time had been a shell, a puppet of the horror that called itself the Ravager, as the present one was. Probably. It would fit into the pattern of things.

At least four chambers were identifiable by remnants of wall, and, of the four of these, only one was large enough to be what he sought. There was rubble strewn over various parts of it, but the placement of the fragments was just a bit too precise. As he suspected, the largest pile was located near one of the far corners. Moving over there, the lionbird began the tedious process of removing the rubble.

He worked for what he estimated to be ten minutes before the fruit of his labors became apparent. The wind had picked up, but the former mercenary scarcely noticed it as he stared at what he had uncovered. A trapdoor. To most eyes, it would have been invisible, but, by careful inspection, he located the edges. The door was puzzling; it had no handle that he could see, and it was such a perfect fit that his claws could not even get a hold on the sides.

"Not now," the Gryphon muttered. "Not when I'm so close to it at last!" In a sense, the freeing of whatever being lay chained within was secondary to at last discovering his true past. Given the choice, however, he would have traded the latter for the former. A few memories were not worth the lives of even one person.

A miniature rock slide from somewhere behind him warned of the fact that he was no longer alone.

Carefully, as if he had not noticed, the Gryphon rose from his examination of the stone door, crossing his arms as he straightened. His back was toward whoever had joined him, so it was impossible for the newcomer to notice that one of the lionbird's hands now rested on the hilt of his sword.

The intruder moved again, creating another tiny avalanche. This time he could not ignore the noise. His grip tightened on the hilt.

"Kill! Kill!"

The shrill, birdlike voice startled him so much that he almost failed to draw the sword on. The Gryphon whirled around even before the second shout began. Surprise was no longer an element in this venture. Not now that he knew what he was up against. The call of the creature had decided it for him. He recognized it, though not because of the words. Rather, the lionbird recalled the cries of its kin as he and Morgis had battled to escape Canisargos.

Surprise proved it had yet one more card to play, for the gryphon that stood overlooking him was possibly the largest he had ever encountered. The ones ridden by the sentries could not have been more than half the size of this great beast. Had he not known how savage it truly was, it would have almost looked majestic. *Almost* majestic, for the blood on its beak and foreclaws eliminated any sort of illusion in that respect.

The blood was still fairly fresh.

It had a terrible rent in one wing, which explained why it had not simply swooped down and finished him before he even had time to react to its presence. There were other wounds, mostly minor ones, but he did notice that the beast was breathing harshly, as if it had been damaged within as well. Knowing this did not raise his confidence. If there was one thing deadlier than a gryphon, barring dragons, it was a wounded gryphon. *That* was one thing he had in common with the creature.

The monster tried to circle around him, but the footing was too precarious, and it started to slide downward. The wings, or rather one wing, spread in a feeble attempt to fly, the failure of which only made the gryphon angrier. It continued to cry out the word that someone had obviously worked hard to make it say.

He tried to reach out with his power and end this quickly, but, to his astonishment, the animal had some sort of protection that was by no means natural in origin.

"There were two of them originally, you know."

The ex-mercenary backed up so that he could keep the animal in sight and yet still confront the newcomer as well.

"What did you need them for?" The Gryphon turned, trying to get both in his range of sight. "You're far more of a mad beast than a dozen of these, D'Shay."

D'Shay, still out of sight, chuckled and, to the lionbird's aggravation, started moving so that animal and master were always one hundred and eighty degrees apart from one another. The Gryphon continued to turn, but he found that, even with his unique eyesight, he would have needed eyes in the back of his head to keep track of both of them simultaneously.

"I'll take that as a compliment. You know, this really shows how fortunes can change at times."

"In what way?" the Gryphon asked, wishing his would change for the better as soon as possible.

"When we met again, after so long, in the cavern of the Black Dragon—Lochivar, wasn't it—I was ending a commitment to the drake lord because we could no longer afford to trade him slaves for an emergency port. We thought we might actually need them. We'd conquered as much of this continent as necessary and had decided it was time to deal with the Master Guardians of Sirvak Dragoth. Imagine our surprise when, even with my aid, they not only held us but they actually pushed us back."

The beast chose that moment to shout, "Kill! Kill!"

D'Shay shouted something at it, a sound more than a word, and the animal quieted. The wolf raider apologized. "They tend to be impatient creatures."

"I can see why. You certainly are long-winded."

He could almost imagine the smile on D'Shay's wolfish visage. "Just a little bit longer. I want to savor this. Until a few minutes ago, I thought I was going to die. Now I am safe. I was trapped in the Dream Lands; did I mention that? The Tzee, who I admit were more cunning than I imagined, had some plan of their own backfire, so they came to the one person who might still be willing to bargain with them."

The Gryphon stumbled momentarily, but quickly regained his balance. "You should never bargain with the Tzee."

D'Shay continued to move. "Yes, I learned that. No time to worry now, though. They only had enough power to create a portal and get me here. I was no sooner here than they were dissipated from lack of power—exactly as I hoped. So much for betrayal."

"Would that they had left you floating in the Void by accident."

"You would have liked that. As I said, fortunes change. The stalemate continued, and I searched for new ports, supposedly to appease unrest in the council, but actually because I knew you still lived. You know the rest. The stalemate finally ended, with us on the side that was winning. As I see it now, we have changed places, you and I. You had a country behind you, and I was forced to slink around; now, I have the power of an empire, and you, you are the lone hope. The predator has become the prey."

D'Shay ceased moving. As if by some unseen signal, the gryphon halted as well. It pawed at the unstable footing, beak open, rage and hunger in its mad eyes.

"I'd like to say," the wolf raider added, "that the blood is from your companions. But I won't. That will come with time."

"D'Rak?" The Gryphon silently cursed himself. He had hoped that he had sent them *away* from the danger.

"Not his, but surely some of his fools'. He is here somewhere, but he lacks complete knowledge. A pity. I think he would've enjoyed the poetry of this moment."

The beast roared, reacting to a new signal, and leaped for the Gryphon.

XXI

Morgis and Freynard, while not yet prepared to consider one another in terms such as "comrade" or "friend," had at least come to the point where they respected one another's skills. Now and then, to keep the boredom of their task from overwhelming them, they would discuss the ways of the warrior and how it was the little things that always seemed to be the deciding factor in the greatest battles.

They had just begun to discuss the Turning War, the war that was still causing changes in drake and human society today— due mainly to Cabe Bedlam and the Gryphon—when Freynard spotted something and called out quietly but urgently. Morgis, regaining his balance for what he considered the "thousandth damned time," rushed as quickly as was possible.

"What is it?" he hissed softly. There seemed to be no one around, but if the warm-blood thought it best to talk quietly, Morgis would not argue.

Freynard pointed at a congealed, dark liquid splattered across some of the rubble. He stuck a finger into it and held it up for the drake to see.

"Blood."

"An animal, perhaps." The drake doubted his own suggestion. It would have been the first one they had seen since arriving here. There were not even any birds.

Freynard's eyes met the duke's. "Follow it, milord?"

Morgis knew that, as things stood, the captain did not have to acknowledge his rank. Nonetheless, the act of respect did please him, and he unconsciously returned courtesy with courtesy. "As you think, Captain Freynard."

"It heads toward Troia and the Master Guardian. We should take a look."

"Haggerth is his name. Yes. Who knows, we may find what we seek on the way."

"Whatever that may be." Freynard smiled briefly.

The trail went haphazardly for several hundred yards, but was always clear enough for them to follow. Knowing the time limit that they had, they dared increase their pace even more. Thus it was that they were nearly over the bodies before they saw them.

There were four bodies. Three mangled forms that could be identified as Aramites and one that Morgis recognized and that gave him pause because of the incredible size. He shivered briefly, but convinced himself it was only the wind.

Most of the blood, it seemed, was from the hapless wolf raiders. The thing that had killed them, the gryphon, had several slashes across its flanks, but something else had finished it off. The drake stepped over to the beast and studied it from head to tip of tail. There was something wrong with its inner structure —as if the bones and organs were not quite in the right places. *Keepers.*

"Freynard!" he spat quietly. The captain looked up from his clinical examination of one raider who was missing most of his midsection. "Check for a keeper!"

While Freynard searched his man, Morgis moved to one that lay broken over the jagged edge of an upturned piece of street. The man's arm was gone, and his face was a pulp—the wolfhelm had been torn from his head, apparently—but his uniform was more reminiscent of those worn by the keepership guards. Better kept. A bit flashier, including a tiny symbol on the chest that, when the blood was wiped away, was revealed to be a tiny crystal.

A hand fell on his shoulder. He was standing straight, sword over his head, before he recognized the human. "You could find yourself without a head if you make a habit of that!"

"You said you wanted me to find a keeper. The last body is one, I think. The only keeper I remember was one named D'Laque, but he had something like this." Allyn Freynard opened his hand to reveal a small, toothlike crystal. Unlike those Morgis had seen, it was dull and cold-looking. He suspected that was one way of knowing that the keeper was dead—the other was to look at what remained of him.

"There were trails of blood," the captain continued. His eyes were not on his companion, but on the area around them. "The one we followed here, and another one moving on the way we were going."

"Toward the Master Guardian and the Gryphon's female."

"Is she?"

"I know it, even if they do not."

"Then"—Freynard rose—"it is my duty to protect her as well. Let's go."

The trail of blood, unfortunately, went only a little farther before dwindling to nothing. Someone had obviously finally had the good sense to either heal the wound or, lacking that power, bind it. That did not deter them. They were more concerned with finding the other two than with finding whatever survivors of the Aramite party still remained. That was a problem best dealt with afterward, when they knew everyone was safe.

After several more minutes of clambering over the ancient wreckage of Qualard, Morgis called a halt by raising his hand. To Freynard, it seemed that the duke was listening to something that he himself could not hear.

That was indeed the case. "There are voices coming from that direction—and I think one of them belongs to someone whose acquaintance I have been hoping to renew."

He did not expand on the last comment, but instead signaled the captain forward again. With the practiced stealth of two survivors, they moved closer.

The voices, especially one, became audible, if not necessarily understandable. Morgis was about to continue forward when Freynard grabbed hold of him and pointed to their left.

A single Aramite, definitely a keepership guard as far as the drake was able to tell, kept an eye out for any intruders. He seemed nervous, a totally reasonable emotion if he had recently survived a gryphon attack. Morgis looked for another path that would lead them closer. It was not that he feared a lone sentry or even D'Rak himself; it was just that charging in would not save Troia and the Master Guardian Haggerth if they were prisoners, which seemed likely. Shifting to dragon form would not help, either; he would be too susceptible to attack by the senior keeper while he was transforming. After all, it was hardly something he could keep secret.

He found a likely route, a place where two large buildings had apparently fallen together. Time and erosion had more or less fused them into one mass, but there was still a tunnel—actually, more of a gap—down between the foundations. It would require crawling, but that was not what bothered him. The tunnel was barely large enough for him to fit in, and any wolf raider who discovered them before they were through would be able to kill them at his leisure. There was no way they could defend themselves properly while inside.

Still, it was the most likely choice. Morgis pointed at the tunnel and whispered, "There."

Freynard nodded and followed as the drake worked his way to the opening. Morgis wasted no time; holding his sword before him, he went down on his knees and began crawling.

Just inside, the duke discovered that the tunnel extended much longer and would bring them even closer to the Aramites than he had first expected. Inside, the voices came stronger, though with an echoing effect, and the words were more or less understandable.

". . . Dragoth! It would go . . . you told me where the Gryphon is now!"

Morgis hissed in barely restrained anger. "D'Rak!"

"You seem to be growing more . . . worried with each passing. . . . There something wrong?" The other voice was unmistakably that of Haggerth. Was Troia there as well?

"We have to move," Freynard reminded him. Morgis grunted quietly and continued on.

"There is nothing wrong," D'Rak was saying, but there was tension in his voice. "How could there be with Sirvak Dragoth falling even as we speak, you two my prisoners, and the Gryphon to follow? Even D'Shay is no longer a problem."

"What is it about Qualard, D'Rak? What is here that you and your god fear so much that you tried to remove all knowledge of it from us?"

The two reached the other end of the tunnel and hesitated. Someone in a heavy pair of boots walked nearby and then moved away again. Another guard. Morgis waited until the sentry's footfalls had faded into the distance and then slowly crawled from the passage. A wall that had stood the test of time stretched in both directions. Morgis realized that D'Rak and the others were on the other side. Freynard joined him, seeming to grasp the situation immediately.

The senior keeper's voice rose slightly. "It's not something that you need to know where you will be going—unless, Master Guardian, you would be willing to trade access to the Dream Lands for that secret and your own miserable life."

"You don't know. He doesn't know, Master Haggerth!"

Morgis nodded to the captain. Troia *was* there, after all—and still fighting, he was pleased to see. Too many creatures gave up when faced with death. Even drakes.

There was a heavy *crack* and a gasp of pain. "I will know all soon enough, misfit. I know many things even now. For instance, it is not a thing your friend seeks, but a being, a being ensnared here long, long ago by the lord Ravager himself—your god, guardians."

"What you say could not possibly be true!" Haggerth was apparently growing upset. The drake frowned; he had thought the man stronger, steadier. This was not the Haggerth who seemed always to find reason when others, like Mrin/Amrin, could not.

"He's going to kill them at this rate!" Freynard practically mouthed the words so as not to alert the others to their presence.

"You should be glad that my veil obscures my face, wolf raider, else my anger would probably strike you dead!"

Drake and man stared wide-eyed at one another. Haggerth knew he was going to die, but like Troia, he was still fighting —and, at the moment, he had only one weapon remaining.

Morgis pointed at himself and then behind him. He then pointed at the captain and indicated the opposite direction. Freynard nodded. They would come from both sides. The drake held up three fingers and then created a zero, indicating a count of thirty once both of them were in position. In case the keeper did not fall into the trap, they would still commit themselves. Before they separated, Morgis mouthed one last word—*D'Rak*.

Freynard nodded once. No matter what else, one of them had to kill the senior keeper.

Silent as a cat, the drake moved swiftly toward his end of the wall.

D'Rak had been laughing, but when he calmed enough to speak, there was poison in his words. "Small wonder they call it the Dream Lands! You've been hiding behind your kerchief much too long to be so arrogant at a time like this. Do you think that you invoke mystery or power with your little piece of cloth?''

So intent was the drake on the Aramite's words that he did not hear the clink of rock upon metal. He was only halfway to the end of the wall when the sentry came around the corner. Both froze, realization and decision delayed by overcomplacency, the guard because he had come this way more than a dozen times before and Morgis because everything had seemed to time itself so right.

The sentry opened his mouth to give the alarm. Morgis jumped at him, knocking the other's sword away.

''Let me show you what your power is worth!'' D'Rak snarled from the other side of the wall.

The guard slipped from the drake's grasp. ''Alert!''

Morgis ran him through as he tried to recover his weapon. The duke rushed to the end of the wall, glanced briefly behind himself, and saw Freynard vanishing around the corner even as D'Rak's shocked ''Ravager's Blood!'' cut through all other noise. The shout was followed by a scream of denial. Troia's scream.

Morgis cursed, shielded his eyes, and charged around the edge of the wall wondering which would get him first, a sword point or an accidental glance at one of the two people he was trying to save. He hoped it was the sword point; at least *that* could be explained to his sire—if someone remained alive to explain it.

''That's it, old friend, delay it! Delay it as long as possible!'' D'Shay's laugh was more of a cackle, a mad one at that.

Blood seeped from the Gryphon's right side where one of the beast's claws had caught him during that initial leap. D'Shay's pet was used to slower prey, not something with a swiftness to match its own. Unfortunately, despite that swiftness, it was impossible to escape from the monster. If the Gryphon turned away for even a second, he knew that the beast would get him.

It was not all one-sided. He still had his short sword, though now he wished he had traded it for something with a little more reach. D'Shay's creature had already received a slash across its chest, and it did not seem too eager to try for a second. Instead, the two of them circled about the area with the master wolf raider the only audience—a partial one at that.

Moving about had at least allowed the Gryphon a chance to study D'Shay. What he had seen had shocked him: D'Shay was dying. Almost half of his visible skin was gray, and some of it was peeling. One of his arms hung loosely at his side and, when D'Shay did move, it was with some hesitation, as if he was uncertain of his own ability to function.

"Why don't you try another spell? The last one might have only misfired!"

Misfired? Not likely, the lionbird knew. D'Shay's pet had been specially bred, but it was also magically enhanced, shielded, and capable of dampening his powers to a level that had proved useless so far. A special treat that D'Shay had raised for several generations just on the off chance that his adversary would return.

There had been *two* of these. The Gryphon gave a brief mental thanks to whatever patron was watching over him that D'Rak had been unfortunate enough to arrive so near the creatures and thus relieved the lionbird of some of the trouble. Two such beasts would have been fighting over his remains long ago.

"It will be nice to rest without wondering when you might reappear. I still think of the last time we were here."

"I'm sorry," the Gryphon interrupted, his eyes remaining on the animal before him, "but my memory is a little hazy about that last time."

"Suffice to say that I would have died because of you. Died, if not for the Lord Ravager."

"Why, what happened?" An idle thought had occurred to the lionbird, an idle thought concerning a similar situation to this. He had to keep D'Shay distracted while he concentrated.

"That, I am afraid, is something I would like you to go to your death guessing about."

"I already know a little about who you have imprisoned down there." D'Shay's pet took another swipe at him; the Gryphon held off the blow with his sword, but his arm was growing heavy and the loss of blood from his wound was slowing him. He could not afford to lose speed, not now.

"Do you?"

"Enough to know that it was not the Ravager that devastated this city."

D'Shay did not laugh. As he came into view once more, the Gryphon saw that he was growing a bit anxious and not merely because of whatever was killing him. "It seems I arrived here just in time, then. I thought you had almost no memory, but now I think you might even know what you did wrong last time and how you could change that."

The lionbird was almost ready to admit his true ignorance on that point, but then found that he suddenly *did* possess the knowledge. The discovery nearly cost him his life, because the gryphon lunged toward him and he barely managed to dodge its paws. It was to prove an unfortunate choice, for he landed on his injured side, and the sharp pain wreaked havoc with his motor functions. The sword dropped from his clawing fingers. The beast shrieked and moved toward him. Tears in his eyes, he rolled away and succeeded in stumbling to his feet.

The sword lay beneath the hind legs of D'Shay's pet.

"I think a conclusion is imminent now," D'Shay said with a growing smile. "The last of the misfits, the special ones. My only regret is never really being certain of where you came from. I don't suppose you remember *that*?"

The Gryphon shook his head, as much to clear it as to answer his foe's question.

"Pity." D'Shay shouted out a command. The beast stood poised, knowing now that its prey was more or less helpless. Even with his claws, the Gryphon had no chance against this mad version of himself. He had a knife, as well, but it seemed unlikely that it would do any better than his claws.

It was now or never. He prayed it would listen to him.

"Kill!" shouted the wolf raider.

"Kill! Kill!" The huge creature leaped at him, aiming for his uninjured side. It knew by instinct that its prey would then be forced to depend on the weaker side, and even a moment of hesitation due to pain was all the skilled hunter needed.

The Gryphon, however, did not move in either direction. Rather, he fell to the ground, an act that, under normal circumstances, would have meant his death. The beast would have landed, turned, and caught him while he was still struggling to his feet. That is, if it had landed where it expected to.

Behind where he had stood, the Gate, doors open, materialized and accepted the unsuspecting gryphon. The animal roared its confusion, a roar that was cut off as the gryphon disappeared and the portal returned to wherever it had come from. It was over before the lionbird could draw another breath.

He could not believe that it had actually worked.

Neither could D'Shay. His uncomprehending face was gray, but it was hard to tell if it was from whatever was killing him or from what he had just seen. "What—did—you do?"

His question went unanswered, for the Gryphon was taking full advantage of the situation. He had rolled to a position that left him facing his adversary, and then his knife was out, ready for throwing. D'Shay finally woke from his madness and began shouting. Two heavily armored figures joined him on the rise, figures that were probably not human, the Gryphon supposed.

D'Shay turned, his body shifting slowly, uncertainly. The Gryphon released the knife, aiming, not for his back, which the two guards were moving to block, but for his leg. One of the servants made a late attempt to put his own leg in the way, but he was too slow.

Had his condition not slowed him, the knife would have flown uselessly over his shoulder. Instead, the blade caught D'Shay in the unprotected backside of his leg near his knee. The wolf raider let out a cry, made a feeble grab at the handle of the knife, and finally fell from sight. The Gryphon, meanwhile, retrieved his sword and prepared to face off against the two armored figures, only to discover that they had stopped moving. He waited, expecting some trick, but the two continued to stand where they were, frozen in the midst of whatever movement they had been making when D'Shay fell. Evidently, D'Shay's will was their will, period. That they were unmoving meant that he was now unconscious—or dead.

Taking a chance, the Gryphon sheathed his sword and climbed to the top. Carefully, for past experience with his adversary had taught him never to take anything at face value, he looked over.

The master wolf raider lay in a very crumpled, very dead heap. In addition to his knife wound, which apparently had resulted in a broken leg on the way down, his head was bent back at an awkward angle. If it was a ploy, it was a very good one—yet, he had seen D'Shay die before. Best not to take a chance, he decided. Hoping he would not regret his decision, he worked his way down to the body.

Had he not seen it happen and been responsible for it, the Gryphon would have supposed that someone had killed D'Shay more than a week before. His skin was nearly completely gray now, and even partially mummified. He remembered some of the things Freynard had mentioned, but they only served to confuse him further. The former mercenary rose. Whatever Shaidarol had become during all those years in service to the mad wolf god, this body would give him no more service. He pulled out the sword, raised it over his head, and brought it down on the neck with all his strength.

The resistance was negligible; his sword dug deep in the

ground, and the rapidly decaying head rolled away. The Gryphon dragged the body a hundred yards away and, just for good measure, buried it under some heavy rubble. He then did the same for the head.

Rest in pieces, he could not help thinking, and then added as an afterthought, *and stay there*.

The Gryphon finally examined his side. It had stopped bleeding, and, if he held his hand on it, it did not hurt as much. With neither D'Shay nor his pet to interfere, he could use his powers to heal himself. It would be a slow process; he had still not completely recovered from his previous wounds, though he had tried not to show that to anyone. Now was not the time to worry about them. Now was the time to worry about finding a way into—what?

He climbed once more over the rise, stopping briefly to inspect the two armored servants. Empty though the suits appeared, he knew better. These were portions of the Tzee that D'Shay had secretly ensnared. They had no consciousness of their own and did not respond to his commands. In the end, the Gryphon decided to leave them to the elements.

His eyes focused on the approximate location of the trapdoor, an action that almost proved fatal, for his foot was just coming down when it hit him that he was staring at, not the well-disguised entrance, but a square hole cut deep into the foundation of the ancient building. The Gryphon slipped and slid halfway down the slope (fortunately, on his good side) before he was able to stop himself. He completed the downward climb in a more standard manner, though it was difficult not to keep staring at the uncovered entrance to Qualard's underworld.

Once down, he raced over to the hole. Someone, somehow, had removed the slab. The prisoner, perhaps? It was doubtful, but there was no way to be certain. At the moment, he could not sense the other. It was almost as if a wall was preventing contact.

A row of steps led into darkness. The Gryphon cursed himself for not bringing a torch or something. He would have to rely on his night vision, which, while excellent, was by no means a substitute for light.

Sword ready, the lionbird slowly descended, feeling much like a bird walking blindly into the mouth of a cat . . . or in this case, a wolf. He moved slowly, allowing his eyes to become accustomed to the dark. The air was dry but breathable and fairly dust free. No small creatures had made their home here, not ever. It was like walking into a tomb only recently sealed— only, the occupant was still alive.

There was light after all. As in Canisargos, small crystals dotted the walls. They seemed to come alive slowly, as if those closer to him were waking those farther away. He thought for a moment that the dim light from above had started some sort of reaction, but then he noticed that those behind him gradually darkened once more. They were responding to *him*.

The city sleeps above us, a memory told him.

"The wolf raiders never sleep," he replied before realizing he was merely repeating something he had said long, long ago.

Can you do it? another memory, seemingly female, asked pensively.

He wondered about that. Could he do what? Free the one entombed here?

Can you die without screaming out your fear!

This was not a memory! The crystals ahead of the Gryphon died abruptly, followed by those near and behind him. He was plunged into total darkness, which his eyes attempted to compensate, albeit inadequately, for.

The clean, dry air gave way to a pungent scent like a thousand years of rotting meat. He heard the sounds of bones rattling as something huge crushed them beneath its massive paws. Hot breath seemed to wash over his face.

Two burning, bloodred eyes glared death at him from the corridor. He was forced to look upward, for the thing, its form indistinguishable from the darkness save for those eyes, towered over him. It snarled.

This is no dream this time. I am so very real, as you can see.

Behind him, the light from above vanished and the Gryphon heard the sound of stone scraping against stone. The entrance was sealed once more.

He was trapped—and alone with the Ravager himself.

XXII

Morgis had charged out into the open, fully expecting to take on any number of opponents single-handedly. That everyone had fallen victim to Haggerth's trap was too much to hope for. If D'Rak alone had suffered the consequences, that would be sufficient.

He stood there for several seconds, his right side virtually blind because he feared to remove his hand. There was no one to fight. One wolf raider, lying facedown, was visible, but he looked to have been dead for some time, perhaps at the claws of Troia, more likely from the gryphon. Another, a keeper, was on his knees and staring blindly into space, mouth open in a pitiful expression of incomprehension—perhaps at the cause of his own collapse. The drake paid no more heed to the unfortunate save to register him as one less threat. He had, of course, no idea how many other, actual threats *did* remain.

D'Rak was here somewhere, and that was what truly mattered. Hand still shielding his eyes, he moved nearer to where he guessed Troia and Haggerth were, hoping one of them would alert him to any nearby danger.

He bumped into something clad in metal. It pulled away from him as quickly as he pulled away from it.

"Rep-reptile!" The voice was slurred, as if the speaker were talking in slow motion, but it was unequivocally D'Rak.

The drake cursed. He'd walked right into the one person who could kill him with little more than a glance! Half blind was no way to fight a battle—and where was Freynard? Had he accidentally caught sight of whatever horror the Master Guardian hid behind his veil? "Haggerth! Turn away from me!"

"He—he cannot—he cannot hear you—you!" D'Rak muttered. "His—his ears—his whole head—are no longer on speaking—on speaking terms!"

"Dead?" Morgis pulled his hand away. Whether or not the Master Guardian's visage would affect him after death was now unimportant; what was important was that someone else had suffered at the senior keeper's hands—and this time was dead. He could not even guess about Troia; was the scream for herself or the elder human? And *why* had D'Rak not laid him low with some spell?

Morgis was not greeted by the sight of his worst nightmares come to life, which was what he had half expected, but then he saw the form slumped against the wall, head turned from him, and knew why. Next to the unmoving body, Troia was struggling, slowly loosening her bonds. It occurred to him that she could use some assistance. Morgis started toward her, calling out. Troia looked up, and the expression on her face was one of sudden fear. He puzzled over it for perhaps a second or two . . . and knew with growing horror that he had fallen under the spell of D'Rak after all.

Without hesitation, he cried out in the name of his father and swung the sword in a vicious arc, not really caring if he struck anything, but hoping he would disrupt the senior keeper's concentration. When his blade suddenly sank deep into something other than stone, something that let out one gasp and then became dead weight, he thanked the Blue Dragon for guiding his aim and quickly pulled the sword back out. Morgis stepped back and turned even as an ebony-clad form fell lifelessly at his feet.

It was not D'Rak. He knew that instantly, for while the senior keeper was indeed in front of him, he was also several yards away. In one hand he held a crystalline talisman; with the other hand, he kept himself from falling over. The body before the drake was yet another guard, probably the one who had been standing lookout earlier. D'Rak himself looked only half alive. The lower right portion of his face was slack, lifeless, and he constantly blinked, as if even the dark, cloud-covered day was too bright for his eyes. His skin was as pale as death. What was most important, however, was that he was now alone.

"You—" Morgis's observation was confirmed. The right side of D'Rak's mouth did not move when he spoke. "You—you are as difficult to kill—to kill as the bird!"

Morgis still had no idea what had happened to Freynard, but that became secondary as he faced what was left of Lord D'Rak. Either through willpower or the protection of his crystal, D'Rak had succeeded in resisting the trap—at least partially, that is. His mind had suffered a strain that the drake, who had caught only a glimpse of Haggerth's face that one time in Sirvak Dragoth, could not begin to comprehend sufficiently. Small wonder that he had not killed Morgis outright. It was hard enough for the Aramite to stand, let alone concentrate. The senior keeper had obviously hoped that his one remaining follower would be able to walk right up to the ensorceled drake and finish him from behind, but either D'Rak's will was too weak now or he had sadly underestimated Morgis. Whatever the case, it was doubtful the senior keeper could summon up sufficient will to do it again.

He smiled slowly at D'Rak, every sharp, predatory tooth revealed in all its glory. "It's my turn now."

D'Rak held up his talisman, as if the crystal alone would be enough to stop the duke. "Not—not yet. Not while—not while I—I control the Eye of the Wolf!"

The keeper smiled defiantly at Morgis—and then the smile faded, first incomprehension and then panic setting in. "I—cannot feel it! The Eye is—Eye is hidden from me!"

"A pity." Morgis raised his sword. He had no compunction about killing D'Rak outright. The Aramite was one of the lords of the wolf raiders. Morgis did not doubt that the path to that position of power was even bloodier than he imagined.

"Fool!" Spittle ran down the senior keeper's chin and onto his breastplate. His eyes spoke volumes; why had his lord abandoned him now? "Kill me and you kill your—"

After D'Rak had fallen, Morgis bent down and opened wide the Aramite's hand, removing the talisman from his limp grip. He stood up and examined it. Like the last one he had seen, it was dull and cold.

Just for good measure, the duke dropped it at his own feet—and crushed it beneath his boot. As a further safety precaution, and one that seemed to come to him out of the blue, he severed the wolf raider's body from his head. Then he went to Troia, who had finally freed herself of her bonds and was leaning over Haggerth. His head was covered by the hood of his cloak.

"How is he?"

"Dead." She was worn. A trail of blood, still fresh, went from her mouth to her chin, the result of D'Rak's anger. "It was a reflex action. I—rolled away when he pulled the veil off, but I saw him hold out his—his crystal in order to save himself. There's not much left. D'Rak *was* senior keeper."

"It was not enough to save him. He was half mad and half crippled, which by no means meant he wasn't dangerous." Morgis scanned the area. "Is this it? Are there any more?"

She touched Haggerth's head lightly and whispered something. Then the feline woman rose. "There was one more, I'm sure of it. D'Rak used his crystal to capture us, but then he had his men bind us. Naturally, I counted their strength, in case I was able to break free. I think there was another guard. That way."

Morgis frowned. That was where Freynard had been. He pulled Troia closer. "You must do something for me."

"What?"

"Cut off the heads of the other wolf raiders. I—I do not understand it myself, but I feel it is important. Meanwhile, I have to find Captain Freynard. Will you do it?"

To his surprise, she actually seemed to draw strength from the suggestion. "Of course I'll do it. It's the right thing to do."

"The right thing?"

Troia shook her head. "I can't explain it. I just know. Like you."

"Curious." Sword in hand, he left her to the grisly task and headed cautiously to the other end of the wall, where he had last seen the Gryphon's man. Freynard, he knew, had not been in the best condition for this trek, but he had not weakened, either. Morgis was no longer concerned with his loyalty; now he was concerned for a soldier whom he had come to respect.

He saw nothing at first. It might have seemed that Freynard had never been there. Then the drake caught sight of something stirring in the rubble nearby. He stepped over what might possibly have been the remains of a stone bench or table and pulled a piece of masonry away.

It was Freynard, pale as if he had just died. His eyes were open, but he seemed not to recognize the drake at first, for he pulled away as if he expected to be killed. Morgis caught him by the shoulders and shook him. "Freynard! Curse you, it's me! Duke Morgis!"

"Morgis?" The captain looked at him oddly, then seemed to collect himself. He put a hand to his head. "I'm sorry. I wasn't myself."

"What happened here? Were you attacked?"

The man gazed around him, as if seeing things for the first time. Slowly, he explained everything. "Guard saw me. We struggled—lost my sword after wounding him. Was chased up there, then everything collapsed."

"Where's the wolf raider?"

"Underneath that." Freynard pointed at a new mound of marble and rock to his left. A boot and part of a leg were barely visible in the middle of the pile. There was no question about whether or not the Aramite was dead.

Morgis helped the human to his feet. "Haggerth is dead."

"Haggerth? Dead?"

"But D'Rak is as well."

That brought a broad smile to the captain's features. "D'Rak dead! The keepership is without a leader now!"

The drake thought about it. "Yes, I suppose that is an important consideration. What's more important right now is to get Troia and find the Gryphon. Suddenly, Qualard is becoming the most popular place on this continent!"

Coming around the wall, they spotted Troia. Freynard began to tremble. "What is she *doing*?"

The cat woman had taken care of the other bodies as Morgis had requested, and now she stood before the one survivor, the keeper who had lost his mind. Before Morgis could explain, she had slit the wolf raider's throat.

Freynard started to struggle. He was proving stronger than the duke had imagined. "Stop her!"

Morgis held on to him. Troia turned at the noise, her borrowed sword raised to strike the head off the Aramite. Clutching the captain tightly, the drake spat, "Cut it off! Now!"

With a precision that spoke of skills he had not imagined of her, she took the head off with one smooth strike.

"Release me!" Freynard nearly pulled free. Morgis turned him so that they faced one another and then quickly said, "It had to be done, Captain! I don't know if I can explain it, and I doubt that Troia could, either! We just know it has to be done!"

The man in his hands shivered uncontrollably, then slumped. "As you wish, then. If you think it was necessary, my lord, I will take your word."

Troia threw the sword down by the decapitated keeper and walked toward them. She seemed more at ease than earlier.

"You might need that," the drake suggested carefully.

She shook her head defiantly and extended her claws. "I'll settle for what my ancestors gave me."

Freynard gazed down at his empty hands. "I need one. I forgot to retrieve mine."

"Take your pick."

His eyes focused on what remained of the senior keeper. "Did he have a sword?"

Morgis squinted. "Possibly, though he did not make use of it. I do not think he had the physical strength or the coordination to lift it."

The captain pulled away from the drake and wandered over to D'Rak's corpse. Morgis took advantage of the time to speak with Troia. "I've been doing some thinking. I'm beginning to believe that the Gryphon decided it might be too dangerous for us wherever he was going. Notice he made certain he remained alone. A hunch, I admit, but I've learned from him, you could say."

"You really think he sent us on false trails?"

"Exactly. . . . And judging from what happened here, he may be in great trouble. I think there is a real gryphon tracking him and, the Dragon of the Depths knows, D'Shay might—scratch that—*will* be there."

"D'Shay?" Freynard had succeeded in returning without either of them hearing him. Held in place by his belt was a long, narrow blade. It was almost too long, more of a zweihander than a longsword.

Morgis looked at it and then at the captain. "Where did you get *that*? I am certain I would have remembered it."

Freynard shrugged. "I pulled back his cloak and it was there. I didn't question my luck. I like it better than the short sword I had."

"Do you even have the strength for that?"

"Like to test me?" A cunning smile briefly lit the man's face.

"Not from the way you are looking at me, no."

Thunder cracked. They had grown used to the wind, even the chill, but this was something new. It did not even sound like normal thunder, for it continued on and on for what seemed like an eternity, before finally fading away slowly.

"Gryphon!" Troia whispered.

The drake nodded sharply. "I think you may be right—and I think we may already be too late to help him!"

"No! I won't believe that!"

"It does not matter whether you or I or the captain here believes it, because we are going after him regardless. Any objections?"

There were none. There were only fears, but those they kept to themselves.

The thunder, rather than being muted by the thick ceiling above him, seemed to reverberate through the passages. The Gryphon went down on one knee, his hands over his ears. Before him, the Ravager laughed mockingly, his laughter blending into the thunder so well that it was hard to say where one ended and the other began. Finally, though, only the laughter remained, eventually dying away.

The Ravager's eyes burned through him. *I shall call the elements and have you broken by each . . . Yet you will never be allowed to die. I shall worry your body and cast it upon my hoard, where I will let you spend eternity, never moving, among the bones of those who have fallen to me. You will beg for release, but I, not being merciful, will never grant it.*

His head pounded, and he felt dry, almost mummified. The Gryphon refused to yield, however. For all his bluster, all his savage threats, the Ravager had not yet touched him. Why? He was trapped with no way out. It was doubtful that the wolf god was merely toying with him.

Plead for mercy—I won't grant it, but it might be humorous to see. Go on. Maybe you will touch some tender part of my . . . soul. The mad god laughed again, but was it forced?

The Gryphon forced himself to his feet. He had dropped his sword, but it was foolish to think that it would have any effect on the Ravager. What choice did that leave him, then?

None, misfit.

He felt a sharp, stabbing pain in his chest, and his first thought was that at last the Ravager was striking. It was too small a pain, though, and, when it did not increase, he realized what was causing it.

Are your fears killing you, old one? Give in to them; you'll die that much easier!

Do you remember what it was like? an old memory asked curiously. *Are you still the same?*

The same what? the Ravager snarled, confusion evident. *What are you thinking?*

Memories. Bits of memories. He reached into his shirt and pulled out a single tiny whistle. Once, he had owned three. His only heritage. Each represented, to a guardian, portions of his heritage. The lionbird had never made use of this one, fearing what he would discover. One had summoned birds from all about, an incredible flock that had destroyed an assault by the clans of the Black Dragon. Another had called Troia, a cat by nature, as he, too, was. But what was his third and final piece of heritage?

Your only heritage is death, Gryphon! Bow to me! Bow to my will or I will tear you to blood-soaked bits of meat, which I shall dine on at my leisure!

Perhaps that was meant to frighten him further, but it had the opposite effect. The Ravager threatened too much, but he still held back—and the wolf god's fear, the fear that the Gryphon had felt that last time, was evident more than ever.

He put the whistle up to his beak. It did not matter that this was not as efficient for blowing the whistle as a human mouth. As before, it was only important that he actually force some air through.

Stop!

A brief note, a curious one. It was a questioning note, as if he were an enigma, a being without a distinct personality to call his own.

The darkness within the darkness, that which was the Ravager, seemed to pull away. The eyes still burned with anger, but uncertainty and fear continued to manifest themselves.

The Ravager snarled and then yelped like a hurt pup as the tunnel was bathed in brilliance. A portal—the Gate itself—materialized in one of the walls. As before, the Gate seemed much taller than the corridor allowed. It also had changed. Not just in its basic physical appearance. The rust was gone; the hinges held once more. The creatures that scurried along its sides moved with new life, with a vibrance they had lacked the last time.

As one, the two great doors swung open—and out stepped the first of at least half a dozen of the Faceless Ones, the not-people.

The Gryphon's people.

He received no blinding understanding of his past. Some memories fell in place, but it seemed others still desired to remain buried. Yet, there was no denying now that he had been one of them, had moved along through the centuries adjusting things here, instigating things there, assisting in other places—but never truly taking sides.

Until the Ravager dared the unspeakable.

He looked at the shadowy form. It cringed, but still put on a false face of power. *I do what I desire to do! The game is mine; it is too late to change that! I've won! Do you hear? I've won! The rules are mine to change as I see fit!*

"*You* made me!" The Gryphon stepped forward in wonder. As he moved closer, the darkness of the Ravager retreated deeper into the tunnel. The Faceless Ones stood by silently. Though they did nothing, their very presence aided. It gave the lionbird the understanding he needed, such as why they had turned from their own ways to help him more than they had ever helped another. Regardless of the change, he was still one of them.

But he was more, as well. The Ravager was apparently not the final arbiter. Whatever he had done to take one of the blank-visaged beings and turn it into a parody of the actual animal had disturbed some power. If there was one rule that could not be broken, it was *there were those who could not be touched.* They lacked a true name, but those who needed to know did. The wolf god knew the penalty but had ignored it in his obsession with "the game."

The Gryphon reached out a hand toward the shadows. He heard a gasp, and then the Ravager was again retreating.

"You have no power over me. Not after that first time. That's why you fear me more than the other guardians. You cannot touch me directly; you have to work through agents, which was why you originally seduced Shaidarol. You knew what I was even though the Master Guardians did not."

Lies! I permit you to live because I have won and can be magnanimous! Look! See! I give you your freedom!

The lionbird glanced back, not worried in the least that the Ravager might try to destroy him. He could not. The wolf god's powers were limited, probably had been limited since the day he had succeeded in trapping one of his own kind down here.

"You have a rival down here, don't you? One who watched over the Dream Lands. That's why they stood so long." He advanced again.

The darkness, the shadows, all that was the Ravager vanished in the midst of one long howl. Even the stench of rotting meat was gone, if it had ever been there. Illusion could be very real —and not all of the Ravager's power was illusion. He did have limited control over the dead, but that was not his chief weapon. First and foremost, he was the master of fear. That fear had created an empire in his name.

Turning, he faced his brethren. Despite their lack of features, he could feel the sadness. His existence was not the purpose they had either chosen or been created for. The Gryphon doubted he would ever learn completely what had happened.

I know a bit—if you will free me, old one.

As if that were a cue, the Faceless Ones began to return through the Gate. They did not look back, and he understood that they considered him lost forever. By listening, he had decided to continue to choose sides. They had broken their own rules to aid him, feeling he deserved that much, but the rest was up to him.

That is about right. Even I cannot say for certain what they believe.

"Who are you?" he called out, his eyes fixed on the vanishing Gate. "What are you? Another god?"

By your terms—almost. Let us say . . . one of a superior group, though he who calls himself the Ravager does not paint us as such.

"Where are you?"

You have not decided whether you are going to release me. What can I do to prove myself? I aided you in Canisargos. I would have done more, but I could not without arousing his suspicions. I am more susceptible to his powers than you little ones are. A fine jest that. It serves me right for underestimating him, but he had been so quiet since regaining his freedom. At the very least, you owe me for saving your life a few moments ago.

"When? The Ravager did nothing but try to scare me."

Not him, but one of his lapdogs, the one called D'Rak—or have you forgotten when he touched your hand? He truly meant for you to die if he did.

It was true; he had forgotten about that. Now, though, it did not seem to matter. The Gryphon, for lack of someone to look at, eyed the ceiling. "You seem to display more power than the Ravager, yet you still cannot escape?"

The bonds that hold me were designed for one of our kind. Once, they held that one called the Ravager. When we saw what he had become, we worried that the same would happen to us, so we turned the—let us call it the key—to the only ones all could trust.

"And—as one of them—I had the key."

You do.

"Then tell me what to do. I'll release you."

He could almost feel the hesitation. *There, we have a problem.*

The Gryphon knew what was coming. From what he remembered and what he could piece together, it made sense. Unfortunately. "You can't. You don't know."

All knowledge of the key was given to your kind. That way, those who would misuse it could not.

"What happened last time? What destroyed Qualard?" The lionbird knew, but he wanted confirmation.

You are wrong.

"Wrong?" It all added up, or so he had thought.

Misinformation and misdirection—the Ravager's forte. Qualard was the birthplace of the wolf raiders. Why do you suppose that was?

This was ridiculous. He was passing the time talking history with an unseen being, while the Aramites must be now seeking out the refugees of Sirvak Dragoth and his own companions might be dead.

We are wasting no time. In here, time goes very slowly. A part of the punishment—the worst part, you can believe me. Besides, it has been so long since I could speak to another.

Qualard the birthplace of the wolf raiders? It made some sense, but why was that . . . "This was the Ravager's prison."

It was. The Aramites were his way to pass the time, but, when we finally asked for his release, his obsession with them continued. I wanted to know why, because it began to disrupt the pattern of life in what you now call the Dream Lands—and then I discovered that his pets, his children, were doing what he could not physically do.

The keepers, the Ravager's sorcerers, had captured, on his command, one of the blank-faced observers. The wolf god wanted his own key—and not merely to the prison he had endured. The not-people were allowed to do many things he could not. As they were, he could not control them.

His faithful followers *could*—but something went amiss.

Yes, they chose, as the mortal link, possibly the worst beast to control. A gryphon. Even I cannot say why. I discovered all and so I came to your plane, to Qualard—and found he was

*waiting for me. He had the key to the prison, and he used it. I
. . . struggled . . . and the city perished. But I had gained control
over his key. Over you. You know most of the rest.*

"The false memories?"

*Partly the spell that he—or rather, his children—cast upon
the Dream Lands, and partly one the Master Guardians cast for
me, though it cost them protection from the Ravager's spell.*

All this subterfuge; for what? "What does he truly fear about
the Dream Lands? Is it simply because he cannot control it?"

*To those who thrive on power, a thing they cannot control is
a thing to fear . . . and thus they seek to destroy it to prove their
mastery.*

"I think I know how to release you—wherever you are. Some
of the fog has lifted."

He felt the pleasure and relief that the other could not hide,
despite its seemingly calm demeanor. *Then I have one request
that you, as one of them as any could be, may grant or not.*

The Gryphon saw what he wanted and nodded. Taking a deep
breath, he steadied himself. "Are you ready?"

*I have been ready from the day I was bound. I am tired of
sleeping.*

The Gryphon summoned the Gate.

XXIII

He met them a hundred or so paces east of where they had agreed to rendezvous. His sword he clutched in his left hand. In his right, he held something so small that his closed fist hid it. That did not matter at the moment; all that mattered then were the words he spoke when they were near enough to hear him.

"It's over."

Freynard was the first to speak. "Over? You've done it, Gryphon?"

He nodded slowly. "The . . . prisoner has been freed, and D'Shay . . . he's dead."

"At last," Morgis hissed. "We can leave this inhospitable place and return to the peace of the Dragonrealm."

The Gryphon could not help cheering a little at the drake's words. Peaceful? He suspected—*hoped*, actually—that Morgis was jesting.

Troia, on the other hand, did not seem so happy. "Is that what you plan to do? Return there?"

He looked at her, trying to tell her some of the things he was too uncomfortable with to say out loud. "Not yet. Not until I'm sure that the wolf raiders are on the run, that their empire is going to collapse . . ." For the first time, his exhausted mind registered the fact that Haggerth was missing. The dark expression on Troia's face deepened. "What happened to him?"

"D'Rak killed him—but he was able to strike a blow of his own, which Duke Morgis completed." She looked up at him. "We gave him a burial of sorts, Gryphon, but I want to go back—"

"We will. Now that the wolf raiders have been removed from the Dream Lands, we can afford to do that."

They all looked at him. Freynard, most disbelieving of all, asked, "How could that be? They should have overrun Sirvak Dragoth by now! There was no way to stop them!"

He thought back to the underworld prison. Releasing the other had proved anticlimactic. After being freed, the joyous presence spoke into his mind once more. *I have already broken many rules, old one, chief of which was compounding the situation by trying to hide your continued existence. That failed. One or two more cannot harm me, and I think they would understand.*

" 'They'?" the Gryphon had coaxed.

The other had not fallen for the bait. *The wolf raiders should have never been able to invade the Dream Lands. Those lands are the last legacy of one I owe a great deal to. A free, untouched land, nothing more, but special because of that. I will remove the blight of the Aramites from it . . . and then I will tell you one last thing of importance. It concerns the one once called Shaidarol. . . .*

That was a memory now. He sighed, a bit bitterly, and, looking at all three of them, replied, "Let us say that the prisoner was grateful."

Morgis and Troia looked confused. Freynard looked pale. They waited for more, but the lionbird was finished with the subject for the present. One thing did occur to him, and he felt the drake had, at least, a right to know.

"It's a pity you weren't there, Morgis. I'm sure there was so much you would have wanted to ask him."

"Why? What was he?" The drake shivered. They were all shivering now that they had been standing in one place. "Could we not return to the Dream Lands and discuss this?"

"As you wish." It was easy now, contacting that which was the Gate. The Gate—the Dream Lands themselves—were a presence of a sort akin to the prisoner and the Ravager, and, as such, he could feel the joy and gratitude—and still a bit of apprehension, which he quickly relieved.

This time, it shone more brilliantly than even the last time.

The doors were wide open, and they could see Sirvak Dragoth, untouched and whole, standing in the distance. There was no sign that there had ever been a battle.

It was an imposing sight, a miracle. Behind him, he heard someone mutter something. "What was that, Allyn?"

"Nothing, Gryphon. Astonishment, though I should be used to that where you're concerned."

"How true," Morgis added.

The Gryphon stood to one side and indicated the duke. "You first, Morgis."

"If you think I'll protest, you are dead wrong." The drake stalked up to the portal and was about to step through when the lionbird caught his arm. "The prisoner, Morgis. Some mortal creatures once called him the Dragon of the Depths, he said."

"The Dragon—" The duke's mouth was wide open, an almost religious awe spreading itself across his face. To the drake race, the Dragon of the Depths was the closest thing they had to a god, a wondrous being whom some claimed had prodded the drakes on the road to power. From the being's tone, the Gryphon thought that such flagrant interference was doubtful, but he was not about to tell his companion that.

Morgis still stood frozen, trying to accept the idea. The Gryphon chuckled loudly, though, within, he felt nothing approaching happiness. "We'll talk about it where it's warmer, remember?"

He pushed the drake through the Gate.

Troia was next, though she wanted to wait. The Gryphon had to insist. He pulled her close and whispered, "Lord Petrac put me under a dream to keep me occupied, but I came to realize that he was merely pulling my own desires from my subconscious. If I get back, I want to tell you about them and see if you might share some of them."

Her eyes said she did—and then she caught the one menacing word. "What do you mean, 'if'?"

He pushed her through and, as he had silently requested of the Gate, the massive doors swung shut. The Gate itself remained fixed in place.

Freynard stepped back, startled. He looked around as if expecting foes to come leaping out of the ruins of the city. The wind whipped his hair about. He looked narrower in the face, more like a fox or some such animal. "Is there something wrong?"

The Gryphon shook his head. "No, I just wanted to speak to

you alone. I still haven't forgiven myself for what you went through at D'Shay's hands.''

"I survived.''

"And I'm glad about that.'' The former monarch held out his right hand. "It was good to see you again.''

Freynard took the proffered hand in his own, a smile growing.

He screamed and tried to pull away, but the Gryphon held his hand tightly. The captain went to his knees, his body shivering uncontrollably, as if he were experiencing a tremendous shock.

The Gryphon glared down at him like a bird of death. "And it was so terrible to lose you so quickly. I should have known better from last time. You always had one last trick.''

He finally released the other's hand. The face that looked up to his, even through the beard, was not Allyn Freynard's. It had fast become another, familiar visage.

D'Shay.

"I held it back!'' the master wolf raider gasped. "I held back the transformation, figuring that somehow . . . somehow I would be the last. My powers were still weak. You couldn't—couldn't have known!''

He held up his right hand for D'Shay to see. On it was a mark similar to that he had seen earlier on Freynard's cheek, but inverted. It had not been visible until the two of them had touched one another.

"A little gift from the senior keeper to both of us. It was supposed to burn your new body out, giving you no time to prepare yet another, and burn me out as well. The Dragon of the Depths informed me and altered it slightly—his last gift. He has gone away, Shaidarol, to atone for all the interference he himself has caused.''

A gleam came into D'Shay's eyes. The Gryphon shook his head, more sad now than angry.

"You'll receive no help from your lord and master. He was going to abandon you anyway. Reach out. See if his power still supports you.''

He watched as his adversary did, the arrogant face slowly draining of the last vestiges of color as D'Shay realized that he had now become very, very mortal. It was as if the Ravager no longer existed. There was nothing.

Reaching down, the Gryphon pulled him up by the front of his shirt. D'Shay's face was no more than a hair's width from the tip of the lionbird's sharp, predatory beak.

"You're looking a little gray. It's all over. You can claim

you were seduced and then forced to be what you are, but I know better. You merely hid what you really were—in mind, anyway—from the other guardians. I remember that much. It was *you* who first contacted the Ravager.''

He knew when D'Shay started reaching for his long sword and caught the wolf raider's wrist with his free hand. He almost did not see that this was a ploy until he realized that, even as desperate as he was, D'Shay would know how useless it was to try to draw such a lengthy weapon when so close to his opponent.

The dagger had been hidden behind D'Shay's back. He brought it around while the Gryphon's eyes were still on the sword. There was nothing the ex-mercenary could do but try to push away. Now, however, it was D'Shay who was holding tight.

''You will join me!'' D'Shay spat. ''You *have* to!''

The knife caught the Gryphon low, but he twisted enough so that it cut only flesh, not an organ. Instinctively, he struck out, and his claws tore through the master wolf raider's unprotected chest as if it were water. D'Shay released him and fell back, gasping as the blood of his new body spilled forth.

His eyes tried to focus on the Gryphon, but instead looked off into empty space. ''No. I cannot—''

D'Shay might have escaped then, for all the attention his enemy was able to give him. The Gryphon pulled the knife free, cursing himself for being overdramatic and acquiring yet another healthy wound to tax his healing abilities on. Emotion still had the upper hand, no matter how hard he strove.

''Gryphon!'' D'Shay forced out. Their eyes met ever so briefly, the hatred still in full flame, until D'Shay finally fell forward, striking the ground just inches from the staggering lionbird.

D'Shay shuddered, then lay limp.

With one hand on his wound, the lionbird pushed the body onto its back. Death would not make it look like Freynard once more; that he knew from the last two times. What was different now, however, was the fact that he knew, under no uncertain terms, that D'Shay was truly dead. The inverted mark on his palm was D'Rak's way of assuring that. In the end, the senior keeper had finally outwitted his rival—and the Gryphon was only too happy to give him the credit. He wanted nothing out of all this save a little peace.

How many times had D'Shay cheated death? he wondered suddenly. Even one had been too many. For this alone, it had been worth it. He only wished he had realized the truth sooner. Staring at the hated face, he could not help saying, "You've stolen your last life, you bastard."

Out of respect for the unfortunate Allyn Freynard, who deserved some memorial, he dragged the body to the Gate. The portal did not open, would not open until he desired it—and, at the moment, the lionbird just wanted to catch his breath. The wound pained him, but he knew that, once through the Gate, he would have no time for himself.

He could not return to the Dragonrealm until the wolf raiders were at least on the defensive. Even with the great loss, the Aramites would not bend easily. They had been born to war and conquest, and to ask them to simply lay down their arms and surrender was madness. He also hoped to still learn more about himself and this land in general. Somehow, he felt that there was a bond between this continent and the Dragonrealm. It went beyond what little the Dragon of the Depths had told him. He doubted if even that incredible being knew everything.

The Gryphon *would* go back, however. He had been here long enough to know that his home lay across the Eastern Seas—and if Troia chose to come with him, so much the better. The lionbird hoped Morgis would stay until they could all sail together, but that was up to the duke. It would be nice to have one familiar face, even if it had to be a scaly, pointy-toothed drake lord.

He looked up at the Gate. The dark creatures seemed to be watching him, but there was no malice in their alien eyes. On an unspoken request, the huge doors slowly began to open.

When they were open wide, he lifted his burden—ignoring the agonizing pain—and stepped through to the arms of anxious, curious friends. Instead of an end, he knew it was only a beginning.

The Gate closed behind him, and the ancient structure faded away, leaving the wind to run alone through the battered remains of Qualard.

_____ **XXIV** _____

The bonds held tight this time. Not in the physical sense, but they served the same purpose in the long run. He could not communicate with the outside, could not touch those who would come to his aid.

The Ravager stirred, tried to shake the bonds loose so that his mind could reach beyond his prison—the prison *they* had forced him back into. With the Gryphon's aid, for he had the key, of course.

It's not fair! he had cried. *The game was won!*

They did not understand. They had never understood.

Despite his latest attempt, he was still fettered to this place. The bonds held, as they always had and always would, and he felt the fear grow uncontrollable, for, this time, they had said they did not know if they could ever ask for his release.

But I won!

The emptiness was his only companion. He could not even hear the wind above. The wind that blew constantly through Qualard, a place *no one* ever came to if they could help it.

Didn't I?

3

Wolfhelm